# fast

Millie Belizaire

**Copyright © 2020 by Millie Belizaire**

**Edited by: Monique J.**

**Cover Design by: Millie Belizaire**

Cover Photo by Nick Owuor (astro.nic.visuals) on Unsplash

# Summary

*fast*
**adj**.
1. *A girl or guy who is quick to engage in sexual activities.*
—Oftentimes used to shame.
—Oftentimes used to blame victims for their own abuse.

After the untimely death of her mother, **Caprice Latimore** has to move in with her grandmother. At eight years old, life as she knows it is turned upside down. The trauma of losing her mother is made worse with the introduction of Marcel, her grandmother's adult son who still lives in the home.

Her uncle Marcel takes an inappropriate interest in her that ultimately results in a tragic breaking point for the child. The only silver lining is that shortly after what Caprice calls "that night", Marcel is booked by local police with a drug possession charge. He's sentenced to prison for twelve years.

Seven years later, however, Marcel is released on good behavior.

Caprice is now sixteen, still dealing with the emotional scars of the past. But things aren't like they were before.

Because now she has **Shaun Taylor**, the boy across the street who will do whatever it takes to make sure no one ever hurts Caprice again.

*fast* is a standalone that spans twenty years. Separated into three acts, we watch Caprice grow from eight years old to sixteen years old to twenty-eight years old. She gets hurt, she falls in love, she grows, and she just might overcome.

*fast* is a story written about victims who were made to feel like their abuse was their own fault.

**TRIGGER WARNINGS**:
Child abuse, assault in prisons, mental instability, etc.

Some themes touched upon in this story may trigger you. Please protect your mental health.

TABLE OF CONTENTS

## *Thank You*

To new readers, thank you for taking a chance on me.
To returning readers, thank you for continuing to support the dream.

I'm so grateful for the opportunity to continue to share these stories with you.

Thank you, Octavia @ Polish Your Pen Editing Services. You made this story better.

Thank you Monique for every time you dragged my writing. You make me better.

I hope y'all like this one.

## *Prologue*

# Caprice

When I was a little girl, I developed obsessive compulsive disorder.

Of course, nobody ever called it that. My grandmother simply liked to say, '*Caprice just has her ways about her.*' So, she never got me checked out.

OCD wasn't something I always had, either. I can pinpoint the exact moment in the timeline of my life where my "ways" began.

I was eight.

Later on in life, I would come to understand that trauma unlocks parts of the mind that sometimes need to stay locked. Some people have it worse than I do. For them, their trauma introduces a new set of behaviors that can't be so readily ignored by saying, "*Oh… they just have their ways about them.*"

In that sense, maybe I was lucky.

As for what my "ways" were—one of them had me feeling the need to take five to six showers a day. If I let too much time pass between washes, and my skin stopped smelling like soap, I felt dirty. And when I felt dirty, I would itch. I'd itch so bad that my skin would scab up and crack.

So, I washed, and I washed, and I washed, trying to attain an unattainable sense of clean.

OCD made it so that I always had to fall asleep facing my bedroom door. If I woke up with my back to it, I had to stay awake for the rest of the night. When the morning would come and I would move about my day tired, I'd take it as a lesson to stay facing the door next time.

My disorder made me really good with numbers. Maybe this can be seen as a positive side effect. When your mind makes you pay attention to every little thing, you get into the habit of counting just about everything.

How many steps did it take to get from my bedroom to the bathroom? Thirteen. How many steps did it take to get from my bedroom to the kitchen? Thirty-two. How many steps did it take to get from my bedroom to school? One thousand nine hundred and forty-six.

Each step was one second. It took me thirteen seconds to get to the bathroom. If somebody was coming to my room from the kitchen, it would take them half a minute. As for walking to school, I needed a little over half an hour to arrive on time.

All that counting accidentally made me a math genius. Numbers came easy.

People? Not so much.

I couldn't always wrap my mind around people and why they would do the things they'd do. People aren't like numbers—they aren't predictable. People lie. People pretend. People don't always make much sense.

Then again, people might've felt that way about me, too.

I lied, I pretended, I didn't always make much sense.

When I was growing up, it was very difficult for me to find people who understood me and my "ways". In truth, it always kind of felt like most people didn't try.

Except for one.

*ACT ONE*

# CAPRICE - AGE 8

1999

# Chapter One

## Caprice

After mommy died, they put me on an airplane.

My mommy had been sick a really long time, with blood coming out of her mouth and stuff. I couldn't remember a time when she wasn't sick, and I knew she was hurting real bad. When she died, everybody told me she wasn't hurting no more. So even though I was sad, I was happy, too, 'cause the hurting stopped.

Plus, I liked the airplane. It made my ears feel funny, and I got to see Alabama turn small when we went up in the air. I thought it was real nice; real pretty.

The lady at the place where all the airplanes be, said mine was going to Orlando. When I got on the plane, everybody was talking about Mickey Mouse this and Walt Disney World that; real happy kids with their moms and dads. I was talking to them, and I thought that's where I was going, too.

So, I was really excited.

When the plane came down and my ears popped back to normal, all the excited families got off and went one way, and I went the other way.

You see, *I* wasn't going to Walt Disney World.

I was going to Parramore.

Parramore is the part of Orlando that they don't put on TV. Here, everybody is poor and angry at somebody. Parramore is a little neighborhood right outside of Downtown Orlando. It's like, there go the big city… And underneath the shadows of all the big tall buildings… there go Parramore. For that reason, even when the sun is out, it's always a little dark over here.

My mommy grew up here, and after she died, this was the

only place where I had family willing to take me in.

"Caprice—" Ms. Walowitz, the white lady who picked me up from the airport, been saying my name like *Cup-Rice,* and I ain't figured out how to tell her she was saying it wrong. It's said like *Cup-Reese.* We were sitting in her car, and she was getting ready to lie to me. "Your grandmother is very, very, very excited to meet you."

"Oh, for real?"

I know a lie when I hear one.

Especially when white folks try it. White folks don't know how to lie. They try too hard to make it sound true, and that's not how you do it. When you lie, you gotta sound like you don't care with it. Like you just be saying stuff just to say it, and if people don't believe you then they stupid.

I was eight years old and even I was a better liar than Ms. Walowitz.

"Yes, of course! If she had a car, she would've picked you up from the airport herself!" Ms. Walowitz was trying too hard. All she had to say was *yes.*

"She don't have a car?" I asked, wondering how I was gonna get to school if my grandma didn't have a ride. It was 1999, at the end of May, so I wouldn't have to worry about getting to school for some time now, but what kind of grownup doesn't have a car?

"You live in the city now, *Cup-Rice,*" Ms. Walowitz told me. "Everything is a short walk away. No need for a car."

"Except when you need to pick somebody up from the airport," I quickly answered.

Ms. Walowitz laughed and told me I was bright. I took that to mean that if we was fighting with words, I just won the fight. Ms. Walowitz's car slowed down as she turned onto a street with houses on both sides.

"Oh, I grew up on a cul-de-sac, too," Ms. Walowitz said when she saw the street my grandma was living on. Somehow, I got the feeling that Ms. Walowitz's house didn't look like none of the houses in this neighborhood. She moved around nervously, running a hand through her curly red hair, pushing up her glasses even though they weren't slipping. She took a quick look at me as she drove. "I bet there are lots of kids here to play with."

We came to a slow stop in front of a bright pink house with brown grass out front. It was an ugly old house, but it wasn't the worst looking one on the block. Maybe the pink house looked so bad because the house directly across the street was kept up so nice.

I undid my seatbelt before Ms. Walowitz could take her key out of the car. Soon as I shut my door, the front door of the pink house slammed open. Out stepped a skinny old thing, wearing jeans up to her bellybutton and smoking a cigarette.

I thought grandmas were supposed to be fat and jolly type folks.

Not mine.

My grandma looked like she was Ms. Walowitz's age; too old to be my mama, but too young to be my mama's mama. She wore a white polo shirt tucked into these baggy blue jeans that she held up at her stomach with a belt. Her hair was cut short and swooped to one side, like she wanted to look like either one of the ladies in Salt-N-Pepa.

She let her half-smoked cigarette fall to the brown lawn, but she stepped on it before it could start a fire in the dry grass.

"You got so big!" she said, which meant even though I didn't remember her, she met me before. When her arms circled around me and lifted me off the ground, she smelled like cigarettes and minty gum. I didn't like the way she smelled, but I liked being held. As she looked at me, she sadly realized, "You look just like my Alice."

That's true. I *do* look like my mommy. Like mommy, I had brown skin with black poofy hair that fell to my shoulders in two pigtails. And mommy was pretty, so I was pretty, too.

I stared at the gold tooth in her mouth when she said, "Call me Gracie. I ain't with that grandma shit."

At the sound of the word *shit,* Ms. Walowitz choked on the air she was breathing. Gracie was still holding me like I was five pounds heavy, noticing Ms. Walowitz was there for the first time. She watched that poor lady struggle to get my suitcase out of the trunk of her car a little before she spoke.

"Thank you for dropping her off," Gracie said, not helping the woman with my bags. Instead, Gracie twisted her head over her shoulder and shouted, "Marcel! Come get these bags!"

She shouted two more times before a big light skinned man with muscles all over his body came from inside the pink house. Marcel looked so scary, but Gracie talked to him like he was a little boy. Stepping down the steps of the porch, his eyes stayed on me the whole time. He didn't even blink; he just stared at me like I stole something from him.

And then he pointed. "Who's this?"

"This is your sister's baby," Gracie said, even though I wasn't a baby.

"*Ohhh,*" Marcel made a sound like he understood. "She got…?" He got quieter and tried asking again, "She got that AIDS virus, too?"

Gracie rolled her eyes, not too worried with being as quiet when she shouted, "Does she *look* like she got AIDS to you? *Stupid…*" Even though I could see it in his face that he didn't like to be called stupid, Marcel didn't say anything. His anger just stayed behind his teeth. Gracie was still shouting at him when she said, "Bring her bags on inside the house."

And so that's what he did.

Gracie talked to Ms. Walowitz for a few minutes, the whole time that poor lady was looking very scared to be outside. It's not a lot of people who look like Ms. Walowitz in Parramore, I came to realize. She got in her car as soon as she could, dang near shouting, "Goodbye, *Cup-Rice.*"

And then it was just Gracie and me on that brown lawn. She put me down and made herself smaller by bending her knees. That way she could look me in the face when she said, "Caprice—" she pronounced my name the right way and pointed at the pink house. "—welcome home."

* * *

I slept in the living room.

Gracie said I'm lucky because that meant I slept in the biggest room in the house. At night, when everyone was sleeping, sometimes I would turn on the TV and put the volume really low and watch David Letterman on NBC. That's how I knew all the good jokes.

The pink house had two bedrooms and two bathrooms. One room was for Gracie, which had a bathroom inside of it, and the other room was for Marcel. The second bathroom was across the hall from Marcel's room and him and me would share it.

Sometimes I would go to the bathroom and get a peek inside of Marcel's room. It was very dirty in there, with food and trash all over the floor and no sheets on the mattress. Gracie said she would've made Marcel sleep in the living room and given me his room, but somebody was gonna have to clean up his mess first, and it wouldn't be her.

I think Marcel kept his room dirty so that Gracie couldn't give me his room.

That was okay, though.

I liked the living room. Plus, the couch was very comfortable. Gracie bought me princess sheets and a pink quilt to cover up the cushions. It was easy to fall asleep on the couch. I never had my own bed when mommy was alive, so I didn't need one now.

There was no TV in Marcel's room anyway.

Most importantly, I didn't *want* to kick Marcel out of his room.

He was a very nice uncle to me, always giving me stuff. Every time he came home from wherever it was he would go, he would always bring me back something like candy or a new toy. Chocolate was my favorite, so he always got me chocolate bars.

He was my best friend in Orlando. Sometimes when me and Marcel would be at the house during the day, I could hear the neighborhood kids playing outside. I didn't feel no desire to go out there. Marcel was the only friend I needed. He laughed at my David Letterman jokes, and he always told me I was smart. He was always telling me I was pretty, too.

And sometimes we would dance.

Marcel would always put on the radio and say, "Go crazy, Caprice!"

So, I would go crazy, just shaking and wiggling and laughing. He liked that. He liked to see me be silly. At first, I thought he was scary, but Marcel really was just one big ole teddy bear. After I would dance, he would give me bear hugs and tickle me until I screamed so loud, laughing for him to stop.

It made him laugh when I laughed. He was happy to see me happy.

After three weeks in the pink house, I had more toys on account of Marcel than I ever had when I lived with mommy. He was almost kind of like my daddy, and I never had one of those before.

One time when Gracie was at work, Marcel even said since I didn't have a mommy, he would be my daddy, if I wanted him to be. We were sitting in the living room watching *Family Matters*, and he said he would be my daddy, like Laura Winslow's daddy. I didn't know what to say, so I said thank you.

So, then he asked me to practice calling him daddy, and I did.

After I said it, he said, "Keep calling me daddy, Caprice," while he was scratching his privates. He must've been itchy or something. "Keep calling me daddy. Say it. Call me daddy. Say daddy."

I called him daddy again and he started scratching harder. After a while, he made a sound like somebody punched him in the gut. When he stopped breathing fast, he called me a good girl, and left me in the house by myself. Later that night, when Marcel came back home, he brought me a *Hershey's* candy bar.

"Thank you, Uncle Marcel," I said after I took it. It didn't feel quite right to call him daddy, so I decided not to do that anymore.

Gracie walked in as I was opening the chocolate and said to him, "You gon' make that lil' girl fat with all this candy."

I took one bite of the candy bar and even though I knew it was all fine, to me it tasted sour.

Gracie walked to the kitchen, which was behind a wall that blocked off the living room. She couldn't see us from where she was, but we could all hear each other. I could hear her getting started on dinner, the sizzling of a pan canceling out the low sound of the TV.

Marcel watched me put the unfinished chocolate bar on the glass coffee table. My uncle got real close and he whispered to the side of my face so that Gracie couldn't hear. His breath was hot against my neck as he spoke, and his rough hand slipped over my back, just rubbing up and down. "Your body is perfect the way it is, Caprice. Eat up. You deserve it."

And just like that, I decided I didn't like chocolate anymore.

# Chapter Two

## Caprice

Sometimes Gracie would talk to Marcel like he was eight years old, too.

Marcel is a grownup, and I know because I asked him how old he was one time. He said he was twenty-one, which seemed old enough to me. That meant he was thirteen when I was born. I did the subtraction.

But Gracie treated him like a kid, and so sometimes he would act like one.

Especially after he would smoke.

Marcel didn't smoke the same kind of cigarettes that Gracie did. His cigarettes were brown, and they smelled stronger. Marcel's cigarettes didn't come in no box neither. He would make them himself on the living room coffee table, and before he would even light them, it would make the whole house smell like plants.

Sometimes, when Gracie was at work, people would come by the house to buy the stuff Marcel would put in his cigarettes. I realized that's how Marcel gets all his money for toys and candy. He had a lot of that cigarette filling; just jars and jars and even more jars. When people would come over, he would give them these *little* tiny baggies, and they would give him ten dollars; sometimes twenty.

Marcel maybe sold to almost twenty people a day, so one time I did the multiplication and I got a really big number. I asked Gracie for a calculator after that because I thought maybe I did it wrong. What I learned was that I got it right the first time, and Marcel… He was *rich.*

My uncle didn't act rich, though. He never wore a suit or

nothing. Marcel liked wearing these baggy black basketball shorts and white shirts with no sleeves. On his feet, he always wore the same *Nike* slides and dirty white socks.

"Caprice," he said to me one time in the middle of June. Gracie was at work again, and since it was summer, Marcel was the only grownup who could watch me during the day. Nobody had come by the house to buy cigarette filling from Marcel today. He was sitting on the La-Z-Boy and I was laying down on the couch where I always sleep. "Come over here and sit on my lap."

I got this cold feeling in my stomach that I couldn't explain. Even weirder, I felt like I could hear everything in the room then. It was like the clock on the far side wall got louder with its *tick-tocks*. All I could hear was that clock and my own breathing. I just laid on the couch for a bit, listening as time passed.

When I finally opened my mouth to speak, I said, "I'm okay right here."

"I didn't ask you all that. Come *here*." Marcel's voice sounded angry, and I didn't want to make him angrier. So, I got up from my couch, and I walked over to his side. His hands came out and picked me up, sitting me on his lap. I could tell he'd been smoking one of his brown cigarettes when he spoke again, because his voice was all slow and dreamy. "Now that's not so bad, is it?"

I shook my head even though I felt the opposite. His hands rubbed at my shoulders, like he was giving me a massage. Rough hands just squeezing at my shoulders and then stopping before it could hurt. Over and over again. It didn't feel good like how massages are supposed to feel.

"Just keep watching the TV," he whispered behind my neck as his hands began to move to places I knew they weren't supposed to go. That cold feeling in my stomach rose to my chest, and even though I didn't know why, I started to cry. From behind me, of course, Marcel couldn't see the tears coming down my cheeks. "That feel good, niece?"

Even as I cried, I somehow knew there was only one right answer, so that's the answer I gave him.

* * *

I was watching Letterman by myself while everybody else was sleeping.

Usually, when I watch David Letterman, I have to cover my mouth so that I don't laugh too loud. Tonight, it was all just noise and moving lights to me as I stared at the screen.

I couldn't sleep. I took a shower before bed, but I still didn't feel clean.

Maybe I was being a crybaby, I thought. What was I crying for? Marcel didn't hit me. He just… he just touched me a little bit. It didn't hurt, so what was I so sad about? I was talking to myself about how I was being silly for being such a baby about this stuff.

*He was trying to make you feel good. It wasn't nothing bad. It wasn't nothing to cry for.*

My thoughts were interrupted by the sound of Marcel's door opening on the left side of the house. I rushed to close my eyes, scared for some reason. I thought maybe if I pretended like I was sleeping, nothing bad would happen. My eyes were kept shut tight as his heavy footsteps got closer and closer. I didn't want to peek, but I could feel his shadow over me, blocking out the light from the TV.

I pretended like I was dead as his hands pulled the covers off of me. Slowly, he took the bottom of the shirt I was wearing and rose it up high to cover my face. So, now my eyes were covered, but my stomach and chest were not. I opened my eyes, and through the fabric of my shirt, I could see his shadow outlined by TV light.

Marcel just stood there and looked at me a little bit. He didn't touch me this time. I didn't move. I barely breathed as the cold of the house pricked at my naked skin. I just listened.

Over the low sound of the TV, I could hear his breathing getting louder and faster. Even though he wasn't touching me, I knew he was touching something. I could hear skin rubbing against skin, like the sound you make when you rub your hands together. He must've been rubbing his hands together awful fast.

Again, he made a sound like someone punched him in the gut. On my stomach, it felt like someone had poured lotion on me. His breathing slowed down after some time. Maybe I was just really surprised, because I forgot to close my eyes, so when Marcel started to pull my shirt back down to cover me up, he saw that I was not sleeping after all.

First, he looked at me real scared like. It was like he'd been caught stealing. When his face relaxed, he put up a single finger to his lips and whispered, "*Shhhh*, keep it a secret."

* * *

Gracie was staring at me like she knew I was hiding something.

She didn't go to work today on account of yesterday being the Fourth of July. Gracie worked as a clean-up lady at the mayor's office in the big city. This year, the Fourth of July was on a Sunday, so just so that everybody could get their day off, Gracie didn't have to go to work on Monday.

"Caprice, you not hungry yet?"

I looked at Gracie and shook my head. It was the middle of the day—lunch time. I hadn't even had breakfast yet. Gracie wasn't one of those types to force people to eat if they wasn't hungry, but I could see she was starting to worry.

"Well, shit," she put her hands at her hips, looking at me like I was scaring her, "you do this everyday when I ain't here?"

"No," I lied, which came easy for me 'cause all you gotta do is act like you don't care with it. "I eat. I'm just not hungry today."

Gracie might've believed me if not for the fact that my bones was starting to show on my arms.

"You've been losing weight like crazy."

Gracie loved me—I could tell—but she don't pay attention to me.

I know this because Gracie would sometimes come home in the late evening, just in time to catch Marcel jump away from me on the couch. She never found that strange. There were days when I would leave my dirty clothes for her to find, hoping she might see the dried-up lotion, but she never noticed. Sometimes I'd just be sitting on the bus with Gracie, on the way to the grocery store, and I'd just up and start crying.

She would pull me to the side and ask what I was crying for, and when I couldn't tell her, she would get mad and promise that she'd give me something to cry about if I didn't stop.

Being with Gracie and Marcel made me miss my mommy in

ways that I can't even begin to say. I missed Alabama, too. I used to think Orlando was better than Mobile, but I don't think that no more. Orlando was too hot, and the heat made Gracie buy me nothing but shorts and tank tops.

I knew Marcel liked it when I wore shorts. When Marcel liked what I was wearing, he would look for reasons to be next to me. So, I just kept wearing the only long jeans that I had, over and over.

"You smell bad," Gracie told me as I sat at the kitchen table. She wouldn't let me leave until I finished the bowl of buttery cheese grits she put in front of me. It had long turned cold. "Child, are you wearing dirty clothes?"

"No," I told her quietly. I didn't talk much these days unless somebody asked me a question.

Gracie got up close and sniffed me, making a sound like she could throw up. "Caprice, what in the *hell*?"

"I took a shower." I would take at least five showers a day. It was very important for me to feel clean. Gracie grabbed at my upper arm and dragged me out of the kitchen and into the living room.

"Get out of these dirty clothes. *Now*."

It wouldn't have been the first time I was told to take off my clothes in this living room. Like a robot, I took off my shirt and then I took off the jeans, just standing in the living room with nothing but my panties on. Gracie didn't look at me like Marcel did.

She didn't look at me like I was something to eat.

Instead, when she saw the bones pushing out of my body, like a living skeleton, she got tears in her eyes. I had never seen Gracie cry before, but something about how skinny I got made her cry like she didn't know what to do anymore. She put me in a night gown that was too big for me now, and then she begged me to eat. I didn't want to see her cry no more, so I put the food in my mouth and swallowed.

I didn't really taste none of it.

The next day, Gracie didn't go back to work again. She woke up early and sat in the living room, thinking I was sleeping. She sat there for a really long time, waiting for me to wake up. She didn't know that I didn't really sleep no more. But I liked that she was there. Marcel wouldn't come into the living room if she was here. When the sun came out, I pretended to wake, stretching and yawning.

"Go get ready, Caprice," she said from the La-Z-Boy chair. "I'm taking you to the doctor today."

Gracie held my hand at the clinic. I was staring at all the kids that was coughing and sneezing. They were sick for real; not me.

I was just sad, that's all.

When people go to the clinic in Parramore, they don't have to pay for it. That's why everybody would go there, and why the lines would be so long. We waited so long that two episodes of *Matlock* had played on the waiting room TV before they called my name.

The doctor at the clinic—Dr. Joe—looked very tired while Gracie explained to him that I was losing weight. He asked me a few questions after, like what I did every day, and what I liked to eat. When he asked me if everything was okay at home, I tried to sneak a look at Gracie. Dr. Joe said, "Don't look at her; look at me, Caprice. Is everything okay at home?"

"Yes," I said, like I didn't care with it. A good lie. Even though it was a good lie, Dr. Joe didn't believe it.

He asked Gracie if she could step outside of the room, and when she was gone, he asked me again, but like he already knew the truth. "What's going on at home, Caprice?"

"Nothing."

"Is your grandma hitting you?"

I was so mad when he asked me that. "Gracie would *never* hit me! Gracie loves me!"

I could see him getting ready to say something else, and I didn't want to hear none of it. I was so angry. I wanted Gracie to come back in the room. Also, I didn't want to be alone with a man. He was big like Marcel, and I didn't like how close he was standing to me.

I started screaming like Dr. Joe was trying to kill me. "Gracie! Gracie!"

So, she rushed back in the room, ready to fight. Dr. Joe

didn't want no problems after that and so he finished up that visit quick. He said Gracie had to buy me something called *Ensure Plus*, 'cause that would get my weight back up.

Dr. Joe also told Gracie to sign me up for summer camp, because maybe I was spending too much time at home and it was making me "stir crazy", whatever that meant.

When we left, Dr. Joe looked at me like he was sorry, even though he didn't really do nothing to me.

Gracie took my hand and from the clinic, we walked to the closest Publix. She took us to the *Ensure Plus* aisle, and she said, "Which one is it, Caprice? Vanilla or strawberry?"

She didn't even ask about chocolate. You see, Gracie knew that I didn't like chocolate anymore, too. Even though I never said it.

So maybe she was paying attention to *some* things.

## *Chapter Three*

# Caprice

At the local library, they had a free camp.

The library was in the big city, so Gracie would take me there in the mornings on her way to the mayor's office, and I would wait for her on the steps out front after the library closed. There was a big clock over the doorway at the library. When the little hand was on the eight, that's when Gracie would come for me.

The library closed when the little hand was on the five, though.

That was three hours. I did the subtraction.

After Gracie started taking me with her when she would go to work, I think Marcel thought I told her what he was doing to me. I think he was scared, 'cause he stopped for the rest of the summer. At night, I would wait for him to come into the living room, and he would never come. He didn't buy me toys or candy anymore, but at least he stopped touching me. For me, that was a good trade.

My weight was coming back on account of the *Ensure Plus*. Drinking one of those bottles was like eating breakfast *and* lunch. Some of my clothes were still too big, but I wasn't so skinny mini like before. Things were starting to change for the better.

I was having a good time at the free camp, just reading and reading. Sometimes we did art projects. Sometimes we watched movies. Best of all, I got to play with other kids, and some of them were even from Parramore, like me.

The free camp teacher was called Ms. Kelly, and Ms. Kelly said I didn't talk right. Every time I opened my mouth to say something, she had to tell me the right way to say it, like I was learning English for the first time. But I was still smart, she promised.

*'We'll get that Alabama out of you soon,'* she'd say.

Ms. Kelly was like my free camp mommy.

She was real pretty. And I liked her hair a lot, too. On her head were these teeny tiny braids that went all the way down to her back. She said her hairstyle was called sister locs, and that she was gonna grow them to the floor if she could. Even though she didn't like it when the other kids did it, she always let me play with her hair.

That's how I knew she liked me the most.

On my first day of camp, I asked her where the shower was because it had been three and a half hours since my last wash. She bent her knees so that she could be small like me, and said, "You have to take a shower every three and a half hours, Alabama?"

Sometimes that's what she would call me. I was the only kid she gave a nickname to.

I was real serious. "Yes, I do."

She tilted her head to the side and just looked at me. "We don't have a shower at the library, Caprice."

And I almost cried.

Before I could start, she went into her purse and pulled out a package of wet wipes and said, "Will this help?"

"Why do you got baby wipes in your purse?" I asked.

Ms. Kelly said, "Why do I *have* baby wipes in my purse. *Have.*"

"*Okay.*" I pulled out a baby wipe from her package, running the little towel down my arms. "Why do you *have* baby wipes in your purse?"

"Because I'm a woman," was all she said. "You want some more?"

All it took was three baby wipes, and I felt clean enough. It wasn't as good as a shower, but it would keep me calm until I got home. I would feel clean enough if I was able to wipe every two hours.

The very next day, when I went back to free camp, Ms. Kelly had brought me a big tub of wipes. In black marker across the top, she wrote my name on the lid so that everybody would know it was mine.

Sometimes I wanted to go home with Ms. Kelly.

She was always saying really nice things to me like, "Caprice, you come from kings and queens."

I don't know about all that, but it was nice of her to say.

Ms. Kelly was always talking about Africa this, and Africa that, so I figured that's where she was from. Once, I asked her what part of Africa she was born in, and she just laughed and said she was from Los Angeles. That didn't make no sense to me.

Even so, she was still the smartest lady I knew.

Ms. Kelly told me that she was a student at the local university, getting her bachelor's degree in education. When I asked her what she wanted to teach, she said high school math. I told her I was good at math, and she said, "I knew you would be."

Yep, out of all the kids, Ms. Kelly definitely liked me the most. She would bring me books that weren't in the library, books with black girls like us on the cover.

When free camp would finish up, and I would stay behind, she used to wait with me and talk. After the second week of waiting with me, I told her she didn't have to anymore because I wanted to read, and she talked too much.

By the middle of my third week of free camp, I started to get bored while waiting for Gracie. There was a basketball court across the street from the library, and I figured since I could still see the big clock from the court, I would know when to start heading back.

I would sit under the bright white lights of the basketball court and just watch. Even though I didn't understand basketball at first, it was easy to catch on. They were all trying to protect their basket, and if they failed, the other team got a point. Easy enough.

All the boys who would play were tall like Marcel, except one.

The littlest one was called Shaun.

I knew his name because he was so small that you'd think he wouldn't be able to keep up with all the older boys, but he was one of the best ones. So, you had to know his name. Especially because Shaun had a group of girls about my age that would cheer him on, screaming and giggling if he looked at them.

Those girls would chew gum and blow big, pink bubbles that made the air smell all fruity. Sometimes they weren't even watching the game, they'd just talk real loud and make sure everyone could hear them laughing. I wished they would talk to me sometimes. It looked like they were having fun.

One time one of the taller girls in the bunch walked up to me and asked, "What are you reading?"

I looked up at her from where I was sitting, holding my hand up to block out the bright court lights. I'm not gonna lie. I got really excited that she was talking to me, and so I rushed to show her the cover. It was one of the books Ms. Kelly told me to read.

"*Assata: An Autobiography*. I don't understand all the words, but it's a book about this lady named Assata Shakur. I like her so far." And then I told her my name. "I'm Caprice."

"Princess," she introduced herself plain like, her eyes looking me up and down. Even though she didn't say anything, the way she watched me made me feel like an ugly weirdo. After breathing out a long sigh, she walked away, back to her group. I don't know what I said, but apparently that's all I had to say for her to decide I couldn't be in her crew. From that day on, those girls pretended like they couldn't even see me.

So, I just read my books under the white lights of the basketball court, and sometimes I would look up to watch the boys play.

Even though I didn't scream like the other girls, I was rooting for Shaun, too. A win for Shaun was a win for all the little people up against bigger people in the world. When Shaun got a point, it made me feel like just because I was small, didn't mean I couldn't be powerful. When I told Ms. Kelly about it once, she said the word I was looking for was, '*inspiration*'.

That's what Shaun was to me. My *inspiration*.

On one of the last nights of summer, Shaun accidentally got pushed down by one of the bigger kids. Before thinking, I stood to my feet, because I was worried about him. He ended up being okay, but Princess and her crew took one look at my face and started singing, "*Caprice likes Shaun! Caprice likes Shaun! Shaun and Caprice sitting in a tree, K-I-S-S-I-N-G!*"

I was so embarrassed.

When Gracie came to pick me up on the steps of the library that evening, I was still replaying that memory in my head. I stopped going to the basketball courts after that night.

* * *

The first day of third grade was *amazing*.

I went to Parramore K-8 Center, a charter school that was a thirty-two-minute walk from the pink house. For short, we called it PK8. My school was one big white building—elementary schoolers on the first floor, middle schoolers on the second floor.

On the first day of school, I learned two things.

One, Shaun from the basketball court lived in the pretty house across the street.

Two, Shaun went to my school, too, and he was in fifth grade.

I was too embarrassed to say hi to him first, on account of Princess and her friends telling him I liked him. He didn't say anything to me, and I didn't say anything to him. On the way to school, he walked on one side of the street, and I walked on the other. When I walked a little bit slower, he slowed down a little as well. When I walked faster, he got faster, too.

We arrived at PK8 at almost the same time.

When Shaun let himself through the front door, he waited for me so that he could hold it open when I walked inside. As I walked through, he finally spoke.

"I'm Shaun," he said, as if I didn't already know.

I smiled, way too happy that he was talking to me, and answered, "I'm Caprice."

"I know," he said, even though I never told him my name before. "You want help finding your teacher? I been here for five years now, so I know my way around."

Unable to find my words, I just nodded.

And that's how I started my amazing first day of third grade. My teacher was nice. My clothes were new. I had a fresh pack of baby wipes in my backpack. And Shaun from the basketball court knew who I was.

I think he even wanted to be my friend.

This is because after school, Shaun asked me if I wanted to go with him to the basketball court in the city. The whole time he was talking, I was just staring at his eyes and thinking they were really pretty. That's why he had to call out my name to get me to pay attention. When he said my name, I got all warm like the sun was on my skin.

Even though I wanted to go, I said no on account of the fact that I had to go home and take a shower. The baby wipes did a good job of keeping me calm, but deep down I knew I was still dirty.

So, I walked home after school by myself, but the whole way there, I just couldn't stop smiling.

* * *

When I got to the pink house, everything was quiet. The little hand on the clock in the living room was on the four, so I knew Gracie wouldn't be home until later.

On my way to the bathroom, I could hear that Marcel was home, listening to music in his room. I didn't say anything because I didn't really want to announce that I was here, so I just quietly shut myself in that bathroom.

It had been a very long time since Marcel played any of his secret games with me. Whether it was because he was scared that I told Gracie, or if he just got tired of me, I was glad he didn't want to play with me anymore.

After leaving the water running for half a minute, I checked to see if it was warm before hanging up my clothes to get in. I scrubbed down every inch of my skin, soaping and rinsing at least four times. It had been seven hours since my last shower, so I had to be extra serious about washing.

By the end of it all, I was so clean that I was squeaky, and that's how I liked it. I stepped out of that shower, still smiling from my amazing first day. With the towel wrapped around me, my eyes rose up from the floor to see the bathroom door that I had shut was now wide open.

In the doorway was Uncle Marcel.

My smile faded.

"Hi, Uncle Marcel. You gotta use the bathroom?" I didn't mean for my voice to shake, but it just did. I was talking quickly as I tried to walk past him. "I'mma be outta here real fast so that you can—"

His hand, rough and dry, came down onto my shoulder, stopping me. I looked up. His eyes were red and shiny, like how they got when he smoked his brown cigarettes, but he must've been woozy from something else too, because his body was all wobbly.

"You always teasin' me," he said, voice slow and deep like a… monster. "You always takin' them showers 'cross the hall from me, swingin' your naked tail 'round this house. What you want Caprice?"

My eyes got big, 'cause I didn't understand, but I understood that he was thinking bad things. Very bad things. I kept the towel around me tight as his second hand touched on my other shoulder.

"You want some dick? That what you want?"

My eyes were filling with water and even though I didn't want it to, my voice shook even more when I said, "I wanna go now."

Marcel pushed me further into the bathroom, kicking his foot behind him to slam the door shut. I tried to fight; I swear I did. At some point, it was like I was in two places at once, with Marcel and watching it all happen from outside of myself. I was on the bathroom floor, with Marcel on top of me. I scratched, I hit, I screamed.

And then I just got quiet.

It was nothing to fight for no more.

He was doing it.

And I was floating above it all, watching myself on that bathroom floor. There were two Caprices in that moment. The one who was watching, and the one who was feeling everything. I have vivid nightmares of being the Caprice who was watching, but I have no memory of being the Caprice who was feeling.

Floating overhead, I saw the blood spread across the bathroom tiles. I saw Marcel kick Caprice softly when he was finished, just to see if she was alive. I watched as he left her and his mess to lie there on the ground. I saw Caprice stay there, bleeding and bruised, staring out into space, softly crying out for her mommy who was dead.

# Chapter Four

## Caprice

I woke up hurting real bad.

I was wearing my pink pajamas and had been sleeping on the couch. When I sat up, I got scared because out of the corner of my eye, I saw somebody sitting on the La-Z-Boy. My breathing picked up, but when my eyes got used to the dark, I saw that it was just Gracie. I calmed down.

Did she find me in the bathroom?

Did she put me in these clothes?

Did she clean all the blood off the tile floor?

"Gracie." My voice was scratchy from screaming, so it came out sounding rough. It hurt a little. Did she know what I did? Was she mad at me? Did she think I was bad? "Gracie—"

She didn't let me finish talking. She was off the La-Z-Boy in seconds, getting close to my face. When her hands came and grabbed me by the shoulders, I started shaking and I didn't stop until she let me go. I didn't want anybody to touch me. Even Gracie.

"Child," she whispered in the dark. All I could see was the outline of her head, and the little bit of outside light reflecting off the white parts of her eyes. Her whispered words came out rushed; angry. "Did you let Marcel touch you?"

I froze up, my back going straight.

*Let?*

Like… did I *want* him to?

Did she think I asked him to do it? Did she think I was bad? When I finally found my voice, I couldn't control how loud it came out. I was practically screaming, "I didn't want him to. I didn't want him to. I didn't want him to."

"*Shhhhh*," she shushed me, trying to hold me in a comforting manner, but I threw my arms out against her chest and pushed her away. "Alright, alright..." Gracie sighed, holding out her hands so that I could see them. "I won't touch you, baby," she understood.

Wrapping my arms around myself, I rocked back and forth, shaking even though I wasn't cold. My grandma's eyes running over me felt like needles on my skin. She didn't say anything for a very long time, just looked at me as I shook, realizing I wasn't about to stop. I think Gracie was scared I was gonna tell somebody because she broke the quiet by saying, "You don't have to go to school today."

I could tell from the way I was feeling that I wouldn't be able to do the thirty-two-minute walk anyway. Gracie promised, "And from now on, you can have my room. I'll sleep in the living room."

She said it like she was doing me a favor, but I heard what she was really saying. If I got her room, and she took the couch, that meant Marcel would still be sleeping in his own room. He was gonna be here every day after school, able to do what he did to me again. Maybe this was Gracie's way of letting me know that even though her son hurt me real bad, he was still her son.

Maybe Gracie didn't love me like I thought she did.

All I said was, "Can I lock the door when I'm in there?"

It was dark, but I could almost hear the water collecting in her eyes. Even though I couldn't see it, I knew she was crying. "Sure, baby."

Somehow, hearing how sorry her voice sounded made me mad.

I didn't like how she let herself cry for me. Something bad happened to me, and yet my eyes were dry. What right did Gracie have to cry? My voice was like a robot now, like I couldn't feel anything. I didn't have no more emotions. "After school, I'm gonna wait for you to get off of work at the basketball court in the city. I don't wanna be here by myself no more."

"Marcel ain't never gon' touch you again when I'm done with him," she promised, as if that was supposed to make me feel better.

It didn't matter if he never touched me again, anyway.

What mattered was that he already had. There wasn't no going back from that. It was burned into my brain now, and so no matter how much Gracie promised to keep me safe, all I could think about was how she couldn't do it in the first place.

I repeated myself. If Marcel still got to live here, then, "I don't wanna be here by myself no more."

* * *

That morning must've been twenty hours long, because when I opened my eyes again, it still wasn't nighttime. Or maybe I slept so long that we had gone into tomorrow.

I woke up to the sounds of shouting in the kitchen. Gracie's bedroom was the biggest room in the pink house. In here, there was a bed big enough for two people, a pair of dark wood night tables, and a dresser to match. It was a lot of space for just one little girl, but it was all mine now. Maybe Gracie thought she was keeping me safer by moving me out of the living room. Maybe she thought Marcel would have a harder time getting to me here.

My new bedroom shared a wall with the kitchen, and it wasn't very thick. Sitting up on the big bed, with my back against the dark wood headboard, I could hear voices through the wall behind me. Gracie and Marcel were having a conversation about me, about the way Gracie found me.

She made it easy for him to lie, almost seeming like she didn't want to fight him too hard. She'd accuse. Marcel would lie to her. And she refused to ask him twice. Like, she was more afraid of the truth than she was of him lying.

So, lying was exactly what Marcel did.

He kept repeating that he didn't do anything to me. My uncle swore he wasn't home yesterday; he said he was out with his boys. The words sounded too true when he said them. Either he was lying, or I was. Listening to Marcel speak made even me wonder if it was me. Maybe I was the liar.

But Marcel's answers only made more questions.

Gracie asked them.

*Why would Caprice lie? Why doesn't Caprice want to be alone with you anymore?*

*If you didn't do her like how I found her, then who did?*

"You don't know Caprice like I do," Marcel shouted, but I didn't know what he meant. I could hear his fists slamming against the wall. He told stories about me that I never heard before. Maybe he knew me better than the self I thought I knew. Maybe that was why he could say things about me that I didn't know were true. "That little girl got some fire in her pants. *Fast* as hell. She probably invited one of those neighborhood boys in, and got roughed up tryna be grown!"

*Is that what happened? Is that true?*

Just listening to him, you could tell Marcel believed the words he was yelling. Maybe I could believe it, too. Maybe Marcel didn't do anything to me. I started to get comfortable with the idea, pushing out memories in my head as leftovers from a bad dream. I must've remembered everything the wrong way.

I got hurt yesterday, while Marcel was out with his boys. When I came home from school, I must've forgot to lock the door behind me. Somebody must've followed me inside. Sitting up on the bed, I closed my eyes and tried to remember it that way.

Like a movie playing in my head, I saw Marcel pressing me down on the bathroom floor. I floated up above, watching both of us from the ceiling, outside of my own body. I don't remember feeling anything; no pain to go along with the blood spreading across the bathroom floor. Nothing. It was like my brain had blocked everything out, just for those few minutes.

So, the pain didn't come until much later, when I woke up in the living room with Gracie. Even now, I could still feel it, feeling like the skin near my privates was scraped and lit on fire.

If I tried to think about what I felt in that moment, though, all I could remember was the heat of Marcel's breath, hitting against the side of my cheek. *Haaah... haaah... haaah...* The sounds of his breaths played in my head like a scratched-up CD.

I rushed to open my eyes again, hoping it would make the sound go away.

"I didn't touch that girl, Mama. The fuck do I look like?" They were still fighting in the kitchen. "It had to have been one of those neighborhood boys."

Gracie fought him on that, telling him that only a "*grown ass man*" coulda done how she found me. I brought my knees up to my chest, hugging myself as I listened to them argue.

Marcel said, "Then maybe Caprice got herself some older friends you don't know about."

All this back and forth made me feel extra bad, thinking about how I didn't remember things the way Marcel did. He was lying about everything, and I was gonna get in trouble if Gracie believed him over me. She probably would put me out her room, back to the living room, where Marcel could keep doing bad things to my body.

"Mm-mm-mm," Gracie made that sound she always made when she would be shaking her head. Soon after that, a sharp slapping noise made everything go quiet. It seemed like even the birds outside stopped chirping as soon as it happened.

Gracie slapped him.

"That's your sister's baby you lyin' on. Alice's *baby*! That lil' girl done lost her mama, and then you went and stole her innocence. For *what*? You can't get nobody grown to *fuck* you at twenty-one?"

"Mama—"

"Don't '*mama*' me, lil' nigga. You lucky I don't call the police on your *raping* ass—"

"I didn't *touch* that girl!" Marcel was shouting now, pretending so good, he could put Denzel Washington to shame. "I swear on Daddy. I swear on Alice. Shit—I swear on *me*! I *don't know* what happened to Caprice yesterday. Bring her out here! Let me talk to her, and she'll tell you I ain't done *shit* to her."

I said a quiet prayer so I wouldn't have to do none of that.

"Marcel, where you going?" I could hear him stomping about, his footsteps getting closer. My breathing started to speed up, my eyes jumping to the door to see if it was locked. "Marcel, don't you bother that little girl. Poor thing can barely walk 'cause of—"

There was a loud banging at the bedroom door. I flinched, and then I started to shake. Marcel continued to bang at the door, calling my name so that I could come out. I brought my hands up to my ears, trying not to hear the banging that sounded like gunshots. When I shut my eyes tight, trying to go somewhere else in my mind, fat tears rolled down my cheeks as Marcel shouted my name over and over.

And then the banging stopped.

Even with my ears covered, I could hear Gracie screaming. "I WANT YOU OUT! YOU HEAR ME? OUT!" I uncovered my ears. She started to talk about things I didn't even know she realized. "Boy, you must think I'm stupid. She was losing all that weight over the summer, wouldn't eat nothing, coverin' up like it was snowing outside. She stopped taking care of herself. And even when that stopped, she developed this habit of washing herself like she just couldn't get clean enough. All that crying she was doing outta the blue. You don't think I had my suspicions then? But when all her issues disappeared once I put her in camp, I wrote it off, thinkin' maybe she was just sad about her mama." There was a minute of quiet. "Get'cho ass away from her door."

"Mama, I didn't—"

"I don't care about none of that. What you did. What you didn't do. But I'll tell you what you *won't* do. You won't be in my house come the first of next month. Get your shit—*get all your shit*—and move on. You got till the end of August. Start packing."

I wasn't sure if Gracie did it on purpose that way, but the last day of August was my birthday. See, that's when I would be turning nine.

After that first fight, I didn't hear fighting for the rest of the day. For hours, I just sat upright on my new bed. The pain between my legs only got worse when I climbed off to walk to the bathroom. I had to pee, so I had no choice but to make the painful thirteen steps to the toilet. My white panties were red with blood when I pulled them down.

I felt like I could cry, but I didn't.

I don't know why, either. I guess just figured crying wouldn't help none. It wouldn't make the blood dry up. It wouldn't make the pain go away. So, I was better off keeping it inside. I did what I had to do, wondering how long it would be until it didn't hurt to pee. Soon, I hoped. The minute I was back in my bed, I heard a knock at the door.

"Baby." I breathed out, feeling the fear leave my body. It was just Gracie. She must've heard the toilet flush. "It's almost five o'clock and you haven't eaten anything. Can I get you something?"

All I asked for was a bag of ice, thinking maybe it would cool the burning between my thighs.

When I opened the door to grab the ice Gracie said I would find, next to the ice pack she made, was a bottle of vanilla *Ensure Plus*.

I took both into the room with me.

* * *

I didn't know what day it was.

The sun outside had gone up and down at least five or six times since I started counting. My new room was decorated for a grownup. My bedsheets were light gray at first, but after Gracie came in to change them a few days ago, they were peach now. That was the only sign of color in the room. Everything else was either dark wood or dark metal, all put together against clean white walls.

A couple days ago, Gracie came in and removed all her things—her clothes, her hair stuff, everything. After that, she replaced it with all my stuff—my clothes, my hair stuff, and a brown box filled with my books and toys.

This was really my room now.

Gracie only came by once in a while to see if I was hungry, dropping off peanut butter and jelly sandwiches, *Ensures*, or whatever else she could fit in a *Ziploc* bag. Most of the time, I skipped my meals. I don't know how it happened, but hungry didn't come so easy no more. My days were mostly spent in bed, listening to the movements and conversations on the other side of my walls.

Marcel was still here, but everyday that passed couldn't come without Gracie reminding him that he had to be out before the end of the month. He must've not been taking her serious, because one night I woke up to her shouting at him. She was angry because he hadn't started packing yet. Gracie said she'd call the police on him if she had to.

Even though I felt bad for it, it made me happy to hear her say that. I fell asleep smiling at the thought of police officers coming to take Marcel away. Did that make me a bad person?

For the most part, my days were quiet; a little bit fuzzy sometimes. I had days where I couldn't tell the difference between being asleep and being awake. Some mornings I'd get up and pick something in the room to stare at until the sun went down. In that room, locked away from the rest of the house, there was nothing to do but sit and count.

I counted everything.

Thirteen steps to the bathroom. On me, I had twenty-six teeth in my mouth, three hundred sixty-one eyelash hairs, and eleven fading bruises on my body. I figured my time in that room must've been what it felt like to die—alone at first, and then forgotten.

At least, I *thought* I was forgotten.

It was days before somebody came around asking for me, but I was awake when it finally happened.

I'd been keeping my blinds opened, because once in a while a bird would fly by my window and I could take a break from counting my eyelashes. Keeping my window opened let me watch the clouds move across the sky. Sometimes I'd imagine they were racing each other. It must've been late afternoon because the sky had that purple color it would get right before it turned into night.

I was sitting up on my bed, halfway asleep. Enough time had passed that I didn't hurt or bleed no more, but I wasn't sure how many days it had been.

There was a knock at the front door. I knew it was the front door because it was too far away to be my bedroom door, but too close to be Marcel's. It knocked one more time before somebody opened the door.

Gracie spoke.

"Can I help you?" She sounded confused, as if she didn't expect to find this person on the other side. This made me curious. I got out of bed, careful not to let the floorboards squeak under my toes. Quietly, I put a crack in my door so I could hear everything better. I pressed my ear to the opening, catching the last half of what the knocker was saying.

"...haven't seen her since the first day of school, so I was just wonderin' if she moved. Since it's been two weeks, and all."

It was a boy...

It was *Shaun*.

Sitting here in my room with nothing to do, I'd been thinking about him, too. Mostly it was to remind myself that Marcel wouldn't have been able to do nothing to me if I'd gone to the courts with Shaun that day.

But sometimes I'd just think about him for no reason at all.

Gracie told a lie. "Caprice is here. She's just been sick with the flu."

"Oh," Shaun answered, and there was a little bit of quiet before he asked, "Do you know when she's comin' back?"

"Monday." Gracie never spoke to me about going back to school on Monday. I didn't even know what day it was *now*. Was Monday tomorrow?

Shaun's next question surprised me. "Can I see her?"

It was like even though Gracie was a good liar, he still wanted to make sure I was okay with his own eyes. I could tell by how Gracie's voice changed that she didn't like that. "Caprice is still a little bit contagious, so I don't think that's a good idea."

"I see what you're sayin. So, you're tellin' me Saturday and Sunday is just enough time for her to get well enough to not be contagious no more, right?"

Shaun didn't believe her. You could see that plain as day. Knowing Gracie, she would think he had a smart mouth for asking her something like that. But his question let me know what day it was.

Friday.

I missed the rest of the first week of school, and the entire second week. There was no telling how much I missed. What if I was the dumbest girl in class when I went back? I didn't have much time to worry about that because I realized something else, too.

It was easy and quick to do the count in my head. My first day of third grade was on August 16th. If today was Friday, the second week of school, then that meant the last day of August was soon.

Marcel didn't have much time left.

So busy doing the math, I wasn't paying attention to what Shaun and Gracie were saying to each other. When I tried to focus again, I could hear my grandma tapping her foot like she was losing her patience. Gracie didn't care for Shaun's questions. You could tell he was bothering her from the way she spoke fast, like she wanted him gone.

"I'll tell Caprice you stopped by…" Gracie paused because she didn't know what to call him. "What did you say your name was?"

He cleared his throat. "I'm Shaun, Shaun Taylor. I live right across the street."

## *Chapter Five*

# SHAUN

I was up extra early on Monday.

Mom was surprised because most of the time she had to beat me with a pillow to get me out of bed. Though, today—before she could even wake up—I was showered and dressed for school. I was eating a bowl of *Lucky Charms* when she walked into the dining room, looking at me like *'Who are you and what have you done with my Shaun?'*

"Good morning, Mom."

She didn't say anything. Instead she just shook her head and rubbed her eyes, like she was trying to wake up from a really confusing dream. When she opened her eyes to find me still sitting at the dining room table, she spoke up. "Since when..." She couldn't finish her question. Instead, she just asked. "Shaun, baby, are you feeling okay?"

I nodded, taking a spoonful of my cereal. "Yeah, mom. What's up?"

"Baby, it's..." She breathed out a yawn, slipping her red hair bonnet off her head before she took the seat at the table. "It's four o'clock in the morning."

"I didn't wanna be late today."

Mom looked at me with squinty eyes, almost smiling. "It's still dark out. School doesn't start for another..." she snuck a look at the silver watch on her wrist. "...four hours. And it don't take you but thirty minutes to walk there."

She stared at me, and I stared back. Neither of us blinked. I waited for her to ask me something. She waited for me to just tell her on my own.

With just me and mom in the house, she had nothing but

time to get all up in my business. A long time ago, I had a dad, too, but when he died, *I* became the man of the house. I'd be turning eleven on the first of September. I was too old for her to be asking me all these questions. As the man of the house, I had every right to my privacy.

"You excited about something?" she asked, starting to remove the pink hair rollers from her head. Mom owned a salon just outside of Parramore, so she was always trying something new with her hair. This week it was curly brown. That's because she liked the way it looked on Whitney Houston when we watched *The Preacher's Wife* last Saturday.

Mom swore up and down that Whitney Houston was her long-lost sister since they looked so much alike. With her hair like that, I could kinda see it. It looked good, but I'd learned not to like her hairstyles *too* much. Just when you start getting used to one style, she switched it up for another.

When I didn't answer Mom's first question, she started digging deeper. "This wouldn't have anything to do with Caprice, would it?"

I shouldn't have told Mom about her.

It's just that… after Caprice missed four days of school, I told Mom. My mistake was that while telling her how worried I was, I slipped up and called Caprice pretty. Mom didn't take my concerns serious after that—she just got real girly and started acting like I said I wanted to marry her or something. Ever since then, she's just been bringing up Caprice every chance she gets.

If I forgot to brush my teeth before bed, she'd remind me by saying things like, *'I bet Caprice likes boys who brush their teeth.'* If I forgot one of my chores, she'd say, *'How are you gonna get Caprice to like you if you can't even get me to like you?'*

Just real annoying with it all. She thought it was very funny.

That's how you know moms are little girls, too, at heart. 'Cause that's the type of stuff little girls laugh about.

After another week of Caprice missing school, instead of talking to Mom, I just marched up to the house across the street and asked for her myself.

Her grandma said she had been sick. I don't know why, but I didn't believe her. Even so, she said Caprice would be back in school on Monday.

Today was Monday.

* * *

I was sitting on the porch steps in front of the house.

The sun hadn't come up yet, so it was still dark outside. Even though I told Mom I wasn't too scared to be outside by myself, she insisted on waiting out front with me. I think it was because she was having too much fun teasing me.

Behind my head, she was leaning on a beam holding the roof above the porch. Dressed in a baby blue sleep robe, my mom stood behind as I sat on the steps, watching the pink house across the street. Mom blew at her steaming cup of coffee, telling me what time it was every couple of minutes.

"Twenty more minutes to seven-thirty," she updated. The school was thirty or so minutes away, if you walked slow. With school starting at eight, Mom figured the girl across the street would come out half an hour before the first bell. "When she comes out, you should offer to hold her backpack."

I twisted my head back and looked up at her from the steps, scrunching my face up because I didn't understand. "Why would I do that?"

Mom rolled her eyes like I was bothering her. "She was sick for almost two weeks, Shaun. Her strength might not be back up yet… and it's the nice thing to do."

I was still confused. "But then I gotta carry two backpacks…"

*How am I gonna carry two backpacks and a basketball?* Every day after school, I played ball at the court downtown, so I always had my ball with me. If I did what Mom was saying, walking to school was just gonna get harder.

I must've kept saying the wrong thing 'cause she rolled her eyes again. "Yes, I know you would be carrying two backpacks."

"What if her backpack is heavy?"

"Then she'll be extra appreciative that you helped her." Mom smiled when she added, "You want her to like you, don't you?"

I was still stuck on the word I didn't recognize. "Appreciative?"

"Shaun, I appreciate you waking up this morning without my saying so," Mom explained, "If I appreciate, then I *am* appreciative. Do you understand?" Mom was a big believer in talking to kids like grown folks. She cared a lot about my "development", so I'd been reading since I was three. Sometimes she would say things I didn't understand, but it was up to me to ask questions. I swear I learned more with Mom than I ever did in school.

"I understand."

"That's my super smart boy," she said quietly, bringing her wrist up to her eyes. "Ten minutes until you better start walking. If she's late, that doesn't mean that you also have to— " Mom stopped talking, and I followed her eyes to the house across the street. Out from the front door stepped a girl who I *think* was Caprice. She looked a little different. Her body was skinnier than I remembered. Mom spoke quietly so that only I could hear. "Aw, she's adorable. Shaun, get up and go hold her backpack—go."

She nudged my back with her bare foot, making me stand up.

"Oh, don't get nervous now," Mom teased in a low voice.

I swiped my head back to give her a look. "I'm not nervous!"

After tucking the basketball under my arm, I jogged up the street to catch up with her. Hearing me get closer, she turned her head at the sound. When I took my last step closer to her, she took a step back. I took one more step forward to close the space… so she took two more steps back. Thinking to myself, I nodded. Some people don't like it when you all up on them and stuff.

"Hey," I said first. I wanted to ask her where she's been, how she was feeling. Even though I didn't believe her grandma when she said she was sick, seeing her now and how small she got, I was wrong to think her grandma lied. Compared to how I remembered her, Caprice *looked* like somebody who had been sick.

But she was still pretty. Her black hair was tied into two ponytails with pink and white ribbon on each one, matching with her white uniform shirt. I liked her eyes best—those shiny, dark brown eyes of hers made looking at her feel extra special. She was pretty like an angel. It kinda made you want to check for wings.

Caprice didn't say anything to my 'hey'. Not knowing what to say next, I looked at the pink backpack strapped to her shoulders, looking heavy—but even worse, girly. My friends would clown me to death if they saw me holding it.

But Mom said it would make her like me.

"Gimme your backpack."

She made a face like she was afraid and backed up one more step. "I don't have anything nice in here."

"No!" I almost shouted. "I don't wanna steal nothing from you. I just… wanna hold your backpack."

Her eyebrows scrunched together when she asked, "*Why*?"

"Because… because… Just *because*, okay?"

"I don't wanna give you my backpack…"

She wasn't understanding. I tried to tell her, "You're not giving it to me, you're just letting me hold it."

"Do you *like* it, or something?" she asked, her eyebrows doing a thing that made me feel like she thought I was a weirdo. "It's for girls, you know."

All I could do then was huff out a breath, turning my head back to see if Mom was still standing on the porch. She was standing there… being nosy. Just so she would know she was wrong, I shouted to her, "Not appreciative!"

When I turned back to say something to Caprice, she was already walking on ahead without me. Jogging to catch up, I tried to talk to her as we walked to school.

"You were sick?"

She looked at me out the sides of her eyes and then quietly nodded. "Uh-huh."

"You feel better?"

Like somebody tryna say as little as possible, she just nodded again.

"What was wrong with you?" I asked curiously.

"Just about everything you could think of," she answered my question in a way that didn't really answer anything at all.

"Did you read a lot of books?" I asked her how she spent the time. She just looked at me after I asked, probably wondering how I knew she liked to read. I explained, "You read books at the basketball court over the summer. Everybody else was screaming, or fighting, or playing… but not you. You barely ever looked up from your books."

When I would play ball over the summer, sometimes I scored points just to get her to look up. I wanted her to see me. I wanted her to cheer me on like the other girls did, but at the same time, I was kinda glad she never tried. I might've been too nervous to play if I knew she was watching me the whole time.

Caprice shook her head at my question from before, sounding tired when she said, "I read all the books at my house already."

She kinda sounded sad, too.

"My mom reads a lot." Even though I didn't have permission to say what I said next, I said it anyway. Wanting to make her feel better and all… "I could let you borrow some of hers."

"That's okay," Caprice said softly, maybe guessing I didn't all the way have the permission to do that. "Thank you anyway."

"You still a little sick?" I asked as we continued to walk. She sounded like she didn't have much energy behind her words. Her voice didn't have the same kind of life it had before. "You don't sound too good."

"I'm okay."

"Are you sure? Pinky promise?" I had to ask again, because even her last response sounded a little blue. Caprice didn't take my outstretched pinky; she just kept walking. Putting my hand down, I stepped a little closer to her as we walked, accidentally bumping my shoulder up against hers.

She jumped back, like my body was made of fire and it burned to feel me touch her.

"Sorry," I said, even though my shoulder didn't bump into hers that hard. "I didn't mean to."

She walked on ahead without saying anything. I didn't say anything either now as I walked alongside her. She didn't seem to mind the quiet. After some time, Caprice's footsteps stopped directly in front of PK8. Before we could go our separate ways, I spoke up again.

"I can walk you home after school."

I hoped she'd say yes, but instead she just said, "I'm not going home after school."

"Oh… tomorrow then?"

She shook her head. "I'll be at the ball courts after school from now on."

Hearing this only made me hold back a smile. If that was true, then that meant I wouldn't have to walk her home, just to turn around and walk the other way to the courts. "Really?"

"Yes, or the library across the street," she added.

"Can I walk with you to the ball courts after school then?"

"Like how we did this morning?" she asked. I just nodded, and she said,"Yeah…" The ribbons in her hair swayed as she gave her answer. "…We can walk together."

## *Chapter Six*

# SHAUN

"How was your first day back?"

Caprice and I walked toward downtown after school. The walk into the city was about the same as the walk home would've been, too. We would be passing Mom's salon on our way to the courts, and I would always stop in to change out of my school uniform. When I told Caprice this, she said she didn't mind waiting for me.

"My teacher gave me a bunch of make-up work so I could catch up," she answered. Unlike me, a day at school seemed to give her more energy. There was a little more pep to her step now, and her voice was alive again. "I have a lot of homework to do."

She actually sounded happy about this.

"I remember most everything from third grade," I told her. "And I'm the best reader in the fifth grade now. I could help you some."

Caprice shook her head, a little smile growing on her face. I don't know why, but seeing that made me smile a little, too. It was good to see she was in higher spirits.

"I wanna do it by myself," she said. "That way it stays in my head better."

We were getting closer to my mom's salon. Mom liked that I didn't go straight home after school. Since she was at the salon till late, it made her feel better to know I was not in her house by myself, messing things up, doing "God knows what".

We worked out a schedule. After school, once I got changed out of my uniform in the salon, I could go to the courts till about seven. After that, I had to walk back to the salon and do my homework until closing. Then, me and mom would head home together.

"You don't talk like the rest of us," I told Caprice, trying to make conversation. "You must not be from Orlando."

"I used to live in Mobile," she told me. "That's in Alabama, and lots of people there talk like me. Do you think the way I talk is funny?"

I was quick to tell her, "No. It's just different." After thinking about it, I decided I could say, "I like it."

She looked away from me when I told her that, looking down at her feet and trying not to smile. Even though I could tell she was embarrassed by what I said, I still felt good about it. Maybe my saying that made up for the fact that I wasn't holding her backpack.

The bell over the front door of my mother's salon rang to announce that we came. I stepped inside first, holding the door open behind me so that Caprice could walk through. *Sylvia's Salon & Spa* was on the border of Parramore and the fancy part of Downtown Orlando, on Division Avenue. My mom—that's who Sylvia is—had been running it for about six years now, since my dad died.

He had a really bad kind of cancer. Mom said even though she was sad he wasn't with us anymore, his last act of love to us was the money he made sure we'd get if he died. She used it to start her salon, and in a way, Dad is still the reason we can take care of ourselves now.

"Hey, handsome," Miss Maya—the front desk lady at Mom's salon—said hi to me when Caprice and I burst through the doors. The shop was busy today for it being a Monday.

On each side of the salon were six chairs facing a wall of mirrors, hair on one side, nails and feet on the other. Most of the twelve chairs were filled today, and mom was busy running a blow dryer through some old lady's hair when we came in.

"Hi, Miss Maya," I said hello back. "This is Caprice," I said before she could ask. "She's gonna wait for me while I get changed out my school clothes."

I was slipping off my backpack in the main waiting area, setting it on a leather black couch, and my basketball on the ground. Just as I was about to tell Caprice I'd be right back, Mom interrupted me.

"Shaun!" my mother called over the sound of a blow dryer. Behind a client, while holding two bobby pins between her lips, she shouted, "There's pizza in the back from lunchtime. Offer some to your guest."

Listening to my mom, I turned to Caprice, and asked, "Do you want some pizza?" Almost kind of embarrassed, she said yes. "Alright, follow me to the backroom."

"Ahem," Mom tried to get our attention just as we walked past her. I stopped to see what she wanted. Caprice might've not been able to tell, but Mom was teasing me when she said, "Introduce me to your friend, Shaun."

If my eyes could talk, they would've been begging her not to embarrass me. "Caprice, this is my mom, Sylvia. Mom, this is Caprice."

"Hello." Caprice's voice was extra soft.

"Aww," my mom dang near sang, like Caprice was a cute puppy or something. "Aren't you precious with those little pigtails… I like your hair, cutie. Who did it for you?"

Mom is always asking people about their hair.

"My grandma."

"Aww," Mom said again at the sound of Caprice's voice. "I always wanted a little girl with hair like yours. It's beautiful."

This wasn't news to me. Mom told me all the time that she wishes I was a girl. I knew it was because she wanted somebody else's hair to mess around in.

"Thank you…" Caprice wasn't sure what to call her.

"Sylvia is fine," Mom assured.

"Thank you, Miss Sylvia," she tried again, adding the *Miss* for respect, not realizing that the little word she added before my mother's name made all the difference to Mom. Caprice didn't know it yet, but she had just won Miss Sylvia's love without even trying.

* * *

I practiced taking shots while Caprice sat on the bleachers with a notebook on her lap.

It was early in the day. The regular older boys weren't out from their high school yet, so the court was dang near empty as I dribbled the ball from one basket to the other. Every minute or so, I'd check to see what Caprice was up to, just to see she was doing the same thing she'd been doing minutes before.

Her homework.

I wanted to ask her to play, but she wasn't dressed for play. She had on a white polo shirt and a khaki uniform skirt, and those might get messed up if she played in them. I didn't know why she was here when it might've been easier for her to do her homework at home.

"Hey Caprice!"

She looked up from her work, her poofy black pigtails reflecting the sunlight shining from behind her head. Her dark eyes were on me, waiting.

"You wanna play ball with me?" Maybe she wouldn't care about messing up her clothes.

She didn't say no right away, her head tilting to the side like she was thinking about it. Almost kind of embarrassed like, she told me, "I don't know how to play basketball."

Did that mean that if I taught her, she would play with me?

"It's easy." I smiled as I nodded, trying to encourage her out of her seat. "Put your books down, and I'll teach you."

A bit later, we stood face to face, about three feet apart. I had the advantage of being dressed in basketball shorts and a plain t-shirt, so I decided I'd go easy on her since she could get hot faster in her school clothes.

"A'ight this is streetball, one-on-one, so the rules are a little bit different. We play for the same basket." Since she was new to this—and a girl—I started low. Like, preschool low. "First one to five, wins. I'mma let you start with the ball, so when you're ready to play, you bounce it off the ground to me, and I will throw it back at you to start the game. You watched us play over the summer, right?"

She nodded.

"So, you know you can't just run with the ball, right? You gotta dribble it on your way to the basket. The whole time, I'm gonna be trying to get the ball from you. I can't push you or trip you or none of that, so don't worry about getting hurt. You can hold the ball in your hand so long as you're not moving, and I can't knock it out of your hand until you try to take a shot. Is this making sense?"

"I think so," she said it like a question.

After we walked to the middle of the court, I tossed her the ball.

"A'ight now, check." She just held on to the ball. "Whenever you're ready, Caprice."

She bounced the ball toward me and right before I threw it back at her, I told her to, "Make sure I can't get it, okay?"

She caught the ball and started awkwardly dribbling to the basket. I let her have a five second head start, coming up from behind her as she started to travel. Sounding like my coach, I shouted out pointers, "You can't hold the ball while you move! Either dribble the ball or stop moving and try a shot."

She stopped moving, holding the ball out in front over her as she tried to get a clear shot of the basket. I started guarding her, standing close behind as I waited for her to try her shot. I wasn't even going to try to block it 'cause I could tell from her form that she was gonna miss every shot she tried this game. Still, I had to act like I was guarding her, so that it could be at least a little fun for her. It would suck if I spent the entire game crapping on her.

Caprice took a step back as she tried to get in a good shot, and since I was guarding her, her back pushed against my front.

The ball slipped from her hands the moment our bodies bumped together. It was like she stopped breathing and the world got quiet all around us.

And then she started screaming.

I'm not just talking about screaming like how some girls laugh and scream when they're having fun outside. No. This was something different.

Caprice screamed like someone was trying to kill her. She covered her ears and dropped to the ground, curling up into a little ball, just screaming and screaming. It was the kind of screaming that had people coming out of their apartments, traffic slowing down, ripping into your ear drums to tell you something was *very,*

very wrong.

It was the kind of screaming that scared the heck outta me.

*Did I play too rough? Did I hurt her? Did she break something?*

"Caprice," I tried to shout over her screaming, leaning down to touch her shoulder.

The moment my hand touched down, her screams changed into repeating words over and over, "Don't touch me. Don't touch me. Don't touch me. Don't touch me."

I let her go, and she stopped.

It was quiet now; no more screaming. For that I was grateful, but I wasn't sure what I was supposed to say. Just before I could ask her if she was okay, she started crying.

And I mean, crying *really* hard.

Caprice didn't cry like someone who was hurt really bad. I don't think she was in pain. At least, not on her body. Curled up in a ball on the blacktop court, she cried like someone she loved had died, like she'd been holding this inside for a really long time.

I couldn't stop whatever was happening, so I just sat down next to her on the court. Her cries must've been ripping out of her from deep down. I could almost feel her shaking the ground underneath us. My eyes were getting prickly with my own tears just from looking at her. I didn't know what to do, but seeing her this sad made me feel a falling feeling at the bottom of my stomach.

Before I knew it, I was crying, too.

It was almost like she snapped out of whatever had her sobbing so hard the moment she heard me sniffling. Slowly she stopped, the ball she was curled into quietly coming apart. Breathing fast from all that crying, she sat up criss-cross applesauce, face-to-face with me. Her voice was croaky when she asked, "Why… why are *you* crying?"

Now I felt embarrassed.

Because I didn't even know. Even though it made me feel like a sissy, I told her that.

"I don't know." And then I asked her the same question. "Why did you cry?"

I don't even think she was lying when she said, "I don't know either."

We both tried to collect ourselves, neither of us looking at the other while we tried to get better.

"Your nose turns bright red when you cry," she said to me, her voice like everything was normal now. My nose changing colors when I cried was on account my skin being as yellow as a pistachio shell. Those were my mother's teasing words, not mine. Caprice stared at it and laughed a little.

Even though I was confused as heck, I was relieved to see her smile. "You think my red nose is funny?"

She nodded.

"You're like if Rudolph the Red-Nosed Reindeer was a boy." She laughed at her own joke, wiping the last of the wetness on her face. Even though she was making fun of me, it made me smile to see her laugh. "I'm really sorry for making you cry," she said.

It's not like she did it on purpose. Even I didn't know that seeing her cry would set me off like that.

"I'm sorry for bumping you," I apologized, too.

"You were just playing the game. I know," she understood. "I just get weird when people touch me, is all... It's not your fault."

What she did wasn't weird, it was *scary*.

Of course, I didn't say that.

"Oh, okay," was all I said out loud, then promising, "I won't touch you anymore."

Caprice's eyes got a little worried by the sound of my voice, and she rushed to ask, "We can still be friends, right?"

At first, I only gave her a smile, my hand digging into one of my pockets to pull out two hard candies. I'd taken them from the candy dish at my mom's salon. One chocolate, one butterscotch.

"Of course, we're friends," I promised, offering up a candy. "Take one. I'll take whichever one you don't want.

She picked the butterscotch.

* * *

The streetlights were on when I got around to walking Caprice home.

After the scene at the court, we went into the library across the street, which Caprice seemed to like more. When it came time to walk Caprice home, I stopped by the salon to tell Mom I'd meet her at the house. She opposed at first, but when I told her it was time for Caprice to go home, Mom let me go so that Caprice wouldn't have to walk home alone.

Now we walked side by side, as close as we could get without touching. I was still thinking about how she cried on the basketball court. By now she had bounced back from her fit, acting now as if it hadn't happened while I was left to replay it over and over in my mind. I wanted to ask her what happened to her. Something had to have happened to her for her to just break like that out of nowhere.

But I didn't want to bring it up again.

Especially not now as she smiled and practically skipped her way home with me at her side. You could never look at this happy little girl and believe she drew a crowd of horrified grown-ups listening to her scream downtown. It's a wonder nobody called the police.

Maybe the people in the city thought it was part of some kid's game we were playing.

"Are we going to the court tomorrow?" Caprice asked, everything about her more comfortable with me than she was this morning.

"You want to?" I asked.

She nodded quickly. "I just wanna watch, though, if that's okay."

I figured.

"Yeah," I agreed as we turned the corner onto our block. "That's okay. We'll go tomorrow."

"Do you go to the courts every day after school?"

"If the weather's good, yes."

"And can I keep coming with you?"

I was in the middle of saying yes when flickers of blue and red lights flashed across her face. We were both close to home and close to where the lights were coming from. Turning away from each other, we looked out ahead of us.

Parked in front of Caprice's pink house were three police cars, blue and red lights on. All around the street, people had come out of their houses, standing in their front yards so they could watch everything as it was going on.

Three police officers stepped out from inside her home. The first one held two big jars of this green stuff that I knew was called weed. The second officer held only one jar of the same stuff, but in his other hand was a big white trash bag of something else I couldn't see. The last police officer was holding onto a man.

I turned to look at Caprice, to see if watching this man arrested out of her home was hard for her to see. I'd hate to see her cry again. Instead, when I turned to get a look at her, all I found was blue and red lights flashing and reflecting off her widened eyes. She was more surprised than she was sad.

"Is that your dad?"

She shook her head quickly, only saying, "Marcel."

I had no idea what he was to her, but soon enough, tears started to collect at the rims of her eyes. Quiet drops ran down her cheeks as she looked on, unblinking and unmoving. Even though her crying wasn't scary like before, I still tried to help.

"Please don't cry. Please don't be sad."

The man she called Marcel was shoved into the back of a police car. Caprice looked on, almost kind of hypnotized by it all, only snapping out of it at the sound of my tries to comfort her.

Her head slowly turned in my direction. I'll never forget how absolutely chilling it was to hear the words that came out of her mouth next. She looked at me square in the eyes, blue and red colored lights shining over one half of her face, and told me, "I'm not crying because I'm sad."

*ACT TWO*

# CAPRICE - AGE 16

2006

# Chapter Seven

## Caprice

Somebody somewhere once said, *'Time heals all wounds.'*

My only question to that has always been… how much time?

I have a different theory.

You see, I think time makes you forget the things that never mattered. However, when things are serious—traumatic, maybe—time has a way of painting unforgettable images into your memory. Trauma is like cement; time only makes it more solid.

Sometimes you can fool yourself into thinking you're "over" something. Then you catch yourself saying things, doing things, avoiding things, realizing you never truly got over anything. You just set new boundaries so that the same thing couldn't happen to you twice.

Time doesn't heal most wounds. If you're lucky, time distracts you long enough so that you can forget.

Time didn't do that for me, but it did it for Gracie.

When I was a little girl, my uncle Marcel did a terrible thing to me. Gracie—my grandmother, his mother—was furious. At the time, at least. She wanted him out. She wanted him to pack his things and get the hell out of her house. For days after she told him he needed to go, he didn't pack not one of his things. She told him he couldn't stay with us anymore, and he didn't pay her any mind. Marcel was being defiant.

Since Marcel made it clear he wasn't going, she called the police on him, thinking they might help her kick him out. In her mind, the worst that could've happened was them ordering him off the property. She wasn't going to press charges or anything. Gracie wanted to scare him just enough so that he could see she was serious about him leaving.

What Gracie didn't know was that Marcel was selling drugs out of her house.

It was mostly just weed, but that was still pretty serious in the 90s.

My grandmother called the police on her son, thinking they would only send one officer over for a simple domestic dispute. When that single police officer arrived, he let himself into Marcel's room and found a felony amount of weed, among other illegal things. Two more police officers were called, and they raided the entire house from the bottom up.

Because drugs were only found in Marcel's room, Marcel was the only person arrested.

Gracie called the cops, thinking Marcel would've been escorted out with a slap on the wrist.

What he got was a twelve-year prison sentence and a felony drug charge.

Even though I didn't tell her to call the police, even though I didn't tell Marcel to have that much weed, even though I was just a child when all this went down… Gracie blamed *me*.

Something about seeing her son in handcuffs made Gracie forget all about what he did. All that anger that she had for him? She turned around and gave it to me the day of his sentencing.

When I was a child, I thought Gracie loved me.

And maybe she did.

But, despite everything, she surely loved Marcel more.

The shift was like day and night. She turned into somebody I no longer recognized—hateful, apathetic, and just *really* mean. There was a time when she used to beg me to eat, and overnight she decided she would feed me just enough so that I wouldn't die. I went from being a welcomed guest in her home, to constantly being reminded that had to be out by eighteen.

I grew to hate being in that house.

I grew to hate her.

By the time Marcel would be out of jail, I would be twenty years old and long gone. Knowing this made me sleep a little easier at night.

In spite of it all, Gracie let me keep my bedroom. She took Marcel's room after he was arrested. And not because she wanted me to have the bigger space, either.

I think being there just made her feel closer to him, sleeping where he used to sleep.

Marcel getting locked up was the thing that finally made Gracie get a car.

Every Sunday, Gracie would make the six-hour drive upstate for prison visits. Over time I learned it was best not to be around her when she arrived home from those trips. Seeing Marcel from behind a glass never failed to put her into one of her moods. She'd just get home from those visits and look for things to go off on me for. She was upset about her son being locked up, so taking it out on me must've helped her cope.

One time, Gracie was on the phone with a friend, talking about one of her visits. Through the paper thin walls, I listened from my room. From what I gathered, Marcel was having a very tough time on the inside. Over the years I put clues together, using what I'd learn about prison, and I figured someone on the inside was doing to him what he once did to me.

I thought imagining it would make me happy, but it didn't. I wouldn't wish that kind of thing on anyone.

Not even Marcel.

* * *

The first day of school is my least favorite day of school.

Something about first days always takes me back to 1999; third grade. Nowadays, I just kinda think about it and push down that looming feeling of anxiety it gives me. When I was younger, like in fourth and fifth grade, first days of school used to make me cry. Thankfully, not today. Not anymore.

Today was the first day of tenth grade, August 21$^{st}$, 2006. Jefferson High School was bustling.

I was the first student to arrive in my homeroom, probably because I didn't stop for conversations in the courtyard.

First days of school are all about being seen.

People don't go through the trouble of getting new clothes,

new shoes, and new hair, just for nobody to see it. It's not a big deal to be late on the first day. So, people take their time getting to class. That way everybody who matters can offer up their compliments.

I'm not judging.

I would've done it, too, if I had new clothes, shoes, or hair.

But I didn't.

So, I had the privilege of walking into an empty homeroom and having my choice of any seat.

I picked a seat in the back-right corner, briefly making eye contact with Ms. Frasier as we both waited for the day to start. Ms. Frasier was my homeroom teacher last year as well, so introductions weren't necessary. She was the mousey type, so she didn't bother making conversation or asking me how my summer was. Technically, as just my homeroom teacher, I didn't know her like that. During the regular school day, she taught remedial English, so I had never taken her class.

I've never taken remedial anything.

It was three minutes after the late bell when students finally began to pile in. The usual faces appeared, nearly all of them dressed in new clothes from head-to-toe. This was another reason why the first day always used to get me down as a child.

Gracie never bought me anything nice.

And when you're a kid, not having anything nice makes other kids look at you some type of way. Over time, I learned to let it roll off my shoulders. *They're just clothes.*

"Hey, gorgeous." Mischa took the desk directly in front of mine, turning around so we could talk. I smiled, happy to see we were in the same homeroom again. Mischa Gaines was my second best friend, after Shaun. We became friends in sixth grade after I let her copy my math work for the entire year. We didn't have a ton in common, but Mischa genuinely liked me, which was more than could be said for most of my other classmates.

I didn't know what it was about me, but it wasn't easy for me to make friends.

"Guess who finally got a RAZR over the summer?"

My friend flashed the thin flip phone excitedly and then adjusted the glasses on her nose. It was trendy right now to be wearing just the frames, so Mischa's glasses didn't have any lenses.

I was happy for her. Really.

I didn't have any kind of cell phone yet. It was one of those things I couldn't bring myself to buy every time pay day came around. Cell phones were really expensive—even the cheaper ones—and the phone plans weren't any better. Every time checks came around at my job, I always talked myself out of it. With only two close friends—one of which who lived across the street—I didn't have much need for a phone anyway.

Once everyone was in the classroom, you could almost choke on how thick the smell of *Victoria's Secret Love Spell* and *AXE Body Spray* was in the room. Kids were still doing the '*check out my new stuff*' song and dance as Ms. Frasier began passing out class schedules and taking attendance.

Jefferson was a uniform-only school, but kids still found a way to make it a competition. If we had to wear khaki pants and polo shirts, then the pants better be *Dickies* and the polo shirts better be *Ralph*.

And shoes?

Shoe game was no joke around here.

This is exactly why the first thing that Princess Knight said to me was, "You still wearin' those ratty *Keds* from last year?"

I've been knowing Princess for quite some time now. When I was much younger, I remember really wanting her and her friends to like me. Looking like an off-brand Christina Milian, Princess was pretty and had really nice style. Unfortunately for me, she was also nasty, and for some reason she decided I was the person she should direct that energy at. As we got older, I did my best to avoid her. Princess had it out for me, and I had no idea why.

Mischa spoke up before I could. "You know what's sadder than wearing old shoes? A bitch who's got another girl's wardrobe memorized like that. Shit, Princess... You couldn't find nothing interesting to do over the summer? Bitch, just tell Caprice you missed her and get gone."

Walking up an aisle of desks, Ms. Frasier caught the last half of that exchange. "Miss Gaines! Language!"

"My bad, Ms. Frasier."

"Good guard dog," Princess praised Mischa mockingly. "Caprice got you trained up real well. She house broke you yet?

With your fat ass…"

"Miss Knight!" Ms. Frasier's reprimands fell on deaf ears.

"Stop," I had to cut in before Mischa messed around and got herself detention on day one. I didn't need Mischa to defend me, and I didn't need Princess insulting my friends to get under my skin. "Princess, you're right. My shoes ain't new. You done?"

Ms. Frasier set a schedule on my desk as Princess turned back around in her seat. I went down the class list, grateful that I'd been placed in every class I wanted. AP US History, AP Psychology, AP Biology, AP Calculus, AP English and P.E.

"We only have homeroom and P.E. together," Mischa said disappointedly after sneaking a look at my class schedule. But I saw the bright side. At least I'd get to start and end my school days with her. Mischa continued to stare at my paper. "Damn, look at all these AP classes. Girl, if you pass all these, you can graduate *this* year."

"That's the plan," I revealed.

The sooner I could get out of Gracie's house, the better.

"Wow, you gon' leave me here by myself for two years?" she asked, halfway kidding, halfway serious. "Graduating at sixteen, though? You'll miss out on our senior prom." Mischa knew me too well to know that wouldn't change my mind. A thought flashed in her eyes. "Eh… now that I think about it, your classes boutta be *full* of seniors this year. One of them might ask you to their prom."

"Pshhhhh," I scoffed, rolling my eyes. "Yeah… that'll happen."

While Mischa checked the schedules of all the other kids in class, I took a moment to look down at my shoes. Princess was right, they *were* ratty. As the poor man's alternative to *Converse, Keds* were already lame to begin with, but mine were falling apart. The fabric was tattered. The bottom soles had cracked, so when it rained, my socks would get a little wet. I'd worn them all last year, and I was trying to keep them together until at least November this year.

Then I'd buy myself some new ones on Black Friday.

Anything to save a few dollars.

I had a job in the city. I was a desk clerk at an African bookstore on Division Ave, close to Miss Sylvia's salon. Actually, it was Miss Sylvia who got me that job. One of her clients, Miss Jacinta, was getting up there in age, and didn't have the stamina to run a bookstore all day anymore. It was Miss Sylvia who she confided in. I was in the salon that day, sweeping up hair and disinfecting tools.

Since I was twelve, Miss Sylvia had been giving me little jobs here and there in her salon; maybe paying me more than I deserved for the little bit I did. I think she knew my grandma wasn't taking care of me like she should've been. Letting me sweep up the salon was just her way of giving me some money without making it feel too much like charity.

I was fourteen the summer Miss Jacinta came into the salon for a wash and retwist. She had these long brown locs that took hours to service, so she stayed past closing. I was sitting in a chair, waiting for Miss Sylvia to finish up so she could drive me home. I could've walked, but Miss Sylvia refused to let me walk through Parramore at night.

While Miss Sylvia retwisted her locs, Miss Jacinta complained about how she didn't know what she was going to do about the bookstore. You see, Miss Jacinta's son was going off to college in Georgia, and there would be nobody to run the store in the evenings.

Without much thought, Miss Sylvia glanced at me and casually suggested, "*Take Caprice.*" Then she went to listing off the reasons. *"She's fourteen, so she can legally work. She's responsible, trustworthy, and actually wants a job. I'll vouch for her."*

It was the summer right before ninth grade. I'd been working at *Kemetic Pages* more than a year now, every day right after school. I saved most of everything I made. Making about seven fifty an hour and working about twenty-five hours a week, I saved almost eight thousand dollars on my own.

Miss Sylvia was the one who helped me start my bank account, and that's where nearly all the money went every pay day.

I was saving up for when I moved out of Gracie's house and went to college.

Before school started this year, I thought about getting some new clothes, shoes, and maybe even getting my hair done, but I decided against it. It would be nice to have those things at first, but then I knew I'd feel regretful over time.

That money was for college.

"I got bad news for you." Mischa pulled me out of my thoughts, putting me back in that energized homeroom. I raised my eyebrows, ready to hear it. "I saw Princess' schedule, and you two have all the same classes again this year."

That's one of the things you can't call Princess—you can't call her dumb. Mean, nasty, bully, but never dumb. The only reason I knew her so well was because she was always in my classes. Even though she didn't wear her grades proudly across her *Ralph Lauren* polo shirts, she took school seriously. I was not looking forward to another year of Princess in every room.

Mischa's brown eyes looked at me sympathetically, her chubby cheeks puffing out the sides, making her look more like Kim, from *The Parkers* TV show, than she usually did. I couldn't think of anything else to say after that bad news. There was nothing to add. Shrugging, I let it go as the bell rang from behind her.

"I'll see you at lunch?" I slid out of my seat and grabbed my things.

"Lunch," she agreed. "See ya later, gorgeous."

# Chapter Eight

## Caprice

AP Biology was my third class of the day, right before lunch.

This was usually a senior level class, but I'd gotten so many high school credits while I was in middle school, I practically started my freshman year as a junior. The science wing of Jefferson High School was clear across a grassy courtyard, detached from the rest of the school. Here we had all the chemistry, physics, and biology classes. I think the idea was that if a fire ever broke out during any science experiments, the rest of the school wouldn't burn.

Cutting across that courtyard had the sun beaming over my head. There were no hallways at Jefferson. Each classroom opened directly outside, but the science wing was the furthest distance from any of my other classes. I was a little sweaty by the time I got to the biology lab, which I hated.

It was too early in the school day for me to feel like I needed a shower. The thing with me is—even when I'm not dirty—if I *feel* dirty, I get really stressed. It was a behavioral tick that had been getting progressively worse since I was a kid. When I was eight, I didn't feel clean unless I took at least five showers a day. Of course, with a regular grade school schedule that just wasn't possible.

I adapted.

Shower in the morning. Shower after school, before work. Shower before bed.

Still, when I didn't feel clean, I got anxious.

It didn't help that I'd been feeling weird all morning. There was a dull ache in my lower stomach, and I felt kind of lightheaded. When I woke up, I thought it was because I was nervous about the first day, but that nervousness should've subsided by now. I checked my backpack for baby wipes. Maybe I would feel better if I felt just a little cleaner.

Unfortunately, I had none. *Ugh…*

When I walked into the biology classroom, I found ten empty black-top tables. There were two stools at each table, five tables on each side of the room.

Dr. Young, my biology teacher, had his desk positioned at a front corner of the classroom, beside the whiteboard. He was sitting there when I walked in, straightening his tie at the sound of the door closing behind me.

"You're early, Miss…"

"Latimore. Caprice Latimore," I introduced myself, still standing by the door, thankful for the cool burst of air conditioning. I hoped he wouldn't kick me out and make me wait for class to start outside. "Can I sit down?"

"Yes," he nodded, a wrinkled brown hand stretching out in front of him. "Pick any seat you want. That's your permanent spot for the year."

Dr. Young was some kind of Asian mixed with black. I didn't know if he was Chinese or Korean or something else, but I knew he was Asian and black. Like Tiger Woods, but balder and fifty years older.

Dr Young was an old man with six degrees—all of which he kept framed on the wall behind his desk. He'd been teaching at Jefferson for thirty years, which was more than enough time to be completely over it. But he wasn't. While Dr. Young was strict, I heard he taught really well. Most everyone who passed his class could pass the AP exam, and I needed to pass all my AP exams this year to graduate early.

I took a seat at the fifth table on the left, choosing the stool on the left as well. Dr. Young stayed behind his desk, reading a newspaper with his feet kicked up, as we waited for the bell to ring.

Princess was the first person to walk in after me, just before the bell. She grabbed a seat at the fifth table on the right, putting her backpack on the stool next to hers to save a seat for someone.

I looked at the empty stool to my right and debated whether or not I should put my backpack there. Did I want someone sitting next to me? I decided not to be immature about it.

Though, it wasn't like it mattered, by the time most of the classroom had filled, the seat next to me was still empty.

AP Biology was about fifteen seniors, three juniors, and two sophomores—Princess and me. Most everyone in this class had their friends and the people they would've preferred to sit with, so I didn't take it personally that no one chose the seat next to me.

Princess only removed the backpack she placed in the seat beside her when Paris Knight, her older sister, waltzed into the room. If Princess was pretty, then Paris was drop dead gorgeous. Paris looked like a teenaged Meagan Good; maybe even prettier.

Although Paris had never said more than three words to me, I figured since Princess definitely wasn't my biggest fan, her older sister wouldn't be either.

All the seats in the classroom were filled except for one. I didn't mind sitting by myself.

Dr. Young was starting to take attendance when Princess directed a "Psssst," my way.

I didn't want to respond, but I knew she'd only do it louder the second time.

"What?" I whispered, turning to face the two girls across the aisle.

"Your hair looks nice," Princess told me quietly. That's all I needed to hear to know that my hair did *not* look nice. "Do you have to leave it like that to keep your job at that Hotep bookstore?"

It was 2006, and big afro-textured hair hadn't been in style since the 1970s and 80s. I wanted a relaxer, but Miss Sylvia swore up and down that natural hair was making a comeback any day now and I was getting a head start. Thinking about how expensive being relaxed was to maintain, I just kinda took Miss Sylvia's word for it. It seemed like the day was never coming, though.

Mostly I just wore my hair in buns or French braids. Today it was gelled down in a low bun, which was fine. It wasn't first-day-of-school flashy, but it was decent enough. Even as Princess tried to poke fun at it, I knew I didn't look *that* bad.

Dr. Young was cut off in the middle of taking attendance when the door to his classroom opened again. Coming in from outside—late—was my best friend, Shaun. We didn't talk about schedules over the summer, so I had no idea he'd be in this class.

As star player on the school's basketball team, I thought it was safe to assume he wouldn't be adding the stress of AP classes onto his last year of high school.

"Mister Taylor, you're late," Dr. Young reprimanded him in front of a full audience. Shaun wasn't embarrassed, like I would've been. He just dug into the back pocket of his khakis and pulled out a small piece of paper.

"I got stuck in a conversation with a college scout. Coach wrote me a pass."

Dr. Young practically snatched the paper out of Shaun's hand, clearly angry that he had to honor it. Shaun pressed his lips together like someone trying not to laugh. "For the time being, *you* are still in high school, so be sure to let Coach Coleman know that recruiter meetings need to be scheduled outside of class time. Find a seat."

Shaun walked down the aisle of tables, a senior so he knew most everyone in class, dapping certain people up as he looked for a seat. My eyes traveled up from a clean white pair of Jordans, to his khaki loose-fit cargo pants, rising to a blue and white letterman jacket that all the varsity basketball players wore, opened out to a white polo shirt underneath.

Even though uniforms were supposed to make all of us look the same, his six-foot-four frame would never just blend in. He was special. Shaun was visibly fit, filling into his clothes in such an attractive way. He had this smile that didn't try too hard, or too little. It was quintessentially him, handsome and vibrant. Like every other male student, he had a fresh haircut that was sharply lined where his black hair stopped, cut close to his scalp and showing off really pretty waves. I let out a slow breath, realizing I was checking him out and quickly looking away, only to find Princess and Paris watching me watch him.

Looking away from them, I ducked my head down just as I felt his shadow shade the light above me.

"Well, damn," I heard him react out loud, looking up to find his amused features. Shaun was just as surprised to find me in this class as I was to find him. "You savin' enough school for the rest of us, Butterscotch?" He grabbed the empty seat beside me. "What you doin' in here with all these seniors?"

"I'm not the only sophomore in here," I pointed out, my eyes glancing at Princess behind his head. Shaun turned around to follow my line of sight, seeing both sisters before turning back around. Even though the girls behind him had no idea what we could've been talking about, they assumed we were talking about them. Their expressions toward me went completely stank.

"You *always* do that," I complained. "Please stop looking *directly* at the people I'm talking about. You make it so obvious."

Shaun laughed, entertained by my whining. "Right, right."

Dr. Young went down the list of his expectations for the year while we continued to whisper.

"You got work today?" he asked.

"Mm-hmm."

"You need company?"

"You don't have practice today?"

"Not until next wee—"

"*Mister* Taylor—" Shaun was caught, and Dr. Young was clearly in a yelling mood. And he was clearly not a fan of Shaun. "—I *know* you did not come into class five minutes late, and then work up the *audacity* to talk while I'm up here."

I covered my mouth to hide a smile.

As soon as Dr. Young went back to his first-day lecture, Shaun was back to whispering. "So, do you?"

Sometimes, when Shaun didn't have basketball practice, he'd hang around *Kemetic Pages* for my entire shift. The bookstore doesn't have a lot of foot traffic and it was easy to get bored during my four-to-nine schedule. Shaun's company was always welcomed. "I need the company."

He broke into a gorgeous smile, and I wondered if he could tell that my heartbeat stuttered. I tried to push out the feeling, looking away to pay attention to Dr. Young, still feeling Shaun's copper brown eyes on me as I did.

He could be really intense without realizing it. Sometimes my heart rate would speed up when his voice got all gentle and up close. Sometimes I'd stop breathing altogether when he looked at me a certain way—like the way I could feel him looking at me right now.

A long, long time ago, I convinced myself I was in love with Shaun. I was eleven. He was thirteen. That "in love" feeling lasted for three weeks, and then he went off and got his first girlfriend—Tasha Neuman.

I cried for six days—one day longer than their relationship lasted—and decided I was better off only seeing Shaun as a friend. As the years passed, I watched girlfriends come and go, soon understanding that I was lucky to just be his friend.

Because Shaun went through girlfriends like he went through shoes. But friends? He kept those.

Different as we were, Shaun was the person I was closest with. Surprisingly, I was that for him as well. It didn't matter that he was popular, and I was not.

And popular might've actually been an understatement.

As star player on the school's award-winning basketball team, Shaun had just about the entire school wrapped around his finger. That included both the students and the administration. To just about everyone, my best friend was *the man*. He was smart, handsome, and even though all the private schools in the area had been trying to scout him for years, he was proud to play ball for Jefferson. It was no coincidence that our school had won the state championship every year since he joined the team.

Shaun brought out the crowds; he made students—both current and graduated—proud to say they were Jefferson Eagles.

On paper, it simply didn't add up that his best friend was a sophomore nobody with beat up *Keds* and a very forgettable impression. It's just that once upon a time in 1999, Shaun decided he wanted to be my friend, and even when I expected him to, he just never grew out of it.

Even now, he was like a magnet, shrinking the space between us as we sat, getting closer to me than I allowed anyone to usually get. Shaun was different; he didn't make me shrink when he got too close. Unlike with most people, he never made me feel uncomfortable.

We could just kind of exist together in the same space, breathing the same air, like it was the most natural thing in the world.

"Miss Latimore." Jumping, I was snatched out of my

thoughts by the sound of Dr. Young's voice. He held up a thick stack of paper, motioning for me to come up and get them. "Could you pass these out, and make sure everyone gets a syllabus?"

Even when you want to, you can't just say no when a teacher asks you to pass out papers. I nodded, pushing out of my seat and feeling all eyes on me as I walked up the aisle between the tables. Behind me, I could hear students gasping and laughing as they whispered. I knew it was me they were laughing at. Were they looking at my ratty shoes from last year? I turned to Princess, who laughed the loudest, honestly confused about why my shoes were *this* funny.

Catching a glimpse of all the students behind me, I realized everyone in the room was entertained by it, smirking and exchanging looks among themselves. Even Dr. Young had a strange look on his face, as if he had no idea how to address what was happening.

Everyone was reacting to something I'd done. I just didn't know what it was.

I looked to my friend for some sort of hint. Whatever it was making everyone else so giggly, it made Shaun just the opposite. He stood, quickly removing his jacket with a deep scowl on his features. Among our laughing classmates, he walked up the aisle with his blue and white varsity jacket stretching toward me. When he was close enough to whisper, he made up for the difference in our heights by leaning down closer to my ear.

"Tie this around your waist," he said quietly, pushing the jacket into my empty hand as he took the papers from my other. "Go sit back down. I'll pass out the papers."

Confused, my brows furrowed with questions.

He didn't say anything, still wearing that impatience on his face. I couldn't tell if he was upset with me, or if he was upset with everyone else. Like this, he wasn't as easy to read. I knew he could be domineering, but his approach was usually much softer with me. It was the strangeness of his behavior that prompted me to simply do as he said.

Without argument, I tied the jacket around my waist, and I handed him the stack of papers Dr. Young had given me to pass out.

On my way back to my seat, it was Princess who cleared things up for me.

Still giggling, she dug in her purse and pulled out a tampon wrapped in a pink plastic wrapper.

"You might need this," she spoke louder than she needed to, wanting everyone to hear. She tossed it over to me, and I didn't reach to catch it. The wrapped tampon hit the front of my shirt, and then fell to my feet. When I looked down at it, it seemed like everyone in the room gave up on trying to hold back their laughter. They erupted.

My face got hot as the laughing persisted, and even though I could hear Dr. Young shouting something at Princess, I couldn't make out what he was saying over the sound of my own heartbeat pounding in my ears. I was too embarrassed to look at anyone directly. Instead, as my hands quickly went to cover my watery eyes, my feet took me out of that classroom just as fast.

# *Chapter Nine*

# SHAUN

After Caprice ran out, Dr. Young slammed a textbook on his desk.

It gave off a loud crashing sound.

That seemed to get everybody to shut the fuck up.

"Miss Knight," he cut into the quiet, hands rubbing on the sides of his head. Just from looking at the man, you could tell these kids irritated the mess outta him. Dr. Young was too old for this shit. "You just earned yourself detention on the first day. No throwing things in my classroom. Go pick that thing up."

She stood to her feet, not having it. "I was *just* trying to help her."

"Two detentions," was all Dr. Young responded with. "You wanna go for three? Pick up the damn tampon, Miss Knight."

I took my time handing those papers out, staring down each of those corny niggas that seemed to think embarrassing Caprice was so damn funny. A girl getting her period in the middle of class was a petty thing to laugh at, but it was an even pettier thing to knock somebody's teeth in over. I resigned to that fact.

When I took my seat, barely five seconds had passed before a Knight was yapping down the side of my face. I could tell by the voice that it was the younger Knight, not Paris.

"You forgot us, Shaun."

I hadn't given either of them a syllabus.

"You can get it yourself, Knight," I suggested, referring to Paris' little sister as Knight because—regardless of what her parents named her—I refused to call that girl princess.

I didn't like her.

Ever since we were kids, Princess acted like it was her job to knock Caprice down. As the saying goes—don't let Princess catch Caprice smiling for shit. It disturbs her peace. Caprice says Princess is just acting out because she must have issues that nobody knows about.

What it is, is annoying.

When I used to mess around with Paris in sophomore year, I remember bringing it up in conversation once. It was a harmless, *"Yo, get your sister,"* comment. I didn't think it was that deep. Paris, on the other hand, tried to turn it into a thing. She wanted to know why it bothered me that her sister was straight bullying my friend, which was a stupid ass question because it answered itself.

Why *wouldn't* it bother me that some chick was bullying my friend? She'd been doing it for years, at that. So, if that chick is your *fuckin'* sister, I'mma tell you to get your sister. Simple.

Paris didn't understand where I was coming from. She saw it as disrespect that I would even mention another girl's name between the both of us. She caught herself asking me to choose between my best friend and herself.

I wish I could say Paris was the first girl to have me make that dumbass decision, but that's how all my relationships ended. With Paris, it just happened a lot faster than it usually did. We lasted *maybe* twenty-four hours.

That was the thing with girls and me. Caprice would say I go through girlfriends like I go through shoes, but that's not actually true. Shoes have never pulled me to the side and said, *'Look, it's either me, or your socks. Choose.'*

Caprice has no idea that none of my relationships worked because girls don't like the fact that my best friend is another girl. Even worse, a pretty girl.

I've been with chicks who were a little more strategic than Paris about how they move. They'd be with me a little longer, let me get used to them, and *then* ask me to choose.

Them or Butterscotch.

The choice is never *truly* difficult. Even when I do really like my girlfriend; hell, even when I love my girlfriend. There's just something about being asked which of the two I can live without—them or Butterscotch.

So, that's why none of my relationships last.

I glanced at the empty seat to my left, getting angry for her all over again. If there's one thing I hated seeing, it's seeing Caprice cry. By the empty seat where she sat, she'd left her notebook and her backpack. She was probably in the nurse's office, so I'd bring it to her after class.

Aside from my mom, Caprice was the person who mattered most in my life. It didn't make sense to a lot of people, but I didn't need it to make sense to them.

It made sense to *me*.

We just started off as friends when we were little, and then one day… One day, it just hit me that she was different from the rest of my friends. More special. I think part of me always knew, from the moment I met her, that she was somebody special. Even when I didn't know what to call it at ten years old, I just knew.

In life, there are certain things that you just need.

I needed food to eat.

I needed air to breathe.

I needed water to drink.

And I needed Caprice.

If not for the fact that she hated being touched, I would've asked her to be my girl a while ago. And that's likely another reason why none of my relationships lasted. I wasn't exactly secretive about who I had *always* wanted.

Caprice made it obvious that she wasn't down for any of it, though. She didn't like hugs. If I got too close, she tried to be subtle when she backed away. She wasn't the touchy feely type.

I'd been friends with her since elementary school, and I could recall every time I'd touched her, because it was so rare. With her, I only took what she was willing to give.

She liked her space. So, I gave her space.

AP Bio ended with a bell. I packed Caprice's notebook into her backpack. It was a raggedy old thing, her backpack. A lot of times, Caprice would use her things until they'd begin falling apart. This bookbag was getting there.

The end of third period marked the beginning of lunch, so I had a little under an hour until fourth period calculus.

Caprice was standing by the phone in the front office, looking as though she had dialed the number she was dialing at least five times already.

Her grandmother, from what I'd observed over the years, was really unreliable.

My jacket was tied around her waist, hiding the blood stain on the back of her khaki pants. Most of my teammates would let their girlfriends wear their jackets. It was a source of pride for them, putting their jersey number on some girl around campus.

Seeing Caprice standing there with my blue and white letterman jacket, my number—28—hanging down the back of her legs… I understood why my teammates liked seeing their girlfriends wear their number.

"Hey." Caprice jumped at the unexpected sound of my voice behind her. She was a jumpy girl. "Hang up. I'll drive you home. We'll get back before fourth period."

Seniors were allowed to leave campus for lunch, and even though Caprice was a sophomore, I knew no one would be checking her for leaving and coming back. Not with her school record, not with her grades.

She let out a long sigh of relief, her eyes conveying her gratitude when they drew up to mine. It was very clear that she had been crying. I hated that. Sometimes I felt like Caprice's sadness was always deeper than it should've been, like everything hit her twice as hard as it did everybody else. To look at her sometimes was to look directly at pain. I couldn't think of a least deserving person.

When she reached out for her backpack, I pulled back. "Nah… I can carry it for you."

* * *

Caprice was still sniffling from the passenger's seat.

Driving down the noon time streets of west side Orlando was easy enough. With the sun so high up in the sky, most everybody was at work or school, so the roads were empty. I could take my eyes off the street ahead briefly, sneak a look at Caprice.

She wiped her face.

"It's really not that serious." I tried to help, doing what I could aside from reaching over to her side and wiping those tears my damn self. I wished I could, but I knew her well enough to know that touching her would just make it worse. "You don't have to cry about it."

She turned and looked at me as my car slowed to a red light. The sun lit up her dark brown eyes, flecks of gold in them shining with the sunlight. "Nobody was laughing at *you*, Shaun."

This was true, but…

"Caprice, fuck them people." The light ahead turned green, and I had to look away from her as I continued to speak. "You think you're the first girl who's ever gotten their period in the middle of class? That shit happens. Niggas is childish out here. You're not the first girl to forget her period was on its way."

"I didn't know," she almost whispered. This conversation was embarrassing for her. She hesitated with what she said next. "I've never… never."

The streets got busier halfway to her house, cars joining us on the road just in time for the lunch rush. If traffic was this thick on the way back to Jefferson, we wouldn't make it back to school on time. I didn't think about it, as what she said before really registered in my mind. "Wait—you've never…?"

She nodded slowly. "It's my first time."

I turned a corner, slowing down we entered our little neighborhood. I could look at her now as I spoke. "Aren't you a little old to be getting your first period *just* now?"

It was August, which meant Caprice was turning sixteen on the last day of the month, in ten days. Exactly one day before I turned eighteen. I remembered middle school being the time most of the girls I knew got their first period. Tenth grade seemed a little late.

Caprice leaned back in her seat, her hands coming up to cover her face as she muttered, "Don't say period. You're not allowed to say period ever again."

I had to laugh, pulling into the driveway of her grandmother's pink house. We just kinda sat there for a good minute, taking in the sounds of the neighborhood around us. At the same time, we turned to face each other, and I privately admired the way the sunlight glowed back against her brown skin.

"You're a woman now, Butterscotch," I got in one last crack, to which she rolled her eyes.

"*Shuuuut up.*" She let herself out of the car.

In all the years I'd known her, I could count on one hand the number of times I'd been inside Caprice's home. On the inside, it was built exactly like my own house across the street. Two bedrooms, two bathrooms, same kitchen, same dining room, same living room. The only difference was how the inside was dressed up.

My mother liked a sleek, color-coordinated house. The inside of our house was nicer, more updated. Mom had plenty of time to decorate it how she liked. She'd been living at our house since before I was born, since *she* was a little girl.

Caprice's house was rundown on the inside. The furniture was tattered and mismatched, with cracks in the walls, and brown spots on the ceiling from neglected storm leaks. Her grandmother was a cigarette smoker, so the whole house smelled like stale tobacco and topsoil. Interestingly enough, you would never guess Caprice lived with a smoker. Caprice always smelled like a fresh shower, being one of the biggest neat freaks I knew.

"Do you mind if I take a shower?" Caprice asked when we got inside.

"Go ahead."

Because our houses were built the same way, I knew that—for some reason—Caprice's grandmother had given her the master bedroom. In my house, my mother had the room with the bathroom on site. In this house, Caprice did.

She shut and locked her bedroom door, ensuring I wouldn't come in unannounced. Not that I planned on sneaking up on her like that. I waited in the living room, feeling the minutes roll by quickly.

Yeah, there wouldn't be time to stop for food on the way, and we were *definitely* going to be late getting back to school.

I snooped around in the kitchen, looking for something to hold me over until the end of the day. There were few cans of vegetables in the cabinets, and I was sure they were expired from how faded the images on them were. In the fridge, there was just a bottle of ketchup and a pitcher of tap water.

There was no food in this house.

Caprice was just letting herself out of her bedroom when I walked out of the kitchen. She was dressed in a darker pair of pants and a different white polo shirt, looking more refreshed than before. My stomach growled, but she didn't hear it over me asking, "You feel better?"

She bit down on her lower lip to suppress a smile before nodding. "Thank you."

I caught myself smiling. Late for class or not, hungry or not, I was glad she was in a better mood. I was happy I could do this for her. If she was anybody else, I would've reached out to attempt at least half a hug, but I knew her better than that. She wouldn't like that sort of thing.

"What class do you have next?"

"AP Calculus," she revealed which made me smile again. Not knowing why, she asked, "What?"

I shrugged. "At least we'll be late to the same class. Let's get out of here."

* * *

We were twenty minutes late to class.

Caprice and I walked in, in the middle of some first day icebreaker, and students were talking amongst themselves when we stepped through the door. The teacher, like most of the students, hardly noticed us coming in. They sat in clusters, talking amongst themselves—breaking the ice, if you will.

Looking for seats, we drew some attention as we walked down the classroom.

Some of the kids in here were the same ones from AP Biology, the class before, whispering among themselves as they took note of Caprice's change of clothes.

I was seconds away from telling Caprice not to let these nosy ass kids get to her, when this kid at a desk reached out and touched her. I didn't know everyone's name at this school, but I think his name was Zavier. He patted Caprice on the back, half teasing, half flirting when he said, "I see you got cleaned up real nice. You look good."

Caprice was not my girlfriend.

Everybody knew that.

However, most of the niggas around here had enough sense to understand that just because she wasn't *officially* mine, did not mean I took kindly to dudes tryna run game on her. Especially not to my face.

*Especially* not while touching her, which I already knew she didn't appreciate.

I leaned in, dead serious. "You've got two seconds to take your fingers off her back before I break your hand."

He snatched his hand back immediately, but so's to not look like a bitch, he got out of his seat, tryna act hard. The wheels were turning in my head.

Coach would take me out of three of the five pre-season games if I tried it.

*It's worth it.*

Caprice knew me better than I knew myself sometimes. Before I could do anything, her hand came out and grabbed my forearm, hands on my skin like water to a flame. Her hand stayed there, evidently hating the idea of me getting in trouble more than she did touching somebody else.

*It's not worth it.*

At the height of the interaction, the math teacher finally took notice of the three standing students in her classroom. And there went our chances of getting away with being so late. She inserted herself into the space between Zavier and I, quickly telling Zavier to find another seat. Her faculty name tag read 'Ms. Kelly Johnson'.

"Now I know you're not late *and* trying to start fights in my classroom."

She was pretty. Young for a teacher compared to most of the staff at this school. A new one, because she wasn't working here last year. Her hair was twisted up in these tiny dreadlocks that I knew were called sister locs because I grew up in a salon. She was one of those eccentric Hotep types—gold on her eyelids, bright red lipstick, and wearing an oversized dashiki that fell over her black tights like a dress.

Caprice's grip on my arm loosened, and then she let go entirely. We were both ushered to the back of the classroom, away from the rest of the students so that they could continue their ice breaker activity undisturbed. I could only assume this was because Ms. Johnson was about to tear us a new one, and she didn't want to distract the other kids by putting on a show.

"I take it you two are Shaun Taylor and Caprice... Latimore?"

She paused after reading Caprice's name from her roster, her eyes snapping up to get a second, longer look at her. She squinted. "Alabama?"

Caprice's voice had that same surprised tone when she questioned back, "Ms. Kelly?"

They knew each other.

Ms. Johnson kinda just stared at her for a moment, giving Caprice that look. You know, the look old relatives give you just before they say something like, '*You look just like your daddy.*' or '*My, you sprouted up like a weed.*'

"Ms. Johnson," the woman corrected in an almost whisper. Oh, they *really* knew each other. They had to if Caprice was going around calling her by her first name. Maybe that meant we weren't about to get written up for walking into class almost thirty minutes late. "Do either of you have passes?"

Or maybe not.

Caprice and I answered at the same time. "No."

Ms. Johnson looked at me with an air of suspicion, as if she knew for a fact that Caprice could do no wrong. So, if "Alabama", as she put it, was late, it must've been *my* fault. Well, I knew which one of us she definitely liked more.

I bit back a smile, telling her what she thought she already knew. "It's my fault."

"It really isn't," Caprice instantly denied. "It's a... long story..."

Ms. Johnson raised her eyebrows, her head shaking from one side to the other. "Well... I'm waiting. The story, then?"

"I, um..." Caprice hesitated, glancing at me before she continued. "I got... my period... For the first time, in, um, Dr. Young's class before... lunch. And, um, Shaun... drove me home to get changed. The time kind of snuck up on us. And then the lunchtime traffic..."

Ms. Johnson nodded, her features a cross between sympathetic and slightly unconvinced. "And if I ask Dr. Young, he'll confirm this explanation?"

"Yes," Caprice and I responded.

We were let off with a stern stare down and then ultimately a warning. With a little under fifteen minutes left of class, Caprice and I didn't exactly have the time to insert ourselves in the ongoing class activity. We took two side-by-side desks on the far-right side of the room, with Caprice sitting to my left.

"You've met her before?"

She nodded. "She was my day camp teacher the summer I moved down here. She kinda put me on to reading."

Caprice was a bookworm. She had been from the moment I knew of her. The first time I ever saw her, she was reading a book under the white lights of the basketball court downtown. I used to make it my mission to get her to look up, to look my way.

"So, you haven't seen her since you were…"

"Eight," she finished my sentence.

"You must've left a lasting impression if she remembered you more than seven years later," I noted, catching Zavier's wandering eyes over Caprice's shoulder. He looked at her a little longer than I was comfortable with. When he noticed me watching him as he watched her, I couldn't help the glare that settled into my expression, knowing I looked every bit as territorial as I felt.

Caprice—whether she acts like it or not—is a *very* pretty girl.

As long as I'd known her, she never had an acne phase. She had this perfect brown skin that stayed clear and lively all the time. Her dark eyes were round and framed by naturally long eyelashes.

Whenever I made her smile, I felt like I'd accomplished something, and seeing her happy was my reward.

Even though she wanted her hair to look like everyone else's, I liked her shiny black hair with all of its puffs and coils. Caprice was perfect. It wasn't hard to understand why every girlfriend I ever had took issue with my friendship with her.

The thing is—Caprice wasn't into me in that way. The best that I could hope for was being her best friend, and I wasn't going to pressure her for anything more than that. She was… sensitive to that kind of thing. And the last thing I wanted to do was make her uncomfortable by expressing how I actually felt about her.

But that didn't mean I was okay with watching other guys express their attraction. As the years went on, they just started popping up everywhere. A growing list of from-afar admirers that clearly made her skin crawl.

Caprice didn't like attention.

So, even though I had my own personal reasons for keeping those clowns away from her, it was an added benefit knowing that she wanted me to.

A win-win situation.

With my mind elsewhere, I hadn't heard any of the last bit of what Caprice was saying when the sound of the bell interrupted her. Students started getting out of their seats, heading out into the hallways. Caprice had English next, and I was gonna walk her to class before heading over to gym class.

Right before we could cross the threshold, her name was called.

"Caprice." We both turned to find Ms. Johnson waiting at her desk at the back corner of the math classroom. "Can I have a word?"

She glanced at me, and then back at Ms. Johnson. I thought I'd be able to wait by the door, but Ms. Johnson quickly shot that down.

"You can go to your next class now, Mr. Taylor." Which was a polite way of saying '*get out*'. "And don't wait outside. You don't want to be late *again*."

## *Chapter Ten*

# Caprice

When the door shut, Ms. Kelly shed that look on her face like taking off a mask, going from strict to absolutely elated.

"Oh, my goodness, you got so big," she was gushing over me like an aunt or cousin that thought about me often. It was nice because I didn't really have any real relatives who would've reacted this way to seeing me.

Not even after seven years.

I did look different, though. Everything about me had changed. I wasn't bony and short anymore. My hair was pulled back into a thick bun. I looked more like a woman now. The last time Ms. Kelly saw me, I was an underweight third grader with ribbons in her pigtails, a squeaky voice, and knobby knees.

Now, I was two inches short of six feet tall, one of the tallest girls at Jefferson. These days, the only time I looked small was when I stood side-by-side with Shaun. Definitely not the same Caprice from 1999.

I couldn't believe she still remembered me. Though, I guess it wasn't too strange since I remembered her. I thought about her often. Working at an Afrocentric bookstore like *Kemetic Pages*, I'd met a lot of women who reminded me of Ms. Kelly this past year.

"I can't believe you still remember me." Time had treated Ms. Kelly well. Still very beautiful, she was probably in her mid to late twenties now. Her locs were now waist length, draped over a black and red dashiki covering her black yoga pants.

"I could never forget that face," she expressed, adding with an edge of disappointment, "And your little southern accent is mostly gone."

"I thought you wanted me to lose it."

"Nooo," she stressed. "I wanted you to lose the bad grammar. The accent, however, was very cute."

My response was interrupted by the late bell ringing outside. I was late for English. Seeing how no students had walked in at this point, now must've been Ms. Kelly's free period. She must've realized the time just then.

"I'd love to keep you longer so we can catch up, but I gotta respect your fifth period teacher's time. Let me just write you a late pass, and we'll talk some other day." She scribbled her signature onto a yellow pass, walking to the door with me. Just before I let myself out, she absently said, "I'm so relieved that you turned out okay."

*What was that supposed to mean?*

I paused, my hand freezing at the doorknob. I got that prickly feeling I usually got when I felt like people were seeing me a little *too* well. I hated feeling seen. "Why wouldn't I have?"

"You were a very, um… You were memorable for a reason, Caprice," was all she said. And from the way that she said it, I understood that this was all she was *gonna* say. "I'll see you tomorrow."

* * *

"What do you wanna do after high school?"

It was a slow day at the shop. Nobody had come into *Kemetic Pages* for at least three hours now, and Shaun and I were nearing the end of my shift. I was organizing hardcover books onto a towering wooden shelf as he made conversation.

"That's a random question."

"It's not," he disagreed, standing with me in the aisle. "I see you tryna graduate early this year. So, what's the plan after this?"

I ran a finger down the spine of a textbook, rising my head to meet his eyes hovering above mine between the bookshelves. He was standing close enough for me to feel the heat radiating off his body. When he would stand this close, I would often wonder if he could hear my heart pounding in my chest. I was comfortable with Shaun in ways that I wasn't with anyone else, but when he absentmindedly did these kinds of things, my body couldn't help but respond in ways that left me embarrassed.

If he could hear my heart, the totally neutral look on his face didn't give that away.

"Miami."

"Miami?" He was confused. Maybe that was the last thing he expected me to say.

"Yeah," I nodded, turning away from him to slip the hardcover in its place along the shelf. I could feel him hovering behind me, waiting for me to expand on what I'd just said. "The University of Miami has this accelerated MD program for entering freshmen. If I got in, it's an automatic acceptance into medical school as well. That, and it would only take me six years to get my MD, instead of eight."

The University of Miami also had a great scholarship program for low income students. To get it, I just needed to finish off this last year of high school and maintain my high GPA.

"If you enter at the age of seventeen, take six years to become a doctor, then you'll be a doctor by age twenty-three." He sounded impressed. "Sounds like you got it all figured out."

"I'll be a resident by the age of twenty-three," I corrected, turning back to face him. "Two years of residency after medical school makes me an official doctor by age twenty-five."

"What's the rush?"

I shrugged, leaning back against the bookshelf behind me, looking up to meet his thoughtful brown eyes. Shaun had these penny brown eyes that you had to really put effort into not getting lost in. Sometimes I felt like he could stare a hole straight through me with how intense they were. I didn't like it when people touched me, and Shaun knew this, but sometimes I'd swear he was touching me in other ways, without his hands.

Shaun had always been this way. He had no idea that's how it felt for me. He was totally unaware of how, to me, his gaze felt like gentle caresses on my skin.

Shaun was *definitely* unaware of how much I liked it.

"The rush," I repeated his previous words back to him, trying to make sense of my response before I offered it to him. He waited, with a thoughtful look about him, *really* listening. "I guess I would just like to feel like I don't need to rely on anyone else… as soon as possible."

Something about what I said made him think. I saw the wheels turning in his head, a question flash in his eyes, and ultimately watched him decide not to ask it.

I asked him a question instead. "Will we still be friends when I'm twenty-five?"

He smiled into a quiet laugh. Shaun had the most beautiful smile, two perfect rows of naturally straight white teeth, always drawing my eyes down to his lips. He said, "I swear you can read my mind sometimes."

"What do you mean?"

"I was gonna ask you that," he told me. "But it sounded lame in my head."

"So, are you saying *I'm* lame for asking?"

Shaking his head, he assured me, "It doesn't sound lame when *you* ask it."

"Well?" I waited. "Answer the question then. Will we still be friends when I'm twenty-five?"

His answer was whispered, like he was saying it more to himself than to me. "I hope not."

I giggled, assuming he was joking. *Hoping* he was joking. "Oh, come on, I'm not *that* bad."

Shaun didn't laugh. My smile faded.

Just before my feelings could get hurt, he spoke up.

"Butterscotch," he used my nickname, head tilted slightly forward, looking at me from the tops of his eyes. Our foreheads were almost touching, and my heart was pounding. This close, I could smell the soap on his skin, and I secretly liked it. Shaun was sincere when he promised, "It's you and me. Till we're old as fuck."

I let out a breath I didn't realize I was holding.

"So, you'll come visit me in Miami?" I asked.

He nodded quietly, adding a little distance to the incredibly small space between us. He was still standing really close, but at least now I felt like I could breathe easy.

"And what about you? Where are you going after Jefferson?"

"North Carolina," he answered, which I found random until he clarified, "Duke."

"Ahh," I made a sound of understanding. Duke University had one of the best college basketball teams in the country. "You finally decided who you wanted to play ball for."

"I talked to a scout this morning—which is why I was late to Dr. Young's, you remember—and he really talked the place up. They want me bad. Even if I don't play in a single game for Jefferson this year, I'm still getting in. I stand a really good chance of getting into the league if I play for 'em."

"Duke has the same school colors as Jefferson," I pointed out. Jefferson High School's colors were also blue and white. "Maybe it's fate."

"Mhm," he absently agreed, his mind seemingly preoccupied with something else. "It could be."

"You don't seem as excited as I thought you would be," I pointed out. "It's your senior year. You just got a guaranteed spot on one of the best teams in the country. You're almost definitely on your way to the NBA. Why do you sound so bummed?"

He just looked at me for a moment, leaning back against the bookshelf behind him. It was almost like he was waiting for me to see the answer right in front of me. I was lost. What was I missing? When he spoke again, he almost sounded ashamed. "What if I told you I wanted more?"

"Well, what else could you possibly want?" I asked, a little exasperated. Maybe I found him a little unappreciative to be so blessed. He literally had *everything*.

Shaun didn't answer, instead pushing out a long sigh and bringing his wristwatch up to his eyes. "It's three minutes after nine," he informed. "Let me help you with closing."

* * *

# SHAUN

The drive from *Kemetic Pages* to home was a short one.

Most of the time, when I either had practice or a game, Caprice would catch a ride home with my mother since the bookstore was across the street from her salon. When I didn't have practice or a game, I always took Caprice home myself. Jefferson rarely had games or practice on Fridays, so, most of the time, quiet rides like this through Parramore were a Friday night thing for us.

I pulled into the driveway of my own home. The yellow porch light emanating from Caprice's house across the street shined through the back window of my silver 2001 Camry. It was a sixteenth birthday gift. Not many kids in this neighborhood got cars as presents, so even though I lived in Parramore like everybody else, I knew I was more fortunate than others.

To a girl like Caprice, I had too much to be complaining about wanting more. *What* else could I possibly want? Caprice didn't understand what I had meant when she asked me that. I didn't want a "*what.*"

I wanted a "*who.*"

My mother wasn't home from the salon yet, so it was just in the driveway. I killed the engine and we didn't get out of the car right away. There was a pause. Call me crazy, but it always felt like Caprice was mentally preparing herself to go home. Just before she could open the passenger's side door, I stopped her.

"Come in and get something to eat before you go home." I remembered how empty her kitchen was earlier on in the day. I'd spent most of today with Caprice, so I knew for a fact she didn't eat anything for lunch, and I didn't see her eat dinner during her shift.

"Oh, I..." she paused. She passed a nervous hand over her hair, unable to look at me straight when she casually added, "I have leftovers in the fridge at home."

*That's not true.*

The only thing in her fridge was an old bottle of ketchup and some cold tap water. I saw it with my own eyes, and I had no idea why she would lie to me about it. Dignity, I assumed.

Even so—whether it hurt her pride or not—I wasn't about to let her go to bed on an empty stomach.

"Come on," I unbuckled my seatbelt. "I've got something better than leftovers in mine."

I was in the kitchen while Caprice sat at the dining room table. In the middle of boiling some pasta, I began to wonder if going to sleep hungry was a thing she did often. It bothered me because I couldn't be sure. If I asked, I was convinced she wouldn't tell me the truth. Now, *there* was something that would keep me up at night.

In the middle of heating up some pasta sauce, I could hear my mother walking through the front door. Even from the kitchen I could hear the pleasantly surprised tone of her voice when she found my friend sitting in the dining room. Separated by a wall, I couldn't see the exchange, but I could hear everything.

There was an unmistakable fondness in my mother's voice, and I knew she was smiling without even seeing her. My mom liked Caprice more than she liked me. I didn't take it personally, though.

Caprice was very likable.

"Oh hey, cutie. How was the first day?"

"It was…" Caprice hesitated and tried to look for the perfect word. "…okay."

"Bad, huh?" Mom caught on quickly. Caprice didn't say anything to that. "Where's my son?"

She told her, "He's cooking something in the kitchen."

My mother's disbelief was on full display. "He's *cooking*?"

*I'm trying to.*

Listening to Mom's footsteps draw closer to the kitchen, I readied myself for the inevitable teasing. She rounded the corner, past the wall that separated the kitchen from the rest of the house. Walking up from behind me, Mom kept her voice low so Caprice couldn't hear.

"You're *cooking* for her now." I could almost hear her trying to hold back a laugh. Something I confirmed when I turned to find her *very* entertained smile. I rubbed a hand over my eyes, chuckling a bit, feeling a little embarrassed.

Even though Caprice had no idea, there was no fooling Mom. She knew what this was for me seven years ago, when she found me up before dawn, waiting to walk Caprice to school.

Hell, the only reason I didn't take Caprice to school

nowadays was because last year I'd made her late so many times that now she absolutely refused to get in my car in the mornings.

Mom leaned in closer to the stovetop, eyeing what I had cooking, an amused grimace on her face when she asked, "Did you at least make enough for three?"

I checked on the simmering pasta sauce, having emptied an entire jar into the pot. There was more than enough for three. "Yeah."

"Well, then," she concluded with a shake of her head, flipping her shoulder-length burgundy hair in an exaggerated way. This hairstyle would probably last a few more weeks before she did something else with it. "You keep on chef-ing, and I guess I'll go entertain our dinner guest."

As I put on the finishing steps, I could hear my mother and Caprice chopping it up in the dining room. Mom was right to laugh. Rarely did I ever set foot in this kitchen for anything more than fixing myself a plate or grabbing something to drink. Cooking wasn't exactly my thing.

But here I was, sustaining a few burns, playing chef so that I could make something for Caprice. If the hopeless fool in here wasn't me, I would've been laughing too. Pasta, as easy as it seemed, was still more work than I bargained for.

My friend and mother were sitting at the table, laughing together like old friends when I brought out three white plates. To help, they joined me on my second trip to the kitchen, my mother getting some drinking glasses and a water pitcher, and Caprice grabbing the pot of steaming spaghetti. I took some forks, some serving silverware, and the pasta sauce, following them back out into the dining room.

"This is cute," my mother mentioned once we were all seated at the dark wood round table. With four chairs evenly spaced around it, Caprice sat between my mother and I. Across from me, my mother caught my eye, still amused when she remarked, "Look at us, looking like a scene outta *Soul Food*."

Family dinners weren't really common in this house. With it just being me and Mom, we tended to just eat when we had time, and our schedules didn't blend enough for meals to be often had together. Mom was right—sitting around the table like this, we almost looked like one of those movie families. Even though none of us looked related.

Not even me and mom.

You see, my mother and I didn't look alike *at all.* I was often told I was a carbon copy of my dead father. I didn't remember him much, but sometimes I might stumble on an old photo of him and mistake it for one of myself. Like my father, I was tall, light, and athletic—the total opposite of my short, feminine, Whitney Houston look-alike mother. If there was one thing mom might've given me, it was probably her mind. She was one of the smartest people I knew, and I liked to think she shared that with me.

"I didn't know you could cook," Caprice commented quietly.

"Hmm," my mother snorted, flashing me a knowing look. "Neither did I."

"It looks good," Caprice complimented, giving me a cute little smile. I knew she must've been starving, but her manners remained intact. "Do you guys say grace?"

Caprice was assuming this was normal for us. Neither of us let her know it wasn't.

"How about you say grace tonight, cutie," my mother suggested, folding her hands together in prayer formation. I followed suit, closing my eyes to the sound of Caprice reciting a short blessing.

Conversation was easy as we moved the serving plate around the table.

"So, you were saying something about a not so good first day," my mother directed at Caprice. "What happened?"

Caprice glanced at me briefly, maybe worried I might say something. I didn't.

"Just some petty drama," she shrugged. "It really wasn't all bad."

"And that's how you wanted your hair for the first day?" Mom asked, sounding a little judgmental. Knowing Mom, she was likely assuming Caprice had a bad day because her hair wasn't done up all fancy. All roads lead to hair with my mother. I shot her a look. It wasn't her place to say that kinda thing. Trying to make it sound less disapproving, she added, "It's just that the salon was packed the week before school started. All these girls wanting to get this or that done for day one… You know, they wanted to look *nice*."

"Mom…"

"Not that you don't look nice!" she rushed to clarify, just now hearing how bad her words sounded. "Caprice, you're *very* pretty."

Caprice offered a small smile, which was more for my mom than anything. I don't think she actually felt like smiling. "Thanks Miss Sylvia."

An awkward silence followed, the sound of forks scraping against plates being the only thing heard for a while. I tried to think of something to change the topic to, but my mom spoke up before I could.

"You know," my mother started slowly. She was still on the hair thing. "I don't have any morning appointments at the salon this Saturday."

I was starting to get annoyed.

"Mom—"

"Let me finish, Shaun," she cut me off before turning back to Caprice. "I have some braiding hair in the storeroom that matches your hair color, and… I know you have a birthday on the last day of the month. Sixteen is a big one. Consider it a birthday present from me."

Caprice was uncomfortable. "Oh, Miss Sylvia, you don't have to do—"

"Those girls in school can be really nasty, can't they?" my mother spoke knowingly. Her dark eyes were sympathetic. "I was a girl once. I was *your* age once. I know exactly how teenaged girls act once they think they've found something wrong with a girl like you."

Caprice was extremely uncomfortable now; her voice was almost shaking. "A girl… like me?"

Maybe it would've been better for her to go to bed hungry, instead of being subjected to my mother's superficial bullshit. Regardless of my mother's views, Caprice was pretty enough. I couldn't stand the idea of sitting here and watching my mom make a beautiful girl feel ugly.

"Yes, Caprice," my mother nodded, ignoring the daggers I was glaring in her direction. "Girls like you—*beautiful* girls. Girls who are *so* pretty without even trying. Teenage girls love to sink their nails into girls like you at the first opportunity. And your hair is *beautiful*, cutie. Don't think I'm trying to say it's not. But I remember what it was like to be young. Girls love to compare, and since I know most of them can't say a damn thing about your face, I bet the first thing they go after is your hair."

It was quiet for a minute until Caprice finally answered.

"Yeah." Her voice was a whisper. She wasn't eating anymore. My mother talked too much and now Caprice had lost her appetite.

I was annoyed.

"So, let me help you shut them up," my mother offered, her hand coming out on top of Caprice's. I watched her tense up, knowing she would've preferred my mother keep her hands to herself. "Saturday morning. Come by the salon and I'll do you up special. You only turn sixteen once. What do you say?"

Without speaking, she nodded, slowly looking up from her plate to give my mother a genuinely appreciative smile. "Thank you, Miss Sylvia."

"My pleasure, babygirl." Mom glanced my way, an '*I told you so*' glowing from her eyes.

Caprice was fine, back to working on her plate.

My mother was just trying to help. I *maybe* overreacted. Mom acknowledged this when she commented, "And now you can stop looking at me like you wanna fight me, Shaun."

## *Chapter Eleven*

# Caprice

It was late when I finally got around to going home; a little after ten-thirty.

I was expecting Gracie to have long been asleep by the time I got to the house. However, after locking the front door and turning for my room, I was startled by her shadowy figure sitting on the living room couch.

"Gracie," I breathed out, my frightened hand going up to my chest. All the lamps were out, with the only bit of light here shining in from outside. If I squinted, I could just make out the outline of her body sitting on the La-Z-Boy. She stood to her feet, stepping closer to me. In the darkness, came a small, glowing red dot near her mouth. She was smoking a cigarette.

When she finally spoke, the warm smoke blew into my face.

"Where you been?" I could tell from the way that she asked that she thought she already knew the answer. "Melinda next door said she seen a car pull up to the house 'round noon today. So, what? You skipped the first day of school?"

"No," I whispered, already deflated because even though I was telling the truth, I knew she'd say it was a lie.

"Mhm," she hummed, totally unconvinced. "She said she saw you and that light skin boy from across the street come into the house, stay about twenty minutes, and then you both left. And you know what's funny?" she asked with exaggerated curiosity. "When you left for school this morning, you wasn't wearing those pants, Caprice."

"Gracie, I…"

She cut me off. "What were you doin' at his house just now?

I know you get off work at nine o'clock. I watched you get out of his car at nine-fifteen. And now it's ten-thirty. So… fill me in. What was you doin' in there?"

"He invited me in for dinner."

"Ahh, dinner," she repeated mockingly, taking another drag of her cigarette. Frighteningly close to my face, I could feel the heat emanating off the red glow of the Newport. More smoke blew into my eyes when she asked, "At this hour? You must think I'm stupid."

"Gracie, I… I got my period at school. It messed up my pants, so Shaun took me home during lunch so I could change."

"Mhm…" She took another drag. "That's perfect. Just perfect."

Perhaps my explanation sounded too convenient; too perfect to be true.

"I—"

"Shut up, Caprice," she cut me off quietly, the bite of her cigarette fog pricking at my eyes, making them water. "Shut your *lyin'* ass up."

I pressed my lips together, trying to hold in the cry I felt coming up my throat. Gracie had no patience for tears.

"You know what this reminds me of?" Gracie asked, stepping closer to me, so I stepped backward. I felt the front door press against my back, forcing me to stop. Gracie got in my face. "That first day of school back in '99. I came home around this time and couldn't find you. When I called out your name, you didn't answer. When I checked the bathroom, there you were, naked on the bathroom floor, blood everywhere, unconscious."

I hated this memory. I didn't want to relive it, so I tried to block her out, my eyes shutting tight. Determined to make me listen, Gracie pushed up to the side of my face, whispering the rest in my ear.

"You know, I never straight up asked you who did it. I thought so highly of my grandbaby then, so I just assumed the only man in the house had to have done that to you. I confronted Marcel about it, and he was so… *upset*. He swore on his daddy *and* on his sister that didn't do nothin' to you. I didn't believe him. I didn't believe him when he said you were fast neither. You were just this sweet, innocent little thing to me then. I didn't think you were like that."

Gracie would do this. She would try to make the villain in her world. It gave her somebody to blame for the things she didn't want to feel guilty about anymore.

If I had always been a whore, then she wouldn't feel responsible for my being raped at eight years old. If I was a liar, then it was my treacherous ways that tricked her into getting Marcel locked up for twelve years.

She could put it all on me. She could forget all logic, all her memories, and just put it all on me. I couldn't blame her entirely. Sadness had driven her halfway crazy.

I understood her game.

But that didn't make it any easier to play.

"But I see you now," she whispered. "I see what Marcel was tryna get me to see about you. I should've believed my boy. I should've known you let somebody in my house to do that shit to you. And you was too scared to tell me it was *your* fault—it was *your* doing—so you let me put it *aaallll* on Marcel. I should've dragged your little fast ass back to that bathroom and made you clean up your own fuckin' mess," she listed all her regrets. "My poor Marcel. It's your fault... It's your fault I called the police to get him outta here. I wouldn't have done it if you didn't make me think he touched you."

I didn't say anything.

My least favorite part of the game was coming.

"Say it, Caprice," she blew more smoke against the side of my face. "Say he never touched you."

That was always her primary objective. Gracie needed to hear me say it so that she could continue on with her edited worldview. The dishonest words *needed* to come out of my mouth, or else she could keep this going for hours.

I remember when I was twelve, when this game first started, Gracie forced me to say it. She made me say Marcel never touched me. I thought she would leave me alone if I just told her what she wanted to hear.

On that day, just a second after I let the words come out... she beat *the shit* out of me. She screamed insults at me, called me all kinds of lying whores and lying bitches, forced me to the ground and started stomping on me.

Saying those words was all the excuse she needed to justify beating me within an inch of my life.

So, I knew better now.

When we played this game, my primary objective was to never say it. "No."

"Tell the truth, Caprice. Say he never touched you."

I whispered back, shaking voice and all, "No, Gracie."

She let out a tired sigh in the darkness, giving up earlier than she usually did. Thinking it was over, I attempted to walk past her. I was trying to get to my room as fast as possible, so that I could lock myself in. There, I would be safe.

As I tried to leave, Gracie's hand reached out in my direction, the cigarette between her fingers pressing into my shoulder, burning through the fabric of my uniform and sizzling on my skin.

In trying to get away from the fire, I dropped to my knees, my opposite hand clutching my burning shoulder. I didn't scream. Even the cries that came out of me were silent.

Gracie hovered above my head, a mere shadow looking down at me, and she whispered the word, "*Slut.*"

* * *

In the hood, women don't go to therapists.

They go to their hair stylist.

You could sit at *Sylvia's Salon & Spa* all day long and hear all kinds of stories. This woman got cheated on. That woman got robbed.

We had just finished washing my hair at the sink, so Miss Sylvia was drying me down with a towel when she said, "Tell me about your week."

I guess it was my turn for therapy next. I was careful with how much information I shared as Miss Sylvia started to rub product into my damp coils. I would've hated to slip up and reveal that my grandmother put her cigarette out on me on Monday and slapped me across the face on both Thursday and Friday.

For now, I was just happy to be out of the house on a Saturday.

Since I didn't work weekends, Saturdays were some of my least favorite days. I oftentimes found myself stuck in the house with Gracie on Saturdays. This week especially, I was grateful for an excuse to not be there.

Sundays were the best. On Sundays, Gracie would spend the entire day out of the house, trying to make visitation at the prison upstate.

Sitting in the salon chair at *Sylvia's*, I was light on details as I shared the more basic parts of my week. Miss Sylvia listened intently separating my hair into parts, starting to gently detangle.

"Ahh, so you hope to graduate two years early," she understood. I nodded. "And Miami for college, too? It's more fast paced down there. You nervous at all?"

"A little."

"I know Shaun will miss you."

My heart fluttered at the sound of that.

"I'll miss him, too," I revealed, adding, "But he said he'd visit."

Miss Sylvia chuckled a bit to herself. Just before turning on the blow dryer, she agreed. "I'm *sure* he will."

Hours passed.

We were finishing up the last braid. Nine AM had turned to three PM and I'd been in this seat for an insane amount of time. Miss Sylvia's hands worked fast down the final strand, finally letting the last one join the rest of the braids at my waist.

"We just need to dip these in some hot water in the back and you're all set." She pulled a black handheld mirror off her piece of the salon counter. "Take a good look for yourself."

The reflection looking back at me in the mirror still looked like me, but with a new, more on trend hairstyle. I felt compelled to run my hands through the nearly one hundred long braids.

"They're going to feel a little tight for a few days," Miss Sylvia explained while I admired them. "But after a few night's sleep, they'll loosen up and you'll also get used to the weight. Just in time for your birthday on Thursday," she explained.

"Thank you."

She smiled at my gratitude. "I'm glad I could do this for you, cutie. Those mean girls are gonna have a hard time finding things to knit pick at you for now. Braids look good on you," Miss Sylvia complimented, removing the yellow styling cape clasped around my neck. "Hot water next. Come on."

## Chapter Twelve

# SHAUN

We had pick-up games going at the court downtown on Sundays.

Mostly it was my teammates from Jefferson, mixed in with a couple of players from rival high schools in the area. We picked our teams at the beginning of each game, schoolyard style—two captains calling out the names of the teammates they wanted.

It was teams of five. I picked three kids from Jefferson and the fourth from the high school in College Park. On the street court, school team loyalty wasn't necessary. Also, I always made a point to add a member from a rival team to my street team. It helped me study the way the competition might play. If I could anticipate it, then I could draft good strategies.

I was team captain at Jefferson for a reason.

The teams were tied twenty minutes into the first game. There was talent on both sides. Even though this game didn't mean anything, my competitiveness wasn't going to let me be okay with losing. The ball was in my hand and I saw an easy pass to the College Park kid, standing about two feet closer to the hoop than I was. The sun was in my eyes.

I passed the ball.

It's important to know when to share responsibilities on the court. Sure, I could've tried for a three pointer and *maybe* gotten it in, but that kinda shit is how you alienated your teammates in the middle of a game. If you're only after personal glory, you won't last long in this sport.

The College Park kid made the shot. Point.

People watching at the bleachers cheered. I glanced in that direction, doing a double take when I saw a familiar face, sitting on the lowest bench, face downward in a book.

Just like the first time I ever saw her.

I stared for maybe three seconds before it dawned on me that I was still in the game. A hand came up and smacked me in the back hard as shit. Adrian, one of my Jefferson teammates, was pissed, "Bruh, wake up! The *fuck* you smiling at?"

My team lost that pick-up game. I was distracted. Knowing it was just streetball, I wasn't invested enough to just shut out my surroundings. Especially not with Caprice sitting eight feet away, looking like… *that.*

After my teammates finished talking their shit about me costing them the game, I jogged up to her. When my shadow fell over her, she looked up, her brown eyes squinting slightly from the sun. My mother did a good job on her hair. She still looked like Caprice—which was a good thing—but the braids that fell to her waist suited her.

"You're blocking my sunlight," she told me.

"It's a library across the street," I pointed out, grabbing the seat beside her, our shoulders barely touching. "If you was really tryna read, that's where you'd be. You wanted me to see you, Butterscotch. Don't front."

She broke into the happiest smile I'd seen on her in a while. "Well?"

"Well, I see you." *And you're the most beautiful person I've ever seen.* All I said out loud was, "And you look nice."

I had to look away briefly to keep myself from returning her goofy ass smile. She was dressed out of the Jefferson uniform today, which I rarely got to see. She was wearing a pale-yellow tank top and a pair of denim cutoffs that stopped mid thigh. Caprice was five-foot-ten, tall for a girl, but the perfect size for me since I was tall as well. She wore the height beautifully, with just about the most perfect set of legs. Her dark brown skin was on total display, just soaking in the sunlight today.

On her feet were her usual school shoes. She'd been wearing them for more than a year, and right about now, the white fabric on them had turned a little brown. There were some rips and tears at the sides.

"Your shoes are fallin' apart, kid," I told her, not trying to make fun, but just pointing it out.

Her smile faded and she nodded. "Yeah. I, um... I'm getting new ones soon."

"How soon is soon?"

"I'm gonna buy some new ones on Black Friday," she told me quickly, hoping maybe if she said it fast, I wouldn't realize that the answer was November. *Fuckin' November*—which was more than two months away.

"These shoes ain't makin' it to November, Caprice," I told her. When she didn't say anything, I tugged at one of her new braids and teased, "Black Friday? *Shiiiiit*. You'd be lucky if they see *this* Friday."

"They'll make it," she argued.

"If you say so."

* * *

## Caprice

"How'd you burn a hole in your shirt anyway?" Mischa asked out of the blue, early that Wednesday morning in homeroom.

I only had three school uniform shirts and I couldn't just throw one away because of Gracie. That would be like burning money. Besides, the hole was tiny. At least, I thought it was.

"Is it that obvious?" I asked, looking at it, panicking a bit.

"Ummm..." Mischa grimaced, popping her pink gloss covered lips before saying, "Kind of."

If Mischa noticed, then Shaun would notice, and he would try to have a conversation about it, like he tried to have a conversation about my shoes on Sunday. "Mischa, you *have* to let me borrow your hoodie today."

She made a face.

"What do you wear—an extra small?" Mischa guessed, flipping her wavy brown Malaysian hair to one shoulder. Adjusting her glasses without lenses, she playfully said, "Baby, it's too big for you."

"That's okay," I was freaking out, stuttering over my words. "It's o-okay if it's too b-big. I just… I just *need* to c-cover up this hole."

"Oh my God, Caprice, *chiiiill,*" Mischa spoke slowly. Her eyes scanning around the classroom, embarrassed. I knew I was making a scene, but I was panicking. "It's not even that *seeerious.* The hole is not even *that* big. It's just a little bit weird because it kinda looks like someone put a cigarette out in it."

She had no idea how right she was.

"Mischa, please," I begged. I knew she had body image issues and taking off her hoodie was like taking away her security. But if Mischa was already unknowingly guessing what Gracie did to me by just looking at the little hole, other people would, too. "*Please*."

"If you make me take off this hoodie, everybody's gonna look at my fat arms," she whispered. "You don't get it because you're skinny. I can't take this off," she whined.

My eyes started to water.

"You have *got* to be kidding," she said when she noticed. Mischa whispered harshly, "*Caprice!* Why *the fuck* are you crying?"

I didn't say anything. My eyes just kept watering.

She started to take the purple jacket off, pushing it to me angrily. "Take it! Take it!"

"Mischa, I'm *sorryyyyy,*" I was apologizing for crying, and even as I did this, I was blinking back more tears. "You're not even big, *Mischaaaaa*. Nobody is looking at your *aaaarms*."

"Put it on before I take it back, you *big fat* baby!"

I hurriedly did as she asked. The hoodie was a size large. It was loose on me, but not as loose as Mischa acted like it would be. Mostly, the loose hoodie's sleeves stretched past my hands.

"And don't ask me for *shit* for your birthday tomorrow," she whispered harshly. We just stared at each other after that. I blinked a few times, bringing my hand up to wipe my face. Mischa glared at me for a spell, but over time, her expression softened. Within seconds, as I sniffled, she just started laughing. "You're *so weird,*" she told me.

I laughed a little with her. "I know."

"Gimme back my hoodie at lunch," she demanded. "And it's not to hide my arms. My fourth period classroom is just cold as hell."

I inwardly groaned. Lunch was after third period, and I had both third *and* fourth period with Shaun. Mischa was already stepping out of her comfort zone by letting me have it for half the day. I couldn't ask to keep it for longer than that. "Okay, I'll give it back at lunch."

* * *

The braids really came in handy.

I don't know why I didn't think of it before. I swept them all to the side at the beginning of fourth period, making sure my hair covered the part of my shirt where the burn was. Shaun sat next to me the entire hour of calculus, more focused on getting answers correct on his quiz than he was on my shoulder.

I snuck a look at his paper in the middle of it, checking his math. Out of the ten questions, he'd gotten eight correct, and would be getting partial credit on number four—because his answer was right, but his math was all wrong. He'd be happy with his B+. I—on the other hand—could never settle for less than an A.

Ms. Kelly caught my wandering eyes. "Eyes on your own paper, Caprice!"

Shaun glanced at me, chuckling a bit before looking away. On a scrap sheet of paper, he wrote a note and passed it to me.

*You cheating off me, Cap?*

Directly under his note, I wrote: *I was checking your math.*

He wrote back: *And?*

I wrote: *You're gonna get an 88%*

He replied: *Bullshit. What did I get wrong?*

I smiled, writing back: *You cheating off me, Shaun?*

Out of the corner of my eye, I saw him smile at that. He passed another note my way.

*Help a brotha out.*

I rolled my eyes, but still decided to help him out: *You forgot to shift the decimal on number nine.*

I sat and I waited. And a second later, he started erasing. Hiding my face, I quietly laughed.

Ms. Kelly had me collect all the quizzes before the bell. She was always giving me these little jobs around class. I think it was because she felt most comfortable asking me for things. Because she knew me the best out of everyone else.

The bell rang just as I placed the stack of quizzes on Ms. Kelly's desk. She started to smile and say thanks, but her smile immediately faded, and her gaze fell from my eyes to my shoulder.

I took a look.

My braids had slipped off from their original spot, and my cigarette burn shirt sleeve was left exposed. Behind me, students shuffled out of their seats, headed to their next class.

Trying to avoid eye contact with Ms. Kelly, I turned on my heel and hoped to see that Shaun had already left. His seat was empty. I breathed out a sigh of relief, wondering if I'd be able to leave without Ms. Kelly starting a conversation with—

"Caprice."

*Shit.*

"Ma'am, I am running *so* late for English," I spoke fast as I gathered up my things. I was the only student left to leave. I watched in my periphery as she stepped in front of the only door out of the room.

"I'll write you a pass," she said simply. "Caprice... is that a cigarette burn on your shirt?"

"Of course not, Ma'am."

"Come here." She beckoned me over with a single finger. Reluctantly, I walked forward. Ms. Kelly's eyes narrowed on my shirt sleeve, her hand coming out to inspect it more closely. When I saw her eyes widen again, I immediately went to making excuses, panicking.

"It's not a cigarette burn. I just left the iron on the sleeve too long."

"That iron must be tiny," she replied flatly, unconvinced.

"It's not what you think." My lies were getting less and less believable. I was hyperventilating. "It's just a misunderstanding."

"Caprice, please lift up your shirt sleeve."

My skin started to feel prickly. "*Please*, Ms. Kelly."

Unwilling to ask me twice, she reached over and lifted my sleeve herself. Underneath it—plain as day—was a black burn mark about the same size as the hole in my clothes. It was a little over a week old, so it was still healing.

"I knew it," Ms. Kelly whispered. "You wanted to know why I said I was glad you turned out okay on the first day? Because I always knew *this* kind of thing was going on at your house." She shook her head. "I always had a feeling."

"You did?" I wondered how that could be the case. I knew Ms. Kelly long before the really bad stuff started to happen. When I knew her before, I was just a little sad because I missed my mom and because Marcel kept playing his little games with me.

"You were such a *weird* kid," Ms. Kelly expressed, and I wasn't sure if I should be offended.

"No offense," she quickly added. "I remember the first day I met you, you immediately told me your shower schedule and started bawling because I told you the library didn't have a shower room. To calm you down, I bought you this big tub of wipes, and for days, I proceeded to watch you wipe yourself down with them in perfect two-hour intervals, every single day. You never even looked at a clock. You could tell time in your own head. It took me a few more days to realize how."

She inhaled sharply, her voice deadpan when she said, "Caprice—you were *always… fucking…* counting."

I didn't expect her to start cursing. Was she even allowed to talk to me like that?

"It was the *creepiest* thing. Even when I couldn't hear you do it, I could tell you were doing it in your head. I had no idea what you were counting either. It's like you just wanted to keep your brain busy—like you'd rather focus on which number came next in your head then allow yourself to *actually* think real thoughts. My mother was a psychiatrist in LA at the time, and I described you to her and she immediately said—'*That child has a textbook case of obsessive compulsive disorder. But eight years old is a little young. Could be a trauma situation.*'"

Ms. Kelly shook her head. "Trauma? *Trauma!* You don't understand Caprice—I was a nineteen-year-old education major, working for free, just trying to get college credit. You were *not* what

I signed up for that summer. But then... you grew on me. And you were so *stinkin'* adorable, with your little country ass accent." She shook her head as she remembered, and then continued, "I got you to start reading books because I figured if you were so desperate to keep your mind busy—you might as well be reading. And it worked! You read everything I told you to. You were so smart. By the end of the summer, you were my favorite student." *I always knew I was her favorite.* "But I was also *very* aware that there was something *fucked up* going on in your house."

She pointed at my arm. "And now I know what."

I just stared at her.

When she realized I wasn't going to say anything, Ms. Kelly announced, "I'm calling the police."

That made me find my voice. "Wait!" I rushed after her. "Don't call the police."

"I have to, Caprice!" she told me.

"Ms. Kelly," I practically shouted, my voice begging when I whispered. "*Please.*"

She paused, hearing the pleading in my voice. Maybe she heard the fear, too.

"I'm fine," I promised. "It's not as dramatic as you're making it seem. My grandmother is good to me. Gracie would *never* hurt me. Gracie loves me." The lies felt odd on my tongue, but I could remember believing them once upon a time. "Please, Ms. Kelly. Don't do it. I'm okay. I *swear*, I'm okay."

She let go of the phone, and just stared at me. Her eyes were practically dripping with pity.

"Gracie would never hurt me. Gracie loves me."

## Chapter Thirteen

# Caprice

My Thursday night shift at *Kemetic Pages* was uneventful, as always.

I had a good day today. It was my sixteenth birthday and things at school went well. Mischa—even though she said she wasn't getting me anything—gifted me my very own hoodie. One in my actual size. A gift that would keep on giving, I realized, as this ensured I would never ask her for *her* hoodie ever again. At lunchtime, Shaun abused his position as team captain to force his teammates to sing to me, which was embarrassing, but it *did* make me feel special.

Princess Knight left me alone all day. That was the best part.

The bell at the store's front door rang. I stood up straight, expecting to greet a customer who'd come in to browse the books. What I got instead was Shaun, coming in from outside. I knew he had basketball practice today, so I wasn't expecting him.

"Hey, what are you doing here?" I asked him as he set his backpack on the front counter. He was still wearing his blue and white practice uniform.

There was a smile in his eyes. "Celebrating."

"Practice ended early?" I asked.

"Nah," he said. "I'm at home gettin' some rest after I twisted my ankle during a drill."

To me, it looked like he was walking just fine. I laughed out loud when I realized something.

"You faked an injury to get out of practice! What exactly are you celebrating?"

He made a face. "You serious?"

I remembered. *Right*—it was still my birthday.

"I'm celebrating *you*, Your Highness," he teased, just so we'd be on the same page. From the other side of the counter, his hand came up and held a grocery bag. Grabbing a stool, he pulled up a seat at the opposite end of my counter, using it like a table, pushing away the opened book in front of me.

From the bag he pulled out a clear package from a grocery store bakery. A single cupcake was set in front of me. I rose a single, excited brow, asking, "Butterscotch frosting?"

That was my favorite flavor. It's how I got my nickname.

"It has to be," he confirmed, placing a single candle in the frosting. From his back pocket he pulled out a box of matches, lighting my candle and urging, "Make a wish."

I stared at the dancing flame, feeling Shaun's eyes on me as he waited. I wished for the same thing I always wished for.

*Happiness.*

When the candle was out, Shaun pulled out a single plastic fork.

"What did you wish for?" he asked me as I grabbed it.

"I wished for you to not ask me what I wished for," I teased, sticking out my tongue. "I guess it didn't come true…"

He laughed. "You're a trip."

"Where's your fork?" I asked when I realized he didn't have one.

"No, Caprice." He shook his head solemnly. "This is *just* for you."

It was one cupcake. Knowing Shaun, he probably didn't have enough money to buy two. Because Jefferson's basketball team took up so much of his time, he didn't have a job, and the little money he did have always went to gas for his car.

It was one *small* cupcake. I took some onto my fork. Yes, it was supposed to be for one person.

But that's not how we worked.

"Open up," I told him, holding it out to his lips, watching his eyebrows momentarily flick up. "*You're* celebrating me, remember? So, celebrate me."

Shaun shook his head at first, but when I just stared in return, he gave in. I fed it to him.

"Is it good?" I asked before I grabbed my own bite.

"It was good," he said quietly as I chewed. Hearing his voice change, I thought I might've said something to make him sad.

"Did I do something bad?" I asked. "You sound upset."

"I'm not upset," he told me. "I promise I'm not. You just... you're just always surprising me."

"What did I do?" I asked.

He wordlessly took the fork out of my hands, taking another piece off the cupcake and fed it to me. The gesture filled my stomach with butterflies.

"That," he said quietly, though I hardly believed I gave him butterflies when *I* did it. Do boys even get butterflies?

Shrugging away the thought, I took my fork back, taking the last piece off the paper wrapper. When I readied it for him, he shook his head. "Caprice, you can't just give me half."

"Why not?" I asked.

"Because it's yours."

"Okay," I accepted this fact. "It's mine... and I can do with it whatever I want. And I *want* to give you half."

His brown eyes on me had a thoughtful quality to them, like I was really making him think.

"It's your birthday, too, Shaun. Tomorrow," I reminded. And eighteen was a much bigger deal than sixteen. "So, let me celebrate you, too," I whispered softly.

He gave in, letting me share it with him. Watching him chew, I found myself smiling.

There was a silence that fell over us then, with his eyes looking into mine, and my eyes looking into his. Something powerful hung in the air between us, but I didn't say anything about it. For a moment, neither did Shaun. We were both quiet. And then, I watched as he took in a deep breath, a slow exhale leading into the sincerest, tenderest confession. "I love you, Caprice."

Something in my chest swelled. And even though I wasn't even a little bit sad, my eyes filled to the brim. I couldn't remember the last time someone had told me they love me. I think my mother used to say it when I was small, but I couldn't remember her anymore.

I could feel hot tears burning my skin as I managed to

squeak out, "You do?"

"Yeah," he nodded, a single tear sliding down his cheek. It's been like this since we were kids. If I cry; Shaun cries with me. No matter how big and tough he gets, he just can't help it, which was probably why I got into the habit of refusing to cry around him. He said it again, "I love you."

"Really?"

"Really."

This was a dream. This had to be a dream. Why wasn't I waking up? "Why me?"

Shaun laughed a little at the question, his hand coming up to wipe his face. "Are you serious?"

"But I didn't do anything to..." I was crying so hard for someone who was so happy. "I didn't do anything to deserve it."

"First of all," Shaun started matter-of-factly, "that's not how love works. And second, even if that was how love worked, you would *still* deserve it. You would *still* deserve mine."

He was slowly stepping off his seat. I didn't say anything as he walked around to my side of the counter. I think he kept his movements extra slow, just so that he could give me enough time to let him know if I wanted him to stop.

I didn't tell him to stop when he was six feet away. I said nothing when he was three feet away. I still wanted him to come closer by the time we were just a few inches apart.

In my periphery, I watched his hand slowly draw up to me. His eyes never looked away from mine; they wordlessly asked for permission to touch me.

"It's okay," I told him in the quietest whisper. I'd always hated people touching me. Even the smallest bumps while walking through school hallways would leave me uneasy. In instances like this, I would've cringed away from anyone else's hands.

But never Shaun's.

"You can touch me."

His fingers settled lightly on me. Gradually, he reached in a little further until he held one side of my face in the palm of his hand, his thumb gently caressing my cheek. Shaun was *way* more experienced than I was—I knew this—but in that moment, I could tell this simple touch was equally as meaningful for him.

In the dim yellow light of that tiny store, surrounded by shelves lined with thousands of books, I looked up at him. Those pretty brown eyes of his were all that I saw, filled with love and something else I didn't recognize at the time. Later on in life, I would come to understand that the haziness in his gaze was desire.

With Shaun, it didn't scare me to be wanted in that way. How ever much he desired me, I knew he would never take anything I wasn't willing to give. With him, I was safe.

Gently, his hand changed position, slipping from my face and tucking underneath my chin. He rose my head up slightly higher, his head ducking down to make up for the height difference. In that moment, the seconds felt hours long, and when he finally closed that space between my lips and his… time stood completely still.

Shaun was so soft.

He was so warm.

His lips were so sweet—they still tasted like butterscotch.

I could feel his other hand gently cupping the back of my head, taking extra care in the way he moved against my lips. Not too fast. Never too fast. Without my saying so, he could feel it in his heart that I was fragile. And for that reason… he was extra careful in the way that he held me.

*He loves me.*

*He really loves me.*

By the time I came to that realization, he'd already told me, but even if he hadn't said it—even if he had just come in for the kiss and that's it—I would've known… From this kiss alone, I would've known. I didn't know if I was doing it right, but I kissed him back, welcoming him in when his tongue slipped passed my lips, sweet like frosting and warm like everything else about him.

My arms rose to close around him, and that was the first time I'd ever held somebody else in my arms. This close to someone—bodies pressed together, lips moving as one, holding one another in each other's arms—it would've terrified me to do this with anybody else.

But never Shaun.

* * *

It was a little after nine when he pulled into his driveway.

"Do you want to come inside and get something to eat?" he offered. Even though I didn't go around telling him that Gracie rarely ever bought food for the house, Shaun just seemed to know.

"I'm not hungry," I told him. It was the truth, and he believed me. "But thank you."

I didn't move from the passenger's side. He killed the engine and relaxed in his seat. Neither of us moved. We just sat back in our chairs, sitting in the darkness, the only bit of light coming from Gracie's porchlight shining through the back window.

Today, I turned sixteen.

For my birthday, Shaun gave me a cupcake.

He told me he loved me.

And then he kissed me.

"I loved today," I whispered out loud. Just us, together… I wanted to stay like this forever. I would've if I could.

I certainly didn't want to go home.

But minutes adding up on the clock were dangerous in my house. I didn't have it in me to play one of Gracie's *'Say it, Caprice'* games. Not after such a perfect day.

"I have to go home soon," I told him.

"Are you sure you're not hungry?" he tried one more time to get me to come inside with him. I wanted to. I *really* wanted to.

"I wish I could stay with you forever, like this," I told him. I didn't care if I sounded clingy or desperate. That's what I wanted. It was better than what I had waiting for me at home. "But Gracie is probably wondering where I am; waiting."

"But before you go," he said quietly, turning around to reach for something hidden near the backseat. He turned on the overhead car light so that I could see as he placed a large gift-wrapped box on my lap. "Happy birthday, Caprice."

"You got me *another* gift?" I asked, taken completely by surprise.

"Butterscotch," he simply said, sounding amused as he explained, "a cupcake is not a birthday gift." He added, "*Especially* since you insisted on sharing half of it with me."

The gift was wrapped in pretty red wrapping paper with a white ribbon cross tied around it. The box itself was so beautiful that I didn't want to tear into it. Whatever it was, nobody had ever gotten me a gift this big, and they'd certainly never taken the time to wrap it like this.

"Why are you crying before you even see what it is?" Shaun was laughing. "God, you are such a baby."

"It's just really pretty," I told him.

"You haven't even opened it yet."

I slowly peeled back the paper, finding underneath an orange colored shoebox with a *Nike* logo written across the top. "Shaun..."

I opened the shoe box to find a brand-new pair of white *Nike Air Force 1's.* At that point in my life, those shoes had just become the most expensive thing I owned. They must've been, like, almost a hundred dollars.

"These are too expensive," I whispered, unsure of whether the tears in my eyes were of joy or of sadness. "Shaun, you really shouldn't have. This is too much. You can't afford this. You don't even have a job."

"That's a really offensive way to say thank you," he commented, amused, "but you're welcome."

"How did you even?" I asked. "You have to tell me how. Did you do anything bad to get them?"

"Accusin' somebody of stealing is an even worse way to say thank you," he pointed out.

"You have to tell me how."

"My granddad sends me a hundred dollars every year for my birthday," he explained, chuckling as he joked, "I didn't rob anybody at gunpoint for your shoes, Caprice."

He used his birthday money. "You weren't supposed to spend that on *me*!"

"Why not?"

"That money was for you," I told him.

"Right," he agreed. "It's mine... and I can do with it whatever I want."

I was just about to argue with that when I realized he was just quoting me from before. "A cupcake is not the same as a hundred dollars."

"Do you like them?" he asked, ignoring the comparison I was trying to make.

I looked down at the shoebox in my lap. The shoes were brand new, not secondhand, like a lot of the stuff I was used to. They were so white, I feared I'd never be able to keep them looking like new. They were so pretty. So perfect. I didn't own anything in my closet nice enough to wear with these. I rose my head to respond, "They're beautiful."

"Are you happy?"

I nodded.

"Are you gonna wear them to school tomorrow?"

Again, I nodded.

"Then as far as I'm concerned—money well spent."

"Thank you, Shaun," I finally thanked him for them. He just smiled at the sound of it, and I watched as a thought flashed in his eyes and made him laugh. "What's funny?"

He leaned over the car's center console, pressing a kiss onto my cheek before whispering, "I told you those old shoes wouldn't make it to this Friday."

* * *

The pink house smelled like freshly made cookies when I walked through the door.

Gracie was baking.

I went to go set my gifts and school bag down in my room, and then I followed the smell to the kitchen. Gracie was in there, wearing an apron over a baby blue tracksuit.

"Caprice, I didn't hear you come in," she greeted me when she saw me lurking in the corner. I stepped further into the kitchen light.

"You baked cookies," I acknowledged, a budding smile on my face. She remembered my birthday.

"Yes, I did." Gracie set the hot tray in her hand on the kitchen counter, dusting the flour off her hands. I looked at them—warm chocolate chip. A little of my excitement fizzled. I wasn't a big fan of chocolate—not since I was a little girl. Gracie knew this. The next thing Gracie said let me know who those cookies were really for. She said, "Marcel's favorite."

My smile faded.

"Oh," I understood, nodding. Not for me. "You're making them before you go see him on Sunday."

But as soon as the words left my mouth, I immediately realized something was wrong. Their meetings were between six inches of bulletproof glass. Gracie couldn't bake cookies for Marcel—she couldn't even give them to him.

"No," Gracie corrected, filling me in, "Tomorrow."

I squinted, wondering if Gracie was forgetting something. "There are no visits on Fridays."

"I know, Caprice. Tomorrow's the first of September," she told me, absolutely beaming from ear to ear. And then—rather casually—she told me what I was missing, "When Marcel had his parole hearing in March, that's the day they set for his early release."

"Parole hearing?" I could suddenly literally hear my blood pumping in my head. Standing under the white lights of Gracie's kitchen, I suddenly felt like I was being cooked by the fluorescent bulbs overhead. "You never told me about a parole hearing."

Gracie gave me that look—that *'I'm in a good mood, so don't start with me'* look.

"Why would I tell *you*? You don't care about him. Seven years he's been in there—suffering! And you ain't *never* visited him."

My body was going numb. I was speaking, but I could barely hear the words coming out of my mouth. "He's getting out tomorrow?"

"I *just* said that, Caprice!"

"Is he staying here?"

Gracie glared at me then, whipping her black and white hair out of her face before she checked me.

"How dare you even ask me that? Do I need your permission to allow *my* son to live in *my* house? Do you have bills here you've been paying that I don't know about? *Check* yourself, lil' girl."

"Gracie…" I was on the verge of begging, but I stopped myself. It wouldn't do me any good.

"*Shiiiiit,*" she muttered to herself. "You lucky I don't make your little freeloadin' ass go back to sleeping on that couch. And you can thank the uncle you forgot all about for that! He's the one who told me he didn't want to take your room from you." She shook her head at the thought. "Imagine that—after all those lies you told about him, and he's still got nothing but love for you."

I could feel the half-eaten cupcake I had earlier climbing back up my throat, but I swallowed it down. Gracie continued to rant.

"And you better act like you have some sense when he gets here. No more of them booty shorts, with your fast self. You can't be running around, half dressed, with men in the house." Gracie rose a thin eyebrow. "You hear me?"

Today was supposed to be different.

For a while there, I had managed to snatch up just a little bit of happiness. It felt *so* good. I felt so free. Today didn't even feel like my life. It felt like a dream.

And now I was waking up to the life that I recognized.

# Chapter Fourteen

## SHAUN

Caprice was leaning on the passenger's side door of my car when I left the house.

This was a pleasant surprise because she hated going to school with me. It was 'cause I always made her late.

Like this morning.

I gave myself a birthday gift and slept in an hour. If I left the house now, I could make it to the end of second period. That senioritis was hitting me hard.

But if I had known Caprice was catching a ride to school with me today, I would've been up earlier. Did she say anything about riding to school with me last night? I didn't think she did.

When I greeted her, it sounded like a question. "Good morning?"

It wasn't until I got a little bit closer that I realized everything else that was out of the ordinary.

Her eyes were set with the determination of someone on a mission. She came to get something done today. I just had no idea what that something could be.

Although she had her backpack, she wasn't wearing her uniform, but instead had on a pink and white shirt, some jeans and the shoes I got her. She looked nice, but she *definitely* wasn't dressed for school.

And now that I thought about it—the fact that she wasn't dressed for school made sense.

Because the Caprice I knew wouldn't have waited for me if she knew I was going to make her *this* late. She wouldn't have waited unless she had no plans to go to school today.

Skipping school was something I often did alone, so I already knew what she was about to ask me to do with her.

Just to make sure, though, I asked. "We skippin' today?"

She just nodded.

Skipping school? On a Friday? On a Friday that is *also* my 18th birthday? "Say less."

* * *

This was her first time doing this.

Caprice is a nerd.

Not in a *'she's lame'* kind of way, but in a *'she loves being in school'* kind of way. Caprice was the only person I knew who seemed to get sad on weekends and holidays. Unlike me, she hated being home.

"What do kids do when they skip school?" she asked me from the passenger's seat like I was some sort of expert on the topic. To her, I might as well have been. I wasn't out here missing a day every week, but once in a while I'd take a little break. My grades were still decent, so I obviously was not skipping too many.

But Caprice? Since that one time she was sick for two weeks when she was in third grade, she has never, ever missed a day.

It was still a little bit too early in the morning for me, but as we were now creeping into 8AM, I was having a brief moment of clarity. I was starting to truly wake up. And, in the middle of driving, I really started to process what was happening.

I was skipping school with *Thee* Caprice. Alicia. Latimore. Little Miss Perfect Attendance for the past six years. At first, I thought it was her way of celebrating my birthday, but nah… She liked me a lot.

But she didn't like me *that* fuckin' much.

Caprice *loves* school.

"Wait—why are we doing this?" I asked suddenly.

Realizing she was no longer dealing with my sweet, innocent, impressionable, vulnerable, sleepy brain, she must've panicked. Because the next thing she said was just about the craziest shit I'd ever heard anyone suggest.

"*Shaun,*" she said, doing *That Thing* with her voice. Caprice wasn't experienced, if you know what I mean, but she knew enough to know that when she did *That Thing* with her voice, she would get the next thing that she asked for. "Let's go to Disney World."

Unfortunately for Caprice, *That Thing* can't make money I don't have, magically appear.

I tried to let her down easy. "Are you on *crack*? No!"

"But I've never *been* to Disney World! And it's only twenty minutes away from heeeere!" she whined, as if I was saying no because I didn't want her to go, and not because a trip like that would cost more than two hundred dollars. Not including the gas it would take to get there. "Shaun, I've always wanted to goooo. Since I was a little girl. Ms. Walowitz wouldn't take me!"

*Who?*

Even though it was absolutely impossible for me to do that for her—which I was *very* aware of, sleepy brain or not—I felt guilty the second time I said no. "We can't."

"Why not?"

I shook my head. "Because I left my Disney World shoes at the house."

"Well, let's go back and get them!" she encouraged energetically, not even realizing I was being sarcastic. It would've been really cute if it wasn't also really fuckin' tragic.

I turned the car into the parking lot of a roadside plaza, ready to lay some sad reality on her newly reckless, adorable ass. I had a little over quarter tank of gas. It would get us to Disney World and get us back, but I needed to make this tank last for the rest of next week, too. And what would be the point? So that we could chill by the gate and watch a bunch of rich white people go in?

"Caprice," I said her name sternly as I put the car in park. "We are not going to Disney World."

She looked at me and did *That Thing* times-two with her voice. "*Please.*"

Why was I feeling guilty for a matter that I wasn't even saying no to? My bank account was saying no. It was easy to assume it wouldn't, though.

I couldn't work because of basketball. But my mother owned her own business, and it was *very* successful. People—both in school and around Parramore in general—would assume that meant she had to be giving me cash every other day.

But she *wasn't* raising me like that.

My mother gave me the absolute bare minimum financially because she "*didn't want to raise a spoiled and entitled brat*"—her words, not mine. But it must've worked because I've never in my life felt like I was entitled to her money.

But damn...

I really wished I had some now.

"I *can't* afford it, Caprice!" It hurt me a lot to have to say that. "I can't do that for you. I don't have enough money for even one ticket into that place."

She grimaced at me like I had just said that to her in Chinese. And then she just said, "Duh!"

"What?"

"That's not shocking," she said. "Don't forget who you're talking to. I *know* you."

"Then why would you ask me to take you to—"

"*You* don't have any money," she said matter-of-factly and then raised her eyebrows, "but *I* do!"

Caprice had a job, but ever since she got it, she started saving like she was getting ready to buy a house. That's why she still used her backpack from seventh grade and up until recently was wearing broken shoes.

It was easy to forget she had money.

"You just have to take me to the bank and drive. I got this!" She looked at my gas meter, and added, "Everything! I *promise* you I can afford it. It would barely make a dent in my savings."

"Oh."

"You thought I was asking *you* to pay?" she questioned, somewhere in the middle of annoyed and entertained. "On your own *fucking* birthday?"

I just kind of sat there in silence.

"Look, Butterscotch." I sighed, ready to explain how I missed that. "It's *really* early in the morning..."

* * *

Today was one for the history books.

Of course, I didn't feel comfortable with Caprice spending that much money on me. She argued that I spent nearly all I had for her birthday, while she was spending less than five percent of what she had for mine.

We went back and forth about it for a hot minute and then she said, "I just want to have *one* perfect day, Shaun. Just me and the person I love most. Please don't think about who is spending what. Just be here with me. Just *one* perfect day. That's *all* I've ever wanted. You and me. Disney World—The Happiest Place on Earth. I want to go to The Happiest Place on Earth. And I want you to come with me."

And it was *the way* she said it.

I didn't even have the time to process the fact that this was the first time I was hearing the word 'love' come out of her mouth in reference to me. All I could hear was how *desperate* she was to be happy.

She wanted one perfect day.

And when I finally let go of my pride, that's exactly what we had.

We were on the drive back when Caprice spontaneously grabbed my hand. I was still getting used to that. We'd touched more today than we had in all the time I'd known her before today.

I didn't realize this until recently, but Caprice's skin was so soft. She weaved her fingers between mine, and just exhaled. Like it was the most comforting thing in the world for her to just be holding my hand.

"Shaun," she whispered quietly when we were almost home. I kept my eyes on the nighttime streets when I spoke.

"Hmm."

"Could you make a left instead of a right at the next light?"

I squinted, surprised by the random request. "Sure, where are we going?"

"I just have something I need to do," she said quietly.

"And what's that?" I asked as I took the left she wanted me to.

"I'll tell you soon."

I really couldn't take anymore birthday gifts. She'd done so much for me today already.

"One more left here, and then the immediate right," she gave more directions, but at this point, because I knew these roads, I knew there was only one place we could be going.

"Caprice…?"

"Please just drive me there," she whispered quickly. At this point, I took my eyes off the road and just looked at her. There were tears reflecting the streetlights off her cheeks. She was crying, her voice breaking a few places in her plea. "Please."

"Why…" I started to feel an uneasy twisting in my stomach, but my stupid ass was still doing as she said. "*Why* are we going to the bus station?"

She turned her whole body around to fully look at me, a regretful sadness in her eyes. There was also a determination there, too. That same determination I saw in her eyes this morning. She let go of my hand. "I have to go, Shaun."

I stopped the car, pressing hard on the brake.

"If you can't take me, then I will get out of the car and walk there from here," she threatened, and I knew she meant every word of it. It was getting dark, and we weren't in the best part of town. If I left her by herself, I left her open to all manner of neighborhood pervs, all manner of people who might hurt her. Even though I didn't want to, I took her there. I didn't want her out here by herself.

"I have to go," Caprice said again when I drove up to the parking lot of the station. She was reaching into the backseat for the backpack that she had with her this morning. I guess that was one thing I should've paid extra attention to. I had never skipped school and brought my backpack along looking that full.

"Why?" Why was she leaving? Things had just started to go right with us. Things had just started to go the way that I always wanted them to. Was it me? Did I do something? "Why are you leaving?"

"I can't…" She could barely get the words out, pushing her braids away from her face. "I can't live there."

"Where? Your grandmother's house?" Caprice was dead serious about leaving. She couldn't tell yet, but I was starting to panic. "You don't have to go back there. Come home with me. You can stay with us. We'll take care of you. You don't have to... have to leave."

"Shaun," she almost shouted, her crying only getting harder by the second. She was in so much pain. I didn't know what was going on, and I had no idea how to even begin fixing it. "It's too close! You live across the street. I'll still have to see... You don't know! You don't understand! I'm so scared! I have to leave!"

Her fear was too potent. Was her grandmother not only neglecting her? Was she...?

"Is she hitting you, too? I promise she won't be able to get to you in our house. *Don't* do this. We'll protect you! *I'll* protect you."

"I love you," she said it like a goodbye, so I hated hearing it. Caprice told me, "I love you so much that it makes me feel like I'll die if I leave you. I've loved you since I was eight years old at that city court. Watching you play—against all those kids who were so much older than you, so much bigger than you. It made me feel like I could be that brave someday, too. It inspired me more than you know. You're my best friend, so please don't be mad at me for doing this. You're *always* going to be my best friend. Please trust me when I tell you that I can't go back there. Please don't be mad at me. And please don't say no to what I'm about to ask you for next."

She was breaking right in front of me.

Everything just happened so... *fast.* One minute we were walking around, hand-in-hand at the most popular theme park in the world, and the next minute we were at a shabby bus station just outside of Parramore. I could've never guessed this was where we'd end up. Not in a million years.

I didn't know how to stop her. I didn't know how to stop any of this from happening. And I was breaking right along with her. Just like when we were kids, matching her despair in ways I had no control over. She was broken, so I was broken, too. Only Caprice Latimore could make me act this way.

Because I hated seeing her cry; I hated seeing it so much.

And then she asked me for something.

"I'm only sixteen," she told me. "I can't just walk up to the counter and ask for a ticket."

I understood what she was about to ask, and I was prepared

to say no. But when she started begging, I didn't really have much of a choice at all.

She explained, "I'm a minor. But not you. Not anymore. You're the only person I know, who's a legal adult, who won't say no. I have to get out of here, Shaun! And *you* have to help me. *Please, please* help me! I will kill myself before I have to go back to that house, Shaun. I mean it. If you love me, *help* me."

# Chapter Fifteen

## Caprice

Shaun got me the ticket.

He hated every second of the amount of time it took to purchase it, but he got me the ticket.

Not because he wanted to me to leave, but because he loved me.

I didn't know where I was going. I had a ticket to somewhere far out west, and it was anyone's guess where I would get off between here and there. It didn't matter. Anywhere was better than the pink house. Anywhere was better than under the same roof as Marcel.

I thought this all the way through last night, after Gracie told me he was coming back. I told myself I would not be there to greet him as he came through the door. It was never my intention to have to see Marcel ever again. I woke up this morning, knowing where I was going to end up by the end of the night.

This bus station.

But I had to have my perfect day with Shaun first.

I had over seven thousand dollars in savings, and while I knew that money was supposed to be for college, *this* was an emergency. I'd rather spend the rest of my life with no degree, no job, no money, than to *ever* let Marcel touch me again.

I shared a bench with a few other strangers at the stop. Like me, they were waiting for the next bus out of here. I wanted Shaun to wait with me. I even wanted to be selfish and ask him to come with me. We could run away together, I thought. The only reason he didn't buy a ticket for himself was because he couldn't afford one. I could've paid for two tickets. I knew in my heart of hearts that if I asked him to, he would've come with me.

But he had his whole life ahead of him. A *very* bright future.

And I could never do that to Miss Sylvia.

So, I didn't dare ask.

But when I asked him if he would sit next to me as I waited for my bus, he told me he could not. He didn't want a hug goodbye. He didn't even want to hear me say the word goodbye. I knew it wasn't because he didn't care, but because he cared too much.

So, he refused to sit and wait with me.

Instead, he was almost a hundred feet away, keeping watch over me while sitting on the front hood of his car. His eyes never left mine, and my eyes never left his. From this far away, I couldn't see the tears I knew were streaming down his face, but I could see how red his nose had become.

From afar, we looked into each other's eyes, as if we were trying to burn the memory of one another into each of our minds. And when the bus finally arrived, it stopped directly in front of me, and I couldn't see him anymore.

Clutching my ticket tightly, I let all the strangers get on the bus before me. Until I was the very last one. Just standing there. The bus driver had to shout a, *'Hey, kid!'* at me to take me out of my own head. I looked at him and he said, "We don't have all day."

Couldn't he see that I was falling apart, walking up the steps to hand him my ticket? Couldn't he see that I was getting on this bus, but leaving my heart?

He told me to hurry up and find a seat.

And so, I took a step backwards.

And then I took another.

And then I just…

I got off the bus.

* * *

Love is *amazing*.

Love is a powerful thing to get to experience. Love keeps your body warm when the September night air breezes past your skin. Love is like no other emotion. Unmatched in every aspect. You don't know what it truly means to be real until you've been in love.

But for me…

Love is also a prison.

I couldn't do it. I couldn't leave him.

When that bus drove away and I could see him again, it filled my heart with the kind of happiness I knew I'd never find anywhere else.

No matter where I went.

There was nothing more fulfilling than running that near one-hundred-foot distance and crashing back into his arms. I was locked up in a prison that I had no will or desire to escape from. Not if this prison was built with Shaun B. Taylor's arms, wrapped tightly around me, lifting me up off the ground. It brought me no greater happiness than to see his tears of despair turn to tears of joy.

I wanted to run away from the pink house, but I wanted to stay with Shaun more.

Today was one for the history books.

How many people could say that the best day of their life was also one of their worst?

We sat in the driveway of his mother's house, drained from the events of the day and drained from feeling all that pain at once. But things were better now. At least—in a way they were.

Because we both knew I didn't want to be here.

But we also knew we wanted to be together.

"Come inside," he said to me softly. "Stay with me."

I wanted to. I really wanted to.

I would've loved to live in the house across the street from mine.

And with his mother's permission, we might've been able to get away with it for a few nights.

But this was America.

And I already had an official guardian, certified by the great state of Florida. I could choose to stay with Shaun and Miss Sylvia, but if my guardian had anything to say about it, she could snatch me right back. And Miss Sylvia could get in serious trouble.

Gracie, as many times as she's told me she didn't want me in her house, didn't want me with Shaun even more than that. She never liked Shaun. The first time she ever met him, he was snooping around, knocking on our door, making it very clear he thought Gracie was suspicious.

She hated that we were friends.

But she couldn't control who I loved.

However, with the law on her side, she could surely control who I lived with.

I might be able to get away with it tonight, but I couldn't just go live with Shaun. I couldn't just ask Miss Sylvia to let me stay in her house. I couldn't just take all my things and move across the street.

I was only sixteen. I didn't have that right.

Shaun was the only reason I stayed in Parramore. And if I was going to stay in Parramore for him, I was going to have to live with Gracie. That was the only *real* way for me to stay here. Because even if we called the police, or asked somebody else for help, I was still sixteen. In the eyes of the law, I was a child.

And when you're a child in the great state of Florida, if the police have to take you away, they send you wherever they want.

And deep down, we both knew this.

"Shaun," I whispered, my voice all croaky from crying. But I had been thinking, and I came up with the best plan I could think of. "I have an idea."

He turned to face me, giving me a listening ear.

"I'll never, ever, ever be home again," I told him. "I'll just be there to sleep."

"Would that really keep her off your back?"

He thought Gracie was my problem. Just Gracie.

I couldn't tell him about Marcel without… *telling* him about Marcel. I never wanted anyone to know that about me. Especially Shaun. It made me feel so dirty. It would've shattered me to pieces if Shaun ever thought I was dirty, too.

What if I told him, and he stopped looking at me with that love in his eyes?

So, as far as he knew, it was just me and Gracie in that house.

"I'll just come home at night, run straight to my room, lock my door for the night, and leave in the mornings before anyone else wakes up."

"And if you get into it with her on your way to your room?" he asked, sounding like he wasn't confident in this idea just yet. In truth, I wasn't all that confident in it myself.

"I can get to my room. That's the easy part," I told him, trying my best to sound brave. "But you have to do something for me, okay?"

"Anything."

"At night, when I'm in my room, I'll keep the door locked," I spoke slowly, trying to manage my breathing so I didn't start hyperventilating. "But I would feel a lot safer if you…" I didn't know how to say it outright. So instead, I asked, "Do you know which window on my house is for my room?"

"Do you want me to stay with you at night?" he asked, guessing where it was going.

"*Could* you?" Would he get in trouble for it? Was he willing to climb in through my window every night? And leave every morning so we wouldn't get caught? I was asking for a lot.

"I'll do it."

He didn't even think about it long. Was it wrong of me to ask him to spend the nights in my home and *still* not tell him about Marcel? It might've been.

But the lock on my bedroom door was for Marcel.

Shaun was for me.

"Meet me by my window at eleven?" I asked him.

"I'll be there," he promised.

## Chapter Sixteen

# Caprice

This was the part of my plan I hated the most.

In order to get to my room, I would have to pass through the living room. Gracie's white car was in the driveway, so that meant she'd already come back from picking up Marcel. I already knew he would be in there with her, probably eating chocolate chip cookies in the living room.

It was a little after ten, and I knew Shaun was in his house, packing a bag for the weekend.

I just had to walk into the pink house, say a few things to its newest resident, and lock myself in my room.

*Say a few things to the pink house's newest resident.*

It was never my intention to have to see Marcel ever again.

But alas…

That was the part of my plan that I hated the most.

I opened the door holding a breath. It was late—a little after ten-thirty—but no later than it had been when I came home on the first day of school. If Gracie asked where I'd been, I'd just tell her I had dinner at Miss Sylvia's after work again. It didn't matter if she believed me.

She didn't believe me the first time either.

When I let myself in, they were both sitting in the living room having a chat. I could hear them. It got quiet as soon as I shut the door. I was doing everything I could to control my breathing.

I stepped further in, and then…

I saw him.

Just as I remembered.

Muscular build, beige skin, scary looking, but… he wasn't as tall as I remembered.

And maybe that was because I was tall now, too. I remember being so little and having to look up at Marcel. Now, as he rose to his feet from the living room couch, we were practically eye to eye.

"Hey, Caprice," he said quietly. *Nervously*. That must've been because he knew I was finally old enough to really understand what he'd done to me. Whether Gracie believed me or not—*he* knew the truth.

"Marcel," was all I said, his name in my mouth tasting like… *shit.*

"You not gon' give him a hug?" Gracie spoke up, offended by my keeping my distance.

"Nah." Marcel put a hand up in the air. "It's a'ight. She don't have to. I don't even really like it when people touch me like that," he said.

And that's when I *really* knew.

What he'd done to me as a little girl—someone in that prison had done to him, too.

"I'm going to my room," I said after that, feeling a single tear running down my face. Before I let myself in, I turned my head over my shoulder and told Gracie a lie, "I got my hours extended at the bookstore today. Starting next week, I work till ten."

* * *

Gracie would always make a point to be in bed by eleven.

She worked as head custodian at the mayor's office in the city. Because of that, she had to be up early every day except Saturday and Sunday. Gracie wasn't walking around the house after eleven o'clock. And since Marcel was sleeping on the couch, with Gracie in bed, he had no choice but to go to sleep, too.

That's why when Shaun quietly knocked on my window at eleven that night, everyone in my house was done for the day except me.

"You good," he checked on me once he'd climbed inside. Maybe he could tell, just by looking at my face, that I was still reeling off the encounter with Marcel. I nodded. Shaun was here. So, I was good now.

Shaun looked around my room, taking it all in. This was the first time he'd ever been in here. Chuckling to himself, he shook his head. When I asked him what was funny, he replied, "You must have OCD or something, because this room is *way* too fuckin' clean."

He was joking about the OCD. And though he didn't realize it—he was also one-hundred percent correct.

I didn't like dirty things.

I took as many showers a day as I could get away with. I tried to always have a pack of baby wipes. My clothes were always double washed before I wore them. And as for my bedroom—this place was never a mess.

I always felt dirty inside and doing these things helped me feel clean.

He glanced at my neatly made bed.

And then the air between us felt a little strange. We'd *just* started holding hands today—and now he was either sleeping on the floor or sleeping with me in my bed. The choice was mine.

"Make yourself comfortable," I told him calmly. We could share my bed. I didn't feel clean at all. I'd been out all day with Shaun, but that didn't magically change who I was. "I'm gonna go take a shower."

He was sitting upright against my headboard when I stepped out of my bathroom. So that I wouldn't have to change in front of him, I had taken my clothes in with me. I stepped out now in a large white t-shirt and some shorts. Shaun had never seen me in pajamas before.

When he noticed that I'd walked into the room, his arm came out, inviting me in. I thought about it briefly before climbing in and letting his arm close around me. His chin rested at the top of my braids, and we just laid there for a bit.

Today was a lot.

"Shaun," I whispered into the darkness of my bedroom. I could feel his thumb rubbing soothingly against my arm where his hand rested. I liked it. I didn't want him to stop.

"Hmm."

"I'm so sorry for doing all of this to you on your birth—"

"It's okay," he said before I could finish. "I saw the fear in your eyes. It was real. You're really scared of her. I can tell. But you came back because of me. I know that. So, I guess I'm sorry, too."

"And you won't mind sleeping here with me at night?"

He pushed out a breath. I couldn't see his face, but I could still feel the gentle caresses of his hand against my arm. Laying in his arms like this, I felt really safe.

"Even if we don't tell anyone—lemme talk to her. Lemme let her know what it is. She'll get off your case once she knows I'm not about to let her keep hitting—"

"No."

If he did that, that would blow the lid off the whole can of worms.

Shaun didn't know the full story. I didn't want him to know it. If Shaun knew the full story, sleeping with me in my room at night wouldn't be enough. I knew him very well, and if Shaun knew about Marcel—a *man* that scared me this much—keeping me company at night wouldn't be his way to fix it.

Just a few weeks ago, on that first day of calculus, Shaun was ready to break Zavier Dawson's hand *just* because Zavier patted me on the back and Shaun knew I didn't like that.

Shaun could easily fight high school boys and win.

Shaun might've even been able to best some grown men.

But I saw Marcel today in the living room. Although he wasn't as tall as I thought, every other menacing thing about him was just as threatening as I remembered. And Marcel just got out of prison. A boy like Shaun, no matter how tough, was nothing compared to what Marcel had to fight off.

Marcel could kill Shaun. Easily.

But to protect me? I had a feeling Shaun was willing to die trying.

So, I could never tell Shaun about Marcel. He had to keep thinking the reason I tried to run away tonight was all about Gracie.

If I only came to the pink house late at night to sleep, there was no reason for Shaun and Marcel to ever cross paths. I could keep them apart. Shaun would never have to know.

"You can't talk to Gracie. And promise me you won't tell *anyone*, Shaun," I whispered. "Not your mom, not the police, not your teammates. *Nobody*."

He didn't want to make that promise. I could tell from the way he said my name. "Caprice, I—"

"Please." I took his other hand into both of mine. "I promise I'm fine."

"If you're asking me to ignore the fact that someone is hurting you, then you're asking me to ignore the fact that I love you," he said quietly. "I won't do either."

"You have to."

"Butterscotch…" He let out a deep, heavy sigh. It was obvious he was exhausted. Today was a lot. "The school year just started," he pointed out. "We could do this sleepover shit for *maybe* a month, but at some point, you're either gonna let me talk to her, or tell someone."

I was stuck between a rock and a Shaun Taylor.

"What would you say to her if you talked to her?"

Shaun chuckled after he thought about it, and responded, "I'd tell her that I don't hit women, but I know a salon full of hairstylists who would *gladly* jump her ass for you."

I cracked a smile, soon knowing this was an argument I wasn't going to win with him.

"Alright," I agreed. "Next time she hits me, feel free to rally in the troops."

"Why do I have to wait till she hits you?" he asked, still not willing to compromise.

"*Because…*" I stressed the word. "I think staying out the house and doing this… *sleepover shit* will work for longer than a month. I think it could last until the end of the school year. So, if it's alright with you, I'd like to at least try it my way before you start your little war."

"We'll see," was all he said.

"So, you'll wait?"

"So, I'll *see*."

I sat up and looked at him. His expression was serious, completely pissed off that we were having this conversation. I asked him, "What does that even mean?"

"It means I'll sleep here every night if it makes you feel safe. I'll do whatever it takes to make sure you're good. If that means doing it your way first, I'll do it," he told me, but just before I could feel some kind of relief, his tone darkened and he promised, "But the second I suspect some shit—Caprice, I'm not gonna ask for your fuckin' permission to keep you safe." I'd never seen Shaun this adamant about anything. I knew he wasn't angry with me, but just angry at the situation. Still, his tone was just as furious when he demanded my agreement. "Do you understand me?"

A little shaken, I only nodded slowly.

All this aggression was because I told him Gracie was hitting me.

So, it was in this moment that I realized—if Shaun *ever* found out about Marcel…

Someone was going to die.

# Chapter Seventeen

## Caprice

It was Wednesday night.

Shaun had been sleeping in my room with me for a few days now, and tonight made night five. If we could forget about the main reason why he was even here, it was kind of nice falling asleep and waking up to each other every morning.

"I don't want to be your girlfriend," I told him that night.

Shaun pulled back a little at the sound of the random outburst, his face the picture of confusion. He rose a single eyebrow and asked, "Why not?"

Today we had lunch together in the cafeteria. Usually, I would sit with Mischa and her friends—who were not my friends—and Shaun sat with his friends and teammates. It wasn't because we didn't like eating together. We'd done it before. But just because you have a best friend, doesn't mean you don't need regular friends as well.

Today though, Shaun took a break from his usual table and sat at mine. Sensing that he wanted the alone time, one by one, the people at my table got up to go. And then it was just Shaun and me, sitting face to face at a table in the Jefferson courtyard. The sun shined light into his penny colored eyes and his dazzling smile kept me completely spellbound.

It must've been the way we were looking at each other…

Because by the time we made it to calculus, everyone at Jefferson was convinced we were together. And to my surprise, the word '*finally*' kept being used.

Shaun Taylor and Caprice Latimore were *finally* together, they said, as if this had always been the predictable outcome.

Perhaps everyone had realized that Shaun was in love with me long before I knew it myself.

But I didn't want to be his girlfriend.

"You've had so many girlfriends," I told him while we were in my bed that night. "Tasha, Joella, Jessica, Lyric, Paris... They were all really pretty girls. And you aren't with any of them anymore. They were your girlfriends, and you... got rid of them. I'd rather stay best friends. You've kept me the longest, and maybe it's because we're best friends."

I could feel Shaun's body grow less tense behind me, relaxing once I'd explained my reasoning.

He laughed a little.

"You don't want to be my girlfriend because you feel like it would be more likely for me to leave you?"

"Well, in terms of probability, there is a statistical connection."

He breathed out another short laugh.

"Not everything is a damn math problem, Butterscotch." He shrunk some of the space he'd created before. I could feel his lips press against the top of my head as his arm around me tightened. "You wanna know why they didn't last?" he whispered against my hair. I just nodded, closing my eyes to the feeling of his body pressed up against mine. "Because they kept asking me to choose."

"Choose?" I questioned, feeling his warm breaths hitting the skin along my neck, just behind my ear. Something about that feeling made something come alive between my legs. I spoke again, sounding out of breath. "What did they make you choose?"

Tucked between my pink and white bed sheets, I wasn't so naïve to not know what most loving couples do together in bed. Here I was, a girl hopelessly in love with a boy who was hopelessly in love with me, and we had nothing but time and privacy.

However, there was a deep seeded fear in me that kept coming up. No, it wasn't the fear of being touched, because Shaun's hands had never felt like fire on my skin. And when they did... it was the good kind of heat. I didn't fear Shaun's hands on my body.

My fear was that I was *broken* down there.

Never in my life had I ever seen as much blood as I did the time Marcel pinned me down to the bathroom tile and broke me.

That kind of injury has to leave a mark.

I'd never seen another girl's thing—or mine, for that matter—so it's not like I'd compared. But Shaun—with all those girlfriends—he knew what that stuff was supposed to look like, supposed to feel like.

So, what would he think of me if I turned out to be broken down there?

"Every relationship I've ever been in has always ended the same way," he told me finally, sounding slightly amused. I must've said something funny. "I've always been asked to either choose them or choose my best friend." He laughed again and added, "And like you said… I've kept you the longest."

I pressed my lips together and then bit back a smile.

"So, if I was your girlfriend, would you keep choosing me?"

Shaun kissed the sensitive skin behind my left ear, and then in it he whispered, "I will *always* choose you."

* * *

It was Thursday night when Marcel tried to get into my room for the first time.

It had been almost a week since he was released from prison. In my comings and goings from the pink house, we didn't have many encounters. Mostly, I'd just see him sitting on the couch on my way to my room every night.

If I got home between ten and eleven, then I knew Gracie would always be home and he couldn't try anything with me.

Even though Gracie hated me, she would not sit around and just watch me be raped.

At least, I hoped not.

So, when I would get home, the first thing I would do was announce it to Gracie. Loud and clear so that she could hear me. *Gracie, I'm home!*

Marcel, I would usually greet with a nod.

And then I would run to my room, wait an hour or so, and then let Shaun in through my window.

Around Monday was when I started to notice that Marcel

was getting more comfortable around the house. He'd spent the entire first weekend home, getting doted on by Gracie. She'd cooked more in that weekend for him than she had in the past seven years for me. After that weekend of pampering, Marcel loosened up a bit. The first couple of days, I didn't talk to Marcel much, and if you didn't consider *hellos* talking, then I didn't talk to him at all.

By Monday, he'd started to ask me flyby questions as I walked to my room.

*Does your job hire people with felonies?*

*How old are you now?*

*You doing good in school?*

*Where'd you get those nice ass shoes, niece?*

He was always trying to have a conversation, even if it was only thirty seconds long. It terrified me. Literally. The first night he was here, he could barely look me in the eyes, and it gave me a little hope. Maybe he was reformed on the inside, I thought at first. If someone touched him in prison, maybe he knew better now, and would never do it again.

No, Marcel was just a little shy. He needed time to acclimate to his new life on the outside.

Within forty-eight hours, he'd gotten comfortable, and by Monday… he was talking to me like we didn't both know he raped me when I was a *child.*

On Wednesday, as I sped to my room, in my peripheral vision, I could see him looking at my behind.

By Thursday, I didn't even need to see him in my periphery to know he was looking at me with desire.

He was making eyes at me.

"Hey Caprice," he said when I'd walked through the door.

I nodded at him and as usual shouted for Gracie, "Gracie, I'm home!"

From the worn brown couch, Marcel stood to his feet, and I immediately shrunk into my shoulders. Seeing this, he grimaced into a laugh and said, "Damn, I can't stand up? I was just gonna get some milk and chocolate chip cookies. You want some?"

I was taken back to my childhood, always accepting Marcel's little gifts. For years I would wonder if taking them was the reason he felt like he could just… take me. I remember his favorite thing to give me was chocolate.

And now I couldn't smell the stuff without wanting to throw up.

"I don't want any," I said quickly, frozen in place because he was standing in the path between the front door and my bedroom. I didn't want to walk past him. So, I just stayed where I was.

"You never eat here," Marcel pointed out, eyes first on my face and then slowly gliding down the length of my body. "You're too skinny."

"I ate at work." In truth, Shaun had been packing me all my meals from his house. Because of my *wonderful* boyfriend, I was eating breakfast, lunch, and dinner every day, which wasn't even something I was doing before all of this. "I'm not hungry."

"You still like David Letterman?" he asked, trying to piece together the few memories of me he had saved. I stopped liking the sound David Letterman's voice the night Marcel pulled my shirt over my face and touched himself until he came. David Letterman had been on in the background.

Back then, I thought the stuff Marcel got on me was lotion.

I was so young.

"'Cause Mama was telling me she was gonna get the cable box back, so maybe we could—"

Going down this unwanted memory lane, I didn't have it in me to keep up the pleasantries. My voice just kind of broke as my shoulders slumped and I quietly interrupted, "Can I please go to my room?"

First, he made a face, staring at me in that rundown living room like I had just insulted him.

He stepped a little bit out of my path, his hand stretching out as if to say, '*go ahead*'. As I walked past him, he moved a bit and my shoulder lightly bumped into his.

"My bad," he said casually.

But it wasn't an accident.

And then three hours later, as Shaun lay sleeping beside me peacefully, I watched the knob on my locked door twist left, and then twist right. My breathing quickened, and even though Marcel would have had to destroy the door to find his way in, it didn't matter. He tried. Which meant Marcel was not a changed man. The doorknob twisted four more times.

And I didn't go to sleep that night.

# Chapter Eighteen

# SHAUN

Something had been off about Caprice for about a week now.

We were sitting in third period biology and she was just staring off into space, a million miles away. Dr. Young was up at the board, explaining the difference between asexual reproduction and sexual reproduction and since I'd failed his last test, I should've been taking notes, but I was too busy watching my girlfriend.

Almost three weeks had passed since the bus station thing, and to the best of my knowledge, Caprice's plan had been working.

But now I wasn't so sure.

I leaned in closer to her, and she jumped, scared at how close I was at first. Caprice had always been a jumpy girl, but something about the way she flinched fired up my suspicious meter.

"Are you okay?" I asked her.

For the last couple of nights, her grandmother had been trying to get into her room at night, and I could see the negative reaction it kept getting out of Caprice. We'd be in the middle of whispering, and then all of a sudden, her doorknob would start moving. You could tell Caprice was really scared of her grandmother because her back would go rigid, and she'd shake a little, every time the old lady touched her door.

In my house, since it was just me and my mom, my mother didn't walk in on me at night. At most, Mom would twist the knob on my door, and know I was home if it was locked. This was how I had been getting away with sleeping at Caprice's every night. I'd just lock my bedroom door and leave through my window. A locked door was all my mother needed to check for to assume that I was in my room.

I figured Caprice's grandmother was doing the same thing.

But it was unsettling to see how scared Caprice was of that old lady even touching her door.

Turning away from Dr. Young, Caprice looked over her shoulder and nodded at me. "I'm fine."

Dr. Young took this one moment of distraction to call on her. "Miss Latimore!"

Her little obedient, nerdy head snapped back in his direction. I couldn't help but crack a smile. From the front of the classroom, Dr. Young used a pointer to direct her attention to a vocabulary word on the board.

"Sexual reproduction in humans requires which two gametes?" he asked.

Even caught off guard, there was no tripping her up. She had the answer instantly. "Sperm and egg."

"Very good, Caprice," Princess Knight's voice rang from our right. *Here we fuckin' go again…* It just wouldn't be a completed day at Jefferson until Princess said something slick. She kept her voice low as she taunted. "I'm sure you know all about that now."

We both turned to look at her.

I don't touch women, but if ever there was a woman more deserving of getting her face mushed in, Princess was high on that list. Caprice was always trying to get me to ignore her, just like she did, but today…

Today was *different*.

"Excuse me?" Caprice said in a tone of voice that I didn't normally hear out of her. She sounded pissed.

"I'm sure you know all about sex now," Princess wouldn't let up. Her eyes flickered over to me and then back at Caprice. Beside her, her sister, Paris, was covering her smile. Princess turned to her sister, and just loud enough for us to hear, she said, "Babygirl got herself some new hair and some new shoes and now she don't know how to act."

"Knight—" Caprice stopped me, her hand landing on my arm, not wanting me to defend her. It was women's business, I know… But I'd had it up to here, and I didn't think Caprice had it in her to put this chick in her place, so I was going to do it *for* her.

I was wrong.

Caprice had all that in her, and *more*.

"What's the problem, Princess? Really," she addressed her head on, refusing to shrink. Dr. Young stopped teaching, and the whole room shifted their attention to the back. You could almost immediately feel what this was building up to. "Did I do something to you and not realize? 'Cause you and *your shit*—I'm losing my patience."

Princess laughed, thinking up a comeback quickly. "Figures you would start losing your patience now that you like moving so—" Princess glanced in my direction again and then back at Caprice. "—*fast*."

The way Caprice got out of her seat—it was like a stroke of lightning. There was no time to stop her. One minute she was sitting next to me, the next minute she was knocking Princess Knight off her seat. Caprice straddled that girl and got six good licks in before Paris tried to jump in and help her little sister.

"Let go of me, Shaun!" Paris tried to squirm free as I held her back. If Caprice wanted to have this fight, I was not about to let it be two against one. Princess had this coming, and nobody in the room was surprised that it had come to this. Even Dr. Young seemed to be taking his time walking to the back of the classroom to separate the two fighting girls. Caprice was his favorite student, and Princess was his least.

You could just see how all sense of togetherness left Caprice's eyes. She was somewhere else. She wasn't hitting Princess Knight for what she'd said at that moment. This… this rage was about more than Princess Knight.

Knight just happened to be the fuse that set off a ticking bomb.

My girl had snapped.

"I didn't want him to." Caprice was shouting this at Princess over and over as each of her blows connected. Princess was getting her shit rocked like I'd never seen before. It was almost too hard to watch. *Almost*. Dr. Young grabbed Caprice by the back of her shirt and pulled her off, instructing Paris to escort Princess out of the room to wash her face. Princess was bleeding. I let Paris go.

Dr. Young told Caprice he was writing her up, but as someone who'd been in school fights before, I knew for a fact that what Caprice had just done to Princess was the kind of thing kids got suspended for. Written up? I'd had worse happen to me for just being late to class. *That's that favoritism,* I realized with a half laugh. Caprice walked away from this with a slap on the wrist and a wrinkled-up polo shirt.

I think I might've been in shock to some degree. Seeing Caprice beat Princess up with that level of aggression and anger created more questions in my mind than it solved. When all the commotion in the classroom had died down, I watched as my sweet, previously harmless Butterscotch took her seat, and returned to taking her notes like nothing had happened.

In the middle of her writing, I leaned in and just went ahead and said it.

"That didn't look like '*I'm fine.*' to me."

* * *

"Something's wrong," I whispered to her later that night as we laid side by side.

She turned on her left side to face me, the white light of the moon outside washing her skin in a silvery paint. It was a little after one o'clock in the morning, and neither of us felt the need to be asleep right now since there was no school tomorrow.

It was Friday, September 22$^{nd}$, 2006.

Technically, since it was after midnight… it was actually Saturday.

A full three weeks since my birthday had passed, and I was starting to feel like Caprice wasn't telling me something. I wouldn't have put it past her to lie to me about things her grandmother was doing to her. Caprice seemed to have wanted as little confrontation with her as possible.

I didn't think I was going to be able to keep doing that for her.

It was obvious something was weighing heavily on her mind, and if she didn't tell me what it was, I would just assume the worst.

"Can I ask you something?"

She only nodded.

"You didn't want him to... what exactly?"

Her brows dipped in confusion. "What are you talking about?"

"That's what you kept shouting at Knight, while you were bashing her head in," I recalled. "*I didn't want him to. I didn't want him to. I didn't want him to.*" I shrugged and just looked at her. "And I don't think you were talkin' about me either. So, who were you talkin' about, and what didn't you want him to do?"

"Shaun..." she started cautiously, and then pushed out a sigh. "I don't want to talk about this."

Boundaries.

But I couldn't help but feel like this conversation had to happen. "Buttersc—"

"Drop it," she urged, creating some space between us. "If you're not going to leave me alone about this, then leave."

"*What*?"

I knew she was bluffing when she gave me the ultimatum, "Go home, or leave me alone about this."

So, I called her bluff. "Okay."

I saw the panic flash in her eyes before she tried to hide it, but I got out of her bed and started looking for my shoes. In my periphery, I could see Caprice rising from her pillow and I didn't look at her as I tied my laces.

"Shaun." Her voice came out nervous. I was scaring her. "I didn't mean..." She hesitated. "I don't want you to leave."

I grabbed my backpack and didn't turn around. I could hear her getting out of bed to follow after me.

"Shaun *please*," she practically begged, her hand coming out to grab my shoulder. "*Please* don't leave me here."

There was genuine fear behind her words, as there had been three weeks ago. However, three weeks ago I had never seen my girlfriend beat the shit outta somebody *and* make it look easy. Three weeks ago, I thought Caprice was completely defenseless and... for lack of a better word, weak.

And then I watched her give Princess Knight two black eyes and chip one of her teeth without so much as breaking a sweat.

Don't get me wrong—I was *relieved* to discover that strength in her. Princess had it coming, and I was sure Caprice would never hear from that girl again. She did what she had to do. But that strength in her was a confusing turn of events. It made me realize two things.

One, Caprice wasn't weak at all.

Two, she was, by no definition, defenseless either.

If she could do that to Princess, then she could do that to her abusive grandmother if necessary.

So, the genuine terror that rang from her voice at this very moment—it *wasn't* adding up. She couldn't be both people—a girl who shakes at the mention of being left alone in a house with her sleeping grandmother and a girl who kicked another girl's ass for talking to her crazy. So, what was Caprice *really* afraid of? Something was missing.

And she wasn't telling me what that something was.

"There's no way you're *this* terrified of that old lady." I let my backpack fall to the floor as I faced her. "Not after what I saw today. But you're scared of *something*—I can tell. *What* are you not telling me?"

"Shaun…" She trailed off, her voice getting smaller like she could barely speak from how scared she was. The moonlight outside reflected off the tears collecting at the rims of her eyes. She was so scared that she was starting to hyperventilate. "…are you really… g-going to… leave?"

This immediately made me feel guilty. I backed away from the window, my hands going to her shoulders. She was shaking. *Ah fuck…*

"No, no, no," I tried to calm her down, pulling her in and holding her to me as I tried to walk back my bluff. "I'm not leaving… *Shh… shh…* Caprice, I'm right here. I'm not gonna leave you alone here."

"I'm so sorry," she apologized for crying like this, but I wasn't mad at her. She didn't need to apologize.

"Please tell me what's really going on," I whispered against her hair. "Why are you so scared that you're shaking? Caprice, I'm not dumb—I know there's something you're not telling me. What is *really* going on?"

I could hear her draw in a shaky breath against my chest, her arms circling around me tighter as she exhaled. Just before she could give me some sort of explanation, someone on the other side of her bedroom door whispered her name.

And it was the voice of a man.

*"Caprice!"*

The shock of it made me pause at first. *Since when does a man live in this house?*

*No, for real – when* the fuck *did a man start living in this house?*

*Maybe I heard wrong and her grandmother just has a really deep voice.*

The voice emerged again. "*Caprice,* who you whisperin' with in there?"

*That's definitely not a fuckin' woman.*

In my arms, Caprice tried to keep her voice steady when she responded.

"Nobody, Marcel," she called back, adding, "I was just having a bad dream!"

*Marcel? Marcel? Who the fuck is Marcel?* I tried searching my memory for any mention of the name in recent years. I was coming up blank.

The doorknob on Caprice's bedroom door twisted, just as it had every night for the past week and a half.

"You don't gotta lock the door, niece," the voice whispered through the door. "What'd you lock it for?"

*Niece? Niece…*

This was an uncle. Her uncle named Marcel. It was familiar. I tried to think and remember, and in my mind, it came to me in flashes of blue and red police lights reflecting against one half of an eight-year-old Caprice's face. This was her uncle that was arrested when we were kids.

*When did he get out?*

*Why didn't she tell me he was living here again?*

"Let me come in and see if everything is alright with you, babygirl."

There was something about the way he said that, that made my skin crawl. I couldn't explain it, but without motive and without explanation, I automatically knew I wanted to kick this nigga's ass. For *something.*

I just didn't know what yet.

The wheels in my head started to turn. This was the missing piece of the puzzle that had the big picture looking weird for so long. Unintentionally, I had just realized what Caprice was *really* scared of the whole time. I could hear it in the way her voice shook when she replied.

"You don't need to come in. I'm going back to sleep."

She was still shaking while we listened to footsteps grow quieter and quieter on the other side of her door. Everything was starting to make sense. I pulled back and drew her head up to meet my eyes. She could hardly look at me.

"When did he get out?" I whispered, my sense of calmness feeling like it was being held up by a single thread. I was ahead of the situation in my mind and already pissed off.

"September first," she answered quietly, and I wasn't surprised to hear it.

That was the same day she tried to run away from home.

I was onto something.

This made so much more sense now.

Except one thing.

"Why are you so *terrified* of this man?" And even terrified felt like an understatement.

Caprice was tense, on red alert. The initial fear of me leaving her here had subsided, but that didn't mean she was okay now. Something else was eating at her as well. She wanted to answer my question. I could see her trying to get the words out, but her body kept forcing them back down her throat.

Now was not the time to force her to talk.

She was having some sort of mental break. Part of it was set off because I threatened to leave her here and the other was because this man just tried to get into her room. I guided Caprice back to her bed, understanding that I was seeing her succumb to an irrational terror. She was freezing up. The man behind the door didn't just scare her.

He scared her to death.

When she tried to run away from home three weeks ago, when she asked me to sleep in her room, the reason why I wasn't allowed to talk about it...

It was never about her grandmother.

The failed attempts to get through her locked door for the past week and a half—those were never her grandmother either.

"I'm not leaving," I promised this over and over as I tried to calm her fearful tremors. Even without her explanation, I finally understood what this was. "I promise I will *never* leave you here."

I didn't ask any of the questions that were swimming around in my head. Sitting at the foot of her bed, I just held her closely until her panic attack subsided. I was hours into rubbing soothing circles against her back when she finally fell asleep. Gently, I guided her head from my shoulder to a pillow, sitting above her as she laid, keeping watch as she slept. With me here, even under the same roof as someone who scared her to death, Caprice slept peacefully.

And I didn't go to sleep that night.

## Chapter Nineteen

# Caprice

I woke up exhausted.

As if sleep had the opposite effect on me overnight. I woke up to the Saturday morning sun, the sound of birds outside, and with an inexplicably cold feeling in my stomach. Today was not going to be a good day. I could tell from the moment I opened my eyes to find Shaun, on his side of my bed, sitting up against my headboard, looking like he hadn't slept at all the night before.

His eyes were on me as I stirred awake, making no sudden movements, and saying nothing. I sat up beside him, understanding that a conversation was coming, knowing I couldn't keep lying.

"Good morning," was all he said at first, tone flat with eyes even less expressive. I couldn't read him this way. I couldn't tell if he was upset with me or not. When he spoke again, his tone was just as ambiguous as before. "Go get ready. You and me need to have a talk..." he paused, something burning behind his eyes before he added, "...but *not* here."

* * *

It was a little bit before 9AM.

The basketball court in the city was empty for now, and Shaun had barely said three words to me as we walked there. When we were kids, Shaun and I couldn't shut up on our walks to the court. We'd stand side by side, a hair's distance away from holding hands, and we'd just talk the entire forty-five-minute trip.

He didn't have anything to say to me this morning.

Shaun was quiet even when he stopped inside *Nikki's Place*

to get us some breakfast to go. He didn't ask me what I wanted, but that's because he already knew. And while we waited for the order to be bagged up, not a word came out of him even then.

We were sitting on the courtside bleachers. I had a half-eaten breakfast sandwich in my hand, sitting one bleacher up from Shaun, who sat on the lowest. Shaun hadn't touched anything in our to-go bag. I saw this as an opportunity to finally say something.

"Your sandwich is going to get cold."

I got his attention, making him look up to me on the higher bleacher, squinting a bit because the morning sun was in his eyes. His silence was starting to worry me. I remembered last night just fine, but I didn't know how to address it. I figured I'd just wait for him to say something about it and I'd use his line of questioning to guide me.

But he wasn't asking me any questions.

He just stared at me for what felt like a million years before finally breaking eye contact and turning his attention to the empty court.

Just before I could ask if he was mad at me for lying, he spoke.

Still looking at the empty court, he asked, "Do you remember when we were kids?"

We had lots of memories together. "Sure."

"Remember that day I tried to teach you to play one-on-one?" he asked, turning to look back at me. "The day we officially became friends."

I only nodded at this.

"I remember it, too," he told me. "Vividly. I remember how just before I handed you that butterscotch hard candy, I had bumped into you while guarding." He let out a heavy exhale. "And then you fell to the ground, rolled into a ball, and… screamed *so* bad that you stopped traffic." He pointed at the apartment buildings that lined the court before explaining, "All these people started coming out of their apartments and seeing what the big commotion was, and then you—"

"I don't want to talk about this, Shaun." I didn't want him taking me back to that day.

He stopped, looked at me, and said, "*Yeah*, we're gonna

have this conversation whether you want to or not."

And I had nothing to say to that.

"Sometimes I think you think I'm stupid, Caprice," he expressed out of nowhere.

"That's not true," I told him.

"It's *okay,*" he stressed, just in case. "Lots of people do. Some people think being an athlete automatically means you have to be dumb, so even if they never straight up call me an idiot… they move like they don't expect me to see the shit that's right in front of me. You might not do it consciously, but… you're doing that crap to me *right now.*"

I apologized quickly. "I'm sorry."

"No," he said, raising a hand. "I'm not mad. Don't apologize." He shook his head, eyes distant as he continued from where he left off, "But anyways… *that* day. You screamed like someone was trying to kill you. And then when you stopped… you cried like you *wished* you were dead." I could see his eyes getting a glassy quality to them just from remembering. "It's one of my worst childhood memories, you know that? I'd never seen anyone… *hurt* like that before. At ten years old, it… did things to me. I remember crying right along with you. To this day, every time you cry, I'm reminded of it. I never bring it up, but that doesn't mean I forgot. Still, I hadn't seen you cry like you did on this court that day *for years* after the fact."

He took in a sharp breath and said, "Until three weeks ago… When you tried to get on the first bus outta this city. You cried that night the same way you did when you were eight years old. And now…" he looked away from me before he guessed "…I'm starting to think eight-year-old Caprice and sixteen-year-old Caprice were crying about the same thing—both times."

And then he came out and asked it point blank, facing me. "*What* happened to you?"

I tried to collect myself best I could when I hit him with my own question. "What do you mean?"

"You're doing that thing again," he told me. "That thing where you act like I'm stupid."

I swallowed the lump forming in my throat. He wasn't asking me any of these questions because he needed clues.

Shaun already knew.

"Last night was *not* normal," he spoke slowly. "But look at you—acting as if it didn't happen. You know what creeps me out?" he asked. "You're so… *good* at it. If I wasn't with you last night, I wouldn't be able to tell by looking at you now." He released a slow, trembling breath. "It makes me wonder how many times bad things have happened to you, and I just… didn't know."

I didn't say anything.

I could hear the exasperation in his voice when he said, "Since you won't tell me what I don't know—how about I tell you what I *do* know. I didn't sleep at all last night. I spent the entire six hours, as you slept, going over our history—combing it with a fine-toothed comb. Just fill in the blanks for me."

It was quiet for a few seconds—possibly the longest couple of seconds in my entire life.

And then Shaun showed me just *how* much he'd been paying attention for the past seven years.

"I first saw you in the summer of 1999. You were eight, sitting under the white lights of this basketball court. I used to sneak glances at you while you read your books, but I never spoke to you… until the first day of school. You came to school *once*… and then you just… *disappeared*. You missed the rest of the first week, and the entire second week. Something *happened* to you. And I knew you didn't have the flu, but I was… *ten*. I didn't have proof. Nobody would listen to me. My mom thought I was paranoid. She thought it was some crush gone too far, and that I needed to stay outta people's business. She wasn't gonna do anything about it. So… I knocked on your grandmother's door, and she…" Shaun shook his head. "Even at ten years old I knew that lady was lying to me."

I remembered that day.

"But I don't doubt that… *something* happened to you," he continued. "The first day you came back, you'd looked like you'd been… through it. I figured maybe I really *was* paranoid, and you really had been sick, but… then the screaming happened. Your grandmother said you had the flu. But… you didn't scream like somebody who'd just gotten over a flu. You didn't even cough *once*. I always thought that was strange." He turned and faced me completely before he let me know, "You know—in my mind there has always been two of you, the Caprice before, and the Caprice after. Before you were… sick. And then after. The Caprice before didn't automatically jump back if I stood too close, she didn't flinch if I moved too fast, she was cute and outgoing, even though she was a little shy. And the Caprice after, my best friend who hates being touched by everyone—except me, recently—who is extremely shy, who tenses up when people move too fast or get too close. She's *very* jumpy, very high strung."

"I don't think the flu changes a personality like that," he proposed thoughtfully. "The same day you showed up back at school, you told me you weren't going home after. Actually—you said you'd be at the courts all the time from then on. But you *never* played with us, Caprice… You just never wanted to go home. That's the thing about you—for as long as I can remember—you *never* wanted to go home. You were always looking for some excuse to stay outside longer. I used to take mad ass whoopins for you, staying out the house for longer than I knew I was allowed to."

He continued, "I was thinking really hard last night, and I remember walking you home that day, late, and us seeing your uncle get arrested. Caprice—I thought I dreamt this up, but no… I *remember*… you cried tears of *joy* to see him in cuffs."

There was an extended silence. I could see cars moving along the busy downtown roads. I could see people walking their dogs. I could see birds flying in circles above us, lounging on the powerlines.

But I couldn't hear any of it.

I couldn't hear anything until Shaun spoke again.

"He did something to you, didn't he?" he asked. "Something when you were a little girl, right? Something that took you out of school for two weeks. Something that made you hate other people touching you. Something that scarred you bad enough to want to run away from home at the first mention of him coming back. *Something*… Strange as it may sound—I think I've always known there was… *something*. I didn't know before, but think I know what that something is now." I realized I was crying when I watched as a single tear traveled down his cheek. Shaun always cried when I cried, but this time, I think his tears were for another reason. I think he cried because he knew. "I wanna hear it from you, though. If you can tell me. What… *happened* to you?"

I didn't want him to think I was dirty. I wanted to lie.

But I wouldn't be able to lie.

My hands drew up to wipe away at my cheeks, knowing the words that were about to come out of my mouth were purely to confirm what Shaun *already* knew.

"It started when I first moved down from Alabama…"

* * *

# SHAUN

Caprice was worried about the wrong thing.

I sat through the entire uncomfortable truth, doing everything I could to not punch a hole through something. I thought I wanted to know why Caprice was so afraid of her uncle, but once I knew, I envied the version of myself that had no idea.

This was some *sick* shit.

She was practically a fuckin' *toddler,* at eight years old. The thought that someone could do that to her—they needed to be shot on sight. I don't know what I expected to hear, but it was nowhere near as graphic as what she told me.

And Caprice…

She was worried about the wrong thing.

She told me all that, practically shaking by the time she got the last word out, and when she was done, she asked me if I still loved her.

Like I would've stopped because somebody else hurt her. I was so confused.

She explained, "Imagine if you bought a doughnut, and then when you unwrapped it, you saw that someone else took two big ass bites out of it. That's gross, right?"

"Except there's one issue with that logic," I told her, trying to keep my tone as steady as I could because I was just… Losing. My. Shit, on the inside. I had to spell it out for her—blunt and slow.

"You're not a *fuckin'* doughnut, Caprice."

Nobody took two bites out of her. Some sick ass piece of shit ripped her innocence out of her little eight-year-old hands and to this day, didn't have enough shame to leave her ass alone even now. That didn't make her gross. That made *him* gross.

Gross *as fuck.*

All those attempts to get into her room this past week… I was there for all of it. I had no idea. She was so scared, and I couldn't even begin to understand why.

But now I know.

There were a million and one things running through my mind, but I kept it together for the girl sitting right in front of me. If I was as angry as I felt deep in my bones, I couldn't be there for her like she needed me to be. If I didn't keep myself in check, I'd be giving her too much insight on what my next move was about to be.

I both needed to be a source of strength for my girlfriend, and I needed to keep my emotions in check in order to carry out the idea that was formulating in my head.

I took her face between my hands and made sure she knew a few things. "I love you. That won't change. I will do everything in my power to keep you safe. I'm gonna get you away from those people. You are *not* gross or damaged or dirty, so get that shit out of your head, okay? I'm gonna take care of this."

It made her cry to hear me say those things, but I knew her tears weren't falling out from sadness. She was relieved.

I was heartbroken that she, even for one second, thought I could stop loving her for something so out of her control. What kind of monster did she take me for? I didn't wrestle with those thoughts for too long. There was no telling what years of abuse had done to her self-esteem. What was obvious to me might not have been as obvious to her.

Caprice was confused about one thing. "What do you mean you're gonna take care of it?"

And this was when I started lying to her. If she knew what I was thinking then, she would've tried to stop me. If she knew what I was thinking, she wouldn't open her window for me tonight. I needed to keep my momentum, so I refused to fill her in.

For her own good, I lied to her.

"You and me, Monday morning. We're leaving. Just like you wanted to three weeks ago. I'll go wherever you go. I just need to take care of some last-minute things this weekend."

"But what about Miss Sylvia? What about Duke? What about—"

"My mom will understand." This was a boldfaced lie. "My spot at Duke is guaranteed. I don't even need to play this season to make the team." This was the truth. "What's important to me right now, is getting that man away from you."

That, I had every intention of doing.

But to do that, Caprice and I were not running away to some bus station on Monday morning.

No, that wasn't my plan at all. My plan was much simpler than that.

I was gonna fuckin' kill him.

Tonight.

* * *

It was a little bit after twelve o'clock when I stopped by the salon with Caprice.

The bombshells of this morning had yet to subside, but I was trying to act natural as convincingly as I could. I told Caprice I wanted to stop by my mother's salon because if we were gonna skip town on Monday, I was gonna need to pick something up. This was half true.

I really was picking something up.

But it wasn't in order to skip town.

"We were just stoppin' by 'cause we were in the area," I told my mother when she asked why we'd come in. I remember her brow dipping slightly, a look on her face like she knew something was up with me, but she didn't ask me anything. I was grateful for that, because even my best lies were never good enough for my mother.

Rather than investigate the energy I was giving off, Mom directed her attention to Caprice, telling her how she could tell she was taking care of her braids since they still looked so new. They chatted for a little over five minutes before Mom offered us some of the leftover lunch in the backroom.

That's what I was waiting for, an excuse to walk to the back. Caprice wasn't hungry, so I left her with my mother as I made my way back there. It wasn't food that I was after, though.

*Sylvia's Salon & Spa* was one of the most successful small businesses in the neighborhood. Because she serviced a majority of the women in Parramore, people naturally assumed there'd be lots of money stashed away somewhere in the salon.

And there was.

In a safe in the back of the salon, you could always find several grand locked away, where it would stay for about a week before my mother took it down to the bank every Saturday. Today was Saturday, so the safe was probably empty, but that's okay because I wasn't here for the money.

In the safe, there was also a Beretta.

With all these people in the neighborhood knowing how successful the salon was, it was ripe for robbery. For that, my mother kept a nine-millimeter handgun stashed away in the backroom safe as well. That way, if the shop should ever get robbed, she would walk to the safe, put in the combination, and pull out her gun.

It was a smart plan, but nobody *ever* robbed the salon.

That's the thing about Parramore. There was poverty on all corners of the neighborhood, but there was just some shit people around here refused to do. Robbing Miss Sylvia was just one of those things.

So, the gun had been collecting dust for years.

That is, until I blew the dust off it and stashed it in the back waistband of my jeans. It was heavier than I thought it would be. Other than a BB gun here and there, I'd never handled a firearm before. However, now was not the time to get nervous.

Caprice was still talking to my mother when I walked back to the salon's main room. I walked in on the middle of whatever it was they were saying, and something about the way I was carrying myself had definitely caught my mother's eye.

"You feeling okay, Shaun?"

If it was this easy for her to tell something was off with me, then I needed to get out of the salon, and soon. I looked at my mother and just nodded. "I had a bit of a rough morning, but I should be fine."

Caprice was better at masking her thoughts and feelings. I suppose she had years of practice. You would never be able to tell the horrific shit she'd been through from the way she casually sat in an empty salon chair and chatted with my mother. You would've never been able to guess what kind of conversation Caprice just had with me on the basketball court from the way she carried herself now.

The ease of it all was unnerving.

I hated how good at that she was, knowing I would have no idea how much she was suffering if I didn't already know. I tried to take my mind off it, my attention going back and forth between my inner thoughts and the salon.

It wasn't until a client stopped in for an appointment that our time with my mother came to a close. Mom thanked us for stopping in. I could feel the iron of the handgun fastened at my back rest cold against my skin as I held the door open for Caprice.

I turned my head and looked at my mother one last time before nodding a goodbye.

* * *

Caprice was in my bedroom helping me pack.

It was her first time in my bedroom, and since I hadn't really been sleeping in here for three weeks now, the space was mostly tidy. It was nowhere near as neat as Caprice's bedroom, but it was cleaner than it usually was.

It was just after seven o'clock in the evening by the time my bag was packed. Packing the bag was just busy work—something to keep Caprice distracted so that she didn't focus too much on my overall vibe. She knew me better than most, and even as I tried very hard to act natural, I knew it was only a matter of time before she picked up on my behavior.

So, I kept her busy.

"Can I tell you something?" she asked as the setting sun was starting to turn the sky purple. Behind her, through my window, I could see that the lights in the pink house across the street were on.

Even though I feared I might agonize over whatever it was she had to say, I told her to, "Tell me anything."

Deep down, I didn't know if I could stand to hear one more childhood story.

Even now, hours later, my stomach was twisted in knots over the fact that I didn't protect her. I was ten years old when it all went down… but still, what if I could've done something? What if there were warning signs, and I missed them? What if I'd become friends with her sooner, during the summer instead of during the school year? What if I could've saved her?

At this point, none of that mattered.

I was saving her *now.*

"I thought when I told you, you'd want to…" Caprice hesitated "…kill him."

Caprice knew me better than she realized. Still, she didn't have to know that's exactly what I had planned.

I wasn't even lying when I said, "I *do* wanna kill him."

She had no idea how serious I was. She pushed out a sigh, taking a seat at the edge of my bed, eyes on me patient, while she waited for me to take the seat beside her. When I filled it, her hand came out and guided my eyes to hers.

"I've never felt as safe as I do when I'm with you," she told me, which made me feel like shit because I didn't do a good enough job of keeping her safe. "It's you and me, right? Forever?"

I only nodded.

"We could just let all that… *noise* fall to the wayside. I matter to you, you matter to me. The past is the past, and despite everything—I really think I'm *healing*. Even if knowing what he did to me makes you angrier than you've ever felt in your life, open your eyes to the fact that I'm here… and I *survived.* As much as I think it would please me to watch him die, I think I'm happier to know that I just get to leave it all behind." She wiped a tear before finishing. "And that you're coming with me this time."

I stretched out a hand toward her tear-streaked cheeks, wiping one before I asked, "You really want to just run away?"

She nodded. "That's all I've ever wanted."

"Where do you want to go?" I asked, curious.

My thumb grazed along her cheek, something in my chest

breaking because I didn't want to just walk away from the gun, but here she was, talking me off that ledge without even realizing it. She didn't want me to kill anyone, she just wanted to go. And I could do that for her. I *would* do that for her.

I didn't have to kill anyone.

Sitting face to face on my bed, I came to that decision while admiring her. She was so beautiful.

Caprice has always been beautiful.

From the day I'd first laid eyes on her. Somehow the reminder brought the image of her from all those years ago back into my mind. She was so bubbly. She was so lively. She was so bright.

She was so… *little.*

*Nah… Fuck it, I'm killing that nigga.*

"Wherever you go," Caprice answered. "If you're there, I'm there. Together. Nothing else matters."

I didn't have anything to say to that. I couldn't lie to her, but I also refused to be peaceful about something so… *violent.* So *fuckin'* violent. Her uncle *raped* an eight-year-old girl. An *Eight. Year. Old. Girl.* And not just any girl.

*Mine.*

So, despite everything… Despite knowing what she wanted, I couldn't just *let it go*. There are just some things you don't walk away from. Some things you just can't forgive. Even if she wanted nothing more than to run—I *had* to do away with that motherfucker. If not for the little girl I couldn't save, then for the young woman I loved.

"Promise you'll never leave me?" she whispered, her lips less than an inch away from mine. Without a word, I closed the gap, feeling her soft lips press against mine. Her hands dropped from my face, settling at the hem of my shirt. She started to lift it up.

There was a gun tucked at the waistband of my pants, hidden underneath my shirt. I didn't want her to find it, so I pulled back.

"What are you doing?" I asked. This wasn't like her.

Misunderstanding, Caprice just looked at me with a vague sadness in her eyes when she asked, "Do you want me?"

My response was automatic.

"Of course, I do." I drew back a little further. "Could you give me a minute? I'll be right back."

I stashed the gun under the sink in my bathroom. I'd be coming back for it later tonight when it got to be that time to start heading over to her side of the road. But right now, she was here and in my bedroom. She wanted to know that she was still loved in spite of everything, and I was all too willing to show her.

Caprice was sitting upright on my bed when I returned. She was completely relaxed as I took the spot close to her side, my hand coming out to guide her lips to mine. Again, she reached for the hem of my shirt, her fingers sliding over the bare skin of my abdomen as she moved to slip it off. I helped her, guiding the shirt above my head, going back to her lips the moment it was gone.

My hands gripped at her waist, feeling every rapid breath. We took turns, bit by bit, removing one item of clothing here, another item there, until we found ourselves covered only by the sheets of my bed. This wasn't the first time I'd ever been with a girl, but it was the first time it mattered this much. It was the first time I was thinking about the other woman more than myself.

"I'll never leave you," I promised honestly against her lips. A person would have to move heaven and earth to make me let Caprice go. The reality of just how much she trusted me wasn't lost on me. For her to let me touch her like this—despite *everything*—her faith in me must've run deep, and it must've been strong.

I led her down against my pillows, needing to live up to that faith. I loved on every inch of her skin, hoping to eclipse every fear, every memory, every nightmare. I couldn't fix the past, but I could promise her a happier future. And I could promise her a love that would last a lifetime.

Starting at this very moment.

## Chapter Twenty

# SHAUN

I hadn't changed my mind.

After Caprice let me into her room that night, it didn't take long for her to fall asleep. Today was a… *heavy* sort of day. She must've been exhausted. Like me, she'd been on a roller coaster of emotions and it didn't let up until the moment her head hit her pillow. I stayed awake as she drifted off, her warm body tucked within my arm, relaxing completely within seconds.

There was so much faith in me in her ability to do that. You could tell she trusted me from that alone.

I was careful not to wake her as I moved my arm out from under her. Slowly, I got out of her bed and walked to her door. All I did was twist the lock. I wasn't going to go hunting for the man. If I shot him, I needed this to feel wholly justified. I would only pull the trigger if he tried to come in.

Seeing how her uncle had tried to come into her room every night for several nights, I didn't have a doubt in my mind that he'd come.

I sat at the edge of Caprice's bed and waited.

My eyes would bounce from the unlocked door to my beautiful girl. Every time I thought I might second guess myself, all I had to do was look at her, and I'd find that anger in me again. Anyone who could hurt her deserved a dozen bullet holes to the head.

I held the gun tightly in my hand.

It was a little after four o'clock in the morning when I started to think that maybe tonight wouldn't be the night. The house was quiet, and the only sounds I could hear for a while were the sounds of my heart pounding in my head and Caprice sleeping peacefully behind me.

I was a little tired.

My vision was a bit blurred.

Even my hearing had started to get a little muffled.

But when those first couple of steps broke up the silence throughout the house, my posture straightened out. Her uncle was awake, and on the other side of the door, he was walking around. I raised the gun until it was level with my eyes, watching the knob on Caprice's bedroom door twist. It opened with a faint creak, but I could hear behind me that Caprice slept undisturbed.

As the doorway widened, a shadow of a man appeared between. It was dark, so most of what I could make out was the outline of his frame. He saw the gun in my hands and froze mid-entry. I watched as his hands slowly rose up from his sides, going up in the air, understanding that he was caught, and that the gun was aimed at his head.

He whispered something, but I didn't hear it as my finger pulled at the trigger, the spark of the exiting bullet giving off a flash of light, blasting out into a deafening pop.

That was easier than I thought.

I waited for his body to drop, and it wasn't until that momentary pause stretched for longer that I realized I'd missed. Just as I gathered my wits about me, I raised the gun again, aiming for a second shot. Unwilling to let me get in a second try, the large shadow at the end of the barrel went into survival mode.

He lunged for the gun.

* * *

# Caprice

I woke up to a sound of thunder.

It was so loud that, for a moment, I feared that I'd gone deaf. In the darkness of my bedroom, my ears buzzed as I felt around on my bed for Shaun. He wasn't there. I could see moving shadows in the darkness, mere black shapes zooming from one side of the room to the other. I rubbed my eyes, trying to see things more clearly, hoping for the ringing in my ears to cease.

Still, other than that high-pitched screeching, I heard no sounds.

I felt around the unlit room for the light switch, only to find it and choose not to believe what I was seeing with my own eyes.

Marcel was in my bedroom. There was a gun in his hands.

And he was slamming the gun's handle repeatedly onto Shaun's unconscious face. The gun was dripping with blood. Shaun's blood. I could hear blood droplets falling like rain onto the wooden floorboards. There was so much of it. Marcel just kept bashing and bashing.

*This is a nightmare.*

I tried to wake up. I shut my eyes, feeling hot tears slip out as I tried to wake myself up. *This is a nightmare. This isn't real. This isn't happening.*

Eyes closed, the ringing in my ears stopped. I could hear the shouting. Marcel was repeating himself over and over again.

"You tryna shoot ME? You tryna shoot ME? I'M GONNA KILL YOU, LIL' NIGGA. I'M GONNA KILL YOU!"

My eyes snapped open.

Of course, Shaun would want to kill the man who hurt me the most. I knew Shaun's reaction to my story was too good to be true. Deep down, I'd known this was the reaction that made the most sense. I knew Shaun too well to allow myself to believe he'd be content with simply running away with me. But I believed it because I *wanted* it to be true. Just like I wanted to believe that what I was seeing was simply a nightmare.

But it wasn't.

This wasn't a nightmare.

I didn't have the time to go into shock. I'd already wasted so much. Marcel was going to kill him if I didn't move my ass to the other side of the room and pull him away. It was like an on-switch went off in my mind—emergency mode. Within seconds I was grabbing onto Marcel's blood-soaked arm, trying to stop the repeated blows to Shaun's head.

Marcel's arm was slippery, slicked with the warm, bright red blood coming out from Shaun. The gun in Marcel's hand went off, startling me. I let him go as the bullet went through the ceiling, raining down dusty white pieces of drywall from overhead.

Shaun's blood was all over my hands.

My breathing started to quicken. My skin felt burning hot. My eyes filled with tears.

No way Shaun was bleeding this much and not already dead.

Still, I tried again to pull Marcel away. He pushed me back, sending me stumbling into a fall flat on my behind. The racing of my pulse made me feel like I might die of a heart attack, watching Marcel flip the gun at its handle, aiming for Shaun's head.

Shaun was unconscious, so Marcel had a clear shot.

An easy shot.

I screamed, crawling on hands and knees over to where he was laid out. "Please! No! *Don't* do it."

Crawling past Marcel, I used my own body to cover as much of Shaun as I could. His skin was warm to the touch, and just faintly, I could see that he was breathing. Even in the midst of my screaming, Marcel didn't put the gun down. My vision was blurred from hot tears pricking at my eyes, my throat turning raw from how loud I begged.

If he was going to shoot Shaun, the bullet would have to go through me first.

Marcel hesitated.

In the opened doorway to my bedroom, Gracie slid into the light, her shouting overpowering mine. "*What's* going on in here?!"

There was blood everywhere, on Marcel, on me, on the floor, on the walls. At the sound of Gracie's voice, Marcel lowered the gun in his hand. I pressed my face into the crook of Shaun's neck, begging him to wake up, begging him to hold on for me. He was warm and he was breathing, but with all this blood, who was to say that would last long?

Behind my head, I could hear Marcel explaining things to Gracie. "I caught this lil' nigga in here with Caprice's fast ass! This young nigga tried to shoot me in my own house!"

Shaun's face was a bloodied mess. There was a long, deep

gash running down the underside of his left eye, where most of the blood was running from. If he survived, there would be bruises. There would be broken bones. There would be scars.

My hands were drenched in his blood, red buried deep underneath my fingernails. So much, I feared I'd never be able to wash it all off.

"Shaun," I whispered his name, my voice breaking on just the one word. I could barely hear my own voice as I whispered, "Wake up, and we can go now."

"But I'mma take care of this, Mama." I could hear the click of a gun cocking before Marcel shouted, "Get outta my way, Caprice!"

I didn't move.

"Marcel, baby, you *just* got out! Put the gun down."

"It's self-defense, Mama!" he argued back. "Lil' nigga came in here with this gun, tryna shoot *me*! Can't fault me none for gettin' the gun and defendin' myself!"

"No!" I cut into their argument. This was not up for debate. Keeping myself draped over Shaun, I'd sooner die *with* him then let Marcel take him from me. "You can't kill him!" My tears were mixing in with his blood as I sobbed. "You can't take him from me! You can't kill him! He's *all* I have."

And I just kept saying that last part over and over again. "He's all I have."

# Chapter Twenty-One

# SHAUN

The beeping wouldn't stop.

Every couple of minutes, I would open my eyes to an all-white room, close them again, and the beeping wouldn't stop. I was confused.

I'd never heard this beeping in Caprice's room before.

This was not what Caprice's room looked like.

This was not what it smelled like either.

The all-white room smelled like rubbing alcohol and cherry cough medicine. *A hospital?* It smelled like a hospital. The all-white room was blinding when I opened my eyes again, but I didn't close my eyes this time. Through the blaring headache and the brightness that felt like staring into the sun, I kept my eyes open, looking around the room as my vision cleared.

Who was I here for?

There were needles pricked into my veins. Oh—I was here for *me.* I was in a hospital bed, in a hospital gown, and the constant beeping was some kind of EKG monitoring my heartbeat. The bright room was small, with my bed tucked into some corner, a bedside table with some scattered papers, and two chairs around a low table.

It must've been morning. There was a window, and standing at it, facing away from me, was my mother. I cleared my throat to get her attention, lifting my needle-strewn arm to wave into her peripheral vision. *Goddamn,* my arm was heavy as fuck. A muscle soreness shot pins and needles down my back, pain coursing through me like a jolt of electricity.

*Fuck.*

I swore out loud.

That got my mother to turn away from the window, noticing that I was awake for the first time. Last thing I remembered was Caprice's uncle grabbing hold of my gun, seeing the handle speed toward my face. And then just darkness.

That nigga pistol whipped me to sleep.

But I could tell from the way that my limbs felt like I'd just deadlifted four hundred pounds that long after I was knocked unconscious, I definitely got my shit rocked.

"Shaun?" Mom called my name like she had little faith in my ability to reply. I looked around the room one more time, hoping I might've missed something. Nah, it was just us two in the room.

I tried to force the word out.

"Ca... Caprice?" My tongue was dry like sandpaper. "Mom, where... where is she?"

She didn't acknowledge the question. Rushing to my side, her hands settled at the railing of my hospital bed when she asked, "How are you feeling?"

I tried again.

"Is she... okay?" I couldn't remember what happened. "What happened last night?"

"Last night?" she questioned, shaking her head. I could see tears welling in her eyes, so I knew I must've looked like hell. She fretted over me like she couldn't hear my questions. "Baby, you lost a lot of blood. Are you lightheaded?"

I was in a lot of pain, but my head was starting to hurt more from the frustration of being straight up ignored. Mom tried to adjust the pillow behind my head, and I tried one more time. "Where *is* she?"

She was talking fast, but not saying anything.

"You're eighteen, stupid! You can't be doing this dumb shit—" her unwillingness to answer my questions was starting to make me panic "—you're not a kid anymore!"

"Mom!" It sent the room spinning to have to shout that loud. "Caprice..."

"She's *gone*, Shaun!" she shouted back at me.

All the blood I had left in my body ran cold.

"Gone?" I choked on the word. I couldn't remember last

night. "What do you mean, '*gone*'?"

*Is she dead? Did something happen to her last night?* Last night was a blur. My last memory of Caprice was of her sleeping in my arms. How could she be gone?

"Her grandmother sent her away!" I was both relieved and devastated to hear that news.

"Did you call the police?" I asked.

My mother looked like she might've smacked me if not for my condition. "And tell them *what*, Shaun? Hello, police, my son broke into my neighbor's house and tried to *murder* one of them. Please arrest my neighbors?"

I shook my head at her sarcasm. "I didn't break in."

"That's not even the worst of the accusations!" She threw her hands into the air, her voice getting louder when she asked, "Did you hear the part where I said you tried to *murder* someone?" At this point I realized my mother was crying, still screaming at the top of her lungs, "Do you have *any idea* how much trouble you would be in if you didn't miss? And with *my* gun? Do you have any idea how much trouble *we* would've been in?"

The room was spinning. Her voice was too loud, and the smell of disinfectant was too strong. I was getting dizzy as I argued. I was holding my throbbing headache as I replied, "Mom, you don't understand! You don't know what they did to her."

She stopped shouting just long enough to let me know in a hushed whisper, "It wasn't hard to guess, baby." She kept going, "You're my son—I *know* you. You're too kind, you're too wholesome, you're too smart to have tried something like that for no damn reason. You did it for a reason. And I think I know what that reason is."

This only served to make it worse. If she knew all this—how could she let them take her away? Where did she go? Was she okay?

"You should've helped her, Mom."

"You should've given me the chance then, Shaun! You should've told me what was going on, and I could've helped her!" Mom was shouting again, but this time not out of anger. She was heartbroken. "I loved her, too! I loved that little girl like she was my own!" She cried like someone who'd just lost a child. "I would've helped her if you had just let me know!" Her hands came up to wipe her face. "Instead, you tried to go Rambo in somebody else's house! Are you dumb?!"

And then she was angry again, just ping-ponging between anger and sadness. To what could've only been the confusion in my eyes, she explained, "Four days ago, I heard the gunshots in the middle of the night, and I *ran* to your room. Your bed was empty. Do you know how it felt to find your room empty? How terrifying that was for me?"

I looked away, unable to meet her eyes. I felt guilty, not just for letting her down, but because my efforts were for nothing. I couldn't even tell you where the girl I meant to protect was right now. I fucked up. I acted on impulse, and I fucked up.

My mother continued to explain, "Not long after, those monsters show up with you at my doorstep. They laid you out on the front porch and knocked. At first I thought you were *dead*—" her voice cracked "—There was so much blood. I thought, no way there's that much, and he's alive... Gracie's bitch ass pulls me to the side and says, '*Get your boy an ambulance. We won't talk to the police if you don't. And by the way, we're holding onto the gun.*'"

Something she'd said before just hit me. Four days ago? I'd been here for four days?

"I got you an ambulance. I didn't say anything in the emergency room. Boy from Parramore gets beaten within an inch of his life—what else is new? So, nobody asks any real questions. While you were in surgery, I drove over to my salon—just to check. My gun is gone. You committed a *crime* with my gun, Shaun. It's registered in my *whole ass* government name!" She was shouting again. "So, then I realize I'm stuck, because... because..." Her voice broke again, more tears streaming down my mother's face. "Because at that point, I realize there's a little girl across the street from my house that *really* needs my help, and because of my *reckless* ass son, I can't call the cops on the people who are hurting her." My mother sobbed like I'd never seen before. "Because they can have my reckless ass son arrested for something he did to them. And they have my gun to prove he did it. I wanted to help her, Shaun! I wanted to help that poor baby *so* much."

*I really, really fucked up.*

Weeping, my mother concluded, "But I had to help *you* first!"

*ACT THREE*

# CAPRICE - AGE 28

2018

## *Chapter Twenty-Two*

# Caprice

As a child, you can't pick your family.

When you get older, you surely can. I have a mother and I have a sister, and I chose them when I was sixteen. Before them, I had a grandmother I didn't choose, and an uncle I didn't want, all in a house I had no desire to live in.

The best thing Gracie ever did for me was let me leave it.

Though, she didn't have much of a choice in the matter. Before I left the pink house, Marcel, the uncle I never wanted, almost killed the person who meant the most to me, Shaun. In one of my last days in the pink house, I spent the night drenched in Shaun's blood, cradling his head in my arms, unwilling to let him go. I couldn't move. If I moved, Marcel would've killed him.

So even as Marcel reached to pull me away, I kicked and screamed until he left us both alone.

They wouldn't let me call 9-1-1 on the house phone, and I didn't own a cell phone. Gracie promised they'd bring him home. She promised she wouldn't let Marcel hurt him anymore. I knew she was being honest, so that's when I finally let him go.

It's always been my belief that Gracie was reading between the lines that night.

Yes, Marcel found a boy in my room.

But she must've been thinking the obvious question—why in the world was Marcel in there, too? What might compel a twenty-nine-year-old man to take a stroll around the house at four o'clock in the morning, and step into his sixteen-year-old niece's room?

That's the million-dollar question, isn't it?

After they carried Shaun's body to the porch across the

street, an ambulance sliced into that early dawn silence throughout Parramore. It wasn't long before the word was out about Shaun. He was Parramore's resident golden boy—a handsome, good student and promising athlete. Everybody there knew him.

Star of the community's high school basketball team… in the hospital with four broken ribs, a concussion, and rumors that he might never play again.

I thought I ruined his life.

I felt so guilty.

My last days in Parramore, I avoided his mother. I couldn't bear to look at her after what I'd done to her son. I skipped school that entire time, just staying in my room, picking something to stare at every morning until the sun went down.

I had been able to scrub the dried blood from my floors on the second day, but the splatters on my bedroom walls could only be fixed with paint. Unfortunately for me, I didn't have any.

After I missed my third day of school, somebody came around looking for me. In 1999, Shaun was the person who came looking for me after I disappeared. In 2006, it was my math teacher, Ms. Kelly.

She popped up on a Wednesday, four days after the incident, and questioned Gracie relentlessly. I listened to her shouting through the walls of my bedroom, eyes glued on the red blood splatters I couldn't paint over. I wondered what Gracie would have to do to get her to leave.

I wasn't sure where Marcel was as all this went down. He wasn't home that day.

Ms. Kelly demanded to see me. Gracie refused.

And then I heard my math teacher barge into my house anyway, stomping about as she called out my name. I didn't respond. I could hear her opening and shutting doors, looking for me around the house. My bedroom door wasn't locked, and I didn't try to lock it either. I didn't move. I waited.

And when she let herself into my bedroom, she saw me first… and then she saw the bloody mess on my walls. Her hand rose to her mouth and she went into shock as Gracie told her, "That's not *her* blood."

As if that was supposed to make the horrific scene any easier to look at.

Ms. Kelly threatened to call the police, pulling out her cell phone. I had to stop her. The blood was Shaun's, and if the police started asking too many questions, Shaun could get into serious trouble for trying to kill my uncle.

I didn't have enough time to come up with a lie, so I just told her that. I told her about Shaun, about how he tried to save me. I told her that she couldn't call the police, because I didn't want Shaun to get in trouble for trying to help me.

Ms. Kelly wanted to know why Shaun would want to kill my uncle. Over her shoulder, I glanced at Gracie, who was glaring daggers at me, but to protect Shaun—I didn't give a shit about what Gracie would do to me for saying it.

"He raped me," I said, tone void of all emotion. I kept my eyes on Gracie when I said it again. "When I was eight years old, my uncle Marcel raped me."

"*She's a liar*!" Gracie stepped further into my bedroom, her voice thick with panic as she tried to step between me and Ms. Kelly. "He *didn't* touch her! She tells everybody that, and that's why she almost got that boy killed. She's a liar!"

Ms. Kelly wasn't looking at her; she was looking at me. Her eyes had that shiny, tear-filled look about them almost immediately. She believed me.

She put up a hand to Gracie's face, silently asking that my grandmother shut up. Her eyes were still on me when she spoke again.

"Caprice, get your things," Ms. Kelly ordered, halfway whispering. My brows had dipped in confusion. Her voice shook as she explained, "Everything you think you might need. I've got some trash bags in my car if you don't have any luggage. Take everything."

"What do you think you're doing?"

Ms. Kelly turned to Gracie's question, that sadness in her eyes morphing into an anger I'd never seen in her.

"She's either leaving with me quietly, or I can turn in every bit of evidence I have on this family. And trust me, I have records of conversations I've had with people about Caprice that date back to the 90s. I could turn it all in, but... I won't call the cops. I won't involve anyone else. I'll just be taking her with me." She uncrossed her arms, gathering her locs up into a ponytail as she promised, "And, old lady, I will fight you if I have to."

Ms. Kelly turned her attention back to me as she fastened a scrunchy around her hair. "You need help packing?"

I shook my head slowly, my eyes still on Gracie as I cautiously climbed out of bed and started stuffing clothes into my backpack. In addition to that, I had filled two trash bags by the time I packed everything. Ms. Kelly was helping me load my things into the trunk of her car when I saw Miss Sylvia watching us from across the street. Guilty, I rushed to avoid eye contact, running back into the pink house to grab my backpack.

As I walked out of my bedroom for the last time, Gracie was standing in the living room, watching me move out without protest. Just before we could leave the house once and for all, Ms. Kelly looked at Gracie with a bit of anger on her brows. She asked my grandmother, "Do you smoke?"

Gracie's eyes bounced confusedly from me to my teacher. She didn't say anything, so Ms. Kelly asked me instead.

"Does she smoke?"

"She does."

Getting an answer she already expected, Ms. Kelly nodded, raising a single hand and striking the back of it across Gracie's face. Hard. Gracie cradled her cheek because no doubt getting backhanded like that hurt. It may sound crazy, but even though Gracie had done the same thing to me hundreds of times before, I didn't like seeing someone do it to her.

But that didn't mean she didn't deserve it.

Ms. Kelly reminded me of that when she told her, "That's for the cigarette burn, you evil bitch."

* * *

I spent two days living with Ms. Kelly.

She lived in a one-bedroom apartment in College Park with her boyfriend, and there wasn't much space for me. Ms. Kelly was only twenty-six years old, which made her more fitting as a sister to me than a mother. It was never her intention to keep me. Especially when I told her about everything I'd been through.

After two days of living with Ms. Kelly, she put me on a flight to Los Angeles. There, I was picked up by Ms. Kelly's mother—Dr. Johnson—a recently retired psychiatrist who was spending her retirement knitting scarves and baking homemade bread.

Naturally, Dr. Johnson was bored out of her mind.

She was sick of knitting scarves and baking all that bread was beginning to be bad for her waistline.

For Dr. Johnson, I was… kind of like a project.

There I was, an abuse survivor with years of psychological damage and trauma to work through, and there she was, a retired mental health professional who desperately wanted to get back to work. In a really tragic sort of way—we were made for each other.

Before she retired, Dr. Johnson had been a highly sought-after psychiatrist in Beverly Hills. Rich people have a lot of psychological issues, and nothing but time and money to work on them. They don't have to vent to their hairstylists about their problems, because that's what they pay people like Dr. Johnson for.

At that point in my life, Dr. Johnson was the richest person I'd ever met.

There's something about living in a place like Beverly Hills that makes you realize how the poverty in neighborhoods like Parramore is one of the biggest crimes in our nation.

Dr. Johnson wore seven hundred-dollar sneakers to go to the grocery store.

And they weren't even fancy, diamond covered sneakers. They were super regular, but for some reason, she was willing to spend seven hundred dollars on them. I remember once she tried to buy me a pair, and I felt sick to my stomach. Nobody—absolutely *no one*—needs seven hundred-dollar shoes.

Dr. Johnson may have been a black woman like me, but that's where the similarities stopped.

Even so, in the year I spent with her before I went off to college in Miami, we grew incredibly close. For me, she worked overtime trying to dismantle years of trauma. She homeschooled me for my final year of high school and she spent just as much time with me in therapy. Dr. Johnson made me her fulltime job. I didn't have to lift a finger in her house.

She took care of me. She would even cut the crusts off my sandwiches.

I would go on to get into that accelerated MD program at the University of Miami on a full academic scholarship. It was official—I was going to be a doctor someday, too. Dr. Johnson threw me a party and everything.

On move-in day at the dorms, while all the other freshmen had their parents with them, I had Kelly and Dr. Johnson. They were like my family. A family that I chose.

I would go back and forth between Miami and Los Angeles for the six years I spent at university. In the summers and during the winter holidays, I spent my off time in Beverly Hills, still getting therapy sessions here and there. But I had stopped calling her Dr. Johnson by the time I was twenty-one.

Like my sister Kelly, I just called her mom.

My mom, as lavish and as bougie as she is, is one of the warmest, most loving people that I know.

She's a hugger, too.

I still wasn't fond of hugs, but when they came from my mom, I loved them. There were only two people in the whole world who could touch me and make me feel safer for it. One of them was my adoptive mother, and the other was Shaun.

But I never saw Shaun again after that night.

At least, not in person.

After I moved to Los Angeles, I used to get updates from Kelly, who continued to live in Orlando.

Shaun didn't play for Jefferson his final year. He needed too much time to heal from his injuries. When the time came for him to commit to a college team—despite everything—his offer at Duke was still valid.

Kelly said it was his grades that saved him in the end. Of course, just because he was an athlete, didn't mean he wasn't smart.

He started at Duke the same year I started at UM. I spent quite a bit of my time looking him up on the internet, watching his college games on YouTube. By his third year, Shaun led Duke to a championship win in 2010. Last I checked, he was a first-round pick in the 2011 NBA Draft.

He went pro, just like he always wanted to.

By then, I was in my second to last year of medical school, with a workload that left me no time to keep tabs on him. I was just happy to know I hadn't *actually* ruined his life.

Of course, I thought about contacting him all the time. My first year in Los Angeles, my mom advised against me contacting anyone from Parramore. It would interfere with my therapy, she said. However, by the time I was seventeen and headed off to college, I was free to call Shaun if I wanted.

But I didn't.

Every time I thought I might, I stopped myself. To call Shaun would be like going back to Parramore. If not physically, then mentally. I didn't know if I was strong enough.

I stopped myself from calling him so often that by the time I'd built up the courage to do it for real, too much time had passed.

For me, life had gone on. And from the glimpses I caught of Shaun's life, he was keeping things pushing as well. I let too much time pass. Before my very eyes, Shaun became a grown man in the fast-paced world of the NBA. This wasn't the teenage boy I left behind.

Who's to say he would've even taken my call if I tried to contact him?

And maybe that's what I was most afraid of.

So, even when I wanted to, I never called.

# Chapter Twenty-Three

## Caprice

The FEEL Center is a non-profit organization in the heart of Downtown Miami.

At the center, children taken out of abusive homes were given room and board, virtual schooling, and intensive mental health care. Although the goal was to rehabilitate victims of trauma, the facility didn't feel like a mental hospital. It was designed to feel like a home. The center was my idea, born out of a desire to recreate the amazing work Dr. Johnson had done on me twelve years before.

After I graduated from medical school, I went on to do my two-year residency in psychiatry, following in my adoptive mother's footsteps. Rather than working in a sterile mental health facility, or start my own practice like my mom, I started FEEL.

Well—I mapped the blueprint out for FEEL. The center itself was a joint effort by me and a few connections I made in college. That's why there were four names on the door.

*Mr. Damien Fine, MBA.*

*Dr. Logan Ezra, PsyD.*

*Dr. Rebecca Emison, PsyD.*

*Dr. Caprice Latimore, MD.*

Fine, Ezra, Emison, Latimore—FEEL. We all had our jobs to do to keep the place running. Mr. Fine was a businessman who handled all the financials. As a wealthy stock trader by day, he was rarely *ever* in the building.

But his money always was.

Dr. Emison and Dr. Ezra were psychologists. They oversaw the day to day mental health needs of the residents. The FEEL Center had just under thirty children living in the building, and they were split in half among the two psychologists on staff who saw each child twice a week. Emison and Ezra handled things like talk therapy, which I could never do.

Even though I was licensed for psychotherapy, being a therapist requires a warmth that I just didn't have.

My job at FEEL was to read data, analyze bloodwork, and determine appropriate drug therapies for our patients who needed more than just talk. We had a lot of traumatized children here, and my job was to determine which of them needed to be medicated. While Dr. Emison & Dr. Ezra had the luxury of never dealing with more than fifteen kids at a time, my job required me to have the brain chemistry of nearly thirty children memorized.

It was rewarding work, though.

FEEL had a success rate unmatched by all the facilities like it in the area. Kids who came to us were the best prepared to rejoin the general public. We had a lot of pride in that. Even as children left our facility, we kept regular tabs on them, and in our weekly meetings, it was always nice to hear how well former patients were doing.

Our meetings were always held on Friday evenings just before closing. None of the doctors worked on weekends since the kids didn't have therapy sessions on Saturdays or Sundays. On weekends, our day-to-day operations staff took over and had activities and field trips planned for the kids.

Friday evening meetings at seven were the perfect way to close out every week. In these meetings Emison, Ezra, and I would discuss patient progress, brainstorm ideas, and get updates on former residents.

When I walked into our Friday meeting one evening in July, Emison and Ezra were already sitting at our conference table. They were whispering before I came and got quiet the moment I walked in. I was used to that by now.

FEEL was turning three years old this year, and from the day we started the center, there was clearly a divide among the medical staff.

You see, Dr. Emison and Dr. Ezra were psychologists. They got their Ph.Ds in psychology, which was still impressive, and some would argue harder than getting a medical degree. I, however, was a psychiatrist, which meant I was the only one of us three who actually went to medical school. It really made no difference—we were all doctors at the end of the day—but they got it in their heads that I must've thought I was better than them.

I didn't think I was better than *anyone.*

I was just a very shy person. They mistook my shyness for arrogance, and I didn't care enough to beg for entry into their little workplace clique. So, it was all too common for me to walk into a room and find the both of them had stopped talking.

Ezra and Emison had more in common with each other than they did with me anyway. Aside from the psychologist thing, they were both Jewish, both in their thirties, and probably also cheating on their spouses with each other.

But you didn't hear that from me.

It definitely wasn't winning me brownie points that I was so different from them; young, black, taller than both, quiet, and not trying too hard to be their friend. They were buddy-buddy with each other—not me. But that was okay. We weren't the only employees at FEEL, we were just the founders. I had other friends here. FEEL was staffed with nurses, counselors, tutors, housekeepers, cafeteria workers, a daily operations team, and office assistants.

While Ezra and Emison mostly interacted with each other, I was cool with *everyone* else at FEEL. Everybody got the same respect from me, whether their title was doctor or nurse or neither. The same couldn't be said about my fellow doctors in this meeting here. Hell, these two *barely* respected me.

That's why I would roll my eyes whenever they implied I was arrogant.

I'm no psychologist, but I know a lack of self-awareness when I see it.

"Caprice, Logan and I need to have a talk with you," Dr. Emison announced the moment I took my seat at the meeting table. She said it in a way that already had me looking at the clock on the far side of the conference room.

We had fifty-four minutes left in this meeting. I inwardly groaned.

"What's the news then, Rebecca?" I tried to keep my tone

chipper, knowing that if I sounded anything but friendly, she would get in her feelings about it.

All my life, every setting had a princess. My first ever princess was Princess Knight when I lived in Orlando. In Beverly Hills, my princess was a next-door neighbor who was always acting like I didn't belong in the neighborhood.

At FEEL, my princess was Dr. Rebecca Emison.

We were too grown for her to bully me, but she had that nice nasty energy that let me know she would bully me if she could.

"Logan and I have a patient we'd like you to take over for us."

I hated to be that person, but...

"Talk therapy isn't in my job description," I reminded. Psychotherapy was their job, not mine. I mean, I didn't go around asking them to read my notes and concoct drug therapies, devise suicide watch plans, or be the liaison to the local hospital. That was *my* job. I did it without complaining, and without shifting any of my responsibilities, either.

Rebecca tucked a pin straight lock of blonde hair behind her ear, smiling at me at first and then looking at Dr. Ezra to back her up.

"Logan, could you talk to her?" she whispered affectionately to him, as if I wasn't still in the room.

*Yeah, these two are definitely having an affair.* I made a mental note to remember to share this with my best friend when I met her for dinner tonight. We loved talking about my sloppy ass coworkers.

Dr. Logan Ezra cleared his throat, pushing up his glasses like I made him nervous. His curly black hair was receding at his forehead, which I noticed when he passed a hand over his scalp stressfully. Was talking to me really that scary? Rebecca clearly wasn't cheating on her husband on account of Logan's overpowering masculinity and sex appeal.

Knowing Rebecca, she was probably only screwing around with Logan because it made her feel more powerful in these Friday meetings. That way, it would always be two against one. She was petty like that.

"We know you have a lot of work on your plate here, but

we're just asking you to take on one of our patients." He pushed up his glasses again and looked at Rebecca. She nodded at him encouragingly, as if they'd rehearsed this pitch before I'd come in, and he was doing a good job presenting. I could've rolled my eyes then. "Last week, you remember how we held that vote for taking the kids to Miami Seaquarium? Remember how we voted against it?"

"No," I interjected. "*Y'all* voted against it. I voted yes. You two voted no."

Those two-to-one votes had been happening a lot more since their little affair started. Me and my best friend had this running theory that their whole relationship was basically a strategic workplace alliance... with a little bit of sex sprinkled in between.

"Rebecca and I are prepared to change our votes if you take on this patient," Logan offered. "You are qualified to do psychotherapy just like the both of us and... it's *just* one kid, out of the thirty that we have. Two therapy sessions a week."

"What's so special about this *one* patient?" My question wasn't a yes. I was just curious.

"Well... he's *racist*, for starters," Rebecca spoke up, and I could tell by her tone that whatever the kid said must've cut her deep. Rebecca had a fragile temperament, *just* the personality to go with her meek stature and her constant hair flipping. Very *strong* Becky energy, if I could be so blunt, and not just because her name was Rebecca.

"His name is Kahfi Williams. Name pronounced the way somebody from Boston might say coffee," Logan explained, producing a folder from under the table and sliding it toward me.

*Ha, they did plan this.*

*I walked into a set up*, I realized, suppressing a sigh.

When I opened up the file, Logan explained, "He spent eight years in the foster care system and now the state has turned him over to our care." This was the case for most of our patients. "He's got dissociative identity disorder—you know, multiple personalities."

"I know what dissociative identity disorder is, Logan," I replied calmly as I paged through the child's file. That's the thing about my coworkers—I was the only medical doctor on staff, and they still felt the need to define medical conditions for me.

"Kahfi has two alters. He calls them Marron and Moreno."

"Really?" I asked, my eyebrows climbing to the top of my head. "*Marron* is the French word for brown. *Moreno* is the Spanish word for brown skinned."

*Brown like coffee. Kahfi.*

"Kahfi is *very* intelligent," Logan commented carefully, shifting uncomfortably in his seat. "Very, very intelligent."

"He called me a *cracker*," Rebecca blurted out, clearly still hot off the memory. You could tell she wasn't fond of the kid. It bothered her to hear Logan calling him intelligent.

A short, quiet giggle escaped me. I covered my mouth. Offering a brief apology for laughing, I checked the file for his age. "Rebecca, he's eleven."

"And he *didn't* call her a cracker," Logan clarified. "Not Kahfi, at least."

"It was one of his alternative personalities," I gathered.

"Yes." He nodded. "*Moreno* called Dr. Emison a cracker. Moreno even called *me* a cracker when Kahfi was seeing me for sessions." He turned to Dr. Emison and added, "Rebecca, you shouldn't take it so personally. He can't help it."

I was still paging through his medical notes as Dr. Ezra explained, "When Kahfi gets uncomfortable, he allows his alternative personalities to take over. At face value, the kid is very sweet. Very polite. Very kind. It's his alters that kind of… muddy the waters. We think that if he was a little more comfortable in therapy, keeping his alters at bay, we could really start to make meaningful progress with him."

"And you both think he'll be more comfortable with me," I presumed.

"Yes," they said together.

"Because I'm black."

"Oh, *come on*, Caprice," Rebecca complained, Becky energy at a nine. "Don't make it weird. Almost *all* of our patients are black. Kahfi is just…"

"…he's special," Logan rushed to finish that sentence before Rebecca could say something offensive. "Caprice…" his pleading voice was soft, running a hand through that balding head of his. "I know you've read the studies that say most patients of color respond better to mental health professionals of color. I bet *your* therapist is black."

"What makes you think I have a therapist?" I *do* have a therapist. Dr. Eloise, a wonderful black woman that I saw every Wednesday evening to work out my issues. But that's not the kind of information I shared at work.

"We own and operate a psychiatric care facility for disturbed children from the ghettos of Miami," Rebecca pointed out. Dr. Emison thinks she can say 'ghetto' in that context because she's Jewish, and historically, Jewish people lived in the *original* ghettos. She looked at me as if to say '*obviously*'; Becky energy on ten. "Trust me, Caprice, with a job like this, we *all* need therapy."

Fair point.

"Is there anything about him I should know before I decide?"

Both were slow to answer, glancing at each other before looking back at me.

"Most of what we have on him is in his file." The file in my hands was at least thirty pages thick. I certainly wasn't going to get through all of it in this single meeting. They were hiding something. Logan continued, "Your biggest hurdle with Kahfi might be in getting him to talk about his last foster family."

According to his file, he was with his last foster family for four years until he ended up at The FEEL Center. Before then, he had no history of behavioral problems.

"So... *nothing* on the last four years of his life," I wrote this down on the folder. "Which is basically... *everything* I need to know to understand why he's like this."

They were giving me nothing to work with.

"I mean..." Logan hesitated. "There's *some* information available."

"From the court case," Rebecca added.

"Court case?" That took me for a surprise. I didn't handle patient intake, so I didn't know this kid's backstory. But I knew most kids didn't get removed from their foster families and placed here because of court cases. "Criminal court?"

"Yes," they both answered.

"What did he do?" I asked curiously. There was an extended silence. Logan just stared at the table for a moment. "Logan, *what* did he do?"

"Kahfi didn't *do* anything," he explained, quickly adding, "And neither did his alters."

"It was his foster parents," Rebecca revealed quietly, tone haunting. "They um…"

She couldn't finish the sentence. Logan picked up where she left off, his voice solemn. "They raped him. Together. Constantly. For four years." A chill traveled up my spine. "And he won't talk about it… Not with us, at least."

*No.*

*Fuck that.*

*I can't do it.*

As the only staff psychiatrist—I couldn't stress this enough—psychotherapy *wasn't* in my job description. If I did it, I would be doing it as a favor to the psychologists on staff. Talk therapy wasn't something I'd done for a patient since I was in residency. I wasn't good at it.

My job was drug therapy, and that's it. I could find the necessary drug cocktail to keep Kahfi together, monitor him for major chemical imbalances, keep track of and analyze his data, but it was—

*Not.*

*My.*

*Job.*

To be his psychologist.

Psychotherapy was *their* thing, not mine. I had *briefly* considered taking Kahfi on as a psychotherapy patient at the beginning of this conversation, but I was no longer up to it.

Not if that was his backstory.

Logan and Rebecca had no idea what they were asking of me. They didn't know my history. They weren't aware of my traumas and triggers. They had no idea that taking on this kid's case would only dig up the skeletons I had buried in my own mental closet. I *could not* sit for those sessions.

*Fuck this. The answer is no.*

I looked down at the file on the table in front of me. Resting at the top of a stack of papers was a single headshot photograph of a little brown skinned boy, unsmiling, with lifeless eyes.

I shut the folder.

"The answer is no."

## Chapter Twenty-Four

# Caprice

On Fridays, we eat dinner at Catfish Carol's.

I met my best friend, Sanaa Montgomery, in my freshman year at the University of Miami.

Like me, she was an early entry college student, so we were both seventeen that year. We lived in a four-bedroom student apartment with two other girls. While our other two roommates jetted off to parties we weren't old enough to get into, Sanaa and I grew close, holed up in that apartment.

Like me, Sanaa had recently lost her best friend in the whole world. The loss happened two months before the fall semester started. Unlike mine, however, *her* best friend was dead. She was so depressed when I first met her. I tried to help the best I could.

Over time, we grew to rely on one another.

By sophomore year she was coming out of her shell, dragging me along with her. By senior year, she was an unstoppable force, healing… and still dragging me along with her. The Sanaa that I met in college and the Sanaa of the modern day were not the same people.

We had a ten-year friendship where I watched her grow from a depressed recluse to a vibrant social butterfly. Around Miami, she was *That Girl*, a popular socialite that everybody wanted to know.

Montgomery was an influential name in this city. And not just because of Sanaa Montgomery. Sanaa's father was a really big deal around here, which made her family very wealthy and very powerful.

She had connections. She was friends with a lot of people,

and everyone who she wasn't cool with, secretly pined for her friendship.

And I, Caprice Latimore, just so happened to be her closest friend. She was my ride or die.

Every Friday night, we would eat dinner at Catfish Carol's, a little seafood restaurant near the beach. We'd sit across from each other and just vent about whatever went on that week.

Sanaa owns an event planning business—*Montgomery Events*. She does everything—marriage proposals, weddings, parties, conventions, rallies, protests, you name it.

Sanaa is a *celebrity* event planner—and when I say that I don't mean to say she only plans for celebrities. I'm saying Sanaa is so good at her job, that *she* is a celebrity.

Because of her circle, most of her customers were celebrities or the generally wealthy around Miami. She always knew the hot celebrity gossip before the media got hold of it. Sanaa thought my job was fascinating, but I thought hers was *way* more interesting.

All I did was complain about my job. Well… not my job, my coworkers.

"Not only do I have to do my job, but now they want me to do their job, too." I was giving Sanaa the recap as she sat across from me in the Caribbean themed restaurant. She was slicing her knife into a piece of fried fish as I continued to unload. "Lowkey, I think they're just mad 'cause I get paid the most. But, girl, I *do* the most! Just because I stay in my office instead of socializing in the break room, doesn't mean I'm not working."

Sanaa casually ate her dinner, swallowing as she shook her head. "Yes, girl. Preach."

I aggressively pierced my food with my fork.

Sanaa's brown eyes flashed with exaggerated concern. Her makeup was really pretty tonight—it was Sanaa who taught me how to do mine. Her brown skin was blemish free, with a thin coat of mocha foundation. She wore a wine-red lip color tonight that accentuated her full lips and a light coat of mascara that made her eyes pop.

Joking, she asked me, "Are you mad at the shrimp on your plate, too?"

Rolling my eyes at her humor, I chewed my food before

asserting, "I'm not taking that kid's case."

"Alright, alright, that's fine." She put both her hands up in surrender, flicking the longer side of her asymmetrical bob behind her shoulder. Sanaa pressed her red lips together before adding, "Fuck them kids."

"No—I have nothing against the kid. It's just not my job."

"Mm-hm, get your check and do the bare minimum, sis."

I realized what she was doing.

"You're being sarcastic," I commented. "You don't really agree with me."

She smiled a little and then shrugged. "Your vibe is crazy hostile right now. And you got that fork in your hand… I'mma tell you whatever you wanna hear, Reese."

"Be serious," I laughed.

"*Personally…*" Sanaa spoke slowly and then twisted her mouth to one side of her face, thinking. She always made that face when she was thinking; it was cute. "I'm sure Rebecca and them know it's not your job to do talk therapy, but they must've asked you 'cause they don't have any options. A black child needs help, and your white coworkers don't know what to do with him. You're not obligated to take on that responsibility, but understand that the only person who truly gets hurt in all of this is—"

She was making me feel guilty.

"Sanaa, you're my best friend! You're supposed to be on my side about this!"

"*Aht-aht,* I'm your best friend, not your yes-bitch. I don't have to agree with everything you say."

I rolled my eyes.

Sanaa rolled her eyes right back, adding, "Reese, it's just *one* little boy."

"Three—if you count his other two personalities."

"Really?" Her eyes lit up with intrigue. That was as much as I would reveal. She didn't need to know about Kahfi's abuse. That was personal. "That shit sounds fascinating to me! Your job sounds so damn interesting. And look at you—bitching."

In Sanaa's defense, she didn't know anything else about Kahfi. And even if I told her, she wouldn't know why his case would have such an impact on me. I didn't go around publicizing my own traumatic history either. We were best friends, but she didn't know about my time in Parramore.

Of course, she knew I was adopted, but she never asked how old I was when that happened. And so, I never told her. The Caprice Latimore she knew had a rich mom in Beverly Hills. That's it. So, even though I never lied to her, I certainly didn't fill her in on my entire past.

I loved her, but we would never get close enough for me to show her that side of me. I hoped to never be that close to somebody. I'd done it once. Never again.

"I don't want to talk about my job anymore," I told her, trying to transition, so I asked about her work. "Fill me in on what's going on in the wonderful world of event planning."

Sanaa let out a deep sigh then. That meant she was stressed about something.

"This should be interesting," I realized, leaning in closer across the table.

"It's just a lot, girl. I'm over here trying to plan my own wedding, but every time I get some free time to work on it, I get a new client. Don't be surprised if you end up being the maid of honor to a wedding at the courthouse. I'm over here making everyone else's event perfect, with no time to do the same for mine."

Sanaa was engaged to marry her longtime boyfriend, Micah. As her maid of honor, I had a bridal shower and a bachelorette party to organize. Her wedding was set for March 2019, so I had plenty of time since we were currently in July. If I had plenty of time, then I knew it was too early for her to be feeling this defeated.

"Why don't you hire a wedding planner then?"

"*Biiiiiitch,*" Sanaa said the word extra slow. "The fuck do I look like hiring my competition? Do you think Martha Stewart is out here paying another bitch to decorate her house? I would rather get married in a courthouse then give those girls my business."

"You're not getting married in a courthouse." Sanaa was way too extravagant to not throw herself an equally extravagant wedding. Micah was a sports medicine doctor—I went to med school with him and introduced the happy couple, actually—and he had way too much money for Sanaa to not feel the need to spend it.

"You're right," she nodded. "I'll push the date back if I have to."

"That's an option." I shrugged. "But I don't think it'll be necessary. Knowing you, you'll figure it out."

"Your faith in me is uplifting. You really do love me," Sanaa gushed, reaching across the table to give me a half-hug. I didn't like hugs, but I didn't tense up as much in them anymore. I was pretty good at working through my discomfort and just hugging back. Sanaa pulled back and her eyes glittered with appreciation. "And since you love me—"

She was about to ask me for something. I knew her so well, that I immediately felt the request coming.

"—I have this *re*-proposal that I've been planning, and I need help setting up decorations," she told me, adding, "I'll buy you lunch and love you forever and ever, if you come."

My friend was swamped with work, and barely had time to plan her own wedding. If I could help her get that work done a little faster, I sure would. I just had one question, though.

"What's a *re*-proposal?"

"My client proposed to his girlfriend two months ago, and she said yes…" Sanaa rolled her eyes and continued, "But the girlfriend is an actress, and she wants him to propose to her again in a more romantic and extravagant way, so she can officially announce it to Instagram. So, he's *re*-proposing, and I'm setting it up."

"She wants him to propose again for an Instagram post?" I questioned. "That's…"

I couldn't find the word for it.

"Silly as hell," Sanaa finished my sentence. "The client thinks so, too, but hey—he must really love her. And it's not like he's doing any of the work. *I'm* the poor sucker that has to organize this ridiculous shit."

"The things people do for social media…"

"I know, right?" Sanaa shook her head and added, "But I can't complain. People wanting to floss on social media is keeping my lights on. So, will you help me set up?"

"When?"

"Tomorrow morning, at the marina at Bayside," she

informed. "He's *re*-proposing on his yacht tomorrow night, so I just need your help decorating the boat with flowers and candles."

"Ooh, a yacht... *Fancy*..." I laughed. "What does he do?"

"He's a friend of Micah's—an athlete." That wasn't surprising. Sanaa's fiancé was a sports medicine physician, so most of his friends were athletes. "I really can't thank you enough for agreeing to help me with this!"

I smiled at her.

"Just don't forget you said you'd buy me lunch."

# Chapter Twenty-Five

## Caprice

Miami in July is a fiery time of year.

The sun beat down on my shoulders as I trekked the boardwalk of the *Miamarina*. The *Miamarina* was a yacht marina off the coast of Downtown Miami. Here, the docks were lined with dozens of shiny white boats belonging to the city's richest residents.

I came here to help Sanaa decorate one of them, but it wasn't everyday I got to spend my Saturday on a yacht. Even though we were both here to work, it wasn't like we couldn't make it fun.

As we carted boxes of decorations and supplies down the wooden planks of the boardwalk, each of us was carrying a little something extra to make the morning a bit more enjoyable for us.

In my hands, I had bottles of champagne and orange juice for mimosas, because yes, we were here to decorate the boat, but nobody said we couldn't turn up while we did it. We were turning business into pleasure.

The whole morning was mapped out already.

With six hours to get the boat set up, we knew we could get the job done by noon, and that would give us another two hours to enjoy the Miami heat on a fancy yacht. We were certainly dressed the part, denim shorts and bikini tops.

"Alright, this is the one," Sanaa pointed out a pristine-looking yacht floating at the back of the marina. It was a beautiful boat, with a shiny white exterior and a silver trim. On the front of the boat, like most of the boats in the marina, the yacht had a name written in beautiful cursive along the side.

My eyes widened, and then squinted.

"Sanaa, do you see that?" I pointed and waited until she

noticed.

Her mouth fell open and then she laughed. "Holy shit, you and the boat have the same name! That's *insaaaaane*. What are the odds?"

Like me, it was Sanaa's first time seeing the boat today. If she knew the boat was called *Caprice,* she definitely would've mentioned it. Curious, I had to ask. "Who does this boat belong to?"

"I told you—a friend of Micah's. Micah's best man, actually."

"Yeah, but what's his name?"

Sanaa shook her head. "I actually can't say. Since the re-proposal is a secret, the client made me sign a non-disclosure agreement to ensure I didn't ruin the surprise. If I break the NDA, I don't get paid, and that's twenty thousand on the line. Can't risk it."

In that moment, I thought… what if? How many athletes were out here willing to name a boat *Caprice*? I could only think of one who might.

But I could've been overthinking it. Caprice is an actual word in the English language—it means unpredictable behavior. If you really think about it, the seas *are* capricious. Why not call a boat meant to sail the ocean caprice, then?

I was most likely overthinking.

"I'll tell you who it is after the proposal gets posted on Instagram!" Sanaa promised, adding, "And after that twenty grand check clears."

I giggled, shaking my head. "You're so annoying."

* * *

We were done setting up the boat a little before noon.

No surface was left untouched. The white boat was decorated with glittery candles and nearly a thousand red roses. Sanaa's client was going to be *re*-proposing to his girlfriend out on the boat deck under the moon and stars, surrounded by roses and candlelight. It was a stunningly romantic set up—just the kind of thing to get a bunch of Instagram likes.

The indoor part of the yacht was about as spacious as a two-bedroom apartment, luxuriously new fixtures that shined like the boat was built yesterday.

Sanaa and I were in the kitchen. Yes, the yacht had a *whole* kitchen, stainless steel appliances with white countertops and a big window that offered stunning views of the ocean.

We found champagne flutes in the cabinets and were mixing our mimosas. Now that the hard work was all done, we were going to use the remaining time we had on the boat to have some fun. Like she said she would, she was going to leave me here a little bit to go buy us some lunch.

"Don't get too drunk without me," she warned as she grabbed her purse off the kitchen counter as I mixed my second mimosa. "I'mma make a quick run to the taqueria. You good with tacos?"

"Tacos are fine," I told her, stepping out of my jean shorts.

Me and my champagne flute were going out on the boat deck to soak in some sun. It was summer, and just because I wasn't on vacation, didn't mean I couldn't give my skin that beautiful melanin-rich look. Not wanting to get tan lines, I decided to remove my white bikini top as well, leaving them in the kitchen with my shorts.

The boat deck was furnished like an outdoor patio. At the center of it all, facing the water, was a double lounge chair with white cushions.

I laid across the top, putting in my headphones on loud. After a draining week of work at FEEL, this was just the relaxing Saturday I needed. The sun kissed every bit of my exposed skin, and I closed my eyes to the sound of music playing in my ears.

There I was, lounging worry-free on a fancy yacht under a flawless blue sky.

I sighed, thinking about how lucky I was to love my life this much.

# Chapter Twenty-Six

# SHAUN

I would do anything for my mother.

Two years ago, after battling breast cancer for three years, my mother went into remission. It took three agonizing years of surgeries and chemotherapy. Lots of people had these ideas about what my life must've been like. Five years ago, I was in Houston, a twenty-four-year-old multimillionaire athlete, at just the beginning of a promising career. There were all these assumptions that I must've been living it up. People thought I was king of the world.

I could've been.

But the most important person in my life at the time had *fucking* cancer.

I'd already lost my father to cancer when I was four years old, and the thought of it taking my mother, too? I most definitely was *not* living it up.

My mother and I were already close before she got sick, but her cancer brought us closer. With my ball money, I got her the best doctors and did everything I could. It saved her life. The cancer had been gone for two years now. I'd do everything I did for her a million times.

When it came time to re-sign my contract with the Houston Rockets, I decided to switch teams. My mother was in Florida, so I needed to be on a ball team in Florida, too. And why not? It was my home state.

Life is too short to be so far from the person I care about most.

And my mother absolutely *refused* to move to Houston. She said Texas wasn't her style. So, for her, I willingly moved back to Florida, signing a four-year contract with the Miami Heat.

By my second season, the Heat won the playoffs, earning me my fourth ring in my career so far. I was named MVP just last month. After this summer, I had two more seasons in Miami on my contract, but I was sure I would be signing on for more. Not just because I was doing so well with the team, but because my mother likes Miami.

It's only four hours away from Orlando, so relatives are never more than a drive away. She likes that, feeling so close to home.

Not too long ago, I asked my mother if she was scared when she thought she was going to die. Call it morbid curiosity. She said she hadn't been too afraid of dying, but her biggest regret was that she would miss out on her future grandchildren.

And that's when I realized that even though I saved my mother's life, I still had to do one more thing.

I had to have a kid.

Now, it was never my intention to do the whole family man thing. I couldn't find anyone I wanted to do that with. Yeah, I had a girlfriend, but we were just… chilling. The relationship was coasting. Not exactly the most passionate thing, but it was working.

Arielle Underwood was an actress, which made her just as busy as I was. When we could make time for each other, we did. We'd been making time for each other for about three years now.

However, we weren't one of those out loud and flashy celebrity couples. She refused to publicly claim me unless I claimed her first, and I wasn't exactly going out of my way to do that.

Arielle was a nice girl, but what did she expect me to do? Jump up and down on a couch for national TV, telling everyone I loved her, on some Tom Cruise shit? I'd rather not.

So, for that, our relationship was really private. Of course, I wasn't the cheating type, but I couldn't say my heart was in it either. In fact, I liked that we weren't too serious.

That is, until I realized I needed to have a kid.

Arielle wouldn't just *have* my kid because I asked her to. She was the type who wanted a ring and a wedding first. I was pushing thirty this year, so it was about time I settled down anyway.

I proposed to Arielle this past May, in the middle of playoff season. In hindsight, I might've been too casual about it. We were in my hotel room, just after a winning game in Boston. I pulled an engagement ring box from my gym bag, tossed it to her, and said, "We should get married."

I was twenty-nine going on thirty, she had just turned thirty-three.

It was about that time.

Arielle was unimpressed. "Three years together, and that's how you propose to me?"

It wasn't exactly the most romantic proposal story she could take to the press. Arielle lived for the spotlight. If she was engaged to the highest paid player in the league, she wanted it to make the front page. She wanted interviews. She wanted all that Hollywood shit.

The celebrity couple shit was something I wouldn't give her while we were dating. If we were married, she wanted that celebrity couple shit.

Obviously, she couldn't tell the public that she got engaged in a Boston hotel room, while her new fiancé still smelled like he just finished playing a two-hour game.

That would do nothing for her public image.

And Miss Arielle Underwood was really fuckin' particular about her public image. That's why she always tried to look perfect. Brown skin always clear, never a hair out of place, body on point—*everything* on point, honestly. She had a pretty enough face and was decent enough conversation. To most, I was a lucky man to be able to call her mine.

Many people would've considered me blessed to call her my wife. Arielle was everything men think they want. Good looking, smart, driven, and respectable.

She was *very* cold, though.

But that was okay; I was colder.

In our entire three-year relationship, I think I told her I loved her twice. She might have said it to me *maybe* four times.

Did I love Arielle? I had love *for* her. There were aspects about her that I really liked. There were probably just as many aspects about her that I didn't like, too. But I had love for her.

There's a big difference between loving someone and having love for someone.

When you love someone, you love them for who they are. When you have love for someone, you love what they can do for you.

And what I needed from her right now was a kid.

To get that, I'd have to marry her first. So, when Arielle told me she would say yes if I just proposed to her again—with a little more effort—I hired the most in-demand event planner in Miami.

Sanaa Montgomery.

* * *

Regular people can't just shoot Sanaa Montgomery an inquiry email.

To hire somebody like Sanaa Montgomery, you need connections. Sanaa was a highly sought-after event planner, with a packed schedule. If you could get her number somehow, whatever you needed her to plan had to be scheduled at least six months into the future.

I needed her to plan my re-proposal for me, and she needed to get it all done in three weeks.

If I was anybody else, I would've never convinced her to do it.

But I wasn't just anybody.

I was her fiancé's best man.

Micah wasn't just my friend; he was my doctor. As a sports physician based out of Miami, he kept me in tip top health. And I could thank him for getting me the connect with Sanaa, as well.

Asking Sanaa to plan something that took months, and do it in three weeks, that was asking for a lot. Her usual rate for planning a marriage proposal was ten thousand. Because I was asking her to do it in so little time, she doubled her rate for me.

No family and friends discount over here.

To make it easier on her, we were going to have the re-proposal done on my boat.

What I was doing was fucked up, really. I was proposing for the *second* time to a woman I didn't love, on a boat I named after the only woman I ever truly cared about. The only woman I'd ever given my heart to.

Caprice Alicia Latimore.

She took my heart, and then disappeared with it.

We grew up together in one of the poorest neighborhoods in Orlando, Florida. When I was ten, she moved down from Alabama and she was the most beautiful girl I'd ever seen. I wanted to be close to her from the moment I knew she existed.

I ultimately did it, too. I got close to her. We were kids then.

But I always knew.

I didn't know what to call it then, but I'm older now and I understand.

Caprice was *the one*.

She was the one I was supposed to be proposing to tonight. *Shit*, to be honest, if she hadn't disappeared, I would've proposed to her on the night I got drafted. I was twenty-two years old then, and the ink on my NBA contract wasn't even dry yet.

But I just knew.

If she had been there, I would've got down on one knee and asked her to share it with me. Twenty-two is young, I know.

But I was sure about Caprice when I was ten years old.

For as long as I could remember, I loved Caprice Latimore to death. Actually, loving Caprice as much as I did *really* almost killed me. It probably almost killed her, too.

I was *so* fuckin' stupid when I was a kid. I made a lot of dumb choices. I have a lot of regrets.

Caprice was a very complex girl. There were a lot of despicable things going on in her house. I had a once in a lifetime love, and all she wanted me to do was run away with her. And I couldn't give her that. I had to solve her problems my way.

And my way was really fuckin' stupid.

I woke up in a hospital with nothing to show for it. I got beat the hell up because my stupid, teenaged ass didn't think fighting a grown man, who *just* got out of prison, was gonna be that hard. With age comes wisdom, and looking back, I know my plan was doomed from the beginning.

I was too confident then. Until that night, I had never lost a fight.

But I had never fought a grown ass ex-convict either.

At my age now, I could get what I was trying to do back then done. But at eighteen? I didn't stand a chance.

After that night, Caprice just disappeared. I didn't know where she was. At one point I got so desperate, I demanded answers from her grandmother, who I fucking hated. And her grandmother didn't know either. That old lady was just as lost as I was.

My last year of high school, I was in a really bad place mentally. I didn't know if she was okay. I didn't know if anyone was taking care of her.

I didn't even know if she was alive.

For a long time I battled with the possibility that my Butterscotch was dead, and that it was my fault. And if she was alive, wherever she was, what if someone was hurting her there? I was a mess.

It was my mother that convinced me that the best thing I could do for Caprice was be successful. I couldn't waste my life away because I missed her. It was a better idea to be the best that I could be so that one day, if she was still out there, I'd have the means to find her.

From then on, the plan was to make it to the NBA, so that I could be rich enough to hire someone to find her someday.

As luck would have it, I didn't need millions of dollars to find Caprice. She told me once where she planned to go. She had her whole life planned out by the time she was sixteen. Caprice wanted to attend the University of Miami and become a doctor someday. She told me that once in the bookstore she used to work at in Parramore.

In my junior year at Duke, I went down to Miami for spring break. Up until then, I had little faith that I would find her there, but I went just in case. The Caprice I knew would've reached out as soon as she got the chance. If she made it to UM, then there was no reason why she wouldn't have called me already. I hadn't heard from her in almost four years at that point.

So, naturally, I was convinced she wouldn't be there.

But I went.

Just in case.

One of my old teammates from Jefferson, Adrian, played ball at UM. That spring break, I was staying with him. I was there less than forty-eight hours by the time I found her. Totally by accident.

I was at some pool party near campus. Just a bunch of college kids around an apartment complex pool, living it up for the break.

I couldn't believe my eyes at first.

She couldn't see me, but thirteen feet away, on the other side of the pool, Caprice stood at the center of a group. Like everyone else, she had a red cup in one hand. In a pink bikini, she stood by the water, laughing hysterically at something her friend was saying.

In her other hand was a cell phone. That's actually what bothered me the most—the cell phone.

Not only was she doing better than I could've ever hoped, but the only thing stopping her from calling me was… I don't even know.

When I brought it up to Adrian, he said, "Oh, you didn't know your ole girl was in school here? Yeah, she must've come up on some big money, 'cause… she drives a fuckin *Benz* to class, and all her little fine ass friends are bougie as hell, too. Yeaaaah, she's deep in that rich girl crew." He shook his head, shrugging. "I thought you knew."

Obviously, I *didn't* know.

What I did know was that I didn't have to keep looking for Caprice anymore. I found her. It took me four years, but I finally had some answers. It helped my mother sleep better at night knowing she was okay. It made me sleep worse.

I used to have all these dreams about how Caprice's hard life would change when I finally found her. Every success I achieved until that point was all part of the grand plan to find her and rescue her. And when I finally did find her, it was clear as day that she didn't need to be saved.

## Chapter Twenty-Seven

# SHAUN

I don't hate Caprice for ghosting me.

I could never hate her for anything. She was out there living her best life, and that's all I ever really wanted for her. Happiness. From where I stood that day by the pool, it looked like she finally found it.

Without me.

Which was fine.

I just wish she would've told me that I didn't have to worry about her so much. It could've saved me from a lot of pain and a lot of wasted time.

Before that spring break, I would sometimes look for Caprice's name online. The search results had always been flooded with random people with the first name Caprice or random people with the last name Latimore.

But now that I knew she was at the University of Miami, I found better places online to look. After that spring break, I kept tabs on her for a few years.

She wasn't on any social media, so most of the little updates I got on her life were inexplicit. I learned that she graduated top of her class in undergrad. Her name was on the school website.

I found out that she tutored kids in math. I discovered this by trying to find her on *Facebook*. All I found was a Facebook page review for a tutoring service. Some mom left a review saying her son passed his math class because of *"Caprice Latimore, best math tutor ever!!!!!!"*.

I remember wanting to know if she was dating anyone. One time, I swallowed my pride and just straight up asked Adrian. If he knew who her friends were, then maybe he knew the answer to my question, too.

He clowned me at first.

"Ahhhhh, you tryna slide back into your old spot?" he had asked, laughing. Actually, no. I was just curious. I wouldn't do anything with the information, but I wanted to know. "Caprice's best friend cockblocks everybody who tries to get at her. Kinda like how you used to do before y'all started going out."

So that hadn't changed. It's just, someone else out there was protecting her now.

Adrian concluded, "And don't worry, nigga. All her friends are girls. She keeps to herself and her crew. Caprice isn't fast at all."

It should've made me glad to hear that, but it didn't. It actually made it worse. You see, if Caprice was dating, then I could *really* move on.

But she wasn't.

So, I was stuck.

I kept tabs on Caprice for three years after I found her. Just gathering little tidbits from the internet. The information wasn't much, but the tiny updates were nice. Even if they were always followed by a general sense of sadness. It didn't make me happy to have to learn about her life that way.

But I still did it.

And then my mom got cancer.

My focus shifted. Almost losing my mother put a lot of things into perspective. So, I stopped checking for Caprice five years ago. The sadness that came from not knowing if my mother would survive didn't need to be combined with the sadness I had over Caprice.

So, that's when I finally let her go.

It took me seven years, but I finally *let her go.*

Since moving to Miami, it definitely crossed my mind that someday I might run into her. That is, if she still lived here. I didn't know if she did and I wasn't looking for her, either.

By the time I moved to Miami, I'd been seeing Arielle for a year.

And after three years of dating, I was going to propose to Arielle Underwood for a second time.

* * *

Sanaa said it would only take her six hours to set up the boat.

I had some free time that Saturday, so I was gonna make a quick stop at the marina and see what twenty thousand dollars was getting me. Just because I was the highest paid player in the league, didn't mean I liked dropping that kind of money on a whim.

I didn't grow up as poor as everyone else in Parramore, but I certainly didn't grow up rich. Twenty thousand, regardless of how much I had, was always going to feel like a lot.

No matter how rich you are, parking in Downtown Miami will forever be an inconvenience. I was parked four blocks away from the marina, and to get there, I'd have to walk. It was a hot day in the city, so I could keep my sunglasses on. It was better that way because getting recognized would've created a crowd. Coincidentally, I found Sanaa at a taco stand on my way to the yacht.

"*Oh heeeeeey,*" she said to me, like someone who just got caught doing something they weren't supposed to be doing. "I wasn't expecting you until later tonight."

This had me feeling like a supervisor who just popped in on a slacking employee. *Look at her getting tacos when she's supposed to be working for my money.* For paying her double what she usually charged, I deserved the *best* service. She knew I was thinking it, too.

"I wanted to see the set up," I told her. When it came to planning, I let Sanaa take complete control. I offered no ideas, no input. This re-proposal was just a means to an end for me. I had to get it out of the way so I could get to working on the more important things.

Sanaa could do whatever she wanted. There was no budget. I only asked that the re-proposal be flashy enough for Arielle to get good pictures out of it.

Because that's what this was about after all, Arielle and her pictures.

"Yeah, we actually finished decorating the yacht just after eleven."

I checked my Apple watch. It was almost one o'clock.

"*We?*" When Sanaa told me that she needed six hours to set up, she didn't say she was bringing anyone. In fact, she wasn't supposed to bring anyone.

The re-proposal was confidential. My girlfriend didn't know about it, and I didn't want information to leak before I could surprise her. I figured Arielle would want to look shocked in her Instagram video, so the re-proposal needed to be a secret. Which is exactly why I made Sanaa sign a non-disclosure agreement.

"Before you say I broke the NDA, my helper doesn't know that *you* own the boat," Sanaa explained. "She is always helping me with stuff like this for my clients. She's my best friend… and she doesn't know anything about basketball either, so even if she did know your name, she wouldn't know who you are." Sanaa's brown eyes shifted nervously as we walked in the same direction. "But I didn't tell her your name. I swear." Then rather bluntly, she added, "NDA not broken. You still have to pay me."

I noticed that Sanaa was dressed in a yellow bikini top and jean shorts. It was a hot day, and she'd been working outside, so it made sense.

"Since you're Micah's best friend, I made sure the set up was extra, extra nice," she said.

I'm not Micah's best friend. Although I'm the best man at his wedding, I'm just his friend. I don't do that best friend shit anymore. It doesn't mean anything.

"I would've preferred a friends and family discount then," I replied with a shrug.

Sanaa gave me the sweetest smile she could fake and said, "You're Micah's friend… *not* mine."

This was our thing—the banter. I didn't dislike Sanaa at all, but it was fun to get on her nerves. And now that I was paying her for a service, she couldn't just pop off like she usually would. This new boss-employee dynamic between us was hilarious to me.

For the past three weeks, she had been so professional. I knew the moment my check cleared, that Sanaa would go back to being stuck-up. But for now, she had to be polite. If paying her twenty G's forced her to be nice to me, I was gonna milk it for what it was worth.

"Can I have a taco?"

Sanaa shook her head, nose in the air, straight black hair blowing with the breeze. "No."

"You got, like, six tacos in that bag, Sanaa. Don't be greedy." I rubbed my stomach. "Boss is hungry."

She rolled her eyes and hissed, "These are for me and *my best friend.*"

I noticed something then. "Well, where's your friend at? Because it looks like you and I are walking to the same place."

"Right..." she hesitated. "...um, so you know how I told you we finished early, right?"

I could tell from her tone that she was about to say something that was gonna piss me off.

"Well... I figured since we had the whole six hours... we could just... you know, relax a little bit on the boat deck. You know... reward ourselves with a little luxury for a job well done. Maybe sip on a few mimosas and soak in that summertime sun. You know... girl stuff."

I wasn't amused. We had finally reached the boardwalk "You left a stranger alone on *my* multimillion-dollar yacht."

"Not a stranger. She's practically family."

Now, I was actually mad, so this was no longer harmless banter.

"I'm not talkin' about *you*, Sanaa. She's a stranger to *me*. I don't fuckin' *know* this bitch. How do I know she's not in there stealing my shit? Ain't nobody told you to bring her. And now you're leaving her on my boat to do whatever the fuck she pleases? Sanaa, this is so goddamn unprofessional!"

Sanaa cleared her throat. "First of all—you need to watch the way that you're talking to me. I'm a Montgomery, and this is Miami. You're Micah's friend, so I will do you the favor of not having you shot. My best friend is not in there stealing *your shit*. She has her own money. Everyone is not from *Parramore*, Shaun. I know *you're* a hoodbooger, but not everybody is from the *ghetto*."

I had nothing to fucking say to that. Not because I couldn't. I just was not about to stand here and denigrate this woman over something so petty. Sanaa was disrespectful as fuck for that statement, but she wasn't about to get me out of character. That, and her fiancé was my friend.

She crossed her arms, tapping her foot impatiently on the boardwalk planks. Her eyes were a little pink with tears pooling at the rims. "Say you're sorry."

"Are you seriously crying?"

"I cry when I'm angry! Say you're sorry!" she demanded again.

To this day, I hate seeing women cry. Even though I didn't feel like I was in the wrong, I still apologized. "Sanaa, I'm sorry."

She didn't apologize for her behavior. Instead she just said, "When you meet her, you're gonna feel so fucking stupid for thinking she'd steal."

Sanaa stomped ahead of me toward the yacht. I took my time as I walked.

"And you wanna know something else really cute? Your boat and my best friend have the same name!" she shouted over the sea breeze, throwing her hands up in the air. "We could've laughed about this as a trio, but *nooooo*, you always have to be such an asshole!"

*That's* when I stopped walking.

"Your friend's name is Caprice?" my tone was totally emotionless. Flat. Sanaa only nodded. "Where'd you meet her?"

She squinted at the random question. "In college."

"Where did you go for school?"

"Here, obviously!" she shouted.

How many Caprices could there be at the University of Miami? Sanaa was the same age as Caprice, so she probably would've been there at about the same time as her. According to Adrian, Caprice was friends with a bunch of bougie rich girls, and Sanaa was just about the bougiest chick I knew.

*This is not fuckin' happening…*

"*Why* are you making that face?" Sanaa questioned. The woman in front of me was staring at me confusedly. I didn't know what my face looked like right now, but if it looked anything how I felt, then I probably looked sick. "Do you wanna see how we decorated the place or not?"

I nodded, but I wasn't curious about what the boat looked like. I wanted to get a look at Sanaa's friend.

Sanaa followed behind me as I walked up the boat steps. She

began giving a tour of decorated corners, showing me where the dinner was going to be set up. She couldn't keep my attention. I was too busy searching the boat for signs of another person.

I didn't see anyone.

Not yet.

As Sanaa led me to the boat deck, pointing out the décor and the roses, out of the corner of my eye, I saw something on the double lounge chair. I walked away from Sanaa in the middle of her sentence, circling the chair to find exactly who I knew I would.

There she was.

She didn't even hear us come up. She had headphones in her ears, relaxing with her eyes closed. She was letting the sunlight beam down on just about every inch of her flawless dark skin. I didn't wake up this morning thinking today was the day I would finally see Caprice again. And I certainly would've never guessed she would be topless when it happened.

"Oh my God!" Sanaa shrieked when she walked over to my side, her hand trying to reach for my face to cover my eyes. Unfortunately for Sanaa, she wasn't tall enough. She was shouting at me to turn around. Clearly, Sanaa didn't want me to see her friend almost naked.

Which was a little funny 'cause… it wasn't my first time seeing her naked.

Standing this close, Sanaa's voice must've been loud enough for Caprice to hear through her headphones. I watched her as she opened her eyes to find the both of us standing over her. First she saw Sanaa and then her beautiful brown eyes flickered over to me and just… stared.

Quickly, her arms came up to cover her exposed chest, and just looking at her face, I could see that she was so embarrassed. So uncomfortable. There was nothing here besides her arms for her to cover herself with.

So, without even thinking about it, I took off my shirt and handed it to her. It must've been the way that Caprice and I were looking at each other, because even Sanaa was quiet.

Caprice silently pulled the shirt over her head.

Time had only made her more beautiful, but there were some things that could never change. She had this beautiful pair of dark brown eyes lined with perfectly long lashes. From her eyes, I surveyed down her cute nose, settling on her memorable set of lips. Even twelve years later, I remembered those lips.

*Damn*, she was still perfect.

I spoke first.

"Hey." That's all I could think to say.

She said a little more, sounding so shy. "Hey, Shaun."

All I had to hear her say was my name and I knew. I thought I let her go five years ago, but I guess that wasn't true. Even now, despite everything she'd done, she was still the one and only. I hadn't seen her in nearly twelve years, but I knew now that these feelings were never just gonna go away.

Over the years, I knew it was possible that what I felt for Caprice back in those days was just puppy love. I was ten years old when I decided I loved her. What does a ten-year-old boy know about love? When I was trying to get over her, I would tell myself that one day, as a grown man, I might see her again and realize that Caprice is just a woman. Nothing special.

Nah…

The feeling in my chest right now was the same thing I got when I was ten years old and I gave her that butterscotch. We were sitting face to face on the basketball court, and I just…

Something happened in me.

I wanted things I didn't even understand. On that day, I realized I wanted to protect her, I wanted to be able to give her things, and even though she didn't want me to, I wanted to hold her.

And even now…

I *still* wanted to protect her. I *still* wanted to provide for her. And I *still* desperately wanted to hold her.

"You two know each other." It was Sanaa who broke the silence.

Caprice nodded, her eyes still on me as she told her friend, "We knew each other."

She spoke in past tense because we didn't know each other anymore.

But whose fault was that?

It wasn't mine. When I was a kid, I loved her so much that I would've given her the shirt off my back. And funnily enough, that's exactly what I *just* did.

My plain gray shirt fit loosely on her, the fabric stopping at her upper thighs. I was trying not to stare at her thighs. This Caprice had a terrific body. Not that my old Caprice wasn't just as good. She was just young and underfed, so it made her a bit too thin. This Caprice was undoubtedly a grown woman, and you could tell she regularly attended a gym.

Those thighs looked *fucking* amazing.

Sanaa realized the obvious. "Holy crap, if you guys know each other, then this yacht.... Shaun, did you name this yacht after my best friend?"

Is it childish that I hated the fact that Sanaa kept calling Caprice her best friend?

"I did," I said, not ashamed to admit it.

When I bought the boat last year, the dealer told me this boat was too beautiful to not name. When I asked him for a suggestion, he told me most men just name their boats after important women in their lives.

It was so pathetic, but it was the first name that came to mind. And it really did look nice, written in cursive along the side.

"Whoa, so you two, like... really, *really* knew each other." I really wished Sanaa wasn't here right now. Her voice was thick with '*I told you so*' when she added, "Hmm, guess she's not a stranger after all, huh, Shaun?"

The apology came a little late, but I said to Caprice, "I'm sorry we scared you like that."

Out of the corner of my eye, I could see Sanaa making a face. The Shaun Sanaa knew was not the Shaun I used to be. I wasn't this cold and abrasive when I was younger. And even though that's what I was now, I could never be that to Caprice.

Even though she was the reason I became this way.

"It's okay," Caprice insisted softly. I could listen to her talk all day. That sweet melodic voice would never get old. "It's *your* boat. I just hope Sanaa isn't blamed for my getting so comfortable."

*You can get comfortable*, I thought to myself. But all I said out loud was, "I don't mind."

"Whatttt?!" Sanaa cut in, her loud voice slicing into the moment. "Like you didn't just curse me the fuck out over bringing a friend on your boat five minutes ago? Why are you pretending to be so nice all of a sudden? Reese, don't buy it. He was not saying all this before."

I ignored Sanaa.

"Reese?" That was new.

We were both ignoring Sanaa at this point

"Yeah," Caprice nodded, a little embarrassed. "I got the nickname in college."

"I don't like it," I told her, comfortable enough to be that honest.

She giggled a little, which made me smile. Her hair was still natural, longer now; she wore her dark curls up in a big messy bun that moved with the ocean breeze. Her smile soon faded, a reminder flashing in her brown eyes. "So…" she awkwardly segued. "…you're proposing to an actress tonight."

My smile faded.

If she didn't know who, then I guess Sanaa really didn't give out names.

Since Caprice was gonna point out uncomfortable facts, I'd point one out, too. "So, you were just never gonna call me."

"I wanted to," she said, wanting me to believe. A memory of a nineteen-year-old version of her, standing poolside with a cellphone in her hands, said different.

"Did you forget the number?" I asked, knowing it wasn't possible. Caprice was always really sharp with numbers. She could memorize a whole deck of cards when we were kids. She could tell time in her head. She counted everything and knew exactly how many steps it was from her front door to our school.

She wasn't the kind of person to forget a phone number.

Especially since mine was one of the few she would ever call. Caprice didn't have anything to say, because she already knew I was aware that she didn't forget. She was so overwhelmed right now. I could see it in how her breathing picked up a bit, and in how a hint of tears collected in her eyes.

I was making her *very* uncomfortable.

"Reese, why are you crying?" Sanaa's concerned voice filled

the silence again.

She rushed to sit beside her friend, easily wrapping a hand around her to console her. I immediately noticed how Caprice tensed up. Twelve years later and she still didn't like being touched, but time had taught her to tolerate it.

I hated seeing Caprice cry, and it was my natural reaction to want to comfort her. But somebody else was already taking care of that. Hating what I was seeing—since I couldn't fix it myself, my only other option was to leave.

# Chapter Twenty-Eight

## Caprice

I was right to have suspected the boat belonged to Shaun.

When I got back to my apartment, I was still wearing his shirt. *So, this is what he smells like now.* I liked it. Until the encounter got to be too intense, I liked seeing him as well.

Shaun was so handsome.

He was always so handsome, but seeing him now after so long just… I never really appreciated just how perfect he was. Shaun was my friend for so long, and sometimes when you get used to someone, you think less and less about what they look like. It's less about their face, but more about who they are. I knew Shaun was handsome when we were growing up. It just wasn't the main thing about him that I loved.

But damn…

He really was something else.

That chiseled bone structure. The way his black waves rippled down his scalp like God's artwork. Those gorgeous penny-colored eyes. I forgot how much I used to adore his smile. Even my dreams about Shaun were nothing compared to the real thing. My memories didn't do him justice at all. Time had been kind to him.

On the outside, at least.

The moment he asked why I never called, I knew that I hurt him far worse than I realized. I had an answer for him, but I knew it wouldn't be good enough to fix the problems I must've caused.

I was scared to call at first. And then when I wasn't scared to call anymore, I was worried that I waited too long. In my mind, I waited so long that I was sure Shaun wouldn't speak to me if I called. That fear of rejection drove me to stretch my silence twelve years long. He was right, I never planned on calling. I just figured that by now, he would've definitely moved on.

But now I wasn't sure.

He looked at me today the same way he always did when we were kids. No hatred, no anger. He was just… hurt.

I felt so bad.

When I was a kid, I was such a crybaby. As an adult, I grew to understand I had every right to be. I had a really fucked up life. Now that I was older, I didn't cry as much. But then again, I didn't have much these days to cry about.

That is, until I saw just how much pain I caused to the only man I ever loved. I knew I was the only one of us in the wrong, but I couldn't face him to atone for what I'd done. How infuriating would it be for him, knowing that I was the one who did this to us, knowing he couldn't go off on me? He had every right to be angry, but Shaun was the type to go easy on me because I was such a fucking crybaby.

Even today, I could see him start to get annoyed in the middle of our short conversation, but the moment he realized I couldn't handle it, he pulled back. Shaun didn't criticize. He didn't force me to face the consequences of my actions.

Because he still cared about me.

Even after all this time.

When he walked away from me, unable to tolerate the tears in my eyes, I cried harder than I had in a decade. Sanaa had never seen me like that. My friend was so mad at him, not completely understanding what had just happened. She assumed if I was crying this hard, he must've done something wrong.

But he didn't.

Shaun did nothing wrong. Not to me. *Never* to me.

All Shaun Taylor ever did for me was love and trust me. I betrayed that trust, and even though I know why I did what I did, seeing him today solidified that my excuses weren't good enough.

I was a bad person. Yes, terrible things happened to me, but that didn't give me the right to be a bad person. To be such a bad friend.

When I was sixteen, I was so confused when I realized just how much Shaun loved me. I didn't think I deserved his love, and he disagreed.

Today he must've realized I proved him wrong.

It was true. I never deserved Shaun.

* * *

I felt like a piece of shit all weekend.

A terrible person.

When I came into work that Monday morning, I marched right into Dr. Rebecca Emison's office and decided to do something noble for once. It was going to hurt me to do this, but I needed to stop being so selfish.

"I'll take Kahfi Williams as a patient."

Rebecca's hazel eyes lit up at my unexpected change of heart. Right now, Kahfi was her patient and she was clearly not enjoying her therapy sessions with him. Realizing just how much she didn't want to be his psychologist, I decided I might do something else for the greater good.

"From now on, when we have a vote for something at FEEL, I want to include the daily operations staff, the counselors, and the nurses. They take care of our patients just as much as we do, so it's time they get a say in how we do things. Deal?"

Rebecca thought about it, knowing her little workplace alliance with Dr. Ezra would be useless if I got what I wanted. Kahfi Williams must've been a nightmare because even though Rebecca knew she would lose her upper hand around here if she made the deal, she accepted.

"Kahfi's alternate personalities take over when he's uncomfortable, and they stay for however long they want. While trying to help Kahfi, I've had Marron and Moreno completely waste entire sessions. Kahfi is not aware of his other personalities, but they are aware of him," Rebecca gave me a quick recap and then some advice. "The really nasty personality is Moreno. That's the one who called me the racial slur. Don't take it too personally if Moreno calls you names, too."

"Understood."

I was surprised when Kahfi Williams stepped into my office later that day. Mondays and Thursdays at twelve PM, that's when he would have his sessions with me. He showed up early to our first one, poking his head through my door to check if I was in.

"You can come in," I told him.

Kahfi was adorable. I think all the kids at FEEL are adorable. They're just all so sweet and bouncing with energy. Yes, some of them have their fair share of problems, but every child is precious. Every child needs to be protected. Regardless of whatever he said to Dr. Emison, Kahfi was a child, and I would treat him no different than any other child at FEEL.

He was a medium toned kid, lighter than me, but not quite light skinned. Like most of our children who came out of rough homes, he was noticeably skinny. Standing at about five-foot-three, he was tall for eleven. His height served to enhance how underweight he was. He had dark brown eyes that kind of reminded me of mine, not because they looked the same, but because they were so filled with secrets.

"You Miss Latimore?"

*Doctor Latimore actually*, I thought to myself, but I didn't correct him. "Yes, I am."

He was still standing at the other side of my desk, looking shy and a bit uncomfortable. He fidgeted with his hands. *Aww, he's nervous.*

"I'm Kahfi," he introduced himself quietly.

*One personality down, two more to meet.* "Nice to meet you, Kahfi. Please sit down."

He took a seat on a white armchair on the other side of my desk.

"It's real white in here," he commented. This was true, my office at FEEL was all white everything—white walls, white desk, white floors, white seats, everything.

"Yes, I like it. It's very clean."

"You must be one of those neat freaks, huh?" he guessed.

I nodded, agreeing, "I like to keep things clean. Don't you?"

Kahfi shrugged. "Yeah, but not like this." He looked around the room and then back at me, commenting, "You doin' too much."

In spite of myself, I laughed. "I might be."

He looked for a really long time, scanning my face like he was sure if he looked long enough, he would understand me. Kahfi's eyes, however secretive, were still preciously childlike. There was an innocence in them that I wasn't expecting. Most abuse victims tend to lose that light in their eyes.

He still had his.

"Am I in trouble?" he asked suddenly.

I squinted. "What? Why do you think you're in trouble?"

"Because I'm here," he answered, meaning my office, "And kids never come in here."

This was true, I usually assessed our patients in the examination rooms. "That doesn't mean you're in trouble, though."

"Are you like the principal of FEEL?" Kahfi asked curiously.

"FEEL isn't a school, Kahfi."

"I know that, but it's a building with a bunch of kids. We got online classes. We got counselors and tutors, too. I'm just tryna figure out what you do. Are you the boss of everybody here?"

"No," I told him. "I'm just a doctor. What makes you think I'm the boss of everybody?"

Kahfi hesitated. "Dr. Emison and Dr. Ezra, they talk to the kids. But you never talk to us. You stay in your office, like a school principal. Me and the rest of the kids see you bossin' the other doctors around, too."

I made a face at that assessment, a little defensive when I said, "I'm not *bossing* them around. I'm *consulting* them on drug therapies and—" *Why am I defending myself against a child?* "Kahfi, I'm not the principal of FEEL."

"You don't gotta get worked up, Miss Latimore."

*Doctor Latimore.* I wanted to correct him, but it was so petty.

"I'm nobody's boss. I'm just here to give you psychotherapy," I told him, trying to sound less defensive.

He looked a little worried. "Does that hurt?"

"No," I rushed to inform, finding that question so cute. "Psychotherapy just means I talk to you. It's talk therapy."

"Oh," he understood, sounding a little disappointed. I realized why when he added, "I kinda liked the idea of you being the boss around here."

"Really? Why's that?"

"'Cause you black," Kahfi pointed out, like this was the obvious answer. "I like to see us be the boss. I don't get to see that a lot."

*That was adorable.* I held back a smile. "Do you know what the L in FEEL stands for?"

"Tell me."

"Latimore. I'm not the boss at FEEL, but this whole place was *my* idea. Everybody else came after. But this center was built by four people who just want to help kids. And everybody here is working together to make sure lives get changed. There's no place for ego in that. There are no bosses here."

Kahfi understood, but he had to ask, "Why they put your name last?"

I shrugged. "FEEL Center sounds better than FLEE Center, I guess. To flee means to—"

"Run away," Kahfi finished my sentence, already knowing. "Y'all coulda been LEEF, though."

I laughed. "Mr. Fine's name *definitely* has to go first."

Damien Fine was the generous billionaire funding this place. As a former child abuse victim, this center was very near and dear to his heart. He didn't ask for anything in return when he agreed to be our primary benefactor. The least we could do was put his name first.

"But it might make you glad to hear that Mr. Fine is also—" I pointed at the dark brown skin of my arm, winking at Kahfi. "If you know what I mean."

His brown eyes just lit up. "Oh, for real? Where's his office?"

"He works from home. Mostly he just pays for everything around here."

"Oh, so he's *rich*-rich?"

I nodded, laughing again. "Very."

"That's the type of stuff I like to hear," Kahfi told me, declaring, "I'mma be rich one day, too."

I encouraged the little boy. "I'm sure you will."

That got a big smile out of him, and he had just about the cutest little dimples. This was not the kind of session I was expecting to have when I spoke to Rebecca this morning. Eventually, we wouldn't be in here having all this light conversation, but for now I knew one thing.

I had been speaking to Kahfi the entire time. His alternate personalities had yet to come out, which meant something very meaningful to me. You see, Kahfi's file said even the slightest bit of discomfort triggered him into splitting. If Kahfi got scared, offended, sad, or uneasy, Marron or Moreno would come out.

Right now, I was just talking to Kahfi.

So, although I hated to prove my coworkers right, it was obvious the child was very comfortable with me.

"Miss Latimore?" he said on his way out of my office. It didn't even bother me that he kept calling me *Miss* anymore. "When is my next session?"

That one eager question put me in such a happy place. Most kids at FEEL don't look forward to therapy. "Thursday. See you, Kahfi."

"Yeah," he agreed, his little dimples sinking in, waving as he stepped out. "See you."

# Chapter Twenty-Nine

## SHAUN

I spent the entire weekend thinking about her.

It's really the weirdest thing, to be so angry with someone, but to feel no desire to act on that anger. It didn't make any sense. Then again, when it came to her, most things didn't.

This past Saturday, Sanaa had the most extravagant proposal planned. A private chef-prepared dinner, a violin quartet, red roses and white candles decorating the entire boat deck, where I was supposed to re-propose. It was really beautiful, what she had prepared.

And I didn't use any of it. Not including the cost to get Sanaa to plan it all, that was thirty-five grand down the drain. I scrapped it at the last minute.

Arielle didn't know I was planning it, so the only people who had to know this was ever supposed to happen were me and Sanaa.

...and Caprice, thanks to my oh so professional event planner.

Seeing Caprice smile last Saturday was just as rewarding as it had always been. Then watching the way her smile faded as she remembered I was proposing to someone else that day was...

I'm not gonna lie, I didn't feel all the way bad that it disappointed her. Though it was never my intention to try to "get even" with Caprice, if my being engaged made her feel anything like I did while I was being ghosted for twelve years... *Good.*

But also *not* good.

Because I fucking hate to see her sad.

That's why it's never a fair fight with her. You can never win against someone if you don't ever want to see them lose.

That was part of the reason why I scrapped the re-proposal. There were other factors, too. Long before I ran into Caprice, I was struggling with the act of getting down on one knee and pretending this all mattered so much. Just for Arielle could get some pictures. Every time I thought about having to do it, I cringed.

Finding out Caprice, of *all* people, was the one who decorated my proposal site just made it all the more disgusting to me. If that wasn't a sign from God that I needed to pause a little on this plan to marry Arielle, then I was just being willfully stupid.

There were a lot of red flags flying in my relationship.

But Saturday's red flag was some next level shit. Saturday was the universe slapping me across the face and telling me to *really* fucking think about this.

Yeah, I wanted kids. Not just because my mother wanted grandchildren, but because I was ready to be a father. I was ready to start that chapter in my life.

Almost losing my mom didn't just scare me to death because I love her, it scared me to death because I realized if she died, I'd have *no one* in this world. What is a life if you have *no one* to live it with?

Sure, I have other relatives—aunts, uncles, cousins, grandparents—but it wasn't the *same*. They are related to me, but my mother is my true family. Even if she lived for thirty or more years, realistically she would *still* die before me.

So, I was ready to start my *own* family.

Arielle just so happened to be the woman I was seeing when I had that epiphany.

What happened on Saturday made me face just how important it is to love the woman in your life. Especially if you want her to have your child. There was no reason to be bringing children into this world, knowing damn well I would never love their mother.

My father, despite the fact that he died when I was four, loved my mother. I knew this because what he did for her, was the reason we had food in our kitchen and clothes on our backs. You really gotta love someone to make plans for how they can move on after you're gone. That kind of love makes a home feel warm.

I owed my future children that.

I owed them that confidence that comes from knowing your parents love each other. I didn't want them to ever worry about whether their parents were staying together. Because I could marry Arielle, but that didn't guarantee we'd stay married forever.

Hell, I barely wanted to be in this relationship *now*.

So, I didn't propose… *again*.

Seeing Caprice on Saturday wasn't the *only* reason I made that decision. However, seeing her did make me think long and hard about all the reasons why I should just wait. Waiting for what exactly?

I wasn't sure yet.

* * *

Since I was paying Sanaa twenty grand, I thought getting Caprice's number out of her would've been easy.

I was supposed to have sent her event planning payment an hour ago, but I thought maybe if I held off, Sanaa would call. I figured while I had her on the phone, I could work out some sort of trade.

When Sanaa ended up calling, she caught onto my game real quick.

And she was sure to let me know she wasn't amused.

"Are you holding my money over my head in order to get my best friend's number?" She asked first, putting it all out there in the open before she continued. "Need I remind you that while you made me sign an NDA, I made you sign an event planning contract. Just because you no longer want to re-propose to Arielle, doesn't mean I didn't plan it. *Run* me my money. Because, nigga, I will sue your ass so fast."

"You'd sue me, Sanaa?" I asked, a little bit entertained. Mockingly, I added, "I thought we were buds. It's just a phone number, *friend*."

"Aht-aht," Sanaa disagreed. "*You* are my future husband's friend. *My* loyalty is to my *real* friends—and you just so happen to be asking for the personal information of my closest one. If she didn't give you her number, then there's no reason why you should have it, Shaun. And you won't be getting it from Micah or from me.

You and I are *acquaintances* at best."

She cleared her throat and demanded, "Send me my money right now, or I will *fucking* sue you."

There was a pause and then she added some more.

"In case you didn't know, not paying me will nullify your NDA. Be aware that, since suing you won't be quick enough, I will be well within my legal rights to talk shit about your sheisty ass in my group chat. Using your whoooole ugly ass government name, too, Mr. Shaun *Bernard* Taylor. I've got a *lot* of friends in this city! And guess what? The woman you named *your boat* after is in my group chat, too. Because. Guess. Who. Has. Her. Number. Shaun? And I'm *not* giving it your raggedy ass! And you are *still* going to *fucking* pay me! You have five minutes."

She hung up.

Micah once told me he hated fighting with his girl because she could drag him like no one else could. I think I just got one of those drags. I wanted to be mad about it, but it kinda made me happy to know Caprice had a friend who would cuss my ass out like that while protecting her privacy.

Even though Sanaa going off on me was nothing new, it was the first time she ever talked to me like *that*. Caprice must've been very important to her. I didn't have her number in the end, but at least I knew Butterscotch was out here making solid friends.

I called Sanaa back.

"I sent you your payment. Do me a favor, Sanaa. Give my number to Caprice."

# Chapter Thirty

## Caprice

Although Kahfi left my office on Monday excited to come back, by Thursday he just wasn't feeling like talking.

I understood. Everybody has those days where they just don't want to talk. Kahfi walked into my office, pulled his feet up on my white armchair and said, "I'm tired today, Miss Latimore. Can I go?"

"Did you get enough sleep last night?"

"Yeah. I slept," he said. "I just feel really tired right now. Not sleepy, though."

I was eying his feet on my white chair, thinking about how I was going to have to get the dirt stains out after he left, when I noticed his shoes. Kahfi was wearing a pair of white high-top *Converse* sneakers, and at the ankle of the shoe, he had written the number twenty-eight. It reminded me of a boy I used to know who would write that same number on all his basketball shoes.

"Do you play basketball?" I asked him curiously.

Kahfi looked down at his shoes and then back up at me, realizing that's how I knew to ask him that. "Yeah… I play ball."

"And your number is 28?"

He shook his head. "Nah… 28 is for good luck. That's the number of the best player in the NBA."

"What team?"

"Miami Heat, of course," he answered, filled with hometown pride.

"Shaun Taylor?" I asked. Shaun had been playing for the Heat for two seasons and I had no idea until this past weekend. I hadn't been keeping tabs on Shaun for about four years now, and I didn't pay attention to sports news, so I had no idea he was living in the same city as me for two whole years.

After Saturday, I finally looked him up for the first time in four years. Not only was he playing for the Heat, but he was creeping into legend status these days. I wasn't surprised to learn this. I always knew he would be one of the best to ever do it. Even at eight, when I had no idea how basketball worked, sitting at that court in the city, I could tell that Shaun had talent.

My knowledge on the topic took Kahfi by surprise. "You know about Shaun Taylor?"

I had to chuckle at the irony.

"Yeah," I replied softly. "I know a little about him."

"S.T. is my inspiration," Kahfi told me, starting to warm up to me now that he was aware that I knew about something he liked. This session wouldn't be a dud after all. "He makes me proud to be from Miami."

I rose a single eyebrow.

"But he's not even *from* Miami," I revealed.

Kahfi made a face, not believing me. "You lyin'."

"Why would I lie?" I asked. "Shaun Taylor is from Parramore. It's a little neighborhood near Downtown Orlando. Far from Miami."

"How you know that?"

I shrugged, and just said, "I'm a fan."

Kahfi wrestled with the new information, ultimately crossing his arms and saying, "Well, then he makes me proud to be from Florida then."

I broke into a smile, shaking my head. "Can't argue with that."

* * *

My sixth session with Kahfi was on the last Thursday in July.

For about three weeks now, we'd been keeping our conversation light. I had yet to meet any of his other personalities, so I knew he was very comfortable around me. If I was going to meet any of them, I was going to have to trigger the child emotionally. I was starting to grow fond of him, so I wasn't looking forward to that.

Most of the bad things I knew about Kahfi's life were from reading his file.

Kahfi had a harsh upbringing. His birth mother got a life sentence when he was three, and he'd been in the foster care system ever since. When he was six years old, he was put in the home of newly approved foster parents, Hank and Bethany Rossi. For four years, Mr. & Mrs. Rossi subjected poor Kahfi to the most horrific sexual abuse I've ever heard of.

Kahfi's case made my own history look like a walk in the park.

To know the child, you would never guess the terrible things he'd been through. I suspected this was because Kahfi blocked the memories out. Trauma's effect on the brain is a fascinating thing. Humans are wired to do whatever it takes to survive. If forgetting all the horrible things that happened to you makes surviving an easier thing to accomplish, that's exactly what your brain will do.

Because of that, I don't think Kahfi remembers what Hank and Bethany did to him.

But his alternative personalities probably might.

That's why I knew our little lighthearted sessions were going to have to come to an end. I needed to make him uncomfortable. I had to trigger him and make him split during a session. I couldn't help him if I didn't know what troubled him. I needed to hear his full story, and to get the full picture, I was going to have to meet Moreno and Marron.

When he came in for his sixth session that Thursday, he looked a little bit sad.

"What's up Kahfi?" I asked.

"I don't feel like talking at all today, Miss Latimore. Can I go?"

"You don't?" I tried to keep my tone positive, because I didn't want to make him feel like he was doing something wrong. It's perfectly natural to not want to talk some days. It's just that skipping sessions was not an option. He had to spend the entire ninety minutes with me. "Well, what about play? Do you feel like playing?"

"Play?"

"The basketball court at the playground around back," I suggested. Behind the FEEL Center, there was a state-of-the-art private park built for the kids. "You and me, one-on-one. What do you say?"

I couldn't believe I was doing this. Before joining Kahfi at the court, I had to change out of my work clothes. I certainly couldn't play basketball in a black dress and white coat. Luckily for him, I would usually hit the gym after work, so I had athletic wear in my gym bag.

Kahfi was waiting at the center of the blacktop court in a plain white shirt and red basketball shorts. Tucked under his arm was a basketball. Once I was close enough, he asked me a question.

"You ever played ball before?"

Smiling, I was completely honest when I replied, "I've never played a single game in my life."

Kahfi looked at me with skepticism in his eyes, asking, "You tryna trick me into goin' easy on you?"

This made me laugh out loud. "I don't know—are we playing for money?"

"How you know how to play if you ain't never played?"

"I've watched almost a thousand games." I looked at my pastel pink nails, inwardly groaning because I *just* got this manicure three days ago. Praying to the nail gods to not break the acrylic, I accepted the risk, asking him, "You ready?"

"First one to twenty."

That would take too long, and I hoped to finish this session inside. "Five."

"*Five*? What is this? Preschool?" Kahfi was outraged by the number. He dribbled the ball casually, circling around me as he waited for me to raise the total.

"Ten, then."

"Fifteen," he bargained.

I was in the middle of accepting, but then I realized something. This kid was tall for eleven, but he was all of five foot three. I was *seven* inches taller than him.

Making a face, I asked, "What makes you think you'll be dunking on me fifteen times, kid?"

"Just because you're *eight* feet tall, doesn't mean you're better than me." That bravery reminded me of someone. His confidence, while adorable, only made me competitive.

"I'm about to humble you kid."

"You keep talkin'." He bounced the ball to me and added, "But let's see if you're still talkin' when I get to fifteen."

* * *

Kahfi was a very good ball player for his age.

He beat me fifteen to nine. By the time we were done on the court, there was a little under an hour left for the session. Straight off the excitement of beating me in a game, he seemed to completely forget he didn't want to be in therapy today.

It was easy to get him back into my office and start asking him questions.

"Kahfi, can I ask you a question?"

He was still smiling when he answered. "Sure."

"Where were you before you came to FEEL?"

I watched as his smile slowly faded into a frown. He blinked at me and squirmed in his seat. "I don't remember."

I hesitated to ask him my next question. "Do the names Hank and Bethany ring a bell?"

"Miss Latimore," his voice was hoarse, like he could barely get the words out. "Why are you… Why are you doing this?"

"Kahfi…" I didn't want to do this either. I could already see him beginning to panic from the way his breathing started to quicken. "I'm only trying to help you. And I can help you if I understand you. I need to hear your story."

His expression darkened, glaring. I watched those bright eyes of his turn monstrously cold. It was so unsettling. It was like, even though I knew this was the same child from five minutes ago, something was definitely different. He was someone else.

And when he spoke, even his voice was a little deeper—

almost menacing.

"I'll tell you my story if you tell me yours."

I paused, freezing up in my seat at the sound of how different his voice had become. A shift had occurred. "Who am I speaking with? Kahfi or—"

"Moreno," he revealed. *Ahh, the famed Moreno.* "Nice to meet you, Doc."

"What did you say to me before?" I grabbed my pen tightly, pressing it hard to the pad of paper I held at my desk. "My story for yours?"

"*Yup.*" He emphasized every letter in the word and then shrugged.

"What makes you think I have a story?" I asked.

Kahfi—or Moreno, I guess—cocked his head to the left, eyes scanning me the same way an adult might look at a child they've caught in a lie. I squirmed in my seat.

Silly as it might be, this eleven-year-old boy was making me uncomfortable.

"I see you," he said, fairly direct. "The way you keep your distance out there. Those crackers be all up on us, be all up on each other, stayin' in everybody's business. Not you though. You ain't never tryna give these kids hugs and shit. You stay in your office. You don't talk to *nobody*. You ain't like the rest of those friendly mothafuckas."

I could not believe these foul words were coming out of sweet Kahfi's mouth.

"What made you like that?" the little boy asked. He revised his question. "*Who* made you like that?"

"Kahfi—"

"Moreno," he corrected immediately.

"*Okayyyy,*" I said slowly. "Moreno, then. This session isn't about me."

"You don't like that shit, do you?" he questioned, an amused smirk growing on his lips, which highlighted his dimples. "It's uncomfortable, huh? Feeling like it's some random stranger walkin' around in your head and—" he looked at my note pad "—writing shit down."

Only the sound of my wall clock came with the silence that

followed.

I lifted my notepad in the air, making sure he could see me setting it down on the far corner of my desk along with my pen. Unbeknownst to him, the session was being tape recorded anyway.

Moreno just stared at me. Whether I wrote notes or not, he was just gonna sit there and stare at me. Time was wasting, and he was willing to spend the entire rest of the session staring at me.

"Moreno," I said after clearing my throat. He only blinked in my direction. "Can I speak to Marron?"

He grimaced, growing hostile. "Why you wanna talk to that *faggot*?"

My eyebrows shot up. "Excuse me?"

"I said—"

"No, no," I stopped him before he could repeat it. "I heard what you said. I'm just confused. What's all this animosity for Marron about?"

"That's none of your business, Doc." Moreno crossed his arms.

*Fascinating.*

Two alternative personalities… and they don't like each other.

"Does *Kahfi* like Marron?"

Moreno made a face like I had just asked the stupidest thing in the entire world. "Kahfi don't know about *us*."

Right. In a healthy human mind, a person might be professional at work and playful at home, but still be the same person. In dissociative identity patients, these personality changes become whole new identities.

So, using the same example, the professional personality and the playful personality become two entirely different people in the brain, and sometimes—like in Kahfi's case—the primary identity has no knowledge of the secondary identity.

Moreno, according to Kahfi's file, is a manifestation of all of Kahfi's aggression and anger. He's the rowdy one. Marron is a manifestation of Kahfi's sneaky, more cunning side. He's the tactical one.

"Where does Kahfi go when you're here, then?"

"To sleep."

"He blacks out?"

"Sure."

"Can you bring him back?"

"When I feel like it."

"You can control when Kahfi comes back?" He nodded, and I followed up with, "Can you control when Marron comes out?"

Moreno spoke slowly as he revealed, "I control *everything*."

*An alter with keys to the mind's control room. Interesting.* "So why do you let them have a turn at all? Why not just use this body all for yourself?"

"We all got jobs to do," Moreno revealed.

"Jobs?"

"Kahfi was here first. And he's a good kid." To hear him say that, if you listened to the recording, you would've thought I was talking to an adult, not an eleven-year-old. "When Kahfi has control, he makes us look normal to everybody else."

"Normal?"

"Kahfi's a regular kid. He don't cause no trouble."

"Well, how old are you then, Moreno?"

Moreno made a face, again looking at me like I was hopelessly stupid. "I'm the same age as Kahfi... *obviously*."

"But Kahfi is a kid and you're..."

"I ain't no kid," he told me. "I'm just Moreno."

"*Okayyyy*," I acknowledged, somehow understanding what he meant even though it didn't make much sense. "What's Marron's job?"

"Marron talks to women."

I coughed, choking on a breath, having not expected that answer. That wasn't how Marron was explained in Kahfi's file.

"He talks to *women*?" I was confused. "Is Marron a boy or a girl?"

"Marron is a boy," Moreno revealed. "But he's a *faggot*."

"I heard you the first time you said it," I rushed my response. "Let's not use that word, thank you."

"I said other cuss words and you didn't care."

"You can curse. This is a safe space. So, if you feel like

cursing… that's fine. But let's refrain from using slurs in my office."

Moreno thought about what I said, ultimately pointing out, "Cracker is a slur."

I paused.

"I called your coworkers crackers just five minutes ago," he reminded. "You didn't care about that neither."

I didn't have a response for that. The kid had me there.

Moreno laughed, understanding, "You must not like them."

"Back to Marron," I tried to change the subject as the child in front of me continued to laugh. "You said he talks to women. Why is that *his* job?"

"That ain't your business, Doc."

"I'm a woman," I pointed out. "So, can I talk to Marron?"

"He's real annoying," Moreno warned, eyes on me like he wanted to ask, '*Are you sure?*'

"That's fine. I'd still like to talk with him."

"Okay," Moreno replied simply.

"But before you go," I interjected before he could do whatever switcheroo mind thing he needed to do. "What is your job, Moreno? What do you do?"

The boy exhaled, and way too many years reflecting back in his eyes. Like this, he had the eyes of a person five times his age, with a hundred times the amount of pain anyone should have to face.

Moreno's answer was simple. "I keep Kahfi safe."

The vagueness of his answer left me with more questions than it answered. How did Moreno keep Kahfi safe? I wanted to ask, but almost immediately after he said it, I observed another shift happen in the little boy sitting across from me.

"Who am I speaking with?" I asked.

He didn't say anything at first. Instead, his posture got a little more relaxed, his little hand rising up to stroke the space beneath his chin, his right leg crossing over his left.

"Marron?" I asked.

"Mhm." The little boy sized me up and down. He sounded bored when he commented, "You look nice."

I was still wearing the gym clothes I'd played with Kahfi in, and I was a little sweaty, too. Even though it was a compliment, Marron's comment sounded sarcastic. He delivered it so condescendingly that it made wonder if I *actually* looked a mess.

"I'm Dr. Latimore," I introduced myself.

"I know who you are," he informed quickly, an attitude-heavy demeanor about him. "I see everything they see."

"They?"

He clarified, "Moreno and Kahfi. I hear everything they hear, too."

"So, you heard Moreno call you the F-word."

"Hmm..." The boy shrugged, unbothered. "I got a couple F-words I could call him, too..."

I rose a single eyebrow. These two personalities *really* had beef. "Like?"

"Foolish, failure, forgettable, forlorn, filthy, foul. Ooh—I got a double F-word for his ass: *future felon*."

"That's a great vocabulary for your age, Marron," I commended.

He accepted the compliment, adding, "That's why I do the talking."

"But only to women," I confirmed.

"Mhm..." Marron rolled his eyes, still stroking the underside of his chin. "Our future felon doesn't think men will *respect* me."

"And why's that?" I questioned.

"It's bigotry, baby."

My mouth fell open, and I had to quickly pick it back up. I absolutely did not want him calling me that again. "Doctor Latimore. Please."

"Mmm.. Aright, I see you, *Zoctor*."

*Close enough.*

"Why can't Moreno talk to women on his own? Without you?"

Marron giggled quietly to himself. "All that rah rah, macho man bullshit. I know you see it. He's a poor communicator. Women don't like that," Marron informed. "Women want somebody to talk to 'em... *soft*. Tell them what they wanna hear."

He said the last statement very slowly, his best attempt at sounding sultry. This was all starting to get *very* weird.

"Moreno talked to *me*," I pointed out. "I'm a woman."

"You keep sayin' that… like we can't tell you're a woman."

*I know this little boy did not just try me.* "I'm just saying… Moreno talked to me. So obviously he can talk to women."

"*Noooo*," he stretched the word slowly, just so we'd be clear. "Moreno can talk to *you*."

"I'm an exception to the rule," I realized.

"Decidedly so."

"Why me?" I asked.

Marron's eyes had that same sagacious quality that Moreno's eyes did, and I felt crazy for thinking of it that way—because they were technically the *exact* same kid.

But Kahfi's eyes didn't look like this.

"I think you know why, Zoctor," Marron mused cryptically. He leaned in from his seat, getting closer to my face. "Because you're broken, too. Just like us."

"That's enough." Leaning backward in my chair, I took in a deep breath, determined to not let this *child* take me back to that mental place.

"I can't answer your questions neither," Marron revealed after a time. "Moreno would never let me come out again if I told you our story before you told us yours."

"Ahh, I see," I understood, nodding, but knowing I wasn't able to give this kid what he wanted. "Can Moreno bring Kahfi back, if I ask him to, right now?"

Marron nodded. "He's the boss around here."

"Then, can I have Kahfi back?"

"You tired of me already?" Marron questioned.

"Of course not." I rose my wrist to show him the time. "The session's over."

The boy across from me stopped stroking his chin, uncrossing his legs. That bored look on his face faded away and a semblance of boyhood innocence returned to his eyes.

"Kahfi?" I checked.

"Yes, Miss Latimore?" He looked at me with confused eyes.

While I sat there speechless, that innocence was back in his voice when he spoke again. "You said my name. What is it?" he asked, completely unaware of the session we'd just had.

*So weird. Where does he go when his alters take over?*

Moreno's answer from earlier echoed in my head.

*To sleep.*

## *Chapter Thirty-One*

# SHAUN

It had been a little under a month since that encounter with Caprice.

Every day since then, my thoughts would always find their way back to her. Much like when I was a lovesick kid, Caprice was on my mind ceaselessly. The thoughts were persistent enough to drive a man on a search. At this point in my life, it would've been easy to track her down, but I didn't want things to go down like that. Our twelve-year gap in communication was her decision. To force myself into her life before getting any indication that she wanted me to—I couldn't.

I wouldn't.

Caprice is different. She's sensitive to that kind of thing. I couldn't just force myself on someone like Caprice. Not unless I was trying to scare her or provoke bad feelings. I would never want to do either of those things to her. Whenever she was ready to have a conversation, we'd have one. I knew it was very possible that she'd never be ready, but only time would tell for sure.

It was August $4^{th}$.

With just a few weeks before the official start of the 2018 NBA preseason, there were social events all over the city. A benefit dinner here, a back-to-school event there. My schedule was packed this month with non-basketball related shit, and it was all politics.

As a pro ball player, it's not enough to just play the game. You gotta do all the press walks, cut ribbons, kiss babies, you gotta be *that* guy—be a role model. It's a million people out there—old and young—looking up at me like some God. Even though I never asked for any of that, rising to that occasion was part of the job description.

That's why I often found myself at these charity events in

and around Miami. Usually I could get away with popping in, signing a check, and leaving, but tonight was a benefit dinner. Which was basically a dressed-up way to say a bunch of boring ass rich people, with nothing better to spend their money on, bought tickets to this dinner because they wanted to rub shoulders with celebrities and athletes. They wanted to feel important.

I couldn't just pop in and out. I had shoulders to rub.

Arielle was my date for the night. I hadn't asked her to be, but she was invited to this charity dinner as well. Since we were still in a relationship, going together was to be expected. It was the first time I was seeing her in three weeks. Arielle had been in Atlanta for almost a month, filming for a movie, and I… wasn't missing her.

Not that I usually did.

We were both pretty busy people, and if we spent too much time together it might dawn on one of us that our relationship is… not worth it. I'd been feeling that way a lot—especially lately.

Her thin brown arm was linked into mine, the wine-red color of her strapless ball gown matching my tie. We didn't plan that, and Arielle took the fact that we wore the same color to mean that we were "definitely soulmates".

The way hearing her say that irritated me couldn't have been normal. It was the kind of visceral reaction that might make a person wonder why I was even with her. It certainly gave me something to think about on the drive over here.

Arielle was wearing her hair natural tonight, which she knew I liked. I had a type. Arielle, like all of the women before her, was picked because she vaguely reminded me of someone.

She didn't look like Caprice facially, but they had a lot of the same attributes—they were both tall, with skin like rich mahogany, and jet-black hair that fell in coils to her shoulders. Though, Arielle didn't wear it that way often. When Arielle spoke, much like Caprice, her voice had that soft feminine cadence to it. After a couple of drinks, if you caught Arielle in the right lighting, she was almost as beautiful as Caprice.

Almost.

My girlfriend and I were seated at a table with a few familiar faces. My friend Micah and his fiancée, Sanaa, were already there when I pulled out Arielle's seat.

"Such a gentleman," Sanaa commented quietly, observing us.

Arielle didn't hear the sarcasm, so she just replied, "I know, right?"

Sanaa Montgomery, if you could look past the ugly ass personality, was a pretty enough girl; brown skin, a sharp asymmetrical haircut, big dark eyes that might've been cute if they weren't so judgmental. Sanaa had a friendly face despite how she actually was. Though, I couldn't blame her too much for how she turned out. Growing up with money all your life must have its defects. It was weird thinking the Caprice that I knew could stand to be around her for more than five minutes. They didn't seem all that alike.

But as Sanaa would remind constantly—she and Caprice were *best* friends.

It made me wonder if Caprice had changed a lot. Or maybe I just didn't know Sanaa like I thought I did.

At my table was another Heat teammate and his wife, making it a round table of six. Price per plate at this dinner had been a fortune. For charity, I realized, because you would've never known how much this dinner was by looking at the first course.

Arielle made conversation with our tablemates as she ate her salad. "Sanaa, I'm so glad they put us together. I've been meaning to get a hold of you. Shaun is going to propose any day now, and I'd love to have you plan my wedding."

Sanaa shot me a knowing look, understanding that "*any day now*", had already come and passed.

And I didn't do it.

As if she were watching someone who didn't realize they were doomed, Sanaa flipped the longer half of her bob behind her shoulder and smiled. "Soon as you get that ring, call me."

It was light conversation after that, with Sanaa sending me knowing glances every time Arielle spoke about our relationship. I wasn't exactly cheating on Arielle, but Sanaa was very aware that another woman occupied the space in my mind.

And unsurprisingly, Sanaa couldn't keep a poker face to save her life. To say that dinner was awkward would've been a monstrous understatement. There were surface level back-andforths across the table, Sanaa and my friend Micah being a picture-perfect couple without even trying, and Arielle feeling the need to compete for some reason.

If Sanaa brushed her hand over Micah's, Arielle suddenly felt the need to lay her hand over my lap. If Micah pressed a kiss to Sanaa's cheek, Arielle would look at me expectantly as if I suddenly owed her a kiss, too. When I wouldn't play into it, she would force the affection herself, pretending she had to tell me something important, and acting as if it absolutely needed to be whispered in my ear. It was all very childish.

I was embarrassed *for* her.

Nobody at the table was competing with my girlfriend. Sanaa and Micah were just that type of couple. They weren't performing for us, so it was embarrassing that Arielle felt the need to perform for them.

When Arielle and I first started out, of course there were things about her that I liked. Over the years, just watching how her personality changed depending on her audience, I would often wonder if I liked Arielle, or if I liked the character she played in our relationship. How she behaved changed so often, I could never really be sure who the real her was.

Arielle was in the middle of mingling with donors when Sanaa found me at the coat check. I was picking up Arielle's purse at the desk because we were getting ready to head out. I was done for the night, and Arielle had to be up early tomorrow morning for a flight back to her filming location.

Now that I had Sanaa alone, I had to ask.

"Did you give her my number?"

Sanaa's gaze darted across the room to my girlfriend, eyes concerned that Arielle might've heard my question somehow from fifteen feet away, separated by a crowd of dinner guests. "Your fiancée is in the room, Shaun."

Sanaa's reminder was thick with disapproval.

That disapproval explained why Caprice hadn't called. Sanaa must've not given her my number. "So, you didn't pass it on."

"I actually *did*," Sanaa informed. "Looks like she doesn't want to talk to you. My advice? Leave my best friend alone."

"Could you *stop* calling her that?" As petty as it was—it was bothering me. Caprice used to be my best friend, and even though she wasn't anymore, I hated having it thrown in my face so casually.

"What's the deal with you two anyway?" Sanaa asked curiously, leaning casually against the wall beside us. "I've known Caprice for, like, eleven years and she's never mentioned you. How do you two know each other? You spend a lot of time in Beverly Hills? You don't strike me as the type…"

I almost laughed.

*"Beverly Hills?" Is that where Caprice told her she was from?* "Is that where she's from?"

Sanaa nodded. "Her mom lives out there."

"Her *mom*?" As far as I knew, Caprice's mom is dead. "Are we talking about Caprice Latimore?"

"Duh."

"Caprice's mother is dead," I explained.

"Well, yeah… I know that," Sanaa huffed, annoyed that she had to clarify this. "I'm talking about Caprice's adoptive mother—Dr. Johnson. Obviously."

"Ohhh." I had no idea who that was. Nodding, I was beginning to understand the timeline. "I knew Caprice before she was adopted. So… Beverly Hills, huh?"

Sanaa nodded, biting down on one of her white nails nervously. Maybe she feared she was telling me too much. Sighing, she tried to change the subject, "I don't know where she was before Beverly Hills, and I don't pry. I'm not sure she'd like it if she knew I was discussing her life with someone this far back into her past. Caprice doesn't talk about her life before she was adopted."

*I bet.*

"I hope you realize I want to protect her just as much as you do."

Sanaa shook her head, like I was missing something. "I doubt that. After you left the yacht that day, it took me such a long time to get Caprice to stop crying. Eleven years of friendship and I've *never* seen her like that… And she wouldn't talk to me. She refused to tell me what you did to her."

*That's because I didn't do anything to her.*

"Seeing me upset her that much?" I questioned. Sanaa nodded, and I asked, "So, why'd you give her my number then?"

"*Becaaaaause…*" Sanaa said the word very slowly, smoothing the fabric of her yellow gown out. "When we were in college, Caprice never—and I mean never, ever—showed interest in boys. She didn't like them looking at her, touching her, talking to her, *none* of that. I thought she'd grow out of it as we got older, but she just… *didn't*. And then… I saw the way she looked at you." Sanaa shook her head, gesturing a hand my way. "And even *you*—asshole of the decade—you were so… *gentle* with her. That was so unlike you. If I didn't hate you, or whatever, I would've thought it was sweet how you didn't even hesitate to give her your shirt that day."

I only heard one thing. "She's been single the entire time you've known her?"

That wasn't good news to me. Hearing that actually kind of made me… *sad*. In all honesty, of course there was a part of me that liked the fact that I was her last, but there was an even bigger part of me that didn't like the idea of Caprice being on her own. If she was lonely, that didn't make me happy. I wouldn't have minded feeling replaced if it meant knowing she was never alone when she needed someone.

If Caprice didn't tell her so-called best friend about her life in Parramore, then there wasn't a doubt in my mind that she would sometimes get lonely. *Who does she turn to when she has nightmares? I know there must be nightmares.*

"Don't get too excited, Romeo," Sanaa pulled me out of my thoughts. "She clearly doesn't want your ass either. Or else she would've called." The woman in front of me shrugged, glancing at Arielle, who was still standing about fifteen feet away. "Can't say I'm surprised, though. Caprice doesn't strike me as the type to be any man's side piece." Trying to throw out hints, Sanaa gave me one last eyebrow raise before she dismissed herself. "Good night, Mr. Taylor."

* * *

I was already planning to do this tonight.

It had nothing to do with what Sanaa said to me at the

benefit dinner.

"You should sleep in your hotel room tonight," I told Arielle from the driver's side of my car as we drove under the streetlights of the city. As I pulled up to the curb of her bayside hotel, she squinted at me with confused eyes.

"You don't want me to spend the night?" Her hands came up and nervously moved her hair to one shoulder. "I wore that lingerie set that you like. I was hoping that maybe we could…" She gave a coy smile. "I gotta get on a flight, one thousand miles away, tomorrow morning, babe. How about we—"

I understood what she was implying, and I wondered if I was being too subtle. I didn't wanna fuck. I wanted to break up.

"Arielle, this isn't working for me."

She exhaled, that coy smile on her face fading. Her expression grew confused, her dark eyes meeting mine in the low light of my car. "What? Where's this coming from?"

"This relationship," I stated. "It's not… This isn't how I want to spend the rest of my life, pretending like what we have is good enough for me. You are Arielle *fuckin'* Underwood… You can do better than this relationship. Do you think this is love?"

"It's… working," she replied after thinking about it for a long time. "It's not storybook romance, but it's… realistic. I'm attracted to you; you're attracted to me. The sex is great, the conversation could be better, but neither of us are cheating, and… we look good together."

"We want different things."

"Tell me what you want then," Arielle stressed, wanting to make this work. "Tell me what you want, and I'll be that." I didn't say anything because my answer wasn't a *what,* it was a *who.* "You want me to stop taking so many roles? I can do that. I can make more time for us—for *you.* I want this to work."

Three years is a long time to be with someone, love or no love. It didn't make me feel good to have to tell her, "I don't want this anymore."

"You mean, you don't want *me,*" Arielle revised.

My hands slipped from the steering wheel in front of me. The white light from the streetlight overhead shined through the windshield to glimmer along the pool collecting at her eyes.

Breakups are so uncomfortable.

I hate seeing women cry.

"Yeah," I had to be honest with her. "That's it."

"You *proposed* to me."

"I shouldn't have," I replied.

"Is all this because I didn't say yes?"

"No." I shook my head. "I'm proud of you, Ari. The way I asked you in that hotel room—it was fuckin' disgraceful. The fact that you didn't say yes—I respect you more for it. If my heart was really in this, I would've proposed the right way the first time. You deserve that." I shrugged and then shook my head. "I just can't be the one to give it to you."

"If I get out of this car, I'm not coming back," she warned.

"Good." I nodded. "We had a pretty decent three years, but don't look back. I want you to move on."

Arielle opened the passenger's side door, pausing a bit to see if I'd try to stop her at all.

I didn't.

## Chapter Thirty-Two

# Caprice

"Mom, do you think I'm fixed?"

I could hear my mother's light laugh on the other side of our phone call.

"Now, little miss doctor," she talked to me softly. "You and I both know trauma doesn't work like that."

"But like…" I hesitated. "I told you about Kahfi, right?"

"And Moreno and Marron," she confirmed, laughing as she added, "And telling me was a total HIPAA violation, by the way, babe."

I smiled. Mom was right, but she was a psychiatrist, too, so it didn't feel like gossip. Even though it was a confidentiality breach, when I spoke to my mom about my patients, it was for guidance. That's it.

"His alters absolutely *refuse* to work with me," I complained. "I'm over here trying to understand this child and what he's been through, and like… I'm stuck."

I was pacing around my Downtown Miami apartment. The one-bedroom condo was in a fancy building, all the way on the thirty-sixth floor. My living room was just a wall of windows, overlooking the twinkling Miami skyline, too high up to capture any of the city noise. It was peaceful up here.

Except for the sounds of me whining to my mother on the phone.

"The kid wants to hear my survival story, in exchange for his, and I'm just like… Is it *that* obvious that I am a survivor of something, too? Like… I thought I was fixed."

My mother paused a bit before saying, "First of all, Caprice, being fixed isn't real. You can overcome, you can grow beyond the past, but trauma cannot be undone, sweetheart. Second, even if being fixed was real, you still wouldn't be fixed."

I stopped pacing. "You said I was one of your greatest achievements!"

"Sweetheart, you are!" she defended. "The woman you are today astounds me every time I see you. It's a far cry from the meek little girl I picked from the airport back in 2006. You are a *survivor*, Caprice. Even though you don't think so, you are *so* strong. You've coped with your past beautifully, but… you still fear it." She rushed to add, "And that's okay."

"I fear my past?" *So, I'm not fixed…*

"When you first moved out here, it was so important for you to separate from your old life in order to begin to heal. Eventually, when the healing started, you were free to revisit your history, to confront it head on. I knew you were strong enough even then. You just… chose not to. Which is fine. It's not my place to tell you what to do about your demons. But you even avoided the good parts of your past—like your friends. It was like you didn't want to be reminded. You chose to leave it all behind."

"Is that bad? Did I do something bad?"

"No," she told me. "You didn't do anything wrong, sweetheart. You did what you had to do to heal."

All that, and I'm still… "But I'm still not fixed."

"Almost finished is a better way to put it," my mother encouraged. "You're not almost finished."

This was supposed to be a conversation for me to vent, and now I was sitting on my living room sectional, getting therapy over the phone. "How will I know when I'm finished?"

"Well, for starters," my mother said. "You'll never *really* be finished. Mental health is an ongoing job, you have to keep working at it forever. But I'll tell you how to know when you're close… When a child asks you to tell your survival story, it won't feel like such a giant request," she advised and then informed, "The reason why it bothers you that Kahfi wants to hear your survival story is because… Well, *deep* down, you don't *feel* like a survivor." My mother made sure to tell me, "But you *are* a survivor, Caprice. You just need to feel it like I see it. But no amount of psychotherapy can give you that. That's a personal journey."

"If you were me, how would you make yourself feel it?"

After thinking about it, my mother asked, "Well, who scared you the most when you were a little girl?"

"Marcel," I confessed.

"Not him," my mother rushed past that one. There was a protectiveness in her voice when she added, "You never need to be around that man again. Someone else."

"Gracie."

"Mm-hm," I heard her hum on the other end. "If I were you… I'd pay Gracie a visit. I think you'll be surprised just how different you feel around her now that you're a woman. Sometimes the monsters we create in our mind – in our memories – are so much scarier than the real thing. Gracie could be that kind of monster for you."

"I don't have work tomorrow." It was Friday night. I thought about it. "It's a four-hour drive up to Orlando."

"If you drive up, you should have lunch with your sister," she suggested. "You know how much Kelly misses you."

I smiled at the thought. "I miss her, too."

"It's settled then," my mother decided. "You're going to Orlando. I'm with you every step of the way, sweetheart. Just a phone call away."

"I don't deserve you, Mom."

"Oh hush," she dismissed. Even though I couldn't see her, I knew she was rolling her eyes and smiling. "Love you. Good night."

"Love you, too."

* * *

Driving up to the pink house that Saturday morning was a surreal experience.

Parramore hadn't changed much. There were some differences here and there. The house across the street from the pink house was closed off around a fence now. It didn't look like anyone lived inside.

Parked outside of the pink house, I just stared at Shaun's old bedroom window, remembering the last time I was in that room. It had also been the first time I was in that room, too. In that bed.

It was a cherished memory of mine. I remembered how natural it all was when he touched me, how *good* it felt. If I closed my eyes, I could remember how happy it made me when he took my body in his hands, how gentle each kiss was against my skin, the way he made me feel so precious.

Shaun is the only man I've ever let touch me.

*Let.*

All throughout college, through most of my twenties, I never really felt the urge to let another man explore my depths. The memory of Shaun and me in his bedroom when I was sixteen was all I needed, if that was all I was ever going to get. Of course, I'm human, so there would be times when I would have instinctual needs, but men are…

Men are self-serving.

Not all men, of course, but a woman might have to go through several guys before she finds one who cares just as much about her body as he does about his own. I wasn't one for playing Russian roulette with my mental health like that. I wasn't sure what it would do to me if a man ever used my body as a tool to simply pleasure himself. It might trigger me to feel so used.

Shaun wasn't like that. Even twelve years later, I could still recall how giving he was when we were together that night. He made me the priority, not himself. It was so unselfish, so loving, so… perfect.

If that was the only consensual sexual experience I would ever have, I was okay with that. I had a feeling no other man would ever make me feel so cherished anyway.

Not like he did.

When I knocked on Gracie's door, there was no response. There was no white car in the driveway, and when I looked through the cracks in the blinds, I could see that there was no furniture inside. Nobody lived here anymore.

After doing a little digging around in the community, I got an update on Gracie and Marcel from the next-door neighbor, Madeline. Six years ago, Marcel had been sent back to prison for multiple counts of credit card fraud. Not too long after that, Gracie was put in a facility after being diagnosed with early onset dementia.

Gracie was in a shabby nursing home just outside of Metro West, about fifteen minutes away from Parramore. The place barely had any windows, looking like a prison in its own way.

I pulled into the parking lot and just stared at the red brick building. Now that dementia was eating her brain, would Gracie even remember me? If she didn't, would I get the closure I needed?

I unbuckled my seatbelt, killing the engine to my car.

"I'm here for Grace Elaine Latimore," I told the front desk clerk at the nursing facility. The lobby was cold and sterile, with a few chairs surrounding a low coffee table covered in magazines. In the far-left corner, a dusty screened TV played muted Lifetime movies.

"I'm her granddaughter," I explained after being asked what my relation to Gracie was. I was given a visitor's log to sign, realizing that in the five years she'd been here, I was her first visitor. While part of me was saddened by that, another part of me felt like she deserved it.

I was led down a long hallway of rooms. The facility was poorly kept; dirty floors, leak stains on the ceiling panels, flickering fluorescent lights, loud air conditioning vents. It was cold here. It didn't feel like a home at all. This place smelled like a hospital, but it wasn't nearly as clean as one.

The nurse that I was following knocked on a door twice before letting herself in.

She spoke to Gracie like how most people talked to children. "Good morning, Miss Grace. You have a visitor."

When she stepped out of the way so that Gracie could see me, I watched as the biggest smile grew on my old grandmother's face. Gracie was sitting in a wheelchair, looking like twenty-five years had passed instead of twelve. She looked so happy to see me.

As the nurse let herself out, I realized how far gone Gracie really was.

"Alice!" she called out to me excitedly.

She mistook me for her daughter—my dead mother. Gracie's decrepit arms stretched out for a hug, begging me to come closer. I didn't move. I just watched as the old lady tried to reach for me from her chair, trying to remember why I used to be so terrified of her.

She was so frail.

Even her voice was childlike and scared when she spoke again.

"Are you mad at me, Alice?" My brows dipped in confusion, not understanding the question at first. Gracie helped me understand when she said, "I tried to take care of her."

Wanting her to continue, I played along. "Of Caprice?"

"Caprice… your sweet-faced baby." Gracie shook her balding head of crinkly white hair. "I tried to do right by her."

"But did you?"

"Are you mad at me, Alice?"

I repeated the question. "Did you do right by her?"

Gracie was growing agitated. I could hear it in her voice as she argued, making excuses. "She made me call the police on Marcel. She got your brother put away for *seven* years."

"Why did you call the police on Marcel?"

"Because I wanted him out of my house… but I didn't know he was sellin' that stuff."

I interviewed her like a robot. "Why did you want Marcel out of your house?"

"Because…" she hesitated. "Because I thought he hurt her. I thought he hurt Caprice."

"Did he?"

Gracie brought her hands to her face, hitting at her temples, shaking her head like she was trying to empty her mind of all her thoughts.

"I don't know! I don't know!" Gracie whined, trying to take some of the heat off herself when she began to drag my name through the mud. "Oh, but you should've seen her, Alice! You should've seen how she grew up to be so fast."

"Was she?" I questioned flatly.

"I know so!"

"What makes you say that?"

"She was always running around with *that boy*. You know—

Sylvia's boy. You remember Sylvia. You two were just like sisters when you were girls."

I took a moment to process that information, pausing. Miss Sylvia knew my birth mother. They were friends. I always thought it was because I was close with her son, but was my birth mom the real reason why Miss Sylvia was always so nice to me?

"What if they were just close friends, too? Caprice and the boy."

"Not the way he would look at her," Gracie whispered.

"How did he look at her?"

"Like…" Gracie shook her head, disgusted by the memory. "Like the sun shined out of her ass. Like nothing else mattered."

"Maybe he loved her."

"Boys that young don't understand love," Gracie informed, brushing it off. "She was lettin' that boy play with her stuff. That's what he loved."

I exhaled, deciding not to argue with her about that. Shaun told me he loved me before he ever got to touch me. Gracie wouldn't understand. I brought back a question from before.

"Why did you want Marcel out of your house?" I asked again.

"Because I thought—"

"You thought?"

"Yes, I tho—"

"Maybe you knew."

"I didn't—"

"Yes, you did."

"I didn't know!"

"Yes, you did, Gracie!" When she didn't say anything, I continued, "Do you remember how you found her? Covered in all that blood?"

"I don't remember!"

"Yes, you do, Gracie!"

"Alice, stop it!"

"You know what he did to her!"

"Alice!"

"You knew he was touching her!"

"I didn't!"

"You took her to the doctor because you knew! You wanted a doctor to look at her and tell you what you suspected wasn't actually the truth!"

"She didn't want his help! Caprice screamed for me to make that doctor go away!"

"She was *eight*!"

"You weren't there, Alice!"

"I saw everything! I remember everything!"

"You don't know! You don't know!"

"You let him hurt her!"

"You don't know anything!"

"Say it, Gracie!" I screamed. There were tears streaming down my cheeks, but I didn't feel weaker for it. I felt strong as I shouted the words again. "Say it, Gracie! Say that you know what he did to *me*!"

Gracie's gaze seemed to gain a clarity to it, like she was seeing me again with a brand-new set of eyes. It was at this point that she realized she wasn't talking to the ghost of her deceased daughter. She was talking to me, the little girl that she brutalized for seven straight years in that pink house, with those lit cigarettes and those God-awful '*Say it, Caprice*' games.

"Nurse!" she started calling for help, looking at me with absolute terror in her eyes. Maybe she thought I was here to do to her what she'd done to me hundreds of times. "Nurse!"

I had no desire to hurt Gracie. She was a shell of her former self, and her former self wasn't much to begin with. When staff rushed into her room, I put my hands up to show I wasn't touching her. I backed up until the space between Gracie and I was big enough for her to stop screaming for help, big enough to be out of her room, big enough to leave the nursing home, big enough to be in the driver's seat of my car.

My mom was right.

Sometimes the monsters we save in our memories are scarier than the real thing.

## *Chapter Thirty-Three*

# Caprice

I had a very rough childhood.

But I survived it.

I overcame it, actually. An abused little girl from Parramore wasn't supposed to be in my position. And yet—here I was. Granted, I had help creating the me I am today—from Kelly, my mom, and from Sanaa—but the glue that put all the new pieces of my identity together had to come from me.

It was always my understanding that my adoptive mother saved me. I thought she took me out of a bad place and helped me grow into the person I became, but…

I've tried to recreate my journey countless times at FEEL. Most of the time, we can do for patients what my mother did for me, but there are always kids we can't save.

That's because you can give a victim every resource in the world, but that final push towards healing and self-acceptance… It comes from within.

Some people have it naturally—like me. By some miracle, I carried that will to survive in me for years, and the moment I could allow it to, my will to survive flourished. Some people, however, find that strength within themselves when they hear stories of triumph from others who are like them. They need to be inspired.

Like Kahfi.

I needed to be his inspiration.

He was sitting in my office that last Monday in August. For weeks, I'd been working on me for a bit, trying to build up the strength it would take to carry out this session. I was ready to be vulnerable with this patient. That's what he needed from me in order to feel safe enough to show his own vulnerability.

I could do that for him.

Sitting in that quiet all-white office, I looked at his little face and announced, "If you're listening, I'm ready to tell you my story."

Kahfi didn't say anything. He just stared.

"Kahfi?" The little boy across from me shook his head. "Moreno?"

He nodded.

"How are you feeling?" I asked him like I didn't just ask this boy the same thing when he walked in. But that boy was Kahfi. This one was Moreno.

"I feel really good. You've been treating Kahfi real nice."

"I like Kahfi," I told him.

"He likes you, too."

I was curious about something. "How did you know I had a story? Really."

Moreno shrugged. "When you talk to Kahfi—you say all the right things."

"Like?"

"I guess it's more what you don't say," Moreno told me, his bearing a little slouchier than Kahfi's usual posture. "When Kahfi first started seeing Dr. Emison, she told him '*What happened to you was terrible. It wasn't your fault.*' I didn't like that, so I came out and called her a dogfaced cracker."

Rebecca never mentioned the dogfaced part.

"Why didn't you like it when she said that?"

Moreno shook his head, his eyes turning pink, getting watery. He looked away from me as he spoke.

"Because ain't nothin' happen to Kahfi. He got to sit everything out. He watched it all from above. He didn't feel anything. He went to sleep."

I knew exactly what he meant. I've experienced that. That disconnect. When I was a little girl, I always used to remember my rape as an out-of-body experience. In my mind, there were always two Caprices in that moment, and I got to be the one who floated above. Who's to say that if Marcel had been given the opportunity to rape me more than one time, that I wouldn't have eventually given the second Caprice a name different from mine?

I was beginning to *really* understand why Moreno was here.

"Then who did it all happen to, Moreno?"

A single tear slid down his little cheek.

"Nothing ever happened to Kahfi," he repeated, still trying to sound strong. I understood even before he told me, "Everything… All of it. It happened to me."

Moreno's volatility, his anger, made all the sense in the world.

"Is that why you're so mean to everybody?"

He laughed a little despite his tears. "But I'm not mean to *you*, Doc."

"And I appreciate that," I said sincerely. "So… that was your job? Keeping Kahfi safe?"

He nodded, wiping his face. "I'll tell you what happened to me. But first, tell me what happened to you."

"If I tell you, will Kahfi know, too?"

He shook his head, patting his palm against his chest.

"Just me…" he paused, revising, "…and Marron's nosy ass."

I cracked a sad smile.

"Alright." I let out a long exhale. "When I was a little girl…"

* * *

Moreno sat in his seat angrily. "I wish Shaun didn't miss."

I shook my head, disagreeing, "I'm glad he did."

"Why?"

"His life would be so different now if he didn't."

"You mad at him for getting his ass whooped?" Moreno asked bluntly.

"Shaun was young, he had a young man's skill. Marcel became a broken man in prison. He was filled with a lot of darkness, filled with so much rage. Fights against kids your own size, on basketball courts, can't prepare you for that kind of fight. Part of getting older is understanding which fights are smart to pick, and Shaun… he was just a kid."

"You *really* think Marcel got raped in prison?"

"I know the vibes. So, I know he was. But even for him, I wish that wasn't the case," I said honestly. "It's a terrible thing, being raped."

"Yeah," Moreno agreed. "But he deserved it."

"Nobody deserves it." Moreno was quiet. Because he knew that was true. "Tell me, Moreno. What did Hank and Bethany do to you?"

You could hear a pin drop in the silence that filled that room. And then he spoke.

"They did everything," he told me. "Whatever they wanted." He swallowed hard, wiping his face before he continued to tell the story. "They started touching Kahfi when he was six. Just touching. Then… it got serious. The first couple of times, Kahfi would just black out. He'd block it out in his mind so good, he'd be back at school the next morning like ain't nothing happened. And then when he couldn't black out anymore… his mind just… split into three different parts. Moreno. Marron. Kahfi. It was my job to deal with all the scary stuff, all the nasty stuff, all the painful stuff. I had to do it so that Kahfi wouldn't have to. I think that's why I get to choose which of us three comes out."

I tried to keep my breathing steady as I continued to probe. "And Marron? What was his job?"

"Bethany liked to play these mind games with Kahfi. She'd take him out to lunch, buy him all this shit. And then she'd say things like, '*You see how me and Hank treat you so nice?*' and I never wanted Kahfi to like her, so I would send Marron out," Moreno explained. "Marron would accept all her gifts, all her little trips. He was *best friends* with that bitch."

Moreno was getting angry just thinking about it. I could see it in how the fire blazed behind his eyes, in how he gripped the white arms of his chair tightly. He continued to tell me everything. "Marron told Bethany whatever she wanted to hear. If she asked him if he liked what she and Hank was doing to us, he would gas her up. He made her think what she was doing was okay. He would say shit like—'*It feels good.*' '*I like it.*' And so, she and Hank would just keep doing it. But Marron's sneaky ass knew he'd never have to stay for the hard part. That was my job."

I nodded, understanding why the two personalities were so

at odds. Though, in his own way, Marron could've just been doing what he had to do to keep Kahfi safe, too. By telling his abusers what they wanted to hear, Marron could've been the reason why Kahfi was even still here.

Hank and Bethany, as evil as they were, would've likely killed Kahfi if Marron hadn't been the one to tell them what they were doing was alright. It was Marron who made Kahfi's abusers feel safe enough to keep Kahfi alive.

Moreno might've hated him for it, but I understood what Marron was doing. They all had their jobs, and Marron was just doing what *he* had to do.

But I wanted to know something.

"If you didn't want Marron telling Bethany what she wanted to hear… why didn't you ever talk to her yourself?"

Moreno breathed heavily, shaking his head and blinking back tears. "'Cause I was scared of her. I was so scared of both of them."

"You were scared of them, but you kept coming out for the worst of it."

"I did what I had to do. I had to protect Kahfi."

"But who protected you?" I asked.

Moreno shrugged, staring out into space before replying, "*Nobody*. I wasn't like you. I didn't have a friend like Shaun."

Despite my best efforts to keep them at bay, tears slid down my cheeks.

"But you have a friend like me," I told him.

"You gon' protect me now, Doc?"

"I will. I promise I will," I answered.

"Yeah," he believed me, "I know you will." He looked at me with tears pooling at the rims of his eyes. "I just… I just wish I'd known you sooner."

Upon hearing that, it took everything I had to not break down. I needed to be strong for this child. Like me, Moreno also tried to collect his composure, wiping his face and sitting up straight.

Like a little soldier.

Moreno was the one who told me what the next step needed

to be.

"Protect me now by keeping Kahfi safe. You have to make *him* happy. You have to make sure he's safe. If Kahfi is happy, then me and Marron don't never need to come out. That's the way." Moreno looked at me like someone getting ready to say goodbye, tears still streaming down his little face. "Me and Marron were never supposed to be here in the first place."

## Chapter Thirty-Four

# SHAUN

I got a call from an unsaved number on the last Monday in August.

It was her. It had to be. The only people who had this number were my closest friends and family. It was the number I told Sanaa to give to Caprice.

I was in my bathroom when I got the call. It was a little after eight o'clock in the evening. I'd just gotten out of a nine-hour day at the training gym. With the season a few weeks out from starting, it was time for me to get back into game mode.

I had just finished emptying a cooler of ice into my bathtub when my phone started to vibrate on the bathroom counter.

An unsaved number.

I picked up on the fourth ring.

"Hello?"

Her greeting was so familiar, as if the time between us had been twelve days—not twelve years. "Hi, Shaun."

There was something about the sound of her voice that just twisted my insides. I can't say that it was a bad feeling, but it wasn't a good feeling either. I thought about how I wanted to pick up a ringing phone for more than a decade and hear that voice. Now I had nothing to say.

She let out a slow exhale from her end. Nervous; she was nervous.

"Can I ask you for something?" she inquired apprehensively. She spoke to me like she feared I might hang up at any moment. Didn't she know that even now, even after all this time, she could ask me for anything? Of course, I felt conquered for knowing this, knowing I couldn't say no to Caprice Latimore even though I had every right. Did it make me a weaker man? Maybe.

But so what?

What did I stand to gain from making her unhappy? Nothing.

"I'm listening."

She hesitated a bit before she spoke again. "I, um… I have this kid—"

That took me by surprise. "You have a *what*?"

"One of my patients," she rushed to clarify. My tense muscles relaxed. "He's just about the sweetest eleven-year-old boy you'll ever meet, Kahfi. He's a really, *really* big fan of yours and it would just mean the world to him if he could meet—"

"I'll do it," I agreed before she could finish.

"Really?" She was in disbelief. Perhaps she didn't think it would be so easy.

"Really," I assured. "There's a back-to-school event at the arena this Thursday. I'll see if I can get you a couple passes. Just text me the address you want 'em sent to."

"Oh my God, that is so nice of you. I *really* can't thank you enough," she gushed like anybody else would, making me feel like I was doing a fan a favor, instead of an old friend. I hated that. "Thank you, Shaun."

The words *'you're welcome'* were frozen on my tongue. I didn't say it, but I waited, thinking she might have something else to say. Caprice was quiet on the other end. An awkward silence crept in.

"Is that all you have to say to me? Seriously?" I didn't mean to sound as irritated as I did. I just couldn't help it. Even then, Caprice didn't say anything, staying silent a little longer. I watched the ice in my bathtub melt for a few minutes before she finally spoke up.

"*Soooo…*" She stretched the word uncomfortably, sounding as if she'd rather be doing anything else but this conversation. "…how've you been?"

"Never mind." This wasn't going to work over the phone. Whatever that weak ass attempt was, I was over it, and I didn't have enough patience to act like she wasn't pissing me off. "Just text me the address to send the passes to. Good night."

That sorry excuse for a phone call had me aggravated for the remainder of my night. I skipped the ice bath and headed for the kitchen. During the season, I don't drink or smoke no matter how stressful the pressure of the game gets.

Luckily for me, the season hadn't started yet.

The phone conversation with Caprice was four minutes and thirty-three seconds, and I already needed a drink. She's a tough road to navigate. Caprice is the only person I know who can clearly be in the wrong, and still not provoke me to go off. There was a lot of tongue biting necessary when dealing with her.

First phone call in twelve years, and all just to ask me for a favor. That's it.

If she had been anybody else, I wouldn't have hesitated to remind her that I don't owe her a *goddamn* thing. I didn't owe Caprice Latimore *shit*. I didn't have to do her favors. I didn't have to meet her fuckin' patients. I didn't have to go out of my way to get her VIP passes to a sold-out event at the arena, either.

But that's exactly what I was gonna fuckin' do.

And that's what pissed me off the most; knowing that even in the face of her bare minimum ass efforts, I was still going above and beyond. It made me feel like the world's most pathetic simp. Caprice was the only woman in my life—past and present—that could make me act this way.

And I hated it.

But at the same time… I wouldn't have had it any other way. After all, what did I stand to gain from making Caprice unhappy?

Nothing.

"Whiskey on a Monday night," my mother noted the drink in my glass when I took a seat on the living room sectional. She was stretched out over a bright pink yoga mat on the living room floor, following an intermediate yoga routine on the flat screen. As she stretched, she sarcastically guessed, "You must be having a *great* day."

"I skipped the ice bath," I told her, downing half my drink, inserting my own sarcasm when I added, "So I'm about to have an even better tomorrow."

After a nine-hour day of training, if I didn't get my body in some ice water right away, I was gonna be sore *as fuck* in the morning. But I couldn't focus on submerging myself in a freezing tub right now. Fuck that—I needed this glass of whiskey more.

My mother smiled a bit, shaking her head as she continued to do her yoga tape. Dressed in a pale pink tracksuit and a matching turban, Mom was the only dose of female energy in this house. It was hers to reign over. The place was mine in name, but hers in spirit.

If it were up to me, I would've lived downtown, closer to the arena, but she liked the quiet seclusion of our private neighborhood near the ocean. It fit in nicely with her new lifestyle of meditating and yoga and plant-based eating.

For my sake, Mom was trying her best to live forever.

"Why are you brooding?" she asked curiously.

"I'm not brooding."

She hit me with an extra sarcastic, "Sure."

Unable to let it go, I asked her a question. "If you hadn't spoken to someone in years, would you let the first time you talk to them be to ask for a favor?"

"Ahhh," she understood immediately, laughing to herself as she continued to stretch. "*That's* why you're brooding. Did you do the favor?"

"Yeah."

She laughed even harder, almost falling out of her current yoga pose.

I asked, "What's funny?"

"You." She shrugged. "Her." My mother shook her head. "Both of you."

I wasn't as amused. "I don't get the joke."

"It's just funny, is all." My mother sat with her legs crossed and shrugged again. "Twelve years later and she's still got you wrapped around her little finger." She smiled brightly, way too entertained by all of this. "I wonder if she realizes how powerful she is. You gotta admire it."

"You're supposed to be on my side," I reminded.

"Baby, I'm always on your side."

"You don't sound like it."

"Well, I'm on her side, too."

Feeling childish, I pointed out, "Mom, you can't be on two sides."

"Who says I can't?" she asked confrontationally. There was a mischievous glitter in her eyes as she looked my way. "Watch me."

* * *

## Caprice

Shaun had two VIP passes delivered to The FEEL Center less than twenty-four hours after our phone call.

I hadn't thought of what I was going to say to him after getting him to agree. In fact, while practicing my pitch before I called, I never imagined it would be so easy. I thought he was going to take a lot more convincing. I was fully prepared to list every positive attribute about Kahfi, to really persuade Shaun into meeting him.

Shaun didn't even hesitate. He didn't even wait to hear the rest of my prepared speech.

He just said yes.

No questions asked. Without asking for anything in return. I was so surprised. Maybe I shouldn't have been.

And then we just sat there on the phone. It was uncomfortably quiet. Shaun asked me if I had anything else to say to him, and when I realized I didn't—I panicked. This wasn't supposed to be our *"it's been twelve years, but how are you"* conversation. I wasn't ready for that yet. I was never going to be ready for that conversation.

Sanaa had given me Shaun's number over a month ago. I could've called at any moment between then and now, but I didn't. You see, I didn't have a good enough explanation for my decade-long silence, and I feared confronting him. Shaun was engaged anyway, so was there even much left to talk about? The best I could've asked for was his forgiveness, and I didn't deserve his forgiveness. So, I didn't call.

But for Kahfi, I dialed that number and waited. Shaun was his idol and meeting his idol would make that kid *so* happy. I called Shaun for Kahfi.

To my surprise, getting Shaun to agree was easy. It was what came after that made me squirm in my bedroom uncomfortably.

Shaun sounded so annoyed with me when he said, *"Is that all you have to say to me? Seriously?"*

And he had every right to feel that way, to be irritated. The first time I called him in twelve years, I asked him for something, and then I had nothing to say. I could tell he was pissed off at me when he said good night.

Even still, when I walked in to work the next morning, there were two VIP passes for a Miami Heat back-to-school event waiting for me in the mailroom. One for me, one for Kahfi. The event was on for this Thursday; August 30th, 2018.

When I told Kahfi, he didn't believe me. The part of him that was aware that I even knew Shaun Taylor was locked away in the mind of a different personality. Moreno knew my history. Kahfi did not.

Years of intensive therapy might allow Kahfi to someday merge his separate identities, ultimately allowing the parts of him that he calls Moreno and Marron to simply be Kahfi, too. By doing that, however, he would be taking on a lot of unwanted memories, so I would never pressure him to do it. Kahfi could reconcile his personalities whenever he was ready. It might never happen.

Though, there was a part of me that hoped for him to heal to that point.

I adored Kahfi, but I also adored his other identities. If they ever merged into one being, Kahfi wouldn't just be fixed. Nobody ever gets *fixed*. In the words of my mother, he'd be *almost* finished. Mental stability is an ongoing job, so Kahfi will have to keep working at it forever. With me, though, he'd never have to do it alone.

Shaun sent a car to pick us up from FEEL that Thursday. I hadn't been expecting that. The arena, like my job, is in the city. Kahfi and I could've walked. We were actually going to, but when we stepped out, a black car was waiting outside the building. A driver was holding up a small poster board, *Dr. Latimore* written in black marker across the middle.

It was a bit much for a three-minute car ride.

But Kahfi loved every second of it. His excitement was infectious. We pulled up to the side entrance of the arena, ushered past a security checkpoint that pulled beside an empty curb. None of the other event attendees were coming in this way. The alley was mostly deserted except for a few employees shuffling in and out of the building through what looked to be employee-only doorways.

"Are we in the right place?" I asked our driver after looking out the window.

He nodded. "Yes, Mr. Taylor said he'd be meeting us out here. I'm sure he'll just be a minute."

"Oh." I hadn't realized Shaun was escorting us inside. Obviously since we were here so that Kahfi could meet him, I knew I'd have to see him eventually. I just didn't think...

Out from the double doors of the arena's side entrance stepped a gorgeous spectacle of a man. I could sense Kahfi practically buzzing with excitement as he saw him, but I could barely hear the kid. My attention was elsewhere.

Shaun looked *so* good, dressed in one of those official Miami Heat courtside tracksuits. Standing tall at about six-foot-five, it took me a minute to draw my eyes up from his pair of crisp Nike sneakers, up his long legs, over his broad shoulders, and by the time I got to his handsome face, he was already reaching to open my car door.

I don't know how long I stared before I finally got out of the backseat. I could feel Kahfi slip out behind me, eager to meet the man who was staring down at my face. It was Kahfi who cut into the long stretch of silence, coming in between Shaun and I and sticking out a hand for him to shake.

"Hi, I'm Kahfi Williams," he beamed as Shaun crouched a little and reached for his small hand. A hint of a smile was blossoming on Shaun's face. Kahfi pointed at his white shoes, where he'd written the number twenty-eight at the mouth. "You're my favorite. You make me proud to be from Florida, sir."

Shaun chuckled a bit at the child's enthusiasm. "Do I? Well it's nice to hear that *somebody* is proud to be from Florida."

Unable to help myself, I brought up a hand and covered my smile. This small bit of movement caught Shaun's eye and his smile faded as he straightened out his posture, tone very serious when he greeted me.

"Hello, Dr. Latimore."

The formalness behind it rubbed me the wrong way. It wasn't disrespectful. In fact, it was almost too respectful. It was like Shaun was talking to a stranger. I didn't like that. Suddenly, I found myself wondering if I looked pretty.

I wondered if my twistout was too big. Was my Ruby Woo lip color still on evenly? Why didn't I check my makeup before we left? What if I looked a mess? Did I look too doctory right now? Should I have left my white coat at work?

Almost too late, I realized I had to say something back. I responded with an equally formal, "Mr. Taylor."

Involuntarily, Shaun made a face at my tone, clearly just as bothered by my formality as I had been bothered by his.

"Damn," he said in response to the ice behind my voice, visibly taken aback. "I can't even get a '*hello*, Mr. Taylor'? It's like that?"

*I was just matching your energy*, I wanted to tell him. *Ohhh, he can dish it, but he can't take it.*

"Hello, Shaun," I gave in, still trying to be serious.

He broke into a smile, dazzling me before trying again. "Hey, Caprice."

I didn't think it could happen, but the air between grew noticeably warmer after that. Shaun turned his attention back to the boy between us, urging for him to follow closely. He led us in through the side entrance of the arena. The only people back here had nametags and walkie-talkies. We must've been backstage somewhere because I could hear a crowd and a speaker on a microphone once we were inside.

Shaun offered Kahfi snacks from what was undoubtedly a staff-only table, urging for us both to follow him through a double door that opened out to a long black hallway. The longer we walked down the hallway, the louder the crowd got. People greeted Shaun as we walked past, some dapping him up, with one staff member wondering who I was.

Shaun introduced Kahfi Williams, his special guest, and then me as Kahfi's doctor.

If he was trying to irritate me, it was working.

When we finally got to the end of the hallways, a new set of doors opened out to a professional basketball court and a crowd of thousands. They couldn't see us, but we could see them. Every seat in the arena was filled with children and their parents. Sitting courtside were about a couple hundred attendees with the same VIP passes around their necks. There was only one available courtside seat.

Shaun crouched a bit to level out his height with Kahfi's pointing to the last empty chair courtside, telling Kahfi that seat was his. I watched as Kahfi ran to it. When Shaun came back up, his eyes glanced at me briefly before sidestepping over to my side.

He explained, "The event was sold out, and that was the last seat. That's okay though, right? Or do you mind standing back here with me?"

All I could think about was how nice he smelled. Standing this close, it wasn't hard to pick up on the soapy scent of his skin; and maybe there was a hint of cologne there, too. Whatever it was, I didn't mind standing next to it.

"I don't mind standing..." For some reason, my heart was thumping. "...with you."

A subtle half-smile turned up one of Shaun's cheeks.

The event went on smoothly. One speaker after another taking center court with a mic in their hands, speaking motivationally to the listening students, hyping them up for the new school year. Shaun and I stood back where the lights couldn't quite reach, me watching Kahfi, and out my periphery, feeling Shaun watching me.

"You haven't changed a bit," he commented lowly as the event went on.

*Is that a good thing?*

"I don't know," I halfway disagreed, drawing my head up to look at him. Along his jaw were the dark hairs of what might've been one missed shave. Shaun didn't have that much facial hair when we were kids. I suddenly felt the urge to take his chin between two of my fingers and draw his angular jaw closer to my lips. "I think I've changed. I feel different."

"You look practically the same," he told me and then his eyes traveled down the length of my body, and then back up to my face. He was checking me out. "Except now your clothes are more expensive."

I looked down at my beige wrap dress underneath my white coat. He wasn't wrong. The dress was designer.

For a while, Shaun and I just listened intently as another guest speaker took the floor. Even though Kahfi wasn't technically in a traditional school, each speaker had such a motivational message for the school year, and I hoped he was internalizing it. Online school or not, Kahfi was too smart to not get good grades. I was glad he was here, getting motivated.

I thanked Shaun again for the invite. "Thank you for doing this for Kahfi."

Shaun's arms were crossed in front of him, standing sturdy, the outline of his muscles through his clothes making him look so solid. Damn, I couldn't remember the last time I wanted so badly to touch a man—to touch anyone, really. He shot me a look, a single eyebrow pulled up, expression unamused. "Don't be cute, Caprice."

I tried not to smile and revised my previous thank you. "Alright, alright… Thank you for doing this for *me*."

He shook his head, a hint of a smile in his eyes before he replied, "You're welcome, Dr. Latimore."

*Are we flirting or fighting right now?*

"You're mad at me," I guessed.

"I'm not."

"Something is bothering you," I tried again. He only looked at me, his eyes saying what his mouth did not—'*You have got to be fuckin' kidding me.*' I couldn't read his mind, but I didn't need to, to know that this was what he was thinking. "Shaun, I—"

"Don't do that," he warned.

"What?"

"That thing," he said vaguely. "*That thing* with your voice."

"*What thing?*"

"You're doing it *right* now," he divulged. Shaking his head, he told me, "We don't have to have this conversation here. You have a kid to watch over after this. We'll do this later."

"Later?" *There's a later?*

"I have your number," he reminded, nodding as he confirmed, "So later."

I bit my lower lip nervously.

"It's gonna be bad, huh?" He rose an eyebrow at my question. "Our conversation, I mean. You don't want to do it right now because you know it's going to be bad."

Shaun was very blunt when he explained, "You cry easily. We can't do it here and now because Kahfi is having a great time, and if you start crying, you'll ruin his night." My eyes started to feel prickly already, proving his point. "See? Look at that."

As if he knew this would happen, Shaun pulled a napkin from his pocket and handed it to me. Was I really that predictable?

"You haven't changed a bit," he repeated himself from before, but it took on a whole new meaning now. I was a crybaby when I was kid, too. Very subtly, I could see the tip of Shaun's nose turning rosy. "And I still hate it when you cry."

"I cry when I'm uncomfortable," I explained.

"I make you uncomfortable?" It wasn't hard to hear how offended he was.

I shook my head quickly. *You make me feel guilty. And feeling guilty makes me feel uncomfortable.* "*You* don't make me uncomfortable, Shaun." I swallowed the lump forming in my throat. "You'll never make me uncomfortable."

His shoulders relaxed a bit.

"Breathe," he told me. "Dry your eyes and breathe. We'll do the uncomfortable shit some other time, okay?"

I nodded, knowing deep down he was going too easy on me. "Okay."

* * *

I was turning twenty-eight tomorrow, Friday, on the thirty-first day of August.

If Shaun remembered this, he made no mention of it. Honestly, I couldn't be mad if he forgot. So much time had passed, and it would be conceited of me to expect him to remember my birthday.

Even though I still remembered his. It wasn't a hard one to remember—his birthday was always the day after mine, September first. This year he was turning thirty, but I would've never guessed if I didn't know him.

Of course, Shaun looked older than how I left him at eighteen, but if I'd never met him before, even now I would've guessed he was in his mid-twenties. He looked so *good,* all chiseled and gorgeous. I really couldn't get over how fine he was, how tempted I was to touch him from looking at him alone. To think I used to love this man for *just* his personality, barely acknowledging the fact that he was literal perfection.

We were still at the arena. The event had been long over, but Kahfi wanted to stay behind with the other VIP kids and play on a real professional court. Practicing for the real thing someday, he said when he asked if we could stay. How could I say no to that? Like Kahfi, most of the kids with VIP passes were children with particular connections to players on the team.

Shaun and I sat side by side on the now empty courtside seats, both of us watching Kahfi play with the other kids. We watched as Kahfi made a shot from the three-point line, his head whipping around the room and looking for me immediately.

"Did you see what I just did, Miss Latimore? Did you see me?" he shouted excitedly. I couldn't help the proud smile that spread across my face as I shot the kid a thumbs up, telling him he was doing great.

From beside me, Shaun made conversation, leaning in a little closer. Shaun was never all that good at giving me my personal space, but I didn't mind then, and I didn't mind now.

"He's better than I was at that age," Shaun commented.

I smiled, unsure in my heart why hearing that filled me with so much pride. I added, "He's taller than you were, too."

Shaun laughed at my candor.

"Why did you just bring him?" he asked curiously, as we watched Kahfi play. "And none of the other kids."

"He deserved a day all about him," I sighed, having decided to make it my personal responsibility to keep this child happy. "Just Kahfi."

"Can I ask you a weird question?" Shaun asked, something about his tone reminding me of the him I used to know. I snuck a quick glance at him.

"Go ahead."

There was a long pause before Shaun pushed out a long exhale and asked, "Is he mine?"

I nearly swallowed my own tongue, almost choking on nothing but the air I was breathing. Pulling all the way back in my seat, I looked at Shaun like he was crazy.

"No! What the f—" I was absolutely bewildered. "No, he's not *yours*! Why the hell would you ask me something like that? Where *the hell* did that come from?"

"Yo," Shaun put up his hands like someone being held up by the police. "I was *just* checking. He has the same look in his eyes that you do. And he's obviously some kind of basketball prodigy in the making."

"He's a talented basketball player, so that means he's yours? That's really *fucking* arrogant, Shaun!" Shaun only shrugged at the criticism. I added, "And *what* look in my eyes?"

With him, I was comfortable enough to be this ill-tempered. I was snapping at him like our days as high school sweethearts were yesterday. It was easy to talk to him this way, like the time between us hadn't made much of a difference.

Shaun brought out a level of comfort in me that I just couldn't explain. There was just no way we could behave like strangers. We used to be best friends... And it was only a matter of time before we started acting like it.

He got a little bit closer to whisper, "That wise... *'I've seen a lot of shit'* look in your eyes."

"Well—" I shook my head with a humorless laugh. "—he's a trauma survivor in intensive psychological therapy... So yeah, *just* like me."

Shaun squinted, not finding that funny.

"You have a dark sense of humor," he commented.

"That's the only kind of sense of humor people like me get to have."

He rose an inquisitive eyebrow. "People like you?"

I just looked at him blankly for a minute, finally offering

clarification. "Doctors. Doctors are known for their dark senses of humor."

He sighed, relieved to know that's what I meant. A moment later, he was chuckling, shaking his head. "You're a trip."

I chose to ignore him. After a bit of silence, Shaun nudged my shoulder with his own, a gentle tap meant to call my attention back to him. Even now, it didn't feel strange for him to touch me. At least—not strange in a bad way. There was definitely a jolt of electricity that shot through me at the first tap, and the part of my shoulder where he bumped was still warm.

I turned to face him, giving him my full attention as he pleaded his case.

"Come on, can you really blame me for asking? The last day I saw you before you disappeared, we had sex," he reminded casually. My cheeks grew warm at the memory. "If I'm not mistaken, I didn't have a condom. Until recently, I hadn't seen or heard from you in nearly twelve years. Kahfi's *eleven* years old. And I feel like if you mixed my characteristics up with yours a little bit, he—"

"You need to stop."

"He looks like he could be ours. Don't tell me you don't see it," Shaun argued with an amused smile, determined to not seem crazy for thinking this up.

"I don't see it."

He urged, "If he's ours tell me now—"

"You're ridiculous."

"—because I'll step up," he finished.

"Shaun, he's *not* my kid. He's not *your* kid either."

"I swear you can tell me if he is."

At this point, I was just laughing, explaining, "Good lord, I have his birth certificate at The FEEL Center right now that proves who his birth mother really is."

"And it's not you?" he tried to confirm one last time, and at this moment I realized he was only doing this because he was enjoying the reaction it was getting out of me.

"It's not me," I promised with a shake of my head. I lifted a pinky. "Pinky promise."

Shaun took my pinky into his and they linked. He lingered a

bit, but then again—so did I. We sat there, side by side, pinkies hooked together, looking into each other's eyes. For the briefest moment, I thought about what would happen if I leaned in and closed the distance between my lips and his.

It was Shaun who took me out of that headspace when his voice emerged to break the silence.

"So… uh," he started conversation up again. "You play favorites."

"What? No, I don't. I treat all my patients the same." I finally let go of his pinky, part of me not wanting to be dishonest in the middle of a pinky promise.

"So… Why did you just ask me to meet one? Kahfi would've still had a great day if the other kids came. You didn't even ask if the other kids could come."

There was a long pause. Shaun just sat there staring at me, his brown eyes in mine making it feel impossible to lie. His smug little smirk was judging me extra hard because he knew, already seeing the obvious truth before us. Eventually, I buckled.

"Okay, okay, you're right," I confessed with a huff, only to be dazzled by Shaun's triumphant smile. "You're right—Kahfi is my favorite."

## Chapter Thirty-Five

# Caprice

Shaun personally drove us back to The FEEL Center.

It was a little after nine o'clock by the time we got back, not too long after Shaun had bought Kahfi dinner at the arena food court. We pulled up to the six-story building in Shaun's very dark gray Audi. Kahfi was quick to thank us both for the wonderful evening. As he undid his seatbelt, I reminded him to wash up before bed, and that I'd see him in the morning.

After Kahfi let himself out of the car and rushed into the building, I reached for my own door handle. Shaun spoke up before I could open it "You headed for your car? I could drive you to where you're parked."

"I walked to work today."

"You live in the city," he realized. Right, I lived downtown, very close to my job. "It's dark. Let me drive you home instead."

It didn't take more convincing than that. In all honesty, I wanted to stay with him for as long as I could get away with. Being around Shaun, for me, was like a drug. The more I got of him, the more of him I wanted. I leaned backward in the passenger's seat, buckling my seatbelt again.

"It's the building on the corner of ninth street and South Miami Ave," I informed.

"Brickell," he could already tell which neighborhood I lived in from the streets alone. "That's really nice."

"Doctor's salary," I shrugged at his teasing. Yes, I lived in a fancy apartment building. I could afford it. "But I'll never make enough to buy a yacht… Unlike *some* people."

Shaun laughed at my sneak diss as he drove underneath the

city lights. "Don't be jealous. I worked hard for *Caprice*."

I was confused for half a second, until I remembered that's what he named it. "I still can't believe you named the boat after me."

"In my defense, I never expected you to find out," he told me. "Now that you know, it's kind of embarrassing."

I turned away from my window to look at him as he drove, his eyes on the road so that I could discreetly admire his side profile. He was like a sculpture, masterfully carved to perfection. "You don't seem all that embarrassed."

Shaun shrugged, briefly taking his eyes off the road to glance at me. "I guess I hide it well."

"You don't have to be embarrassed," I promised. "Not over this kind of thing. Not with me."

I wondered if my words felt empty to him, if they meant less because they were coming out of *my* mouth. How dare I try to urge him to be comfortable with me when I treated him like a stranger for years and years? That's what he must've been thinking.

"You're interesting," was all he said, his car finally pulling up to my familiar building. I wanted to ask him what that meant, but if it was less than friendly, I also didn't want him to hurt my feelings. So, I didn't ask.

Instead, before I let myself out, I did something bold. Shaun made no mention of my upcoming birthday tomorrow, but I knew his was the day after, so I asked, "What are you doing this Saturday?"

It didn't matter if he forgot mine. I still wanted to celebrate his. And if he was willing, I would've liked to celebrate it with him.

"Saturday?" he asked, not giving me an answer right away, but instead replying with his own question. "Why?"

"Since it's your birthday…" I trailed off, feeling a little silly at first, but ultimately finding my nerve to just go outright and say it. "Do you want to get dinner, or something?" Before he could think I didn't respect his relationship, I added, "As friends."

*Maybe we could try and have that talk, too.*

"As friends," he repeated it like there was something funny about it. There was a regretful quality to his voice when he spoke again. "I'm sorry, Caprice. I already have plans on Saturday."

"*Oh.*" I tried to make my reaction sound lighthearted and unfazed.

It came out sounding like I was in pain.

Of course, he would have plans. People in relationships always celebrate birthdays with their significant others. No matter how Shaun made me feel, I couldn't ignore the fact that I *wasn't* his significant other. Even though I had just told him he never needed to feel embarrassed with me, I was humiliated. My face fell to my lap.

Shaun offered me an alternative. "But I'm free Sunday if you still want to do something… as friends."

Slowly, I looked up from my lap, hoping he couldn't tell just how much I felt like crying. "Yeah… I'd love that."

* * *

One of the best parts about being best friends with Sanaa Montgomery is that, on my birthday, I just have to show up.

No planning, no decorating, no sending invitations. That kind of thing is fun for Sanaa, so she would always take care of it. I never used to have birthday parties when I was a child, but Sanaa, without even realizing it, was making up for all those lost opportunities.

She treated my birthday like it was a national holiday. Sanaa treated *every* birthday like it was a national holiday, really.

Instead of our usual Friday night dinners after work, today's dinner was at Sanaa's house. Unlike me, she lived out in the suburbs, in an upscale neighborhood in Coral Gables. Her pale-yellow house sat on a large piece of land, giving her Spanish style home quite a bit of space between her and her next-door neighbor. Sanaa kept her front yard pristine, not one brick out of place along her grand driveway, with a gorgeous garden that grew gravity-defying vines up the outer walls of her home.

Besides Sanaa's, there were five cars parked in the driveway by the time I arrived. I didn't bother knocking because Sanaa never locked her doors, inviting myself into the homey smell of warm cinnamon and something else delicious. Sanaa's home was more sentimental than one would expect. Yes, she was chic and stylish, but her home was a shrine to the things she cherished the most, her friends and her family.

In addition to my birthday balloons, every room was decorated with framed photos of the *gigantic* Montgomery family, of Sanaa and me, of countless memories. Her house, with its earth tone color scheme, did a really good job of giving you that warm, comforted feeling. I didn't live here, but there was a reason why I felt like I would always feel like I had a second home in Miami.

Just as I stepped into the kitchen, six shrieking voices startled me out of my skin. "Happy birthday, Caprice!"

Of course, Sanaa would've found a way to get every member of our little girl squad from college in town for my birthday. I was pummeled with hugs from all different directions. These days, I was better about receiving them. I would still tense up, but most people didn't notice.

Any other year, a birthday like this would've had me overflowing. My friends really cared about me, and I appreciated that, but tonight all I could think about was how I wished someone else was here. It wasn't like me to feel like something was missing in the midst of all this love and celebration, but… I just *did*.

Regardless, dinner was lovely. It was a lot of catching up with old friends and being showered with compliments. I could always count on my girls to tell me exactly how they felt about my latest look. Tonight, I must've looked good.

My thick hair was tied up in an elegant bun, with a few strands let out to frame my face. The champagne colored dress I had on complimented my deep complexion and worked even better for my shapely figure. I briefly wondered if I should recreate this look for Shaun on Sunday. Would I be in the wrong, trying to doll up like this for him, a man with a whole fiancée?

Would he look at me and gush over my beauty like my girlfriends? Did I want him to? Would I even measure up? Was his fiancée prettier than me?

I tried looking for news of Shaun Taylor's engagement on the internet not too long ago, but I found nothing. Maybe they were waiting for the pictures to be retouched for social media, or something. I had no idea who Shaun was engaged to, and I didn't want to ask Sanaa.

One, because I couldn't ask Sanaa questions about Shaun without being obligated to answer her questions about him, too. And when it came to mine and Shaun's history, I wanted privacy. Two, I simply didn't want to have a clear image in my mind of Shaun with someone else.

It was late by the time I made it back home in the city. When I got back to my apartment building, a little tipsy off more than a couple glasses of champagne, I almost didn't realize the front desk receptionist calling out my name in his thick Cuban accent.

"Mees Lateemore, Mees Lateemore!" I twisted my whole body back once I realized he was calling for me, holding my black clutch in one hand, my house keys in the other. In accented English, the receptionist explained, "I was just about to call you. For you, a courier stopped by with a delivery just a few minutes before you arrived."

"Oh, I have a package?" I realized. That wasn't out of the ordinary; it was my birthday today. It was probably something from my mom. She had a spending problem and was always sending me random packages in the mail.

"Not exactly," the building receptionist replied, his head ducking behind his desk some before coming back up. In one hand he held a bouquet of what must've been two dozen red roses elegantly wrapped in brown wax paper, tied together with a satin red ribbon. In the other hand, was a simple pale brown gift bag. "These were for a Dr. Caprice Latimore. That's you!"

My mother never addresses my packages to *doctor* anything.

"Who are these from?" I questioned.

"I didn't touch anything, so I don't know, but I'm sure there's a card somewhere," he reasoned before commenting, "Any man would definitely want to take credit for this. These roses smell *lovely*."

"They do," I agreed quietly as I took the bouquet from him. Before that night, no one had ever given me red roses before. They're such an intimate and romantic flower. I could only think of one person who might send them, and coincidentally, that one person discovered where I lived *yesterday*.

The scent of the roses was strong enough to fill my entire apartment, I realized when I arrived. I set the gift bag on the kitchen island as I fished through my cabinets for a vase. After filling one with water, I let the roses be a center piece at my dining room table, breathing the spreading floral smell in deeply.

Inside the gift bag was a small white box. From the smell alone, I knew what it would be before I opened it. Smiling a little to myself, I lifted the lid to find a jumbo vanilla cupcake, iced with a gorgeous swirl of butterscotch frosting.

There didn't need to be a card to tell me who this was from. My memories had already narrowed down the possible suspects to one. The cupcake, I noted, was definitely big enough for two this time.

It was fancier, too. Definitely from a real bakery, and not the grocery store kind. There were three more items in the gift bag—a single candle, a new box of matches, and a card.

My hands shook a little as I opened the envelope. No name was left on it, but the handwriting was familiar. I could feel tears beginning to well in my eyes when I read the short message.

*Happy birthday, Butterscotch. Don't forget to make a wish.*

He remembered.

* * *

# SHAUN

Caprice walked into the empty restaurant wearing red.

I wanted to have this dinner in private so every table at *The Lotus* was paid for tonight so that nobody else could have dinner in here. *The Lotus* was a Japanese restaurant in Coconut Grove, closer to Caprice's apartment in Brickell than my house in Miami Beach.

Even still, I arrived before she did. She wasn't late; I was just early. I got here a few hours ago because me and the maître d' needed to have a conversation about shutting *The Lotus* out to guests for the night. So, by the time Caprice arrived, I'd been here for quite some time, sitting at just the right spot to get a full view of her as she walked in.

And what a view it was.

When I was a ten-year-old kid, I was convinced that Caprice must've been an angel on earth. I had never seen a girl that beautiful, and even twenty years later, I'd yet to find anyone else who could compare.

She walked into *The Lotus* wearing a strappy red dress, hugging at her womanly shape in all the right ways. Her hair in a pretty half tied, half down style, keeping her tight curls away from her face. Around her neck was a white pearl necklace that gave off an aesthetic contrast with her dark brown skin. Her form-fitting dress stopped a few inches above her knees, displaying not just those beautiful long legs of hers, but also showing a bit of her sexy thighs.

That was new—seeing Caprice as sexy now.

When I was a teenaged boy, Caprice was the main character in most of my erotic fantasies—not because she was a particularly sensual person, but mostly because I was in love with her and… hormones. However, now? I couldn't blame adolescent hormones for the thoughts rolling around in my head anymore. This physical response was all her; nothing chemical about it. I was seeing her for who she was, fully blossomed, and my body was responding to it.

Caprice wasn't just my pretty childhood crush anymore.

She was fine as hell.

I stood to my feet, welcoming her to our private table with a hug that felt entirely too short. I noted how nice she smelled, and how she didn't tense up in my arm.

"You look amazing." She definitely didn't wear that dress for me to not say anything.

When we were young, I didn't often tell Caprice how pretty she was. I thought it to myself a lot, but I didn't usually say it out loud. Partly because she was a shy girl who cringed away from too much attention, but also because even though Caprice was pretty, that wasn't what I loved about her most.

Her full red lips stretched into a radiant smile, flattered by the compliment. "Thank you."

I pulled out her chair, waiting for her to sit down before I took my own seat.

"This place is completely empty," Caprice realized, looking

around the Japanese restaurant, staggered. I picked the restaurant, but she had mentioned that she'd been here before. "It's never like this."

I didn't tell her that I bought the place out for the evening. "Must be one of those slow nights."

She squinted a little, so I was unsure if she believed that. Shaking her head, she moved on to something else. "The roses were beautiful by the way. My whole apartment smells like them now."

That drew a faint smile out of me. "I'm glad you liked them."

Her smile shrunk a bit. "We're going to have that conversation tonight, aren't we? The uncomfortable one."

I shook my head.

"It doesn't have to be uncomfortable." And then I reminded her, "It's me you're talking to, remember? Let's just... start from where we left off. Twelve years is a long time to stop talking to someone. Just tell me what I missed, because I know I missed a lot."

"Yeah, and it's my fault—"

"You don't have to do that," I stopped her. "I already know it is." Her face fell sadly to her lap, but I continued. "Right now, however, I just wanna know what I missed. Tell me something about you that I don't know anymore."

"Do you remember that last night we were together?" she asked.

Of course, I remembered. I still had a faded scar along my left cheek to remind me every morning. "I remember."

"He almost killed you," she whispered, pain resonating in her soft voice. It appeared the memory of that night had stayed with her in the worst way. I had the scars, but no true memory of how close to death I got. Caprice had the memories, though. "I felt *so* guilty."

She didn't need to. What happened to me that night was on me—on my dumbass decisions.

"A few days after, while you were still in the hospital, I got an opportunity to leave. You remember our math teacher, Ms. Johnson?" I nodded. "I missed a few days of school. She came by the house to check on me, and she just... she took me with her. I wanted to go. For a few nights, I'd been sleeping in my room, alone, waking up to your blood all over my walls, knowing Marcel was just behind a very thin partition. Every night I spent in that house on my own, I was terrified he would barge in. I got an opportunity to leave… and I did."

I didn't fault her for that decision at all. I couldn't have protected her from a hospital bed. "And where did you go?"

"California," she replied. "Ms. Johnson's mother was a recently retired psychiatrist, and with her, I got the help that I needed. For the first year, it was intense therapy and coping exercises. I was advised to work on me before I reached out to anyone from my past," she explained. "But once I got the opportunity to call you, or Miss Sylvia, or Mischa… I just *didn't*. I kept putting it off. One year turned into two years, and then three, and by the time I wasn't too scared to call anymore, I figured I'd waited so long that you must've hated me."

I was beginning to understand. "You didn't call because you were afraid I would be mad at you… for not calling sooner."

"It sounds so silly when you say it like that," she mumbled.

"Because it *is* silly," I told her bluntly. She flinched, taking my words to heart. I told her the truth. "I waited for you for *seven* years, Caprice. So, if you had called three years after you left…" I trailed off, just filled with so many regrets over the time lost. "Three years is *nothing* compared to twelve."

"I used to watch your college games on the internet," she told me. All I could think about was how she could've been there, live and in person, sitting in the stands with my mom, wearing my jersey. "I followed your entire college ball career, and I think the closest I ever got to calling you was the night you got drafted."

"Really? Why that moment?"

"Because I was *so* proud of you," she whispered, meaning every word. "I remember when we were kids and you used to tell people that you'd be in the NBA someday, and they'd give you that *look*. You know, that '*keep dreaming, kid*' look. But you *actually* did it. Number one draft pick in the first round. I was so, so proud of you." Something at the pit of my stomach twisted and then grew heavy. It was a strange hybrid of emotions, happy to hear her say the words, but sad because I wished I could've heard them sooner.

"I dialed the number and everything; even four years later, I still remembered it. But you had just signed a multimillion-dollar NBA contract, so just before I could press the call button… I thought about how bad my timing was." She brought the back of her hand up to wipe a tear that slipped down her cheek. "How convenient was it that I suddenly wanted to talk now that you're rich, right? I didn't want you and Miss Sylvia to think I was… like that. So, I didn't call. I knew then that I'd waited too long. I had to move on."

"That's funny," I remarked quietly. Not funny as in humorous, but funny as in interesting.

"Why's that?"

"Because the night I got drafted, you were on my mind the entire time. I thought about how you could've been watching it on TV somewhere out there. I had my phone in my pocket the entire night, just in case seeing me reminded you to finally call." I shook my head, hating the fact that all this time was wasted, hating how it all could've been prevented. "I wouldn't have thought you were *'like that'* for choosing to call that night… 'Cause I was waiting for you, Caprice. I was waiting for that call."

Of course, I anticipated the waterworks, so I already had a small pack of tissues in my pocket. When I pushed them across the dinner table toward her, she chuckled, her smile more sad than happy.

"I know you're lowkey calling me a crybaby 'cause you keep bringing me tissues."

"That's 'cause you *are* a crybaby," I affirmed with a short laugh, telling her, "But you know I hate to see you sad." I sighed, urging for a mood shift. "So, tell me something happy about your life. Like me, you did everything you said you were going to do. Look at you… Dr. Caprice Latimore. I'm proud of you, too." She smiled as she pulled out one of her tissues, and I repeated myself. "Tell me something happy."

"I have a mom again," she told me, her voice still really emotional.

"Yeah?" I urged her to keep going. "What's she like?"

"She's *the best,*" she gushed, a little smile starting to grow into her features. "She's a little eccentric with a really bad shopping habit, but she's just so full of love. Dr. LaToya Johnson—by the time I started calling her mom, I was a legal adult, but she still went through the channels to adopt me anyway. She wanted to make it *official*."

"You kept your last name."

She nodded. "Yeah… I didn't want to go through the hassle of changing all my identification documents. I've been Caprice Latimore all my life. I was used to it."

I found myself wondering if she'd change her last name for another reason. The thought made me laugh a little.

"What's funny?" she asked curiously. I shook my head, deciding to keep that thought to myself. "Can I ask you something?"

"You can ask me anything," I told her.

"I know us growing apart is all on me," she started, "but did you ever look for me?"

"I *did* look for you. And I found you, too." That news took her by surprise. "It was 2010—so I guess right around that three-year mark that you decided was too late to call. I was in Miami for spring break. I saw you at a pool party. Pure coincidence." I chuckled even though nothing was funny. "UM is one of the biggest universities in Florida. Plenty of kids from Jefferson went to UM. I knew where you were eight years ago."

"2010?" she questioned, having not expected that at all. "You saw me at a party? Why didn't you approach me?"

"From what I could see, it didn't look like you wanted to be found." I shrugged. "And I suppose a lot of it had to do with my pride. I was a little embarrassed, feeling like I was the last to know that you were okay after all. I figured you had your reasons for ghosting me, and I didn't want to impose. But you looked really happy, though. So, that was a relief."

She shook her head, not wanting me to misunderstand, more tears slipping down her face. "I didn't know you were there. And I *was* happy, but I would've been happier to see you that night."

How could she say that to me now, knowing she never even tried to reach out? She pulled another tissue from the package, bringing it up to her eyes.

"You're gonna run out of tissues if you keep this up," I pointed out.

She must've realized I was holding back, because she asked, "Are you going easy on me because I'm a crybaby?"

I shook my head. "That's not it."

"What is it then?"

*It's because I love you.* I didn't say that out loud. "I'm not angry, Caprice."

This was true. I wasn't angry. I was hurt, I was confused, I was a lot of things, but I wasn't angry.

"You should be," she whispered.

"I should be," I agreed. "But I'm not. Go ahead and tell me something else happy."

She filled me in on the happiest moments of her life that I missed. It was bittersweet. While there was a part of me that was relieved to hear about how her life turned out amazing, I was so sad that I couldn't be there for any of it. I didn't get to celebrate with her when she got into college, or when she graduated. I wasn't there when she started her non-profit.

And then there were little changes about her that I didn't get to see happen. I regretted those, too. Her ears were pierced now. She was extremely girly now. She wore makeup and jewelry now. She could drive now. She wasn't uncomfortable with eye contact now. She was quicker to laugh now. It was easier to make her smile now. Caprice was so bright, almost glowing as she spoke about her new life.

*So* damn happy.

I loved the old Caprice with all my heart, and I could've never imagined the old version of her could be improved upon, but one look at her overjoyed smile now, and I just knew I loved this version of her more.

It would've been a privilege to have been able to watch her gradually transition into this woman. It was hard not to feel robbed, knowing I was there for none of it. But she just talked, and I just listened, trying my best to relive all the years spent apart in that single conversation.

It was a little after midnight when the restaurant staff regretfully told us they couldn't keep the place open any longer. They were supposed to have closed at ten. By now, Caprice must've realized I'd bought the place out for the evening, as nobody but us had been here the entire night.

When the check came, Caprice and I reached for it at the same time.

Earlier on in the day, when I spoke to the maître d' about buying *The Lotus* out for the evening, we'd agreed on a reasonable price. There were fifteen tables at *The Lotus*, so in order to buy the place out for the night, I just had to multiply the cost of my dinner with Caprice by forty-five.

Caprice might've been able to easily afford the little two-hundred-dollar dinner we just had, but I seriously doubted she could pay for it forty-five times. Even on a doctor's salary, nine thousand dollars is still a lot of money. I would've preferred that she didn't even see the check.

"I've got it," I told her.

"*Nooo*," she whined softly, not letting the check booklet go. Caprice was adamant about this one. "I didn't get you anything for your birthday—" she was doing *That Thing* with her voice "—let me celebrate you. I've got it."

Trying not to laugh, I didn't let go of the check. "I *really* don't think you do."

"I've eaten here before, Shaun," she told me matter-of-factly, a little too self-assured. "Trust me—I can afford it."

"You sure?"

She nodded confidently. I let the check booklet go as Caprice reached into her purse for her wallet. I leaned back against the backside of my chair, just waiting. She pulled out a VISA credit card, and I wondered if this dinner was about to max out her credit limit. But who knows—maybe she had a high credit balance.

And then she opened the receipt booklet.

She squinted at the number, staring at it for a *really* long time. I casually drew a hand up to my mouth to hide my smile. Without looking up from the check, she realized, "Is this why nobody else was eating here tonight?"

"You still got this?" I asked, unable to mask the amusement in my tone. She looked up from the check, a lot less enthusiastic about paying for dinner now. Without a word, I reached across the table for the booklet in front of her. "That's what I thought."

"That's a lot of money for just one dinner," she commented

as I pulled my credit card from my wallet.

"Privacy isn't cheap."

"Oh right," she was reminded of something. "You're a professional athlete. I *totally* forgot." That was refreshing. As I reached for a pen to sign the receipt, Caprice added, "Wanting privacy makes sense. This kinda looks like a date, and I'd hate for your fiancée to get the wrong idea."

My pen stopped moving. I looked up from the receipt, meeting her eyes briefly, before going back to what I was doing. Even after this intimate ass exchange, she was really under the impression that I was *still* engaged.

To make matters worse, she didn't even realize that this *was* a date.

*That's cute.*

*In a really, really annoying kind of way.*

"Did you drive here?" I asked randomly when we stood to our feet. The heels she had on were long ones, allowing the top of her head to reach a couple inches below my hairline. I've never been all that fond of short women, and I had Caprice to blame for that. Standing at about five-ten without the heels, and six-three with them, she was the perfect height for me.

She shook her head at my question. "I hate taking my car out of my building's parking garage. I took an Uber. Why do you ask?"

"The restaurant is closing," I pointed out, "but that doesn't mean we have to go home."

She actually sounded surprised when she asked, "You want to spend more time with me?"

*Unbelievable.*

"Sure." I nodded casually. "I was enjoying the little update. Come on, I know somewhere else we can go."

## *Chapter Thirty-Six*

# Caprice

For the first few minutes of the drive, it looked like Shaun was headed for the city.

From the passenger's seat, I was still giving him a rundown of my last twelve years, the whole time wondering if he was headed for my apartment. In truth, I wouldn't have minded inviting him up because I didn't want our night to end either.

When I was getting ready for dinner earlier on in the day, I had been a little worried. I was highly aware of the fact that I'd done Shaun dirty. I completely ghosted him, and he hadn't done anything to me to deserve it.

It would've been totally justified for Shaun to spend the entire dinner ripping into me, making me feel like a monster for what I did to him.

But he didn't.

He just wanted to hear about all the good times that he missed. Even though he had every right to be, he wasn't angry with me. He didn't seem to be comfortable with the thought of me feeling bad for what I did. He didn't even appear to want an apology. It was obvious that the time apart was what he truly regretted. So, all he asked of me was to fill him in.

I just talked, and he just listened.

Nostalgia wasn't a feeling that I got a lot. That's because there weren't many memories from my past to feel nostalgic about… but sitting in the passenger's seat of Shaun's car gave me that warm feeling. It was a comforting feeling that made me feel like I was home, even though I didn't really have a home when I used to know him.

When he drove past my building, I realized we weren't headed for my place. Instead, he was driving towards the edge of the city, near the bay. Shaun parked his car on an empty street a few blocks away from the *Miamarina,* where I knew his boat was docked.

"Are your feet alright in those shoes?" He asked me as we walked side by side along the late-night streets. I turned my head up and nodded, admiring the fact that I still had to look up. Men who were taller than me when I had heels on were hard to come by.

There wasn't much distance left to the boardwalk of the marina. My feet didn't hurt terribly. Shaun kept asking me questions as we walked. He wanted to know simple, seemingly insignificant things, like who taught me to drive, what I liked to do on my downtime, why I was friends with Sanaa. I answered everything, giving him a detailed history. When I was done, I let him in on a little secret.

"Sanaa doesn't like you," I told him, just in case he didn't know.

"That's 'cause I'm from Parramore, and she turns her nose up at people like me."

I corrected, "You mean, people like us."

He raised an eyebrow. "Nah… as far as she's concerned, you're from Beverly Hills."

"And you didn't correct her?"

"Why would I do that?" he asked. "If you wanna leave out parts of your past, that's your business." Shaun laughed a little. "It's just funny to hear her call you her best friend when she don't even really know you like that."

"She *is* my best friend," I argued.

"Oh," Shaun nodded, something a little deflated about his tone. "If you say so."

"Do you think you know me better?" I asked curiously.

He was honest with me, his answer coming just as we reached the marina. "I'm not sure anymore."

For reasons I can't describe, it hurt so much to hear him say that.

"You do," I told him, and his eyes met mine underneath the dim boardwalk lights. I assured, "Even considering the decade-long chasm. Sanaa knows all the superficial stuff about me—my preferred nail color, my favorite place to meet for brunch, how long my hair is when I flat iron it. But you… you're the one who knows all my deepest, darkest secrets."

"Yeah," he whispered, accepting that with a nod, "but I wish I knew the superficial stuff, too."

I don't think he was trying to make me feel guilty, but I felt it so hard then.

In the low lights, the cursive letters etched into the side of Shaun's yacht were visible. *Caprice.* A testament to the fact that even several years of silence couldn't make him forget me. Shaun helped me step onto the boat with my heels on, telling me he'd join me on the boat deck in a minute.

I found the same double lounge chair he'd found me sunbathing in weeks ago. It was a wide lounge, seeming more like an outdoor bed than a chair. I sat on the left side of the white cushion, unclasping and removing my heels, looking up at the night sky.

That's when I realized we were moving.

The boat was floating further out to sea, away from the dock. Shaun didn't meet me on the deck until we were about a quarter mile from the shore. From here the vast ocean surrounded us on all sides, and then off in the distance was the Downtown Miami skyline. The yacht stopped moving, anchoring far enough so that the only noise was the sounds of the open water moving with the sea breeze.

It was easier to see the stars this far away from the city lights. If Shaun truly valued privacy, I could see why he got this boat. This far out into the ocean was the ultimate seclusion. He took the empty spot beside me on the double lounge.

There was something about knowing just how alone the both of us were that made this moment all the more intimate. I briefly wondered if he was doing all of this on purpose. This didn't feel like a moment meant to be shared between two old friends. Two old lovers, maybe, but friends? I wasn't stupid.

Was this what he wanted from me? This kind of intimacy? Did I want this? I mean, part of me knew I did—look at what I was wearing. I *wanted* to be pretty for him. But was I that kind of person? Loving Shaun was no excuse to carry on with a man who belonged to another woman. I knew that. I knew this was wrong.

There was a dim white lamp shining from behind us, adding to the moon and starlight so that we could see each other in the midst of the darkness. Shaun was sitting so close—close enough to reach toward and…

I tried to keep us talking. Anything to take my mind off his lips.

"We talked so much about me," I said quietly. "What about you? Could you tell me what I missed? Tell me something happy."

He was quiet for a really long time, those brown eyes on me the whole while. At first I thought he was straight up ignoring me, but as I looked into his eyes, I realized something truly heartbreaking.

Shaun actually *was* looking for an answer to give me, trying to remember something happy in the past twelve years, and he just… couldn't think of anything.

"I'm sorry," he apologized for his inability to come up with a good response. "I was happy when I got drafted, and every single time I won a game, but… those are all common knowledge."

I felt my insides twist. Were things really that bad for him all these years that he couldn't think of one happy memory? I remembered when we were kids, Shaun used to talk about all the things he'd do for his mom when he was rich. Surely being able to do those things for her now made him happy.

"How's your mom?" I asked after a long, but comfortable, silence. "Does she still have the salon in Parramore?"

"Nah." Shaun shook his head. "I got her to move in with me a couple years ago. She sold the salon a little bit before that."

"You live with her?"

"I do," he answered. "She was, um…" he hesitated a little before he broke the news. "She was battling breast cancer a few years ago, and I felt more comfortable having her close."

"Oh, my Go—"

He stopped me before I could start, putting up a quiet hand. "Don't sweat it. She's been cancer free for years. The chemo got her good."

*Chemotherapy*… I realized something. "But her hair."

"Yeah," Shaun whispered, a noticeable sadness in his faint smile. "She, uh… she was really sad about that, too. You know how my mom is about hair…" Yeah, I remembered. "It doesn't always grow back the same. Sometimes it just comes back in patches," he told me, which I already knew. "She's different now."

"Different?"

"*Depressed*," he put it bluntly. Sighing, he continued, "Some days she's in high spirits, but most days… There's just something about almost dying, I guess. It changes you. When I was a kid, I had all these dreams. I thought I was gonna put my mom in a big ass house, buy her whatever she wanted, and really make her happy. Who would've thought the moment I was able to give her all those things, she'd be the saddest version of herself she's ever been?"

Giving him my full attention as he looked out unto the ocean, I got a full view of his side profile. Even like this, sad like this, Shaun was beautiful beyond comprehension. Sitting out here on the boat deck—side by side underneath the stars—it was reminiscent of the many evenings we used to spend together at that city basketball court, when we were kids.

It was quiet now, and I just looked at him as he looked out unto the ocean's great beyond.

A two-inch scar below his left eye was barely visible, a faded brown line that ran along his cheek. I was taken back to the night when he got it. The Shaun of my past would've died for me back then. I vividly remember him nearly doing just that, trying to protect me from my uncle, his attempts leaving him bloody and—evidently—forever scarred.

My chest swelled.

The only sound for miles was the chorus of waves, crashing at the shore in the distance. The boat wasn't too far out, but it was far enough that we couldn't hear the rest of Miami. It was ridiculously peaceful out here.

In its peacefulness, I was finally beginning to crumble underneath the overwhelming guilt I felt. I did something terrible to him, and I felt so bad for it.

"Shaun," I whispered. Without saying anything, he turned to face me. His handsome face held no resentment, no anger. He was just here. He was just with me. My eyes filled to the brim with tears, even though I had no right to cry. Quietly, I whispered, "You can be angry with me, if you want."

"You think that'll make you feel less guilty?" he asked, not trying to be mean, but definitely still cutting me deep. His eyes held that watery glassiness to them; like he might cry, too. "You think if I make you feel bad about it, we'll be even?" He exhaled with a shake of his head. "But that's the thing, Caprice... I never wanna make you feel bad about anything. It'll do me no good. 'Cause when you feel bad..." A single tear rolled down his cheek. "...I feel bad *with* you."

My hand came up to cover my mouth, my body buckling under the weight of all these feelings. Soundlessly, I cried like a baby.

"You cry, I cry. It's been like that since we were kids," he reminded, just pure unadulterated pain in his voice. He wasn't angry, but that didn't mean he didn't feel *something*. He was... *broken*. I couldn't deal with the fact that *I* had done that to him. It was my fault he was in so much pain. "You hurt, I hurt. That's how it's always been. That's how it's always gonna be. So, you see... There's really no reward in making you feel like shit about this."

I had no right to be crying this much. What happened to us—I did that on my own. All Shaun ever did was love me, and I... I broke his heart. And yet... Here we were, on the deck of his boat underneath the September night sky, and *I* was the one who was bitterly falling apart.

Without asking, without warning, Shaun's arm came out and wrapped around my body, holding my shaking frame to his chest. I didn't tense up. I didn't pull back. I just let him hold me.

I *wanted* him to.

His second arm came around and closed the hug, and I just stayed there, pressed against his warmth. I crawled in closer and my arms moved to wrap around him. This was as close as we could get, his arms surrounding me, my head resting on his shoulder, seated on his lap while he held me to his body tightly. This was the only person in the world who could hug me and have me wishing it would never end.

"I left you," I whispered against his neck.

"You did."

"I made you promise you'd never leave me, and then... I left you."

"I remember."

"I never called. I never texted."

"I know."

"And your mom getting cancer..." Knowing how he lost his dad; he must've been so scared. "I should've been there for you."

"You should've."

"I betrayed you."

"Maybe."

"I'm a terrible friend."

"You're a terrible friend," he agreed. He pulled back, keeping me between his arms, and holding my face in his hands. His eyes had that shiny, wet quality to them. I reached over to wipe his cheeks as he whispered, "But you had your reasons."

"Shaun..."

"I'm not stupid, Butterscotch," he told me. My chest swelled to hear him call me that. He had no idea how much I missed that. "Even though you don't think I do—even though you think *no one* does—I understand you. You might not even really realize *why* you did it, but I do. There were just some things about you that I couldn't fix... Those were the wounds you tried to heal the best way you knew how. Even if that meant forgetting—forgetting the version of yourself it all happened to."

He wiped my tears as they fell, and I wiped his.

"Listening to you tonight, hearing about the life you got to live... I get it. You got to move... Start a new life, create a new self... And, unfortunately for me... I was part of the life you wanted to forget. And I really can't blame you. Remember, Caprice—I *know* you. Your childhood, Parramore, that pink house... Those are *terrible* memories to have to hold onto. I understand why you did it. I understand you."

"But... but I could never... I could never forget *you*," I told him, holding his face between my hands. "Even when I tried to."

His hands fell from my face, coming around and holding me at the small of my back, fingers resting naturally at my waist. "I can tell."

"I loved you," I told him.

"You did."

"You were the only person who ever really made me feel safe."

"I remember."

"I made a mistake."

"I know."

"I should've come back for you."

"You should've."

"Leaving you behind like that was so unnecessary."

"Maybe."

"I didn't deserve you."

Shaun paused, for a moment just looking at me with such a meaningful intensity. Quiet as a whisper, he said the words, "I disagree."

He *couldn't* mean that. My heart sank. I looked away, my face falling down in shame. I felt so *guilty*.

"Look at me," he demanded softly. "*Look* at me, Caprice."

Shaun tucked a single finger under my chin, bringing my eyes back to his. His eyes… Those penny brown eyes were still perfect windows into all of him. More than ten years later, and there was still no change in them. They were just as love filled as they'd always been.

The already small space between us was closing. When his lips touched down on mine, I shut my eyes, melting in his hands. The gentlest kiss. Shaun was the only man I could ever let touch me like this.

With him, I was open. I was free.

I was safe.

How could I not feel that way? Shaun kissed me like I was the only thing that mattered to him between the earth and space. In his arms, I felt protected.

In his arms, I *was* protected.

His lips fit perfectly with mine, tailor made for me. He was warm and his lips were soft, moving against mine with unmistakable passion. Shaun still kissed me the same. Nothing had changed. Things that felt unnatural with anybody else, always felt natural with him. Kissing him, touching him, tasting him. I could've stayed with him forever like this.

But he didn't have forever.

He was engaged.

I pulled back, reluctantly breaking the kiss. I didn't want to, but if I didn't stop now, it would only hurt more when I had to face the fact that I couldn't have him.

Breathless, I whispered, "We can't do this."

Shaun's eyes on me were like a dream. I could've pinched myself just to make sure it wasn't. But alas, all of this was *actually* happening. Even though he was engaged to marry another woman.

Shaun wasn't a cheater.

I wouldn't make him do that for me.

He looked at me and didn't have to ask what I was thinking. He must've been thinking about her, too.

"Go ahead, Caprice," he whispered softly against my lips. "Ask me to choose."

# Chapter Thirty-Seven

# SHAUN

"Okay," Caprice whispered so delicately.

She sounded so anxious when she began to speak. Her voice shook, as she made her lengthy appeal, not even realizing that she didn't have to try so hard.

"I know I was the worst—absolutely the *worst*—best friend and girlfriend for what I did to you. And I don't know how to convince you that I'd never hurt you again, but I won't. I promise. Shaun, I love you. Your fiancée probably loves you, too, and she's probably never broken your heart like I have, but I… I still hope you pick me." Wordlessly, I ran a thumb over her face, wiping the tears that were slipping down her cheek. And then Caprice said, "*Please.*"

And all things considered, that really hurt me. A naïve man might think making the woman who left him beg for him back would be a good feeling.

It wasn't.

Not for me.

I hated it, actually.

"Do you remember that one night in your bedroom way back when?" I asked her suddenly. "The night you told me you didn't want to be my girlfriend?"

"I said that?" she asked, her nose sounding all stuffed up. *Cute.*

"You forgot," I chuckled. "Yeah, it's true… You didn't want to be my girlfriend. You know why?"

"Why?"

"Because you said I went through girlfriends like I went through shoes," I reminded, watching those words jog her memory.

"You told me you would've preferred to stay my best friend because I never kept my girlfriends, but I always kept you." She smiled a little at the memory. "Remember what I told you?"

Caprice nodded. "You said you kept breaking up with them because they kept asking you to choose."

"Right. That's how all my relationships ended in those days," I informed. "Once you found that out, I remember right before you agreed to be my girlfriend you asked me that if it ever came down to it, if I would choose you." I laughed a little at the memory, and I could already tell Caprice knew where this was going. Her spirits were lifting. "I remember thinking how ridiculous the question was, 'cause in my mind—who the fuck else could compete? So, I promised I would. Remember? Easiest promise I ever made, by the way."

"You choose me," she realized, her tone a combination of hopefulness and relief all rolled into one. It made me much happier to see the smile that blossomed on her face than I felt to hear her beg. With that joyful smile was how I liked her best.

Of course, I chose her. I would *always* choose Caprice.

I mean—really—there wasn't a woman on this planet that could dream of competing.

"I chose you several weeks ago," I confessed. That same day I saw Caprice on this boat deck, and then decided to not re-propose to Arielle, that was me choosing. "You can ask your *'best friend'* all about it later."

I could feel her body relax underneath my hands, which made me smile. Her happiness was really contagious.

"I can hear the sarcasm in your voice when you call her that," Caprice mentioned.

"That's 'cause she's *not* your best friend," I emphasized, not caring that I was coming off immature or childish. "It's me."

Caprice didn't argue with my claim, her hands rising to hold my face in her hands as she nodded. "That's true. It is you."

"Yeah, 'cause you don't need to be calling a chick that told me all your business your best friend," I advised, half joking, half serious.

"All my business, huh?" Caprice doubted that. "Well, Sanaa told me that she had to curse you out because you threatened to not pay her unless she gave you my number."

"Sanaa's exaggerating," I assured, however Caprice still knew me well enough to know that I was lying. Since Sanaa threw me under the bus, I'd go ahead and do the same, "Now was Sanaa exaggerating when she said you haven't dated anybody for the last twelve years?"

Caprice's eyebrows rose high, her voice totally shocked when she whispered, "She *did not!*"

"She sure did." I was amused, knowing that whatever conflict created by telling Caprice this was sure to get under Sanaa's skin. Of course, I wasn't trying to end their friendship. I was fully aware that this wasn't enough to cause a rift, but I was definitely getting the last laugh. "Just thought you should know. You might wanna talk to her about boundaries."

It's fun to get on Sanaa's nerves.

In all honesty, I knew I'd have to thank Sanaa for her unprofessionalism someday. If she was out here conducting her business the right way, it would've taken me much longer to find Caprice. Even still, Caprice was the maid of honor in the same wedding I was the best man at. I was gonna run into Caprice eventually, but if things hadn't happened the way they did, then I would've been formally engaged by the time I saw Caprice again.

Granted, officially engaged to Arielle or not, I would've still chosen the same, but this outcome was a lot less messy. For that, I'd be sure to get Sanaa a nice wedding gift, or something. Her unprofessional business practices saved me a lot of time.

And after twelve years of separation, every little moment with Caprice was precious.

"Why didn't you date?" I was curious.

Caprice looked at me for a bit, her hands on my face falling gently to my neck. "I'm still really scared of men."

I knew the reason why, so hearing that response was fucking tragic. Caprice shrugged with a sad smile, but there was nothing funny about this. Her hands on me traced soothing lines along my skin, as if I was the one who needed comforting. I didn't want to be comforted. I just wished the past was something I could fix.

"Men are takers, Shaun," she whispered to my sympathetic expression. "They don't always mean to be, but they usually are.

Men oftentimes know what they want, and when someone is unwilling to give it, they just… take it. I don't know what I would do if a man ever took something from me again." Shaking her head, she added, "But you're different. With us, you've always been a giver, while I've always been the taker, and you just never seemed to mind. Besides… you weren't always a man. I watched you grow into one. And by the time you were a man, I already knew you well enough. You're the only man I've ever trusted."

She tugged softly at the back of my neck, willing me closer to press on the gentlest kiss. Caprice's lips were soft, and her red lipstick tasted like berries. The kiss was slow, teeming with a heat that was born out of natural chemistry. It was just a kiss. She sat on my lap with her hands at my neck and my hands at her waist. She let me in past her lips, giving me access to her warmth, savoring every second and her intoxicating taste. It was just a kiss, but it was one of the most passionate things I'd ever done.

Caprice pulled back, her breath hitting against my lips as her sheer happiness made her laugh. Her hands at my neck moved further down to my shoulders and her arms wrapped around my back in a tight hug. My grip at her waist tightened and I hugged Caprice in return as her head fell to my shoulder, resting there.

"I remember when you were a little boy," she reminisced, and even though I couldn't see it, I could hear the smile in her voice. "The only thing you wanted to take from me back then was my Disney Princess backpack."

I chuckled, shaking my head.

"I didn't want to take it," I argued quietly, remembering. "I just wanted to hold it."

"You *liked* it," she teased. "Admit it."

"I wanted to hold it *for* you." I was honest with her when I revealed, "I just wanted you to like me."

Caprice pulled back so that she could look me in the eyes. "At that point, I already did."

That drew a faint smile out of me as I moved in closer for another kiss, feeling the sea breeze rub her soft coiled hair against the side of my face. Close like this, the warmth of her skin underneath my hands cancelled out the chill of the breezy September night air. With my hands at her waist pulling her further in, I could feel every contour of her body against mine, pressed hard against my lap, all the while the heat was steadily rising.

Since she stayed single all this time, then that meant the last time she'd done anything remotely like this, it was with me, and she was sixteen.

"You okay?" I checked in, never one to take something she wasn't ready to give.

"I trust you," she whispered, eyes still closed for a moment before she opened them and assured, "And I want this."

Wordlessly, I laid her down on the double lounge cushions. She was face down with her back to me as she laid on her stomach. I let my hand drag up the length of her dress, catching the zipper just below the nape of her neck, and slowly glided it down. The red sleeves dropped, exposing her soft bare shoulders, brown skin reflecting the moonlight overhead.

My hands slowly removed the dress, savoring the softness of her skin on the journey downward. A shiver ran down her spine, but not because she was cold. Caprice was unbelievably sensitive, nerve endings ablaze by the simple brushing of my fingers down her thighs.

I was thirty years old, and the last time I was with anybody this sensitive, I... I couldn't even remember. Caprice wasn't experienced enough to be with me at my maximum performance. That was not arrogance talking—that was just fact. I'd have to take my time with her. We would get there someday, but right now I absolutely refused to overwhelm or hurt her.

I'd be gentle.

As I was the first time we did this.

In a sheer black bra and white lace underwear, Caprice rolled over onto her back, with eyes looking up at mine, trusting. Her hands rose from where she laid, settling at the buttons of the navy-blue dress shirt I had on. Fingers steady, with only a slight hint of anxiety, she popped every button all the way down. Her hands reached out for my naked chest; her fingers warm against my skin as I pulled the shirt completely off.

Her hands explored my body almost curiously.

Hidden in the privacy of the open water, underneath the stars, I slipped a hand underneath her and unclasped her bra. She helped me guide the straps down her arms, baring herself to me. She was absolutely perfect. Her round breasts looked – for lack of a better word – delicious, with hardened peaks that showed that she was either aroused or cold. I think she was both.

An almost hum-like moan came out of her when I took one of her nipples between my lips, that sensitivity about her making her back automatically arch up to meet my mouth. I took turns loving on each of her mounds, smiling a little to myself at how much of a task it was to keep her still and pull her lace panties down.

Caprice's hands at the waistband of my pants tugged at my belt, clumsily doing her best to get them off while I worked on her chest and my fingers slipped between her legs. At the first touch of my fingers to her sex, she moaned against my neck, her arms pulling me down closer to her.

She was adorable.

I was reminded of the first time we did this, how after it was all said and done, she turned to me in my bed and asked, *'Was I okay? Was my… you know… Was it broken? Did everything work normal down there?'*

Silly as the question sounded, it wasn't funny at all because she was *so* serious.

And I was the most honest with her I had ever been when I whispered back, *'Butterscotch, you were perfect.'*

Back then, she was so relieved to hear me say that, but I was *so* angry that she had to ask. Everything had been amazing up until that point, but when she asked me that, it completely ruined the moment. I didn't show it, but I remember feeling so sad as I held her in my arms.

Caprice was perfect then, and she was perfect now.

Right underneath the stars, on the boat deck aboard *The Caprice*, I had every intention of letting the woman who it was named after know how precious she was to me. She was beautiful. She was whole. She was perfect.

Caprice trembled a bit, that sensitivity about her making her quiver at the touch of my thumb to her clit.

"Shaun," she moaned my name softly against my neck as my hand moved against the lips between her legs, flesh dripping and hot, and knowing she was ready. I knew it before she whispered, "I want you."

I pulled back and got a look at her face. Her dark eyes were dreamy, practically euphoric. She was smiling up at me like I had already made her come. *Holy shit. Did I?*

I realized I did.

*That's cute as shit.*

The realization made me smile a little as I laid her back down against the double lounge's white cushions. I used to dream about having this much access to Caprice, and now here I was, about to make love to her underneath the moonlight.

And she trusted me so much.

Caprice wasn't scared, and she barely seemed nervous as I guided myself between her legs. Her hands wrapped around and settled at my back, pulling my lips to hers at the moment I pushed in. Underneath me, I felt her body go a little tense, her nails dragging down my skin. She was so wet, which helped with the stretch, but a little discomfort was inevitable as she didn't do this often.

I didn't rush anything.

My hands moved a few strands of her hair away from her face. She offered me a reassuring smile; just effortlessly beautiful. Her breathing was stable; she was so calm, completely trusting me with her body, just knowing I'd take care of it. Of course, it wasn't lost on me how meaningful that was.

After giving her body some time to acclimate to me, for her sake, I started *very* slow. Unsurprisingly, she had a significantly tight grip. *Goddamn…* Pushing in and pulling out didn't come without noticable effort. Her hands at my back loosened, the alignment of her body relaxing after some time. It felt amazing to be back, buried deep within her depths, as she whispered little incoherent encouragements in my ear.

With increased speed, her steady breaths grew shorter and shorter, eventually turning to soft moans against my neck while I left a trail of kisses down hers. This moment was all about Caprice, all about her pleasure. I'd get mine eventually, but she had to get hers first.

Little by little, I could stop holding back as much as she

grew accustomed to each shift in momentum. She took each thrust in stride, her hands on my body opening and closing, her voice rising in pitch each time. Sex was *never* this intense with anyone else. God, she was perfect. Her body was warm, but it was the love that exuded from her that felt like the sun on my skin. That heat mounted and climbed, rising between us until her body shook from underneath mine, and she whispered my name.

Voice soft as can be, "Shaun, I love you."

That was beautiful. I could hear Caprice say that for a lifetime, and it would never get old. Her legs wrapped around me tightly, face buried deep against my neck, as she repeated my name over and over again in soft whispers. Her shallow breaths hit quick against my neck, slowing down and then speeding up as she kept hitting new peaks, climaxing and then climaxing again.

Everything about the moment was a turn on—Caprice's body, her scent, her beauty, her voice, her breathing—but it was watching the way she climaxed so unreservedly that sent me over the edge. Just watching how much she was enjoying herself was sexy as fuck. She wasn't shy at all. Not with me, at least. It wasn't long before I knew it was time to get out of her. Caprice wasn't sexually active, so I doubted she was on any kind of pills. Without a condom, I needed to pull out before my own peak hit. I slowed, but her legs were still linked behind me, hands at my back clasping me there tightly.

I was trying to pull away from her hold. "Baby, I'm about to—"

"Don't let me go," she whispered, and there wasn't a doubt in my mind that she knew exactly what she was asking for.

I didn't let her go.

I didn't pull out. I understood the possible risk that came with what I'd done, but is it really all that risky if that possibility is something that I want?

Caprice's breathing slowed down after a time, with me still holding her close to my side as my own breathing normalized. Her head rested on my chest, her soft hand in mine. Caprice drew her eyes up, her ear still against my heart, and just looked at me. The sea breeze was blowing her hair, and no longer cloaked by the heat of mutual passion, the September chill hit her naked skin.

"Shaun," she said suddenly, "I'm really cold."

I told her to grab our clothes as I sat up on the double lounge, hooking an arm behind her knees and a hand behind her back to carry her inside. The interior of the yacht was a two-bedroom, two-bath living space complete with a full kitchen, media room, and two living rooms.

The boat was a little extravagant, but when I bought it last year, I figured I'd grow into it. *If a man can afford a boat and he lives in Miami, it'll be the gift that keeps on giving,* my sales agent said. Seeing Caprice under the light of my kitchen now, I agreed.

The gift that keeps on giving, for real.

In the kitchen, she sat on the white stone countertop, wearing only my dress shirt with just two buttons done. I just had my briefs on as I rummaged through the fridge for two bottles of water. Offering her one, I asked if she wanted to stay the night.

She didn't even think about it before she quickly nodded. The first Monday in September was tomorrow, which meant it was Labor Day, so Caprice didn't have to wake up early for work.

We stayed up late together.

It was a little after three o'clock in the morning when she started to get sleepy. Underneath a throw blanket, she was curled up by my side on the living room sectional, her head resting on my chest. She started to doze off in the middle of our conversation. I was listening to one of her stories from the past twelve years when she yawned, and her eyes started to get droopy.

She was tired.

"Before you go to sleep," I interjected quietly, "I have a question."

"You can ask me anything," she promised.

"What did you wish for?" I'd sent her a cupcake, a candle, and a box of matches on her birthday. I was curious. I wasn't a broke eighteen-year-old kid anymore. With everything I had access to, maybe I could make her wish come true.

"You know, it had been such a long time since I made a birthday wish," she told me, her voice a little tired. "When I was a kid, I always wished for the same thing—happiness."

And those wishes ultimately did come true. This version of Caprice had to be the happiest person that I personally knew.

Caprice smiled a little, looking up to my face with sleepy eyes.

Delighted, she confessed, "But this time around… I wished for you."

## *Chapter Thirty-Eight*

# Caprice

It was November.

For the past two months I had been living some kind of fairytale life. My life before these past few months hadn't been bad, but these days, I would wake up every morning, happier to be in reality than in dreamland.

Some mornings, I could expect to wake up with an arm around me. It was lovely. Shaun would sleep over three to four times a week, his habitual presence in my apartment starting to make me feel like I had a roommate.

Though, I wasn't complaining.

Living with Shaun part-time had me feeling like I never wanted to live alone again.

Luckily for me, being here so often was convenient for him. His house was near the beach, but his job was in the city, and I lived in the city. Our routine was a useful little arrangement.

In all honesty however, we both knew convenience had nothing to do with why he was here all the time. We liked being together. On the nights when Shaun didn't have games, he would only be at the arena for practice and to train. Those were the days I would come home from work, finding him fresh out of the shower, chilling in my living room.

Shaun had his own key.

I gave it to him after the second week, upon realizing these sleep overs were about to be an ongoing thing. Very much like when I was sixteen, falling asleep with Shaun beside me was one of the best feelings.

It was the second week of November. I was sleeping alone

that night because Shaun was in Cleveland for a game. Because of my job, I watched it from home, bursting at the seams with pride as I watched him play. The Heat won that game and a few hours after it ended, Shaun's name was lighting up my phone.

"I've got a four o'clock flight tomorrow morning." His background was quiet, so he must've been in his hotel room. "I'll be around your place about seven-thirty. Do you need me to bring you anything?"

"From Cleveland?" I questioned.

"Yeah. They're known for…" he paused, trying to think of something, "…pierogies."

I laughed, shaking my head. I really didn't need anything, but since he was asking, "Ummm, you should get one of those souvenir magnets for our fridge."

"*Our* fridge?" he repeated.

"Definitely," I replied, thinking about how differently my kitchen was stocked now that a professional athlete lived with me part time. To stay in top shape, Shaun was a *very* clean eater. "No one who knows me would think that refrigerator is mine. There's way too much salmon and veggies in there now. It's *ours*."

Even though I couldn't see him, I already knew he was smiling. Shaun's last twelve years weren't the best. Of course, his unhappiness wasn't entirely my fault, but I certainly played a large part. So, now I only wanted to make him as happy as possible for the years to come. I had a feeling that these past two months, while amazing for me, were even better for him.

He was so full of light and energy, and I loved that.

I loved making him happy.

"Tomorrow at seven-thirty?" I asked. So, an hour before I had to head to work. "I'll see you in the morning."

* * *

I was still getting dressed when I heard my front door shut that early Thursday.

It was just ten minutes before seven, so Shaun was home earlier than expected. *Home*. I smiled at the thought, wondering if he thought of it that way. From my bedroom, I could hear him setting his travel bag on the hardwood floor in the foyer, and then his footsteps getting closer to my door.

I was wearing a sheer white bra and a black pencil skirt when Shaun let himself into the room. I put the blouse I had in my hands down onto the bed and hurried for a hug. His strong, muscular arms wrapped around me tight, lifting me up off the ground. Shaun smelled nice; the cologne he was wearing had hints of sage and peppermint.

I wondered if we'd ever stop doing this, welcoming each other home like we'd been apart for months. Wrapped in that warm embrace, I couldn't picture myself ever getting used to this. I really, really, *really* liked hugs when they came from him.

We pulled apart, but not all the way as Shaun still held me between his arms when he greeted, "Good morning."

I was smiling when I replied, "You're early."

Shaun's eyes traced down my half-dressed body and he disagreed. "I think I'm right on time."

In the weeks we'd spent together, I'd come to realize that with the right person, hands on your skin could be invigorating. Sometimes I would watch films and see how desperate some movie characters would be to hop into bed with other characters. Some movies are completely based upon who's sleeping with who, and that's it—that's the film. Movies can make sex seem like such a necessity.

I never used to understand movies like this. I never saw what the big deal was.

And then after just two months with Shaun, I truly understood the hype.

My first experience with anything remotely sexual came in the form of abuse. Hands in the shadows touching parts of my body that I didn't want touched. Before getting therapy, there were parts of my body that always brought back awful memories. I was conditioned to feel fear and dread if anything touched me in my intimate spaces—even my own hands. For so long, I associated any sensation down there with terror.

When I was sixteen, I had sex with Shaun one time. It was in his bedroom, on the last day we were together before I moved away. And the fear never came. With him, I was so comfortable in my own skin. You see, with Shaun, I *always* felt safe. It was in that safety, that I got to experience what a sexual encounter was *supposed* to feel like.

At sixteen, there was a little part of me that felt guilty for liking it. Maybe Gracie was right all along. Maybe I *was* fast. Even still, it wasn't until I'd gone through years of therapy that I was able to feel that level of comfort with my own body, alone, without Shaun's help.

I was twenty-six when I touched myself for the first time. *Twenty-six.*

Just *two* years ago.

And while touching myself could be nice given the right mood, it still wasn't enough to make me understand why some people talk about sex the way that they do.

But now I understood.

Shaun wasn't eighteen anymore. While our first time had been magical and so full of love, we were still just kids then. Some might say we shouldn't have even been doing things like that. Some might say we were acting too grown, and while I don't agree, I could see the difference.

Because *this* Shaun? This Shaun was a grown man, and it showed.

When we were together, time and experience were evident in his hands and it had me feeling like a *very* lucky woman. He was so patient, letting me set the pace, but little by little I grew comfortable enough to let him surprise me.

We were in a place where he was learning by body and I was learning his. He was learning my likes and dislikes. He was teaching me how to make him feel as good as he could make me feel. And, man, was he good at it… Shaun could do things to me that would have me daydreaming about him all day long; wanting him, watching the clock until I could get back to him.

For the first time in my life, I had a sex drive.

For the first time in my life, I understood how fun it could be to pleasure a man. When I got a physical response out of him, it would make me feel amazing. I could derive pleasure from simply knowing he felt it. Shaun had always been a giver, and he made me want to be a giver, too.

Shaun and I already had a great relationship, but our physical intimacy was like icing on an already *perfect* cake.

"I got you the magnet," he informed, head hovering above mine as I took slow steps backward, stopping only when I felt the bed behind my legs. His words were casual as he spoke, but the tone of his voice exposed his actual intentions. "It says, '*Greetings from Cleveland – The Metropolis of Ohio*' with a little red bird. You know, they really like cardinals over there."

"It's their state bird," I pointed out, sitting on the bed behind me and then laying down.

Shaun shook his head, descending with me until his face was at my knees. Chuckling, he asked, "Now why in the hell do you *know* that?"

Slowly, he spread my legs as I laughed. "What? You've never randomly decided to read an entire *Wikipedia* article about Ohio on a Saturday night just because? You're missing out. The state beverage is tomato juice, by the way."

"You just made that up," he opposed, his hands pushing up my skirt and guiding my panties down my legs.

"Now why would I make that up?" I questioned, anticipating the first touch as his head drew further between my thighs. "It's true. It's tomato juice, just like how Florida's is orange juice. I'm sure you knew that, though, since we *literally* grew up in Orange County."

"I didn't see anybody drinking tomato juice in Cleveland."

"That's because tomato juice is – " I gasped at the first touch of his tongue. " – *nasty*."

With one hand, I grabbed at the covers draped over my bed, squeezing the sheets within a tight fist as heat rose up from my neck to my cheeks. My other hand landed urgently on the back of Shaun's head, as he worked expertly between my legs. As he licked me, his hands dragged up from my knees and pulled my bra down, freeing my breasts before he took them both into his hands. My entire body was electrified. I whispered his name in soft moans as he tasted me, as he savored me slowly. As if we had all the time in the world.

It was still early. I wasn't late for work.

But I was willing to be.

Shaun held me down on the bed, hitting my most sensitive spots as I did everything I could to keep from melting underneath his hands. My back lifted a little, arching as dizzying sensations surged from Shaun's tongue and spread out to the rest of me. My soft moans morphed into louder declarations of love and encouragement.

And just as the first wave coursed through my body, powerful like electricity, Shaun rose up and buried himself deep within me. I could've cried from how amazing it felt, just feeling every inch of him disappear within my depths, skin to skin in the most intimate sense.

Even though I wasn't sexually active before, I've been on birth control since I was nineteen.

As a girl, I was a pretty late bloomer, getting my first period just a few days before I turned sixteen. It was the first of what would be a very irregular, sometimes painful, cycle. Birth control pills aren't just for unprotected sex. They could be really good at preventing painful cramps and regulating one's cycle. So personally, I took them to keep everything down there running smoothly.

I broke the good news to Shaun the morning after that first night on his boat.

I might've been imagining this, but when I told Shaun I was already on the pill, he almost seemed disappointed… Like he had been *trying* to get me pregnant.

But I was probably only thinking that out of a desire for it to be true. Because honestly, someday I wanted to have his babies. At his age now, he didn't have kids, so I wondered once or twice if he didn't want any. If he didn't, would he be willing to have just one or two for me? I would ask him someday.

Whatever the case, for now, our sex life was without hiccup.

Together we messed up the bed that I had just made. His arms wrapped around me, a hand settling at the back of my head, holding my gaze to those penny brown eyes. I brought up a hand to his face, using my thumb to wipe my essence from his lips, compelling him down for a passionately long kiss. I could taste me on him, and that just… did things to me.

The kiss deepened; lust, desire, and love mixing into a

nameless emotion. The temperature of the room seemed to be climbing, my skin growing hot to the touch as each of his thrusts sent the pressure mounting.

I was *screaming*.

But it was the good kind.

It was the *really* good kind.

Shaun held me in his arms as an uncontrollable quake took over every muscle in my body, my pulsating orgasm being the trigger that finally took him over the edge. And we both climaxed. Together.

I made a conscious decision to be late for work.

Shaun had completely disrupted my morning routine. I wasn't as bad as I used to be, but I certainly *still* had OCD. I had to remake the bed. I had to take another shower. I had to change my outfit for the day.

But most importantly, I couldn't just do that with him and then gather my things and leave.

I wanted to spend a little more time in his arms, cuddled close and giggling. Yeah, I might be walking into work two or three hours late, but I'd be in a *great* mood when I got there. And who was gonna check me? There were no bosses at FEEL.

I sent a quick text to the main office secretary, letting her know that something important came up and I'd be in at eleven-thirty. Just in time for my twelve o'clock Thursday session with Kahfi.

Work-life balance.

"I have another away game this weekend," Shaun told me from his side of the bed.

"A weekend game is good." That meant I could go with him and cheer for him live. I wondered where we were going. "What team?"

"The Lakers."

The smile on my face grew. "If we're going to LA, then you can meet my mom."

"And it only took me two months," he teased, already knowing we weren't on traditional time. Shaun and I had history, a *meaningful* history. If he had asked me to marry him five minutes after we first had sex, I would've said yes. No wait necessary. "I can't wait to finally meet her."

"I'll call her today. Knowing her, she'll probably already want to start shopping for dinner."

Shaun laughed at this; his handsome features were made brighter by his smile.

"Speaking of dinner," he started, "what are you doing for Thanksgiving?"

"FEEL," I answered simply. "I went home last year, so this year I'm spending Thanksgiving with the kids at FEEL. We take turns. The kids don't have families, so on holidays like Thanksgiving and Christmas, some staff stays behind, and we try to give the patients that cozy family vibe."

"That's beautiful," Shaun complimented. He was really proud of me for starting FEEL. He told me all the time, and I could tell he meant it from the admiration in his eyes. "What time do you have to be there?"

"About six."

He nodded and then asked, "You wanna join me and my mother before that, for Thanksgiving... lunch?"

Even though we'd been going steady for about two months, I still hadn't been around to see Miss Sylvia. Knowing how much pain I'd caused her son, a little part of me was afraid to face her. What if she didn't like me anymore? I wanted her to. I wanted to be close with her like I was before. And maybe I could even ask her about my birth mother.

But what if she didn't like me anymore?

As if reading my mind, Shaun assured, "My mom still likes you more than she likes me. Relax."

## *Chapter Thirty-Nine*

# SHAUN

My mother was hosting the entire family this year's Thanksgiving.

In my family, nobody ever just shows up right on schedule. Dinner was at six, so we could expect guests to start rolling in around eight. A bit before that, amidst all the Thanksgiving commotion in the kitchen, my mother had a light lunch planned on the patio by the water. Mom had gotten her contributions to tonight's dinner out of the way, leaving my aunts and cousins to finish up the rest.

My mother was setting the table for lunch now, humming to herself with a little more energy than usual. She was excited, a faint smile along her lips as she placed three sets of everything along a yellow checkered tablecloth. When we were growing up in Orlando, Caprice was like the daughter my mother never got to have.

After she disappeared, I could say my mother was almost as devastated as I was. Years would pass and my mother would let me in on a secret.

Caprice was *special*.

You see, Caprice wasn't *just* my childhood best friend. Caprice was also the daughter of my *mother's* childhood best friend, Alice Latimore. My mother grew up in the same house that I grew up in, which I already knew, but it had never dawned on me that this meant my mother was living in our house at the same time that Caprice's mother was living in the pink house across the street.

They were a year apart, with Alice being the older one. Together, they grew up in that same quiet cul-de-sac in Parramore, the best of friends. Alice left home at seventeen, for reasons my mother still doesn't understand, but judging from the way Caprice was treated in that house, it isn't hard to guess.

My mother told me once that she and Alice had always hoped their future kids would be close.

Caprice and I were more than just close.

For the past couple of months, life had been… good.

Lately, my time was separated between Caprice's apartment in the city, hotels across America for away games, and occasionally my own house by the beach. I was happier these days.

Believe me—I'd be the first to say that staking your happiness on a single person is dangerous and leaves you wide open for all kinds of heartache. I did it when I was eighteen, and I could feel myself doing the same thing now, at thirty, but this was different.

With time came realistic expectations. With experience came strength and preparedness for any outcome. I would be devastated if I lost Caprice again somehow, but it didn't kill me before, and it wouldn't kill me now. Age allowed me to understand that pain is unavoidable, and you'd live a very meaningless life trying to avoid it.

I understood the risk I was taking by loving Caprice with all my heart again.

And I was taking it.

Even still, I hoped for a long and fulfilling future. I had her in this moment, and I had no intention of ever letting her go. But the best part in all this was… she *didn't* want to leave.

Not this time.

Caprice had always been *the one.*

The beginning of our journey just didn't happen when I wanted it to. Ours was a '*right person, wrong time*' type of dilemma. Knowing Caprice now, a wiser part of me understood why I had to lose her before I got her back.

When we were growing up, Caprice was shy and apprehensive around others. To some, she might've been considered soft, and not in the best way. Without my help, she blossomed into a passionate, kindhearted doctor with her own non-profit, helping kids like the one I used to know. And she was so humble about it, too. Every time it crossed my mind, it'd fill me with so much pride. I've never been more proud of someone.

Knowing who she'd become, it was hard not to respect the process.

Even though I wasn't a part of it.

There were things about Caprice, things about her history, that I could've never given her the space and opportunity to confront. I wasn't mature or credentialed enough. I know myself, so I know I would've babied her. I would've let pity influence my actions. I don't know if that would've helped her heal. Despite everything I knew about her past, Caprice *was* healing. The journey to becoming the woman she was today couldn't have been easy.

If she had stayed with me, could I have been able to help her become this person? Probably not.

When we were kids, Caprice was so fragile, and I don't know how well I would've dealt with her feelings in the long run. Of course, I loved her, but… I was young.

In my early twenties, with all the pressures of a new career and a new routine, I might've neglected her. When my mother got cancer, with all the depression and uncertainty that it came with, it's possible that I could've taken my frustrations out on her. I was so used to Caprice always being there when we were kids, so it's not hard to imagine that I might've taken her for granted as adults.

The time apart put a lot of things into perspective. The time apart allowed us to grow.

Things were stable now. *I* was stable now.

I was at a point in my athletic career where I had nothing to prove anymore. With four playoff rings and an MVP title, my place in history wasn't up for debate. At this point, no matter what happened in my career, I would still be remembered as one of the greatest to ever do it. Basketball was still a priority, but not as much as it used to be.

Caprice was a functional, grown woman who didn't need my help with anything, but I had all the time, resources, and desire to take care of her *now*. I was substantially more mature than I was just five years ago. And after twelve years apart, I could get the next fifty with Caprice, and I'd know not to take it for granted.

Because I knew what the other side looked like. And it would be very hard to not appreciate every moment I didn't have to live in it.

So, despite the fact that I hated to admit it, this timing

might've just been perfect. And those miserable years might've just been part of some grand cosmic scheme that turned out to be necessary.

Caprice was wearing a pale pink sleeveless dress that tied behind her neck. It wasn't tight, but it did come in at the waist and flow out at her thighs. She liked to wear dresses and skirts, which hadn't been the case when we were younger.

Clothes always looked really nice on her, though she didn't wear them much when we'd be alone. In her apartment, Caprice liked to wear shirts with no pants, and on the occasion that she would wear shorts, they were usually paired with a sports bra. She was very comfortable in her skin, with a natural confidence that didn't feel forced at all.

I could only assume that this was because her body was a damn *masterpiece.*

In her pale pink dress, I watched her slow walk from the driver's seat of her red car, the clicking of the white heels she had on drumming a beat along my paved driveway. My eyes trailed up from her feet up her long brown legs, over her toned thighs, scanning over every flowy detail of her dress, and then finally her eyes.

When she was close enough, I pulled Caprice in by holding her at the small of her back, just above the curve of her behind, and pressed a kiss on the top of her forehead.

She was stiff.

"I can't believe you're nervous," I commented, liking what she did with her hair tonight. The front was pinned down with some pearly clips, but the rest of her textured tresses were left to fall backward against the top of her back and along her shoulders. I pulled on one of her curls as I teased, "Loosen up; she doesn't bite."

My mother halfway raised Caprice. Yeah, I loved Caprice and yeah, she broke my heart, but Mom would be the first to say that Caprice never owed me love in return. No matter what irrational thoughts were brewing in Caprice's head, my mother could never hate her.

Just like me.

"This house is massive," Caprice commented, her dark brown eyes moving up the hacienda architecture. She wasn't wrong. The house *was* pretty big considering only two people lived here most of the time. With eight bedrooms, I just figured that someday, I'd have a big enough family to fill them all. She added, "But it's beautiful, though."

"Do you wanna see the inside?" I asked, as we were still standing by the front door underneath the ceiling light. I could feel Caprice's back grow a little rigid underneath my hand at the sound of my invitation. She was so nervous. "Come on; she's waiting for us out back."

We passed through the kitchen on our way to the back of the house. In the kitchen we ran into one of my aunts, working on a dish for the dinner tonight. She gushed over how pretty Caprice was, mentioning how, just from looking at us, she could tell we were a better match than I was with Arielle.

In the two months we'd been spending time together, of course I told Caprice about Arielle, mentioning the women that came before my ex-fiancée as well. It was only natural for Caprice to be curious about the woman I almost proposed to. I didn't mention anything about doing it because I wanted kids. All I said was that when it all came down to it, Caprice was infinitely more important to me.

This was the truth.

There was a sliding glass door all the way in the back of the house that opened out to a beachside deck. On the deck, a table was set, and my mother was waiting. She didn't want to ruin anybody's appetite for dinner tonight, so she had prepared some light sandwiches, and *just* for Caprice, butterscotch chip cookies.

When the door slid open and my mother and Caprice came face to face, it was like watching two long lost family members reunite. Caprice stepped once ahead of me, and there was a noticeable pause in the air just before they both rushed toward each other, stopping directly into a long, heartfelt hug.

She didn't tense up in my mother's arms at all.

There were tears in Mom's eyes when they pulled back, still holding each other.

"Hey, cutie," Mom whispered softly, a good six inches

shorter than Caprice, so she had to reach up to wipe away the tear that raced down her cheek. Her hand moved slowly into Caprice's hair. "I told you natural was making a comeback. I'm glad you listened."

And with tears in their eyes, they both laughed.

In the quiet that followed, she apologized.

"I'm so sorry Miss Sylvia," Caprice whispered.

My mother shook her head. "For what, baby?"

"My last day… I saw you outside when I was loading my things into the car. I was too ashamed to face you. I ran away from you. I should've… I should've said goodbye at least."

"I forgot all about that day," my mother replied, still wiping Caprice's tears. "All I wanted to know was that you were safe. And I got the answer to that a long time ago. You don't have to apologize for not doing this or that the perfect way. You were a *baby*."

"I'm so sorry for what I let happen to Shaun that night," she cried, and it was clear that she'd carry that guilt for the rest of her life. Realizing that made my insides twist with remorse because it wasn't her fault. I made that stupid choice. Caprice wanted to run away, but I chose something else. What happened to me that night was my own fault.

My mother was sure to let her know.

"Shaun did that to himself, sweetheart." She quickly wanted to move on. "But enough about the past—look at you, *Doctor* Latimore!" My mother pushed her further out so that she could get a better look at her. "You are just absolutely stunning. And my goodness, this hair is so healthy and gorgeous."

My mother and hair—some things just never change.

Lunch went on without consequence. My mother and Caprice got along like the time had never passed. It was just story after story, with Caprice telling my mom about all the new updates on her life. Mom finally told Caprice that she used to be friends with her birth mother, but Caprice revealed that she already knew. When Caprice mentioned her adoptive mother, my mom mentioned how she looked forward to meeting her someday.

I'd gotten the chance to meet her last weekend when Caprice and I were in LA for the *Laker* game.

Meeting Dr. Johnson, Caprice's mother, made Caprice's friendship with Sanaa make a lot more sense. Dr. Johnson and Sanaa Montgomery were very similar personalities, with Dr. Johnson just being a little more mature, but both were just as peppy and eccentric as the other. However, Dr. Johnson warmed up to me a lot more than Sanaa did. Meeting her was nice, getting to put a face to the person who took care of my girl all those years ago. I was grateful for her.

After my mother expressed interest in meeting her new mother someday, Caprice confessed something that I could just tell broke my mother's heart.

"When I was a little girl, I used to wish that you were my mom," she said.

My mother's smile was a little sad, her hand reaching across the table to settle on top of Caprice's.

"You were already like a daughter to me, Caprice. Everything I ever wanted in a daughter, really. When I realized just how much my son loved you—" My mother glanced at me before looking back at Caprice, and I knew what she was about to say. "I realized that it was only a matter of time before you *really would* be."

* * *

## Caprice

When all the kids crowded around Shaun, Kahfi stood at the center of the circle, introducing every child to him personally.

Shaun hadn't planned on coming to FEEL, but after such a great lunch with his mother, he decided to stop in for a few minutes before going back home to his family. It wasn't much, but any moment we could spare to be together was always taken up. I left my car at Shaun's house, and he drove me here. After dinner with his family, he'd be back later tonight to drive me home to my apartment, where we would be spending the night.

Standing off in the distance, as I helped Rebecca set the table for the kids, it made me smile to see how important it made Kahfi feel to be able to say he got to meet *Thee* Shaun Taylor first. It was obvious how proud he was that he got to be the one to introduce him to the other kids.

They circled around him excitedly, hands coming out to shake his hand or simply just touch him. To the kids, Shaun was a celebrity, and the fact that he was here electrified the space. The children were absolutely elated. Him being here made for a decent enough distraction while the staff got the finishing touches on dinner set up.

"He's even more handsome in person," Rebecca made conversation as we set little ceramic red plates on the white tablecloth-covered cafeteria tables. I glanced at Rebecca out the sides of my eyes. Yes—Shaun was gorgeous. I already knew this. But hearing it come out of the mouth of the coworker I was least fond of might've rubbed me just a little wrong.

I looked over my shoulder and snuck a look at Shaun, who was practically drowning in excited little hands and voices. Unable to help myself, the display made me smile.

He *did* look really good tonight, halfway between formally dressed and business casual, with his white dress shirt tucked into black slacks and paired with a dark pair of oxfords. Shaun had a fresh cut, his waves rippling subtly down to a chiseled hairline that transitioned seamlessly into a sexy five o'clock shadow.

Rebecca wasn't wrong. Shaun was fine, but that didn't mean it didn't bother me that she was comfortable enough to let me know.

"I didn't realize you had friends in such high places," she commented as she placed napkins on each set plate. "I'm impressed, Caprice. An *NBA* ball player…"

It was petty of me, but I corrected her. "Boyfriend."

"Right," she nodded, her smile just as forced as a smile could be. She passed a hand through her blonde hair and stared at me. Rebecca sounded like she was accusing me of something when she mentioned, "And he already knows Kahfi."

"Yes," I confirmed simply. "Kahfi was doing really well in therapy, so I took him to a *Miami Heat* event."

"That's not where you met him, is it?" She was definitely

accusing me of something with that question. As if I would use Kahfi to bait a ball player. That seemed more like her thing, not mine.

"I've known Shaun since we were kids." Not that it was any of her business.

"Oh, how cute…" Her tone was flat, a little bummed to learn the truth was less interesting than what she was cooking up in her head. "But speaking of Kahfi—he's been doing so well lately."

I agreed. Kahfi hadn't split into any of his alters in three months now. "He has, hasn't he?"

"Yes," Rebecca nodded. "Logan and I were thinking about referring him to an external psychologist and beginning the necessary paperwork to have him discharged from the center. He still needs the mental health maintenance, but you've set an amazing foundation, Caprice. I must give you your props. Thanks to you, Kahfi doesn't *need* FEEL anymore. As his doctor, you would need to sign off on it."

My hands on the napkins froze. Again, Rebecca wasn't wrong. FEEL was saved for the most egregious psych cases, for the kids who couldn't thrive without the extra care. Over the past few months, Kahfi had become one of our most well-adjusted patients. She was right. While he still needed the mental healthcare, he didn't need to be *here* anymore.

But that didn't mean it didn't bother me to hear her say it. We only had so many spots at the center. The longer Kahfi stayed here, the longer a child who might need this place more was left out.

"So, how soon do you think we can get him back into the system?"

"Um…" I hesitated. My throat was a little dry when I forced the next few words out. "…I'll see about the discharge paperwork next week."

It was probably unprofessional for me to be this attached to one of my patients, but Kahfi was special to me. Even though I only worked weekdays, some weekends, I'd come into work just be sure he ate his lunch that day. So, there wasn't a doubt in my mind that I would lose sleep thinking about his wellbeing once he was discharged.

Kahfi didn't have a family to go back to, which meant he was going back to foster care.

With him back in the system, I couldn't be given any guarantees. Not really. Of course, social workers are good at their jobs and most foster parents are well-meaning individuals, but… what if? What if someone hurt him again?

I told him I would protect him.

And what if I failed?

"Hey, I'mma be back to pick you up around ten," Shaun informed once all the kids stopped crowding around him and began eagerly taking their seats at the dinner tables.

My mind was far away when I nodded. "Okay, that's perfect."

He sauntered closer over to me, the expression on his face inquisitive. Ducking a little, he spoke lowly into my ear when he asked, "You alright, Butterscotch?"

I nodded a quiet yes, looking up at him to add, "I'll tell you later."

Shaun understood that this meant that there was *something*, but I didn't want to talk about it here. I'd tell him all about it when we were in bed together later tonight, in the privacy of my apartment. Accepting this Shaun's hand briefly pulled at my waist, drawing me closer for a conservative kiss on the cheek goodbye, conscious of the fact that we were among children… and at my job.

The little peck on the cheek was still enough to get hooting and hollering from my young patients anyway.

"Oh my God, you two… In front of the *children*?" I could feel the wind of Rebecca's words behind my neck. When I turned to shoot her a look, she was looking up at Shaun like he had sunlight streaming from out of his pores. *I know this woman is not making eyes at my boyfriend in front of me…* "It was so nice to meet you, Mr. Taylor. My husband is such a big fan."

She stuck out her hand for him to shake.

Shaun, ever the polite one, responded graciously, though his hand never left my waist. She tried to nonchalantly put her hand back down. I could feel Rebecca getting ready to ask him for a photo, and maybe he could, too, because he immediately asked, "Could you excuse us for a second, Reba?"

"Rebecca," I whispered, when I realized she wasn't going to correct him.

"Right, sorry… Rebecca." In just about the politest way you can tell someone to *go away*, he repeated himself. "Could you excuse us for a second?"

"She was about to ask you for a picture," I whispered to him as soon as she walked away.

"Yeah, I know." Shaun's hand at my waist rose to my cheek, his thumb gently caressing as he asked, "You sure you're okay?"

"It's just work stuff," I made sure to let him know, not wanting him to worry about it the whole night while he was with his family. "I'll tell you all about it when we're home."

Shaun smiled to hear me call it that, but why wouldn't I? He had his own key.

"See you at ten," I whispered before giving him one last kiss goodbye.

# Chapter Forty

# SHAUN

Caprice was so stressed.

"And I'm just so scared about putting him back into the system like that," she confessed, a little teary eyed. "Kahfi is so… He's been through so much, and it would just destroy me if anyone ever hurt him again. I would feel responsible."

I was sitting up against the headboard, and Caprice had her head laid in my lap as she vented. Her hair was braided against her scalp in two halves, feeling soft against the skin of my thigh. To bed, she wore just a bra and a pair of shorts, but I was used to that by now.

"Well, does he have to go back into the system? What happened to his folks?"

"No father on record, and his mother is serving a life sentence upstate. She's all Kahfi has in terms of family in this world."

"*Damn…*" That was a tough hand to be dealt for just a kid. I made an observation. "You're so worried about him."

Caprice looked up at me from my lap and nodded, the anxiety she was feeling weighing down on her brows, turning her eyes a little reflective. "I am."

I weaved my fingers through hers, holding her hand as I asked her a question.

"Do you want to know why I asked if Kahfi was mine that first time you brought him by the arena?"

"Because you think if we mixed our DNA, we'd have a kid who looks like him," she guessed.

"Well, yeah… I do." She wasn't wrong about that. If Caprice had told me Kahfi was ours, I would've believed her. He looked like us. "But that's not it. It was *you*, actually."

"What do you mean?"

A faint smile spread across my face. "You don't see yourself when you're with him," I told her. "Your energy, the way you hover, the way you keep your eye on him at all times, the way he makes you smile—it's all very... *maternal.*" I shrugged. "You don't act like his doctor. You act like his mother."

"I do?"

"You do," I doubled down with a nod, dropping a wild idea in her lap. "This might sound crazy, but... Why don't you just adopt him? That'll take him out of the system, right?"

Caprice sat up from my lap, facing me as she tried to find her words. Her heart must've been racing because her hand was at her chest, and her breathing had picked up. "*Adopt* him? Am I even allowed to do that?"

"I play ball for a living," I reminded. "I don't know anything about adoptions... But I can help you, if you want me to."

I knew adoptions could be difficult and expensive. Without the proper connections, they could be particularly time consuming and draining. If Caprice needed me to, I wouldn't mind calling in a few favors for her.

"Adoptions are so hard," she reasoned doubtfully. She was right about that. Even with all the resources I could offer, adoptions are *still* hard.

"So, it'll be hard," I concluded, "but how bad do you want him? If I could be so bold—you *love* this kid. I can tell from just looking at you that your heart won't be at ease unless you know Kahfi is safe and taken care of. So, why not personally interfere to make sure that he is?"

This conversation was getting very real for her. She could see that I was serious. "And you wouldn't... you wouldn't mind if I...? Like... would *we* be okay if I...?"

After everything we'd been through to get to this point? "We'll be fine."

She was talking so fast, breathing a little hard as she tried to get the words out.

"Because I plan on spending the rest of my life with you, and if I adopt a kid... We're going to get married someday, right? If we do, Kahfi technically won't be *just* mine." She asked me a very blunt question then. "Do you even *want* kids, Shaun?"

And I just had to laugh at the irony.

"What's funny?" she wanted to know.

"Adopt him," was all that I said in response. "I'm in this for the long run. Whether you marry me tomorrow or next year, I won't let you do this on your own. I'm fully aware that if he's yours, then he's mine, too. I'm fine with that."

For a second, all Caprice could do was blink in my direction.

"I can marry you tomorrow." We both knew that sounded ridiculous, but she was dead serious about it, too.

I broke into a smile, saying, "I know you can." But this wasn't how I wanted to ask her. "But I'm not proposing to you at one o'clock in the morning on a Friday, in your apartment, with no ring, wearing nothing but boxer briefs. If you give me some time, I can make it a bit more meaningful."

It was the last Friday in November, and I had every intention of asking Caprice to marry me on Christmas Day. Unbeknownst to Caprice, I'd already gotten her mother's blessing when we were in LA.

I didn't need to hire an event planner for it this time either. This proposal mattered to me. This one was coming from the heart, but I just needed a little bit more time.

"It doesn't have to be too over the top. I don't have an Instagram," she whispered, which made me laugh.

"You've got jokes." I pulled her in for a kiss, feeling her soft lips give in completely to mine. Her arms circled around my naked torso, and her skin felt warm against my own. I was taken back to the nights I used to spend with her in her bedroom all those years ago. Caprice used to hold onto me just like this, her arms circled around my waist, her head resting on my shoulder, with soft breaths hitting against my neck.

It was interesting—how I could just tell that I put her at ease. She felt safe here, with me, held close. I didn't have to ask to confirm; I just knew. How refreshing it was to understand a person this much. I never had to do much guessing with Caprice. She opened herself up to me in a way that I knew she didn't open up to anyone else. I got to see a side of Caprice that nobody else knew existed, which made me understand her in ways that nobody else ever could.

"We really are soulmates," she broke the silence. It was like she already knew about the thoughts running through my mind. And maybe she almost did. It was just as likely that Caprice understood me just as much as I understood her. So, why *wouldn't* she know what I was thinking?

"Yeah," I quietly agreed, letting my arms close around her in an equally tight hold. "We really are."

* * *

## Caprice

Christmas at FEEL is always such a joyous time.

Since the center's inception, Mr. Fine, our organization's biggest benefactor, has spent an obscene amount of money each December, ensuring each child at FEEL didn't just get a new donated toy, but gifts they *actually* asked for. The kids would submit their Christmas lists at the end of November, and if their requests were within reason, Mr. Fine spared no expense.

The kids really look forward to this day every year.

This year, for his first and last Christmas at FEEL, all Kahfi asked for a new pair of *OMN1S* basketball shoes. He got them, and he might've smiled for maybe one second before his smile faded again.

Kahfi was sad today.

All the other kids were playing outside that Christmas morning with their new toys and gadgets, but Kahfi stayed inside, brooding in the center's main lobby.

"Why are you brooding?" I asked him, taking a seat beside him on one of the lounge area sofas. Across from us was Shaun, knowing what about to unfold, and claiming a front row seat to it. Since Thanksgiving, Shaun's presence at my job stirred a lot less commotion. He'd been back two or three times since then, so by the time Christmas rolled around, the kids weren't as starstruck anymore and Rebecca did eventually get her picture. "It's Christmas. Where's your Christmas cheer?"

Kahfi turned his head in my direction, a slightly annoyed dip to his brows. "The housekeeping staff took all my clothes to the laundry yesterday."

"Clean clothes are nice," I commented, trying to keep from smiling as I snuck a quick glance at Shaun who was also trying to keep a straight face.

"No, Miss Latimore." Kahfi shook his head, looking like he felt sorry for me because I didn't understand. "They only do that if kids are about to get evicted. Y'all about to evict me. I know it."

"We don't use the word evict, Kahfi."

"Oh, I'm *sooooorry*," Kahfi exaggerated the word, extra sarcastic. Out of the corner of my eye, I could see Shaun bringing a hand to cover his mouth and his shoulders moving a little with his quiet laugh. "Discharge. Y'all about to discharge me."

"That's a good thing, sweetheart. It means FEEL worked for you. You're better equipped to go back out into the outside world."

"The foster care system and the outside world ain't the same thing, Miss Latimore," he pointed out, sounding more like Moreno than he did Kahfi, but I knew it was Kahfi speaking because Kahfi would call me *Miss* no matter how many times he was corrected.

"I got you something," I told him. "For my one and only psychotherapy patient."

Kahfi perked up a little at the sound of that. "You mean—for your favorite patient, Miss Latimore."

He wasn't wrong, but I made sure to tell him, "I don't play favorites."

"What did you get me?" Kahfi asked instead of arguing with it. I pointed out a red paper-wrapped box underneath the Christmas tree in the main lobby and told Kahfi that it was for him. As any child would, he rushed out of his seat in order to get his hands on it. I left Shaun in the lounge area as I followed Kahfi to the tree. Kahfi showed no regard for the wrapping paper as he tore it to shreds.

When the gift paper was removed, Kahfi did his best to not sound unimpressed when he said, "Oh, it's a suitcase." For my sake, he tried to rouse up as much excitement as he could fake when he said, "Thanks, Miss Latimore..."

As he inspected the blue hard-shell rolling suitcase, he let out a dejected sigh. "I guess this really means y'all really kicking me out."

"Don't say it like that," I discouraged.

"How do you want me to say it?" He looked up from his suitcase, a little redness starting to appear in his eyes.

"You're going home, Kahfi."

He shook his head. "And where's that anyway? I thought FEEL was my home. Home don't mean anything if you don't get the choice to stay when you wanna stay."

"FEEL was your home, but now you have a new home."

"I can't call no house full of strangers my home, just because you call it that," Kahfi argued.

"You're not going to a house."

"An apartment full of strangers, then," Kahfi amended, adding sarcastically, "Even better. How many beds per room at this place? Four? Six?"

"You're actually sleeping in the living room for a couple of weeks. You see, your new guardian is in the middle of a move, because she was living in a one-bedroom apartment, and now she's gotta transition into a two-bedroom." I told him. "And then it's just you and her."

"I get my own bedroom?" Kahfi asked, interest piquing at the idea.

I nodded. "You will."

"Where does she stay?"

"It's actually just a fifteen-minute walk from FEEL, so you could still visit your friends on the weekends."

"And I could still see you?" Kahfi asked, a little hopefulness in his voice. I nodded, smiling a little. Kahfi sighed, obviously a little less apprehensive at the idea of leaving, and then he asked, "Is she nice?"

"She's fair."

"That means she's mean as hell," Kahfi deduced, sounding almost a little defeated. It was like he already knew he had no choice in the matter, and he wasn't going to bother arguing with me over things he couldn't control. He wasn't looking forward to leaving, but he knew he was powerless to stop it.

That's when I decided to tell him. "It's me, Kahfi."

He didn't get it at first. With an eyebrow raised, he asked, "What's you?"

"*I'm* your new guardian." I was still going through the steps to outright adopt Kahfi, but that would take a little more time. With Shaun's help, I was able to get some legal work done so that I could at least be Kahfi's caretaker in that interim period. It would probably be a year before Kahfi was *legally* my child, but I could rest easy knowing he was going to be safe with me while we waited. "You're coming home with me."

I could already see water collecting at the rims of his brown eyes, his lower lip subtly quivering when he quietly asked, "Is this a prank?"

A tear slipped down my cheek when I chuckled at the question. "I'm serious."

"Really?" His shoulders had yet to relax. He wouldn't allow himself to be happy about it unless he was absolutely sure I wasn't kidding. Stepping closer to me, he left his suitcase behind when he asked, "You mean it?"

"I mean it," I nodded.

Kahfi looked around me, his eyes settling on Shaun, who was still sitting in the lobby's wait area, watching this all unfold.

"And is he…" Kahfi pointed, barely able to get the words out. "Is he gonna be there… be there, too?"

This question, and the excitement in his voice, made me laugh. I shrugged before I nodded. "Yeah… he's around a lot… *if* you don't mind."

"I don't…" Kahfi shook his head vehemently, eyes bouncing from me to Shaun in the distance. His little hand came up to wipe the tears that were falling. "I don't mind."

"Well then," I pivoted, resting two hands on his shoulders, "let me help you put all your clean clothes in your Christmas gift."

Kahfi grabbed at the blue roller bag's handle, a lot more enthusiastic about the gift now than he was before. For someone who was so upset about leaving just five minutes before, he was practically speed walking toward the hallway that led to the patient rooms. I stopped to have a word with Shaun as Kahfi rushed ahead.

Shaun stood to his feet when I was close enough. His hand came up to wipe the tear that had slipped down my cheek while my hand settled at his chest. I whispered, "That was just perfect."

"That was like watching one of those cheesy Christmas movies," he agreed.

"I'm gonna go help him pack." It was still early in the morning and Shaun had plans for us later tonight. We planned to spend the day getting Kahfi settled in at my apartment, and Miss Sylvia was coming by my place tonight around nine, after Kahfi was put to bed, so that Shaun and I could have some time alone for the remainder of the holiday.

I looked at my freshly done red manicure, pressed against the front of Shaun's gray shirt, knowing I was ready for tonight.

Shaun was doing his best to be subtle about it, but I knew him better than I knew anyone. The big surprise was out the moment he told me his mother would watch Kahfi so that we could have dinner tonight. Proposing to me on Christmas was *exactly* the kind of thing Shaun would do. But for his sake, I'd pretend to be surprised.

I smiled, getting on my tiptoes to press a kiss onto his cheek before I announced, "We'll be right out."

Kahfi was waiting for me at the end of the hall when I caught up. His happy dimpled smile was just about the best part of my morning so far. Standing there with his blue suitcase, in his plain white shirt and black basketball shorts, he suddenly looked like he couldn't get out of FEEL fast enough.

The stark change in attitude was honestly *really* amusing. Soon as I was close enough, his head tilted back to look up at me and he asked, "How long do I get to stay with you?"

It was a natural question for a foster child to ask. Foster homes are often transient, and foster kids learn all too soon that it's better to not get attached.

But Kahfi was no longer in the foster care system. I shook my head at his question, unable to help my smile when I answered.

"For as long as you want."

# Epilogue

## Caprice

Leave it to Sanaa to throw herself the most outrageously extravagant wedding I've ever been to.

It was March 3rd, 2019, Sanaa's wedding day. As maid of honor to just about the most ruthless bridezilla I'd ever had the pleasure of dealing with, I was probably happier today than Sanaa was. Happy that all of this was finally about to be over.

The ceremony was gorgeous.

Sanaa got married in a mansion by the beach. Just her and one thousand of her closest friends. I knew Sanaa's family was pretty well-connected, but I was still shocked to see that even the governor was here. With the grand house decorated in a white and yellow color scheme, coming to the ceremony was like walking into a dreamland. Sanaa clearly had spared no expense.

White roses covered just about every corner, streaming down iridescent yellow ribbon that matched with the bridesmaid dresses. The entire female half of the wedding party was forced to wear this loud shade of lemon yellow, with me getting the privilege of wearing paler shade, closer to lemon cream. For Sanaa, I flat ironed my hair, even though I usually preferred not to straighten it.

The ceremony was held outside on the beach sand, and inside the mansion was where the reception would be held.

There was all manner of fanfare; with guests like Shaun Taylor acting as her groom's best man, Grammy award-winning singer, Eden Xavier, singing live as Sanaa walked down the aisle, and countless other local celebrities. Sanaa's wedding was no doubt the event of the year, and we were still in *March.*

I had no desire to compete.

My wedding was in five months, on the first Saturday in

August, and I was fine with it being small. Of course, my over-the-top best friend was my event planner, so who's to say my wedding would ever be considered "*small*", but it certainly wasn't going to be as extravagant as today's event.

I had just finished giving the customary maid of honor speech over champagne at the reception.

After months and months of best-friend-of-the-bride duties, I could finally catch my breath. The ceremony had gone through without consequence. All twenty-five—yes, *twenty-five*—of Sanaa's bridesmaids showed up on time. None of the guests arrived wearing white. And my speech at the reception was delivered with clarity, receiving just the right amount of applause—enough so that I knew it went well, but not so much that I was stealing Sanaa's shine on her big day.

Now I could just sit beside my fiancé over dinner, and just breathe.

"You seem tired," Shaun commented from my left. Underneath the table, I could feel his hand on my lap, keeping me grounded, letting me know he was with me. I leaned to the left a little, letting some of my body weight rest on him as he encouraged it. "You should relax."

"Easy for you to say," I replied, looking towards his face. He looked super handsome tonight, with a fresh haircut and in that tux. I was already thinking about getting my hands on him the moment we were alone. From that glitter in his eyes, I could tell he was thinking the same thing about me. "Micah is really laid back, so all you had to do as the best man was hire strippers for his bachelor party last night and then show up today, pretending like you're not still hungover."

"It was just poker and cognac," Shaun muttered, lifting a hand and swearing, "No strippers were hired." He rose an eyebrow then. "Why? Did *you* hire strippers for Sanaa's bachelorette party last night?"

"No." I shook my head. "Sanaa thinks strippers are dirty."

"Of course she does." I could almost hear the eyeroll in his voice. Shaun chuckled, shaking his head at this information. It was no secret that my fiancé and Sanaa had this sort of love-hate thing going on—mostly hate. It was pretty funny to behold—they bickered like estranged siblings. "So, you would've hired them if she wanted them," Shaun concluded.

"Not for *me,*" I emphasized. Of course, Shaun already knew this. He, more than anyone, knew I wasn't giving any other man the time of day, ever. But yes, if Sanaa had wanted strippers, I would've been powerless to deny her. To call Bride-Sanaa demanding would be an understatement.

"Just *lie*, Caprice," Shaun laughed, not caring for my honesty.

"Like you lied about poker and cognac?" I asked.

Shaun shook his head, "No. Unlike *you*—regardless of what Micah wants—I'm loyal to my fiancée first."

"Oh *stoooop,*" I whined, not wanting him to make me feel guilty. "So, Micah *did* want them?"

"Nah, he was too scared Sanaa would find out, so he told me not to hire any," Shaun replied with a smile, indirectly admitting that he, too, would've hired strippers if Micah had wanted them.

I playfully nudged at his shoulder with my own. "You're so annoying."

"There's that smile," he mused. "As tired as you look, are you ready to do this all over again in August?"

"Our wedding isn't going to be as exhausting as this one," I assured confidently, admiring the nearly five carat diamond on my finger. I never got tired of looking at it; it was so pretty, clear as spring water, and always catching the surrounding light. "Our wedding is going to be lowkey and intimate and… *not* Three. Hours. Long."

Shaun snickered before cutting a piece off the steak on his dinner plate. He extended his fork to me, and I took a bite. "Did you eat breakfast this morning?"

There was no time to eat a full breakfast when I woke up this morning at Sanaa's house. At best, I was snacking during the little free moments I did get in between helping Sanaa prepare for the day. "No. How did you know?"

"I can just tell," he answered, cutting me another piece.

"I can feed myself, you know," I mentioned after the second bite.

Shaun nodded, cutting a third. "I know… But I like this.

Open up."

Our little moment was interrupted by Sanaa's hands hitting against the table to get our attention. Shaun looked at her pointedly, while I kept a straight face and waited.

"I hate to interrupt your little adorable display—" no, she most likely didn't hate to at all "—but, Reese, it's almost time for me to throw my wedding bouquet."

"Okay?" I squinted, unsure of why she was telling me this. "Do I really have to be in the circle? What's the point? I'm *already* engaged. We are all aware I'm getting married next, so—"

"It's *traditionnnnnn*," she cut me off, stretching the word impatiently, like she wasn't about to argue with me about this. Sanaa turned her attention to Shaun. "You wouldn't mind letting me borrow my *best* friend—" Not liking the sound of that, Shaun discreetly squeezed my thigh under the table, and I had to hold back a giggle. "—for just ten minutes, would you, Shaun?"

"Your what?" he asked, which made Sanaa scowl.

"I know you heard me," she whispered quickly. Sanaa urged me out of my seat with her eyebrows. "Reese, come on."

I stood to my feet, trying to keep the peace.

"You better throw it at me, Sanaa," I warned once I'd gotten around the table. "If I don't catch it, that has to be bad luck."

"After all the work I've put into planning your wedding—shit, you *better* catch it," Sanaa retorted. We walked together, leaving Shaun behind as she complained, "Do you have any idea how hard it is to plan an August wedding in Miami?"

"You remind me every day," I giggled quietly. Sanaa usually didn't take wedding clients on such short notice, but she made an exception for me, her best friend. Shaun had proposed to me last Christmas, and we wanted to get married before the year was up. Eight months, for Sanaa, was an obscenely short amount of time to plan a "decent" wedding.

Sanaa was way more stressed about it than I was. I could've married Shaun in a courthouse, for all I cared. The wedding ceremony was for family—his and mine.

August was a good time to do it. It was just before the next basketball season, on the last full month of Shaun's break after this season.

We had plans for this summer.

I was getting off the pill in June, right after the playoffs, and then we would start trying for a baby immediately after, so that if I did get pregnant, I wouldn't be showing on our wedding day.

Shaun and I were very methodical about it. We knew exactly how many kids we wanted, and so the timeline was already set in motion. If everything went according to plan, our son Kahfi would have a brand-new sibling this time next year. I wanted another boy. Shaun didn't have much of a preference.

Unlike how I originally planned, I never ended up moving into that two-bedroom apartment. By the time my lease had aged out, Shaun and I were already engaged, and it just made more sense to move in with him. There, Kahfi always had Miss Sylvia to look after him when I was at work, and she loved having him around.

Kahfi reminded her so much of when Shaun was that age, and she'd often say helping out with him was like reliving the happiest times of her life. This was great for me because Miss Sylvia was just about the only adult in Miami, besides Shaun, who I trusted alone with him. Even now, at Sanaa's wedding reception, my heart was at ease because I knew Kahfi was safe at home with my mother-in-law.

It was me and twenty-five bridesmaids huddled in a half-circle around Sanaa while her back was turned. The bouquet of white roses swung above her head. I didn't move as dozens of hands sprang into the air, clamoring for the flowers desperately. The bouquet bounced off the tip of someone's fingers pivoting to my direction and falling directly at my feet.

All I had to do was bend over and pick it up.

Sanaa turned around to find the bouquet in my hands, and very discreetly, I could see her exhale as if a source of great stress had dissipated. Even the universe approved of the engagement ring on my finger, and so Sanaa was relieved. She wanted me to catch it. Even though she wasn't Shaun's biggest fan, she could tell that I loved him.

And it was obvious that he loved me.

* * *

# SHAUN

We were at the arrival hall in the Orlando International Airport.

Caprice and I had just come off a two-week honeymoon in St. Lucia, and she was under the impression that our stop at Orlando International was a layover on route to Miami. I had a surprise for her, though.

Today was her twenty-ninth birthday.

"This airport has changed so much since I was a little girl," Caprice observed, her eyes having an almost distant quality to them, like she was remembering something from a long time ago. The last time she must've been here, she could've been about eight, flying in from Alabama more than twenty years back.

As always, Caprice looked pretty this morning. Her dark brown skin had seen a lot of sun these past two weeks, and so she was absolutely glowing. Though, that couldn't have been the only reason. After two months of trying, we were together in an oceanfront hotel room in St. Lucia when a pregnancy test finally came back positive.

Just when I thought the island getaway with the love of my life couldn't get any better… it got better. Caprice wanted a boy. As of late, since we *already* had a twelve-year-old son, I was leaning more in favor for a girl. Either way, it didn't matter at this point. Both Caprice and I wanted lots of kids, so this pregnancy wouldn't be our last one.

"You're going the wrong way," she told me as I rounded a corner, rolling our luggage towards car rentals instead of flight connections.

I shook my head, telling her, "We don't have a connecting flight. I'm driving us to Miami instead."

It was only a four-hour drive south from Orlando, but it was still an inconveniencing choice to make. Naturally, Caprice was curious, an eyebrow poking up when she questioned, "Why are we doing that?"

She kept walking alongside me, holding her purse while I

pushed our bags. I filled her in a little.

"I got you something for your birthday, and we have to be here for you to see it."

"You didn't have to get me anything."

"I've been wanting to do this for you since I was eighteen," I confessed, which then made her curious.

"What is it?" she asked as we passed through the automatic sliding doors, and into the car rental garage. I pressed my lips together and shook my head. It was a surprise. "Oh, come on, give me a hint," she pressed.

"Nope." After confirming the car reservation, I loaded our bags into the back of a white SUV, coming around the passenger's side to hold the door open for my pregnant wife. Keeping eye contact, she tried to will me into submission as she stepped into the car. That look wouldn't work. I didn't budge. "You can wait."

I took the scenic route, the whole time watching as distant memories of the past flashed across her eyes. She watched the familiar Orlando roads turn into Semoran Boulevard, from East Michigan Street to West Michigan Street and then finally up that familiar stretch of Downtown Orlando, on Division Avenue.

That's when she realized we were going to Parramore.

She tried not to show it, but I could tell that being here—back in *this* particular neighborhood—it still bothered her a little. This place held a lot of dark memories for her, and Parramore is already kind of a dark place on its own. Tucked underneath the shadows of the downtown high rises, this was the forgotten part of Orlando.

While many people picture Central Florida as this hub of orange orchards and talking cartoon mice, places like Parramore are cast to the wayside. *People* in Parramore are cast to the wayside.

But I, for one, would never forget where I came from.

Though, that didn't mean it had to stay exactly the same.

Caprice was silent as we pulled into our old, dingy cul-de-sac. Most of the homeowners on this street hadn't survived the 2008 financial crisis, so a lot of our old neighbors had just up and abandoned the block, leaving behind deserted houses, deteriorating day by day.

One such house was the pink house across the street from

my childhood home.

I bought it last month.

And then I had it torn down.

"It's gone," Caprice whispered as I pulled up to where the old house used to be. Across the street was my old house, which my mother still owned, but hadn't been back to in years.

Caprice got out of the car and I followed, coming around the back of the white SUV to join her on the passenger's side. I weaved her fingers between mine, standing close behind as I circled my arms around her waist and settled my hands at her stomach. Resting my chin against the back of her head, neither of us said anything as we just looked on at the empty lot.

Caprice turned her head back slightly and looked up at me when she asked, "What happened to it?"

"I bought it," I told her.

"So that you could tear it down?" she asked, a little smile starting at the corner of her lips. I simply nodded. She looked again at the empty piece of continuous lawn. It was worth every penny when I heard the relief in her voice when she whispered, "It's *really* gone."

She exhaled, relaxing her back more against my chest as I leaned against the car behind me.

"I hated this house," she told me quietly as the light breeze blew the floral scent of her hair in my direction. Her hair felt soft against my chin as I just quietly breathed her in. "Every time I have a nightmare, it always takes place in the pink house."

"I know."

And now the pink house doesn't exist.

"I know I said you didn't have to get me anything, but this..." She laughed a little before she turned back around to look at me. "This was the perfect gift."

I ducked down to press a kiss onto her soft lips, tasting a hint of her cherry-flavored lip balm against my tongue. Her hands shook away from mine, leaving my hands at her stomach as she brought up a hand to the back of my head and deepened the kiss. Who's to say how much time passed? It could've been hours, or it could've been minutes—I certainly couldn't tell the difference. When we separated, my lips were still close to hers when I told her,

"That's not the whole gift."

*"Oh..."* She giggled a bit. "Then what is it?"

I lifted a hand and pointed so that she could follow my line of sight.

"That house and that house, too," I pointed at the two next-door houses on either side of where her grandmother's home used to be. I bought those ones as well. "These ones are getting torn down next week, and we got a permit from the city to combine all three lots for a construction project."

"Really?" There was an excited curiosity in her voice when she wondered, "What are we building?"

I smiled before I told her.

"The Dr. Caprice Latimore Youth Center." She was Mrs. Taylor everywhere except professionally, where she still went by Dr. Caprice Latimore, which was only fair. She didn't go to medical school so that she could put that title on *my* last name. Caprice *Latimore* did the med school course work, not Caprice Taylor. "What you do for the kids at FEEL—it's *really* inspiring. I guess you could say you're my inspiration. I wanna be able to bring something similar here, in Parramore. A place for kids growing up in this community, like me and you did once, to just... feel at home."

I had ideas; a park, so that kids in this neighborhood wouldn't have to walk to the city to find someplace to play, a food bank so no child in this community ever had to go to bed hungry, tutors, computer rooms, weekend activities, and counselors. This youth center wouldn't just help the kids in the area. It would also bring jobs into this community.

Most importantly, everyone on staff would be a mandatory reporter.

"Okay," Caprice nodded after I told her. "I changed my mind—*this* is the perfect gift."

My arms at her waist tightened, pulling her in closer. "I'm glad you think so."

"I love you," she whispered.

I pressed a kiss against the back of her head, as she relaxed even more in my arms, exhaling.

"I love you, too."

*"Shaun."* Caprice was doing *That Thing* with her voice, so I

knew she was about to ask me for something. I suppressed a smile, ready to give her whatever she asked for, since it was her birthday and all. "Can we get a hotel and leave the day after tomorrow?"

"You want to stay in Orlando longer," I realized.

"Yes." She nodded; her enthusiasm was cute. "Just a little longer, for your birthday."

"Because?"

Caprice turned around, facing me with a smile when she replied, "Because I wanna go to Disney World. Remember how much fun we had on your eighteenth birthday?"

I should've known.

"Kahfi will be pissed if he finds out we went without him," I mentioned.

"We're technically still on our *honeymoon*," Caprice emphasized, looking up at me with those big brown eyes of hers. "What we do while we're on it… That's grown folk's business." Caprice did *That Thing* with her voice again when she whined, "He doesn't have to *knooooow*."

"*Grown folk's business*, says the woman who wants to go to Disney World." I leaned forward and pressed a kiss at the top of her forehead. For a little extra push, she batted her eyelashes as she waited for my answer, which made me laugh before I conceded. "I don't see why not, Butterscotch."

## *Author's Note*

The book that you just finished was not based on anyone's life. **Thank God**. In fact, the inspiration came because I was listening to *Dangerously in Love* by Beyoncé on repeat. That's it. *However*, there are millions of children like Caprice and Kahfi all over the world.

So, if you see something, **say something**.

Thank you for reading.

- Millie Belizaire

Text **MILLIE** to **81257** to be notified of my next project.
Please follow Millie Belizaire on Amazon and other social media platforms.

@milliebelizaire

I **love** getting messages from readers.
And **please leave a review** if you can.
Feedback is vital.
Thank You (:

## *Other works by Millie Belizaire*

*The Collide Series*

- When Worlds Collide
- When Hearts Collide
- When Souls Collide

*The Garden of Eden*

More information @ MillieBelizaire.com

Coming Soon…

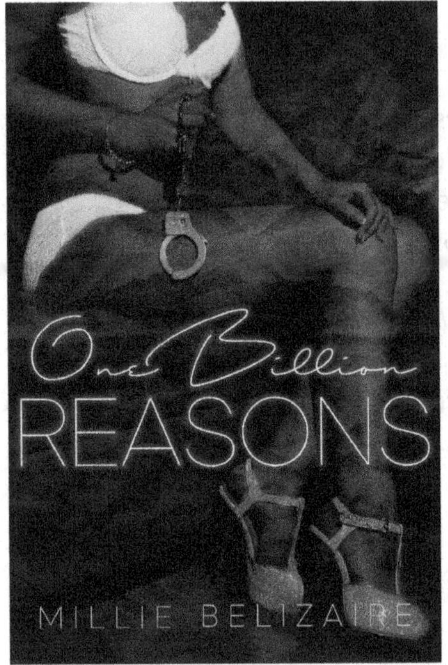


**One Billion Reasons**

Up next, Millie has a billionaire romance featuring the briefly mentioned Damien Fine (The F in FEEL Center) and Morgan Caplan, a familiar character from **The Collide Series**, a previous work by Millie Belizaire. You do not have to read **The Collide Series** in order to read **One Billion Reasons**. (*But you should because I think The Collide Series is dope*)

**One Billion Reasons** is a standalone in a series of billionaire romance standalones, **The One Billion Series**.

**One Billion Reasons** is a little different from what Millie Belizaire has put out in the past. There's a 10-year age gap and some strong BDSM themes, among other things. It's a modern-day reimagining of Pride & Prejudice, but with BLACK people and not nearly as (boring) traditional.

More information coming soon.
Text **MILLIE** to **81257** to be notified.

Made in United States
Orlando, FL
02 October 2024

52293074R00202